"Don't be stupid, Maggie. The answer must be as obvious to you as it is to me. I have arranged to be married on the sixteenth, and that's what I mean to do."

"But you haven't got a bride," she said incredulously. "What are you going to do? Call in one of your conquests? Will any woman do?"

The strange light was there in his eyes again. "Not any woman," he said. "You."

Something caught in her throat and she forced herself to give a brief choking laugh.

"I'm not laughing," he said quietly.

"You're right. It's the unfunniest joke I've ever heard."

"I was never further from making jokes in my life. You don't understand Spanish honor. The one who does the injury is the one who makes reparation. You have injured me, and it is you, and nobody else who must make it right."

Lucy Gordon cut her writing teeth on magazine journalism, interviewing many of the world's most interesting men, including Warren Beatty, Richard Chamberlain, Roger Moore, Sir Alec Guinness and Sir John Gielgud. She also camped out with lions in Africa, and had many other unusual experiences which have often provided the background for her books.

She is married to a Venetian, whom she met while on holiday in Venice. They got engaged within two days, and have now been married for twenty-five years. They live in the Midlands with their three dogs.

Two of her books, *His Brother's Child* and *Song of the Lorelei*, won the Romance Writers of America RITA Award in the Best Traditional Romance category.

Next month, look out for the third story
in Lucy Gordon's THE ITALIAN GROOMS miniseries—
Bride by Choice #3684!

Books by Lucy Gordon
HARLEQUIN ROMANCE®
3655—WIFE BY ARRANGEMENT
3659—HUSBAND BY NECESSITY

THE STAND-IN BRIDE
Lucy Gordon

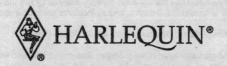

HARLEQUIN®

TORONTO • NEW YORK • LONDON
AMSTERDAM • PARIS • SYDNEY • HAMBURG
STOCKHOLM • ATHENS • TOKYO • MILAN • MADRID
PRAGUE • WARSAW • BUDAPEST • AUCKLAND

ISBN 0-373-03681-7

THE STAND-IN BRIDE

First North American Publication 2001.

Copyright © 2000 by Lucy Gordon.

Visit us at www.eHarlequin.com

Printed in U.S.A.

CHAPTER ONE

CHRISTMAS weather had come early. Although it was only the first day of December there was already the promise of snow, making the air sparkle and the street decorations gleam. High over London's West End they shone against the darkness, multi-coloured confections of angels with long golden trumpets, elves, fairies dancing with long streamers, silver bells hanging in clusters.

But the two young women hurrying along the glittering street had no attention for the beauty overhead. They were arguing.

'Catalina, please don't be unreasonable,' Maggie begged for the third time.

'Unreasonable!' Catalina snapped. 'You want me to spend an evening looking at men wearing nighties and little skirts, and *I'm* unreasonable? Hah!'

'*Julius Caesar* is a great play. It's a classic.'

Catalina made a sound that might have been a snort. She was eighteen, Spanish and looked magnificent in her blazing temper.

'It's Shakespeare,' pleaded Maggie.

'*That* to Shakespeare!'

'And your fiancé wants you to see it.'

Catalina said something deeply uncomplimentary about her fiancé.

'Hush, be careful!' Maggie urged, looking around hurriedly, as though Don Sebastian de Santiago might appear from thin air.

'Pooh! I am here in London; he is in Spain. Soon I

5

shall be his prisoner, and behave myself, and say, "Yes, Sebastian," and "No, Sebastian," and "Whatever you say, Sebastian." But until then I do what I like, I say what I like, and I say I don't like men with knobbles on their knees wearing skirts.'

'They probably don't all have knobbles on their knees,' Maggie said, trying to lighten the atmosphere.

Catalina let forth a torrent of Spanish and Maggie hastily seized her arm and steered her along the road, weaving in and out of the seething crowd. 'It was supposed to be part of your English education,' she said.

'I am Spanish; he is Spanish. Why I need an English education?'

'Why *do* I need—' Maggie corrected her automatically.

'Why *do* I need an English education?' Catalina repeated in exasperation.

'For the same reason you needed a French education, so that you can be a cultivated woman and host his dinner parties.'

Before her rebellious charge could answer, Maggie steered her into a teashop, found a table and said, 'Sit!', much as she would have done to a recalcitrant puppy. The young Spanish girl was delightful but exhausting. Soon Maggie would see her off to Spain and retire to the peace of a nervous breakdown.

For the last three months it had been Maggie's job to perfect Catalina's English and share chaperoning duties with Isabella, her middle-aged duenna. The two Spanish women lived in one of London's most luxurious hotels, courtesy of Don Sebastian, who had also arranged the highlights of their schedule, and paid Maggie's wages.

The whole thing had been arranged at a distance. It was six months since Don Sebastian had last found time to see his fiancée, and that had been on a flying visit to Paris, during which he seemed to have checked the improvement in her French, and little else.

Day-to-day decisions were in the hands of Donna Isabella, who hired teachers locally, communicated with Sebastian and relayed her employer's wishes to her employer's bride-to-be.

He was in America at the moment, expected to arrive in London the following week, after which Catalina would accompany him back to Spain to begin preparing for her wedding. Or possibly he wouldn't have time to come to London at all, in which case they would travel without him. Whatever else he could be accused of, Maggie thought, it wasn't flaming ardour.

She couldn't imagine what he was thinking of to choose a wife so totally unsuitable. Catalina was ignorant and empty-headed—clothes-mad, pop music-mad, boy-mad. By no stretch of the imagination was she a proper consort for a serious man with a seat in the regional Andalucian government.

Catalina's efforts to master languages were half-hearted. She managed fairly well with English because she'd watched so many American television programs, but her French was dire, and her German had been a waste of everybody's time.

Yet Maggie was fond of her. Exasperating Catalina might be, but she was also kind, warm-hearted and fun. She needed a young husband who would be entranced by her beauty and high spirits, and care nothing for her lack of brains. Instead she would soon be imprisoned in a world of premature middle age.

'All right,' Maggie said as they ate tea and cakes. 'What do you want to do this evening?'

'Die!' Catalina declared passionately.

'Short of that,' Maggie said, firmly dousing melodrama with common sense.

'What does it matter? In a few weeks my life will be over anyway. I will be an *old* married woman with an *old* husband and a baby every year.'

'Is Don Sebastian really old?' Maggie asked.

Catalina shrugged. 'Old, middle-aged. So what?'

'I wish you had a picture of him.'

'Is bad enough I have to marry him. What for I want his picture?'

'Anyone would think I hadn't taught you any English,' Maggie complained. 'It's not "what for I want his picture?", it's "Why should I want his picture?" Now, let's try it. *I* say, "I wish you had his picture", and *you* say—?'

'I say if I have his picture here, I stamp on it.'

Maggie gave up.

'Maybe he's only middle-aged outside, but he's old *in here*.' The girl tapped her forehead, then her chest. 'And it's in there that counts.'

Maggie nodded. She knew only too well how a man could look one thing and be another. Four years of marriage had taught her that. Blissful happiness, followed by disillusion, then heartbreak, disgust and despair. To cover her sudden tension she ordered more tea.

The two women made a study in contrasts—the one still in her teens, all proud, passionate Spanish beauty, dark, glittering eyes and a warm complexion, and the other in her late twenties, with soft fair skin, dark brown eyes and light brown hair. Catalina was tiny, built on dainty lines, but her lively temper and excitable personality tended to make her the centre of attention.

Maggie was tall and statuesque, but her manners were so quiet that she could be overlooked beside the magnificent Catalina. Yet she too had a touch of the Mediterranean. Her grandfather had been Alfonso Cortez, a Spaniard from Andalucia who had fallen madly in love with an Englishwoman spending a week in Spain. When it was over he'd pursued her all the way home, never seeing his own country again.

From him Maggie had inherited her large, dark eyes that suggested unfathomable depths. They were alluring in themselves, but doubly so against the Anglo-Saxon pallor of her skin. Observers would have summed Catalina up in an instant, but would have lingered over Maggie, puzzling over her mystery, and the pain and bitterness that she strove to hide. They might have read the sensuality and humour in her mouth. The sensuality she tried to conceal, even from herself. The humour was her weapon against the world. Once, and it seemed a long time ago, she had laughed all the time. Now she laughed to protect her privacy.

'If you feel like that about your fiancé, you should tell him,' she said.

'You think Sebastian would let me go, after he's spent two years grooming me? Everything I do is under his control. I am taught what he wants me to know—languages, how to dress, how to eat, how to behave.

'Even on this tour of Europe, I have no freedom because he has organised everything. In Rome, in Paris, in London I stay in hotels he chooses, and do what he say.

'And now, it's Christmas and there are so many lovely things in London: decorations and Christmas trees, and children singing carols, the stores are full of lights, and we buy lots of lovely presents, and visit Santa in his grotto...'

'I'm not taking you to any more grottoes,' Maggie

interrupted with a shudder. 'You nearly got us thrown out of the last one for flirting with an elf.'

Catalina giggled. 'Wasn't he the most handsome boy you ever saw?'

'But you're practically a married woman.'

The girl's laughter faded. '*Si!* And when all these lovely Christmas things are happening, Sebastian want me to see a worthy play. Why not a pantomime? Widow Twanky and Principal Boys. We don't have that in Spain, so is part of my English education, *si*? But no! *Julius Caesar!*'

It would be impossible to convey the depth of loathing and disgust she put into the last two words. Maggie sighed in sympathy.

Having exploded, Catalina settled to submerge her sorrows in chocolate éclairs doused in cream. 'And always there is Isabella,' she sighed. 'Spying on me.'

'That's not fair,' Maggie protested. 'She's kind and very fond of you.'

'I'm fond of her, but I'm also glad that tonight we could come out without her. She means well, but she is Sebastian's poor relation, and she thinks he's God. Always she say, "Don Sebastian's wife would never do this," and "Don Sebastian's wife would always do that." One day I will reply, "Then Don Sebastian's wife can do it, but *I'm* going to do something else."'

'Good for you. Tell him that the wedding's off.'

'If only I dared! Oh, Maggie, I wish I was like you. You had the courage to follow your heart and marry the man you loved.'

'Never mind that,' Maggie said hastily. Catalina's curiosity about her marriage was making her tense and edgy. To change the subject she said, 'We've still got time for a show.'

'Oh, yes, we must go somewhere, or we shall look nice for nothing,' Catalina said fervently.

She seized any excuse to wear her loveliest clothes, so even for an outing with her chaperone she was done up to the nines. The floor-length peacock-blue dress looked glorious with her warm colouring. The diamonds, perhaps, were a little old for her, but she knew she looked beautiful, and was happy.

Maggie would have preferred to dress with restraint, but Catalina viewed restraint with horror. She had insisted on a shopping trip and, with an unerring eye, steered Maggie towards a black silk cocktail gown that moulded itself to her womanly curves.

'It's a bit low,' Maggie had said hesitantly.

'So what? You have a magnificent bosom; you should show it off,' Catalina had said imperiously.

Even Maggie could see that the dress had been made for her, and she bought it, compromising with a black silk chiffon scarf that she could whisk about her shoulders. She was wearing the scarf now but, even so, she wished that the dress was a little less revealing.

'What shall we choose?' she asked now.

'*Your Place Or Mine?*' Catalina said at once. 'I have wanted to see that ever since I read that it was very rude and naughty.'

'Just the sort of thing Don Sebastian's wife shouldn't see,' Maggie teased.

'No, she shouldn't,' Catalina said happily. 'So let us go *immediately*.'

Isabella turned her heavy bulk over in bed, trying to ignore the nagging pain in her side. She wondered when Maggie and Catalina would return, but a glance at the clock told her they had been gone barely an hour.

A sudden noise made her stiffen. It came from the other side of her bedroom door, where there was the large sitting room of the luxurious suite she shared with Catalina. Somebody had entered by stealth, and was looking around.

Summoning her courage she slipped out of bed, found her bag, dropped a heavy ashtray into it, and crept to the door. Then, with one wild movement, she yanked the door open and swung the bag at the intruder.

The next moment her arm was seized in a grip of steel, and she was looking at the astonished face of Don Sebastian de Santiago.

'Merciful mother of heaven!' she moaned. 'What have I done?'

'Nearly brained me,' her employer said wryly, feeling into the bag and removing the ashtray.

'Forgive me, Señor. I thought you were a burglar.'

The habitual stern, haughty look on Don Sebastian's face softened. 'It is I who should ask your forgiveness for intruding on you without warning,' he said courteously. 'I ought to have knocked, but knowing it was your night for going to *Julius Caesar* I assumed the place would be empty, and persuaded Reception to give me a key.' He regarded her face with concern. 'Are you unwell?'

'A little, Señor. It is nothing, but I preferred not to go out, and I knew I could entrust Catalina to Señora Cortez.'

'Ah, yes, you mentioned her in your letters. A respectable English woman, who teaches languages.'

'And the widow of a Spaniard,' Isabella said eagerly. 'A most cultivated and reliable person, with a mature outlook and the highest principles.' Fearful that her chaperonage might be found wanting, she continued to

expatiate on Maggie's virtues until Don Sebastian interrupted her gently.

'I don't wish to keep you from your bed. Just tell me
how to find them.'

Isabella produced her own unused ticket from the bag.
'They will be sitting here.'

He shepherded her kindly to the door of her room, bid
her farewell, and departed. In fifteen minutes he was at
the theatre, arriving in the middle of the first interval.
Rather than waste time searching the crowd, he went to
the seat number on his ticket, and waited for Catalina
and her companion to join him.

Your Place Or Mine? was only mildly shocking, but to
a girl from a sheltered background it seemed deliciously
risqué. Afterwards they walked to a nearby restaurant,
Catalina blissfully remembering tunes and jokes from
the show.

'Sebastian would be so cross if he knew where I'd
been tonight,' she said cheerfully as they sat waiting for
their food.

'I can't imagine why you agreed to marry him if you
dislike him so much.'

'I was sixteen. What did I know? Maggie, when you
live in a convent boarding school with nuns saying,
"Don't do this," and "Don't do that," you will agree
to *anything* to get out.

'And along comes this old man—OK, OK, middle-
aged man—who was a friend of your Papa—also he is
your distant cousin, third or fourth, I forget. But
Sebastian is the head of the family, so when your Papa
die this man is your guardian. And he say he has decided
you will make him a suitable wife.'

'*He* has decided?'

'He is a decisive man. It is his way.'

'What about what you want?'

'He says I'm too young to know what I want.'

Maggie appealed to heaven. 'Give me patience!'

'Anyway, you say yes, because if you don't get out of that school you will scream,' Catalina explained, adding with a big sigh, 'but he's much worse than the nuns. A girl should go to her wedding joyfully, full of adoration for her groom. How can I adore Sebastian?'

'Since I've never met him, I don't know whether he's adorable or not,' Maggie pointed out.

'He is not,' Catalina said firmly. 'He is a grandee, an aristocrat. He is proud, fierce, haughty, imperious. He demands everything and he forgives nothing. He believes that only honour matters, for himself, for his family. He is *impressive*. But adorable—no!'

'Well, adoration is fine for the wedding day,' Maggie observed. 'But a marriage needs to be built on reality.' She poured them both a glass of the light wine she had ordered.

'What are you thinking?' Catalina asked, looking curiously into her face.

'I—nothing. Why do you ask?'

'Suddenly your face has a strange expression, as though you could see something very far away that nobody else could see. Oh, no!' Her hand flew to her mouth in a conscience-stricken gesture. 'I have made you think about your own husband, and that makes you sad because he is dead. Forgive me.'

'There's nothing to forgive,' Maggie said hastily. 'It's four years since he died. I don't brood about it now.'

'But you do. You never talk about him, so you must be brooding in secret,' Catalina said with youthful romanticism. 'Oh, Maggie, how lucky you are to have known a great love. I shall die without *ever* knowing a great love.'

That was the thing about Catalina. One moment she could discuss her predicament with a clear-sightedness that made Maggie respect her, and the next she would go off in a childish flight of melodramatic fancy.

'I wish you would tell me about Señor Cortez,' she begged.

'Start eating,' Maggie advised quietly.

The last thing she wanted to discuss was her husband, whose name had been Roderigo Alva. After his death she had reverted to her maiden name of Cortez, determined to cut all connection with the past. Normally she kept her secrets, but in an unguarded moment she'd let slip that she'd once had a Spanish husband, and Catalina had naturally assumed that Cortez was her married name. Rather than correct her, and prompt more unwanted questions, Maggie had let it pass.

To divert the girl's attention, Maggie said, 'I'm sure Don Sebastian will see that he can't hold you to a promise given when you were sixteen. If you just explain—'

'Explain? Hah! This isn't a reasonable Englishman, Maggie. He only listens to what he wants to hear and insists on his own way—'

'In short, he's a Spaniard. And I'm beginning to think any woman who marries a Spaniard is crazy,' Maggie said with more feeling than she'd meant to reveal.

'Oh, yes,' Catalina agreed. 'Let me tell you what my Grandmama used to say about my Grandpapa—'

Maggie was a good listener, and Catalina poured her heart out in a way she could never do with the easily shocked Isabella. Maggie already knew much of the story of her childhood in the old Moorish city of Granada, motherless, because her mother had died at her birth, leaving her with a bewildered father who was already middle-aged. But Catalina told it again anyhow, talking about southern Spain, its vineyards and olive groves, orange and lemon orchards.

Just outside Granada stood the Santiago estate, or at least part of it, for it also included extensive property in other parts of Andalucia, all owned by the rich and powerful family head, Don Sebastian de Santiago. Catalina had met him once, when she was ten, and she was taken to the Residenza Santiago, his great home that was like a palace. For this visit she wore her Sunday dress, and was warned to be on her best behaviour. She recalled little of that meeting, save that he had been formal and distant. Soon after that she was sent to the convent school. When she emerged at sixteen her father was dead, and she found herself the ward and betrothed of a man she hardly knew.

She was still chattering as they hailed a cab to take them the short distance to the hotel, travelled up in the lift and walked along the corridor to the suite.

They found the main room almost dark, except for a small table lamp.

'We have a cup of tea, like true English people,' Catalina said. While she called room service, Maggie took off her coat, yawned and stretched.

'I so envy you that dress,' Catalina said longingly. 'No straps and only your bosom is holding it up, so when you stretch your arms over your head it look like maybe it fall down, and maybe not. And all the men are watching and hoping. I wish I can have a dress that look like it fall down.'

'Catalina!' Maggie said, half-amused, half-horrified. 'You make me out a terrible chaperone.'

Impulsively the girl hugged her. 'I like you so much, Maggie. You have an understanding heart, I think.'

'Well, you take my advice. Stand up to this ogre and tell him to get lost. This is the twenty-first century. You can't be forced into marriage against your will—certainly not with an old man. One day you'll meet a nice boy of your own age.'

Catalina chuckled. 'I thought you believed a woman was crazy to marry a Spaniard of any age.

'I meant any English woman. I dare say if you're Spanish they might be just about tolerable.'

'How kind of you,' said an ironic voice from the shadows

They whirled and saw a man rise from the armchair by the window, and switch on a tall standard lamp. Maggie felt a frisson of alarm, and not only because of his sudden appearance, the way he seemed to loom up from nowhere. It was to do with the man himself. There was something inherently dangerous about him. She knew that by instinct, even in that brief moment.

Before she could demand to know who he was and how he came to be there, she heard Catalina whisper, 'Sebastian!'

Oh, heavens! Maggie thought. Now the fat's in the fire.

Obviously he'd heard every word she'd said. But that might even be a good thing. A little plain speaking was long overdue.

She surveyed him, realising that she had been seriously misled. Catalina's notion of elderly was coloured by her own youth. This man bore no relation to the greybeard they had been discussing. Don Sebastian de Santiago was in his thirties, perhaps his late thirties but certainly no older. He stood a good six foot two inches tall, with a lean, hard body that he carried like an athlete.

Only on his face did Maggie see what she had expected, a look of pride and arrogance that she guessed had been imprinted there at the hour of his birth. And right now, to pride and arrogance was added anger. If she'd cherished a hope that he hadn't heard all her frank words, a look at his black, snapping eyes would have dispelled it.

But for the moment anger was just below the surface, almost concealed by a layer of cool courtesy. 'Good evening, Catalina,' he said calmly. 'Will you be so kind as to introduce me to this lady?'

Catalina pulled herself together. 'Señora Margarita Cortez, Don Sebastian de Santiago.'

Sebastian inclined his head curtly. 'Good evening, Señora. It is a pleasure to meet you at last. I have heard much about you, although I admit that I had not expected to find you so young.'

His eyes flickered over her as he spoke, as though he were sizing her up, prior to dismissal.

Maggie raised her chin, refusing to be discomposed.

'I was not informed of any age qualifications for my job, Señor,' she replied crisply. 'Only that I should speak fluent Spanish, and be able to introduce Catalina to English customs.'

He seemed a little surprised that she had turned his remark back on him. He surveyed her ironically.

'Then permit me to say that you seem to have exceeded your brief. Was it part of the terms of your employment to criticise me to my bride, or is that an English custom I've never heard of before?'

'You take a light-hearted conversation too seriously, Señor,' Maggie said, managing to sound amused. 'Catalina and I have enjoyed an evening at the theatre, followed by a meal, and we were in the mood to talk nonsense.'

'I see,' he said sardonically. 'So you were talking nonsense when you told her that she couldn't be forced into marriage with an ogre. I can't tell you how greatly that relieves my mind. For if you were to seriously oppose me, I tremble to think of my fate.'

'So do I,' she riposted. She wasn't going to let him get away with that.

He raised his eyebrows slightly, but otherwise didn't deign to react.

'It's time for me to be going home,' Maggie said. 'I'll just call a cab—'

He moved swiftly to put himself between her and the telephone. 'Before you do, perhaps you could favour me with an account of your evening. Did you enjoy *Julius Caesar*?'

'Very much,' Catalina burst out before Maggie could stop her. 'Such a great play, and an inspired performance. We were thrilled, weren't we, Maggie?'

'Yes, do tell me.' He turned to her. 'Did you enjoy the performance as much as Catalina—?'

Maggie's alarm bells rang. 'Don Sebastian—'

'Or will you, at least, have the sense to admit the truth?' he cut across her sharply. 'Neither of you were there tonight.'

'But we were,' Catalina plunged on, unwisely. 'Truly, we were.'

'That's enough,' Maggie said, laying a hand on the girl's arm. 'There's no need for this, Catalina. We've done nothing to be ashamed of. Perhaps it's Don Sebastian who should be ashamed, for spying on us.'

'That was a most unwise remark, Señora,' he said in

a hard voice. 'I do not owe you or anyone an account of my actions, but I will tell you this. I arrived unexpectedly and decided to join you at the theatre. When it was clear that you weren't there, I returned here to wait for you. It's now past one in the morning, and if you know what's good for you, you will explain exactly where you were, *and who you met*.'

'How dare you?' Maggie snapped. 'We met nobody. Catalina has been in my company, and mine alone, the whole evening.'

'Dressed like that?' he asked scathingly, taking in the elegantly sexy contours of her dress. 'I don't think so. Women flaunt themselves for men, not each other.'

'Piffle!' Maggie said, losing her temper. 'Catalina likes to dress up for the pleasure of it, as does any young girl. I dressed up to keep her company.'

'You'll forgive my not accepting your word,' he said coldly.

'No, I won't forgive you, because I don't tell lies.'

'But Catalina does. Under your chaperonage she feels free to deceive me. Now I know the kind of example you set her. You take her out gallivanting heaven knows where, and encourage her to lie about where you've been.'

'I didn't encourage her—I couldn't stop her. Yes, it was a stupid lie, but only a small one, and it wouldn't have happened if you didn't act like a man bringing the word down from the mountain. Stop making such an issue of something so trivial. She's eighteen, for pity's sake, and entitled to some innocent fun.'

'I will be the judge of that.'

From behind the bedroom door came the sound of a groan.

'Poor Isabella,' Catalina said hurriedly. 'I was forgetting that she isn't well. I should go to her.'

'Yes, do,' Maggie advised, regarding Don Sebastian out of glinting eyes. 'We'll fight better without you.'

Catalina scuttled away, leaving the other two eyeing each other like jousters. Again Maggie had the sensation of danger that she'd felt in the first moments of meeting him. She wasn't frightened. There was something about danger that exhilarated her when she could meet it head-on. Perhaps *he* should be afraid.

CHAPTER TWO

'You are right, Señora,' Don Sebastian said. 'My bride is innocent in this matter. The blame lies with the woman charged with her welfare, who has so notably failed in her responsibilities. For the last time, I demand that you tell me where you have been.'

'To the theatre.'

'To see what?'

'A light-hearted musical. Not as worthy and improving as *Julius Caesar*, but it's Christmas and neither of us was in the mood for war and murder.'

'And does this light-hearted musical have a title?' he growled. He knew she was prevaricating.

Maggie sighed. 'Yes. It's called *Your Place Or Mine?*' she said reluctantly, realising how it sounded.

'*Your Place Or Mine?*' he echoed. 'I suppose that tells me all I need to know about the kind of sleazy entertainment you think suitable for a sheltered young girl.'

'Rubbish,' Maggie said firmly. 'The title is misleading. It isn't sleazy at all—just a little bit naughty, but basically innocent.'

'Indeed?' Don Sebastian snatched up a newspaper he had been reading to pass the time, and pointed to an advertisement for the show they had just seen. 'Outrageous,' he quoted. 'Titillating! Don't take your grandmother!'

Maggie struggled to stop her lips twitching, and failed.

'I am amusing you?' Don Sebastian asked in a warning voice.

'Yes, frankly, you are. If you knew anything about theatre advertising—which you clearly don't—you'd realise that this kind of publicity is deliberately angled to make the public think a show more shocking than it is. "Don't take your grandmother," really means that even your grandmother wouldn't be shocked. My own grandmother would have loved it.'

'I can well believe that.'

'Meaning? *Meaning?*'

'Do you wish me to spell it out?'

'Not unless you enjoy making yourself unpleasant, which I'm beginning to think you do. What a fuss about nothing! Catalina is young, pretty. She ought to be out dancing with friends of her own age, and what do you offer her? *Julius Caesar*, for pity's sake! Men in nighties and little skirts, with knobbles on their knees.'

'Since you didn't see the performance you are hardly equipped to comment on their knees,' he snapped.

'I'll bet they were knobbly, though. A sheltered girl like Catalina would probably have been shocked at the sight.'

But humour was wasted on this man. His eyes had narrowed in a way that some people might have found intimidating, but Maggie was past caring. She had never met anyone who made her so angry so quickly.

At last he said, 'You have your values and I have mine. They seem to be entirely different. I blame myself for hiring your services without checking you out first.'

'Don't you have your finger in enough pies?' she demanded in exasperation. 'Must each tiny detail come under your control?'

'With every word you betray how little you understand. When a man is in authority, control is essential.

If he does not control all the details, his authority is incomplete.'

'Details!' Maggie said explosively. 'You're talking about this poor girl's life. And if you regard that as a detail I can only say I pity her.'

'How fortunate that I'm not obliged to consider your opinion,' he snapped.

'I don't suppose you've ever considered anyone's opinion in your life,' she snapped back.

'I don't tolerate interference with my private affairs. It's not your place to criticise me or my forthcoming marriage.'

'If you had any decency, there wouldn't be a marriage.'

'On the contrary, it's only my sense of duty that makes me take a feather-headed ninny as my wife. On his death-bed her father made me promise to protect her, and I gave my word.'

'So be her guardian, but you don't have to be her husband!'

'A guardian's power ends on the day his ward marries. I protect her best by remaining her guardian for life.

'Well, of all the—'

'You know Catalina by now. Is she intelligent? Come, be honest.'

'No, she isn't. She has a butterfly mind. All the more reason to marry a man who won't care about that.'

'And how will she choose her husband? She's an heiress, and the fortune-hunters will flock to her. Can you imagine the choice she'll make? I don't need her money. I'll make a marriage settlement that ties it up in favour of her children, and then I'll give her everything she wants.'

'Except love.'

'Love,' he echoed scornfully. 'What sentimentalists you English are. You think marriage has anything to do with romantic love? My wife will be protected and cared for. I will give her children to love.'

'And she'll have to be content with the small corner of your life that you spare her.'

He regarded her cynically. 'I see how it is. You think a man only makes a good husband if he prostrates himself and worships the woman, like a weakling. But I tell you that a man who truly worships is without pride, and the man who only pretends is not to be trusted.'

'You think a strong man patronises the woman?' Maggie demanded sharply.

'I think men and women each have their roles, and their duty is to fill them well. And since you ask, no, I don't think that my role is to look up to any woman. I suppose you've been filling Catalina's head with your pretty nonsense.'

'Catalina is young. She knows what she wants out of life, and it isn't you.'

'I'm sure you're right. She'd like some fast-talking boy who'll sweep her off her feet, spend her money and turn on her when it's gone. Is that the fate you want for her?'

'No, of course not, I—' Something was making it difficult for her to speak. His words had touched a nerve. She turned away and went to the window, so that she didn't have to look at him. But the darkness outside reflected the room within, and she could still see him, watching her, frowning.

'What is it?' he asked at last.

'Nothing,' she said quickly. 'You're right, this is none of my business. Soon you'll take Catalina away, and I won't see her any more.'

'What was your own husband like?' he asked, with a flash of insight that alarmed her.

'I'd rather not talk about him.'

'I see,' he said harshly. 'You discuss my marriage, which—as you so rightly say—is not your concern, but if I wish to discuss yours, you feel entitled to snub me.' He pulled her around to face him. 'Tell me about your husband.'

'No.' She tried to get free but he held her firmly.

'I said, tell me about him. What was he like to put that withdrawn look on your face when he's mentioned?'

'Very well, he was Spanish,' she flashed. 'Everything else I prefer to forget.'

'Did you live in Spain?'

'That's enough. Let me go at once.' But his long fingers clasped on her arm did not release her.

'I'd rather stay like this. I don't want to have to follow you about the room. I asked if you lived in Spain, and so far you haven't answered me.'

'No, and I'm not going to.'

'But I intend that you shall. I've been very patient while you interrogated me and favoured me with your insulting opinions, but my patience has run out. Now we talk about you. Tell me about your husband. Was he a passionate man?'

'How *dare*—? That's none of your—' His glintingly ironic eyes stopped her, reminding her of how frankly she had spoken about his private affairs. But that was different, she told herself wildly. It didn't entitle him to invade the secrets of her bed, or to look at her with eyes that seemed to see the things she kept so carefully hidden.

'So tell me,' Sebastian persisted. 'Was he passionate?' Maggie pulled herself together. 'I'm surprised you ask.

You just told me that love has nothing to do with marriage.'

'And so it hasn't. But I'm talking about passion, which has nothing to do with love. What a man and a woman experience together in bed is a life apart. It matters little whether they love each other or not. In fact, a touch of antagonism can heighten their pleasure.'

She drew an uneven breath. 'That is nonsense!'

He didn't answer in words, but his fingers twitched, catching the silk chiffon scarf and slowly drawing it away, leaving her shoulders bare. A tremor went through her at the sudden rush of cool air on her skin.

'I think not,' he said softly.

His eyes held hers. His meaning was shockingly clear. The hostility that had flared between them in the first instant was, to him, an attraction. He was inviting her to imagine herself in bed with him, naked, turning their anger into physical pleasure. And he was doing it so forcefully that she couldn't help responding. Against her will the pictures were there, shocking in their power and abandon: a man and a woman who'd thrown aside restraint and were driving each other on to ever greater ecstasy.

She was intensely aware of the sheer physical force of his presence. Once, before passion had played her false, she had responded to it fiercely: so fiercely that in disillusion she'd turned away from desire, fearing it as a traitor. She'd fought it, killed it. Or so she'd thought.

But now it was there again, not dead but only sleeping, waiting to be awoken by a certain note in a man's voice. *Not this man!* she swore furiously to herself. But even as she made the vow she became conscious of his body, how lean and hard it was, how long his legs with their heavy thigh muscles just perceptible beneath the conservative suit. The touch of his fingers was light, but force seemed to stream through them so that she could think of nothing else but that, and what a man's strength might mean to a woman in bed. Power in his hands, in his arms, in his loins...

She tried to blot out such thoughts but his will was stronger than hers. He seemed to have taken over her mind, giving her no choice but to see what he wanted her to see, and to reflect back that consciousness to him.

'Yes,' he said softly. *'Yes.'*

As though in a trance, she murmured. 'Never.'

'Then he was not passionate?'

'Who?' she whispered.

'Your husband.'

Her husband. Yes, of course, they had been discussing her husband. The world, which had vanished for a heated moment, seemed to settle back into place.

'I won't discuss him with you,' she said, echoing words she'd spoken before because her mind was too confused to think of new ones.

'I wonder why. Because in bed he was a god, who showed you desire that no other man could ever match? Or because he was ignorant about women, knowing nothing of their secrets and too selfish to learn, a weakling who left you unsatisfied? I think he failed you. What a fool! Didn't he know what he had in his possession?'

'I was never his possession.'

'Then he wasn't a man or he would have known how to make you *want* to be his. Why don't you answer my question?'

'What question?'

'Yes, it was so long ago that I asked, wasn't it? And such a little question. Did you live in Spain?'

'For a few years.'

'And yet you know nothing about the Spanish mind.'

'I know that I don't like it, and that's all I need to know.'

'Just like that,' he said, 'you condemn a whole race in a few words.'

'No,' she said defiantly, 'I condemn all the *men* of your race. Now let me go, *this instant.*'

He laughed softly and released her. Something in that laugh sent shivers up her spine, and her sense that he was a man to avoid increased. It was unforgivable that he should have called up old memories that still tormented her. She backed away and turned from him, resisting the temptation to rub the place where his fingers had gripped. He hadn't hurt her, but the warmth was still there, reminding her how he had felt.

'All Spanish men!' he said ironically. 'But surely, some of us are "tolerable"?'

'None of you,' she said coldly.

'How very tragic to have fallen under your displeasure!'

'Don't bother making fun of me. I don't work for you any more.'

'That's for me to say.'

'No. There are two sides to every bargain and I've just terminated my employment. And let me say that you made that very easy.'

'Not so fast,' he said at once. 'I haven't finished with you yet.'

'But *I* have finished with *you*. Now you're here, my job is finished—which is fortunate because, having met you, I have no desire to work for you. You can take that as final. Goodnight.'

From the look on his face she guessed that he had

been about to give her the sack, and was furious that she'd gotten her word in first.

'And may I ask if you expect me to give you a reference, Señora?'

'You may do as you please. I'm never short of work. In short, Señor, I'm as indifferent to your opinion of me as you are to mine of you.'

That really annoyed him, she was glad to see.

'I'll just say goodbye to Catalina and Isabella,' she said, heading for the bedroom door, 'and then I won't trouble you again.'

But when she entered Isabella's room an alarming sight met her. The duenna's plump form was tossing and turning, and her flushed face was twisted with pain.

Catalina was sitting on the bed. She turned quickly when Maggie entered. Her face was frantic.

'She's so ill,' Catalina wailed. 'I don't know what to do. She won't let me call a doctor.'

'She needs more than a doctor,' Maggie said swiftly. There was no telephone by the bed so she looked back to the sitting room and called, 'Get an ambulance.'

'What has happened?' Sebastian asked, heading for her.

'I'll tell you later,' she said impatiently. 'Call the ambulance. Hurry!'

'No,' Isabella protested weakly. 'I will be well soon.'

'You're in great pain, aren't you?' Maggie asked, dropping to her knees beside the bed and speaking gently.

Isabella nodded miserably. 'It's nothing,' she tried to say, but the words were cut off by a gasp. Isabella clutched her side and her head rolled from side to side in agony. Sweat stood out on her brow.

Maggie hurried out. 'I've called them,' Sebastian said. 'They'll be here soon. You evidently think it's serious.'

'Earlier tonight she said it was a headache, but the pain seems to be in her side. It may be her appendix, and if it's ruptured it's serious.'

Catalina came flying out. 'I don't know what to do,' she wept. 'She's in such pain, I can't bear it.'

'Pull yourself together,' Maggie said, kindly but firmly. 'It's poor Isabella who has to bear it, not you. You shouldn't have left her alone. No, stay there; I'll go to her.'

She hurried back to the bedside. Isabella was moaning. 'No hospital,' she begged. 'Please, no hospital.'

'You must be properly looked after,' Maggie said.

She began to talk softly to Isabella, sounding as reassuring as possible, but she couldn't reach the old woman, who seemed maddened by terror at the mere word 'hospital'. At last, to her relief, Maggie heard a knock at the outer door. Through a crack she could just see Sebastian admit the paramedics. But Isabella was now in a state of hysteria.

'No,' she screamed. 'No hospital, *please*, no hospital!'

The next moment, Sebastian appeared. Maggie rose as he came to the side of the bed and took Isabella's hands between his. 'Now, stop this,' he said in a gentle voice. 'You must go to the hospital. I insist.'

'They took Antonio there and he died,' the old woman whispered.

'That was many years ago. Doctors are better now. You're not going to die. You're going to be made well. Now, be sensible, my dear cousin. Do this to please me.'

She had stopped writhing and lay quietly with her hands in his. 'I'm afraid,' she whispered.

'What is there to be afraid of, if I am with you?' he asked, smiling at her.

'But you won't be there.'

'I shall be with you all the time. Come, now.'

In one swift, strong movement he pulled back the bed-clothes and gathered her up in his arms, making nothing of her considerable weight. Isabella stopped fighting and put her hands trustingly around his neck as he lifted her from the bed and carried her out to where the paramedics had a stretcher. Maggie heaved a sigh of relief that somebody had been able to get through to her.

At last Isabella was settled on the stretcher, and the paramedics hurried away with her. Sebastian prepared to follow the little party, but in the doorway he stopped and looked back. 'Come!' he commanded Catalina.

The girl shuddered. 'I hate those places.'

'Never mind that. Do as I say. Isabella is our respon-sibility. She mustn't be left alone without a woman's comfort. These will be your duties in the future, and you may as well start now.'

Catalina looked helplessly at Maggie.

'All right,' Maggie sighed, recognising the inevitable. 'I'll come with you.' She met Sebastian's eyes. 'I can always leave later.'

'To be sure,' he said ironically. 'My bride will mag-ically become strong-minded and responsible, won't she?'

In the flurry of departure she didn't need to answer this. Downstairs the paramedics eased Isabella gently in-side the waiting ambulance. Sebastian followed, nodding towards a car just behind.

'Follow us to the Santa Maria Infirmary,' he said curtly. Maggie's eyes widened at the name of the most expensive private hospital in London.

'Of course,' Catalina said, when they were seated side by side in the back of the chauffeur driven car. 'Isabella is one of his family. He feels responsible for her.'

'He must do if he's gone in the ambulance,' Maggie mused. 'Most men would die, rather. But you should have gone, my dear.'

'I hate sickness,' Catalina wailed. She saw Maggie looking at her in exasperation and added shrewdly, 'Besides, Sebastian is the one she wants. He makes her feel safe.'

'Yes, I noticed.'

Maggie had been unwillingly impressed by the kindness and patience he had shown the old woman, and the way she had clung to him, as though to a rock. However overbearing Sebastian might be, he clearly took his patriarchal duties seriously.

At the Santa Maria Infirmary, doctors were waiting for Isabella. As they prepared to wheel her away she cried out to Sebastian. '*No, no!* You promised not to leave me.'

'And he won't,' Maggie said at once, taking the old woman's outstretched hand. 'But he must stay out here a moment to give them your details, and I shall come with you. You and I are friends, aren't we?'

Isabella gave a weak smile of assent, but her eyes rolled to Sebastian. At once he clasped her other hand.

'Señora Cortez will be my deputy,' he said. 'Trust her as you do me, and it is as if I myself were by your side.'

Isabella gave a sigh and allowed herself to be wheeled into the cubicle. Now her eyes never left Maggie and it was clear she regarded the transfer of trust very seriously.

It took only a brief examination to confirm that

Isabella had acute appendicitis, requiring an immediate operation. The word brought her terror rushing back.

'Why are you so afraid?' Maggie asked gently.

'My husband, Antonio, had an operation in a hospital. And he died.'

'When was that?'

'Forty years ago.'

'A lot of people died then who wouldn't die now. You will recover, and be well again.'

She continued talking in this way, glad to see that the old woman was gradually relaxing. There was a shadow in the doorway and Sebastian looked in. He was smiling in a way that transformed him, and his manner to Isabella was almost teasing.

'Not long now,' he said to her. 'And then all will be well.'

'And I won't die? You promise.'

'You won't die. Word of a Santiago.'

He leaned down and placed a gentle kiss on Isabella's forehead. Her eyes remained on him as she was wheeled away, until she was out of sight.

'I must stress the dangers of surgery on a lady of her age and weight,' the surgeon explained. 'But there is no choice.'

'I take full responsibility,' Sebastian said at once.

The doctor left. Almost to himself, Sebastian murmured, 'I have given a promise I had no right to give.'

'But there was nothing else you could do,' Maggie said. 'It was her only chance.'

'True. But if she dies—when she trusted me—?'

'She would have died if she had not trusted you,' Maggie insisted. 'You did the right thing.'

'Thank you for saying that. I needed to know that someone—' He stopped and looked at her with surprise, as though he'd only just realised what he was saying, and to whom. His face became reserved again, but he said, 'I mean—that I must thank you for what you did for her. It was kind. You have the gift.'

He didn't elaborate and she looked at him with a frown.

'It is a gift that some have,' he said quietly. 'They calm fear and inspire trust.'

'It seems that you have the gift yourself.'

'It's natural for her to trust the head of her family. She trusts you for yourself.'

Then he seemed to become embarrassed, and looked around for Catalina. They found her sitting in a corner, playing with a small child who was waiting with his mother.

'I think I'd better be going,' Maggie said.

'No,' Sebastian said at once. 'Isabella will look for you when she comes round. You must stay here with us.'

Maggie was silent, confused. Despite their truce she still felt an instinctive need to get right away from him. While she hesitated he added gravely, 'I would be grateful if you would oblige me.'

'Very well. But only until I know Isabella is safe.'

He gave her a curt nod. 'I shan't ask you to endure my company longer than that.'

CHAPTER THREE

DESPITE the surgeon's fears Isabella came through the operation well, and awoke in the early hours. The three who had waited for the news emerged into the dawn, tired and slightly disorientated. Sebastian hailed a cab and urged Maggie into it.

'I should go home,' she said, yawning.

'Later. We have matters to discuss.'

In the short distance back to the hotel she slipped into a half doze. Through it she could just hear Catalina prattling away in a non-stop monologue, punctuated by Sebastian's bored 'Really?', 'Indeed!' and 'Quite!'

At the hotel he ordered breakfast to be sent up. While he made phone calls the two women went to Catalina's room, where she stripped off and announced that she was going to have a bath. Maggie would have liked to do the same but she had to settle for borrowing one of Isabella's 'granny' cardigans in a shade of deadly grey, which she slipped on over her bare shoulders.

When she returned to the sitting room, breakfast had arrived. Sebastian grimaced at the sight of her dowdy attire. 'It suits Isabella better,' he said wryly. 'She is past being attractive to men.'

'And I,' Maggie retorted with spirit, 'am indifferent to men.'

'That is a lie and we both know it,' he asserted calmly. 'But this is neither the time nor the place to discuss that.'

'Never and nowhere! That's the time and place to discuss it.'

'Sit down and eat. We have to decide what to do.'

'We?' Maggie enquired ironically.

He refused to rise to her bait. 'Catalina and I will leave for Spain tomorrow. I need you to come with us and remain until the wedding.'

'Certainly not!' Maggie said without hesitation. 'And leave Isabella alone here where she doesn't know anyone? How can you be so inconsiderate?'

'If you would allow me to finish,' he said with some asperity, 'I could tell you that while you were out of the room I arranged for her sister to fly to London. She will arrive this afternoon, and stay until Isabella can travel.'

'I'm very happy for them both, but I gave you my notice yesterday, and nothing has changed.'

'Nonsense, everything has changed,' he said impatiently. 'Even you must see that.'

'Yesterday I was a disreputable woman who was dragging Catalina into dens of vice. Now you're ready to forget that because I can be useful to you.'

He had the grace to redden. 'I may have spoken hastily. Catalina has given me a full account of your evening, including the fact that she pressured you into buying that erotic dress.'

'It's not erotic,' she said quickly, drawing the edges of the grey woolly together.

'If it wasn't erotic, you wouldn't be wearing that thing over it.'

'I'm surprised you believed Catalina,' Maggie said, hastily changing tack. 'Surely you know that under my influence she tells lies?'

'She's told lies since she was a little girl,' Sebastian admitted wryly. 'You have nothing to do with it. Besides, I always know when she's lying, and this time she wasn't.'

'When did she tell you all this?'

'In the cab, half an hour ago.'

'Oh, that's what she was saying. I was half asleep and just heard her voice distantly. And, of course, your replies. I could tell you were simply fascinated.'

He gave her a black look. 'It's true I don't take easily to the prattling of children,' he said defensively.

'Well, you'd better get used to it, if you're going to marry her.'

'Can we stick to the matter in hand?'

'That's easy. You say, "Come to Spain"; I say, "No way." End of conversation. What do you want me for, anyway?'

'I'm Catalina's guardian as well as her fiancé. From tomorrow she will be living in my house. She must have a chaperone.'

'In this day and age?'

'Spain is not England. Our belief in propriety may seem a little old-fashioned to you, but it's important to us. I hope that you'll change your mind, for her sake. She'll need a female companion in the last weeks before our marriage.'

Something constrained in his manner caught Maggie's attention and a suspicion crept into her mind. 'I see what it is,' she said. 'Propriety, my foot! You want me to keep her occupied so that you won't have to listen to her chattering.'

A hint of ruefulness crept into his eyes, and for a moment he almost allowed himself to grin. 'I feel sure she would be happier for your presence. Please oblige me in this.'

'But this is December. Your wedding isn't until next March.'

'I forgot to mention that I've arranged for it to be moved up to the second week in January.'

'*Forgot to mention—?* Did you forget to mention it to Catalina, too?'

'I have every intention of telling her when she comes out to breakfast.'

'And suppose she has other ideas?' Maggie demanded, incensed almost past bearing by this high-handedness.

'We'll ask her, shall we?'

Catalina appeared at that moment, dressed in slacks and sweater. 'Oh, good!' she exclaimed when she saw the breakfast table. 'I'm so hungry.

'I was just explaining to Señora Cortez that official business obliges me to bring forward our wedding date to next month,' Sebastian said smoothly.

Catalina gave a little scream. 'But I can't be ready by then. I haven't even chosen a bridal dress.'

'Señora Cortez will help you decide when we return to Granada.'

'Oh, Maggie, you're coming to Spain? That will be wonderful.'

'Now, wait—I haven't said—besides, you've missed the point. He's changed the date without consulting you.'

Catalina gave a resigned little shrug. 'He does everything without consulting me. This bacon looks lovely.'

It was hopeless, Maggie realised, trying to make an impression on Catalina's butterfly mind. Last night Catalina had talked bravely under the influence of Maggie's strong personality. Today she was under Sebastian's even stronger influence. She listened while he explained that Isabella's sister would be arriving that afternoon, and the three of them would be leaving next day.

'As easy as that?' Maggie said, nettled by this casual way of arranging matters.

'Of course it's as easy as that,' he said in some surprise. 'Why shouldn't it be?'

'It would take too long to tell you.'

'Everything is easy for Sebastian,' Catalina said, tucking into her food with relish. 'People just do what he tells them.'

'Other people,' Maggie said firmly. 'Not me.'

'Oh, Maggie, please!' Catalina wailed. 'You can't just abandon me. I thought you were my friend.'

'I am, but—'

How could she explain to this wide-eyed girl that she had sworn never to return to Spain, and especially to Granada, where her heart had been broken and her spirit almost destroyed? If it had been anywhere else...

But perhaps, after all, it had to be Granada, where the ghosts she'd fled still raged. Maybe she'd run for long enough, and it was time to turn and face them.

'All right,' she said slowly. 'Just for a short time.'

'Oh good!' Catalina exclaimed. 'I'm so glad you've given in.'

Before Maggie could take exception to the phrase 'give in', Sebastian said, 'You're mistaken, my dear. Giving in is for weaklings. A strong person like Señora Cortez makes tactical concessions for reasons of her own.'

And this time there was no doubt of it. He smiled.

It was annoying that everyone and everything seemed to jump to do Sebastian's bidding, but that was the reality, Maggie had to recognise. Isabella's sister arrived later that day, full of effusions at Don Sebastian's 'generosity'. He took her to the comfortable little hotel just around the corner from the hospital, and then to see Isabella. Watching the sisters greet each other, Maggie conceded that he'd done exactly the right thing.

She was less delighted by his insistence that she take over Isabella's old room for their last night in England. 'I can't stay alone in that suite with Catalina,' he said firmly. 'The world would assume that I'd allowed my—er—ardour to overcome me, and she would be compromised.'

He gave her a look in which humour and cynicism were combined, and she suddenly had to look away.

The next day the snow began in earnest as they reached the airport. Maggie knew she would miss spending Christmas in England, but it might be nice to fly away to a warmer climate.

In no time the plane had climbed out of the snow and they were heading south to Spain, where the land was still brown. For the last half hour of the flight Maggie resisted looking out of the window, but she shut out the thoughts that troubled her. Far below lay all the stark magnificence of the country that she wasn't quite ready to face yet, to which, eight years before, she had come as a bride.

In some respects she had been like Catalina, barely old enough to be called a woman, eager for life, sure that every mystery could be explained with reference to her own limited experience. And so terribly, tragically wrong.

At eighteen she'd lost both her parents in a car crash, and at first had been too stunned to realise anything but her loss. When she finally overcame the worst of her grief, she found that she was well off. Two insurance policies and a house didn't amount to great wealth, but it was financial independence.

She had been close to her parents, and still living at home in a happy cocoon. Suddenly she was pitchforked into the world, deprived of the loving protection she'd always taken for granted, and with enough money at her disposal to make stupid mistakes.

She made several, mostly harmless ones. But then she met and fell in love with Roderigo Alva. And that had been the stupidest mistake of all.

They were introduced by friends on what was to be his last day before returning home to Granada. By the end of the evening he had deferred his departure indefinitely, to Maggie's delight. At thirty, he was older than any man she had dated before, yet he'd kept the light-heartedness of a boy. He was full of laughter, and he plunged into life's pleasures as though afraid they might be snatched away. His face was swarthily handsome, and his lean, elegant body moved with the grace of a cat. How wonderfully they danced together, and how desperately every dance increased her mounting passion for him.

He told her about his import-export business in Granada, the wonderful deal he had just pulled off. Everything about him seemed to confirm the picture of a successful man, son of a wealthy family who'd made his own fortune by hard work and skill. He was always well dressed and he showered expensive gifts on her.

He was enchanted to find her one quarter Spanish, and able to speak his language. Her dazzled eyes saw only a man of the world, who might have had any woman, but who declared that she was his first true love. She was eighteen. She believed him.

When she announced their engagement, the few family members she had left begged her to wait. 'You know nothing about him—he's so much older than you—' She brushed the warnings aside with the blind confidence of youth. She loved Roderigo. He loved her. What else mattered?

Unlike the boys of her own age, he kept his hands to himself, insisting that his bride must be treated with respect. But he wanted to marry her in England. She would have liked to have the wedding in Spain, with his family there, but Roderigo overbore her.

Later she wondered what would have happened if she'd held out and seen his home before committing herself. Because then she might have discovered that his 'business' was little more than a shell, that his creditors were dunning him and some of his activities were under investigation by the law.

Or suppose he'd come to her bed before the wedding? With her passion slaked, she might have seen him with clearer eyes, and not rushed headlong into legal ties. That too he had prevented, ensuring that when they reached Spain the cage door had already slammed shut behind her.

She rubbed her eyes, knowing the moment was drawing nearer when they would land. Beside her, Catalina was checking her face in a small mirror. On the far side of the aisle Sebastian sat absorbed in papers, as he had been since they took off. There was something down-to-earth about that sight that made Maggie feel she had been fanciful.

Now she forced herself to look out of the window at the white-capped Sierra Nevada mountains far below her, just like her first view of them on her honeymoon. Then she'd been blissfully happy. Now her heart was grey and empty. But the mountains were unchanged.

Had any bride ever had such a romantic honeymoon, skiing by day and making love by night? Roderigo was technically a skilled lover and in many respects their physical life was good. Perhaps even then she sensed something wrong, but she was too young and ignorant to know what it was—that she was doing with her whole soul what he was doing only with his body.

She met his family, not the solid merchants he'd described, but shysters living on the edge of the law, prosperous one day, hand-to-mouth the next. If they made money, they spent it before it was in hand. His mother wore expensive jewellery which would vanish—reclaimed by outraged shopkeepers, tired of waiting for payment.

The only one of the family Maggie took to was a young cousin, José, a boy of fifteen, who idolised her and constantly found excuses to visit their house. His infatuation was so youthfully innocent that neither she nor Roderigo could take offence.

Maggie had blotted out many of the details of that time, so that now she could no longer be sure exactly when she'd begun to see that Roderigo lived mainly on credit. He had expensive habits and very little way of servicing them. The 'business' was a joke through which he could claim tax breaks without making a profit. And why should a man bother with profit when he'd just married a wife with money?

He went through Maggie's modest wealth like water. When the ready cash had gone the house in England was sold and the money brought to Spain. Maggie tried to insist that it should be banked for a rainy day, but he bought her an expensive gift and swept her off on vacation, both of which she paid for.

He silenced her protests with passion. In his view, as

long as he was a good husband in bed, she had nothing to complain of. When she argued he began to show the other side of his character, the bully. How dared she criticise her husband? This was Spain, where the man was the master.

Maggie began to see with dreadful clarity that Roderigo was a fair-weather charmer, delightful while things were going well, but unpleasant when life was hard. And over the four years of their marriage, life grew bitterly hard. In that time she grew up fast, changing from a naive girl into a clear-eyed woman, surviving the disintegration of her world. Romantic dreams vanished, replaced by a realism that was almost, but not quite, cynicism.

She managed to cling onto a little money, standing up to Roderigo in a way that once wouldn't have been possible. But it was a waste of time. When threats didn't work he simply forged her signature, and then the money was gone.

Why hadn't she left him, then? Looking back, she often wondered. Perhaps it was because, having paid such a terrible price for her love, she couldn't bear to admit that it had all been for nothing. And besides, she was pregnant.

When she found out she entertained one last pathetic hope that Roderigo would finally discover in himself a sense of responsibility, and put some work into his business. Instead, he resorted to crime, petty at first, then more serious, always just managing to get away with it. Success went to his head. He grew careless. A theft was traced to him, and only the best efforts of an expensive lawyer got him off. His confidence grew. He was untouchable.

Then the police called again. A man had broken into

a wealthy house in Granada, and been disturbed by the owner. The thief attacked him and fled, leaving the man in a coma. Roderigo's fingerprints had been found in the house.

He protested his innocence, swearing falsely that at the time he had been at home with his wife. Sick at heart, Maggie refused to confirm the lie. He was arrested, tried and found guilty.

The day before the trial began she went into premature labour. Her six-month daughter was born, and survived a week. During that time Maggie never left her side. The news that Roderigo had been found guilty and sentenced to ten years seemed to reach her from a great distance.

She would never forget the last time she saw him, in prison. Once this had been the man she loved. Now he stared at her, hard faced, his eyes bleak with hate. 'Be damned to you!' he raged. 'You put me here. What kind of a wife are you?'

Exhausted and grief stricken from the loss of her child, she fought for the strength to say, 'I couldn't lie. You weren't with me that night.'

'I wasn't in that house—not then. I went there once before, that's why my fingerprints were there—I stole a few trinkets, but I harmed nobody. I swear I wasn't there that night. I never attacked that man.'

She gazed at him, wondering why he seemed to be at the end of a long tunnel. 'I don't believe you,' she said bleakly.

'But you must believe me. My lawyer—there is to be an appeal—you must help him—'

'I'm going back to England. I never want to see you again.'

'Curse you,' he raged. *'Curse you for a false bitch!'*

'You curse me Roderigo, but I also curse you, for the

loss of our child. I curse the day I met you.' The tunnel was getting longer, taking him further and further. 'My baby is dead,' she whispered. 'My baby is dead.'

His anger collapsed, and he began to weep. 'Maggie, I beg you—don't go! Stay here and help me. *Maggie, don't go!*'

She had left the prison with his cries ringing in her ears. José, now a lanky young man of nineteen, was waiting for her. He took her to the airport and kissed her goodbye with tears in his eyes.

It was José who wrote to her three months later to say that Roderigo had died of pneumonia. He had simply lain there, refusing to fight for his life, waiting for the end. Maggie, who'd thought her misery could get no deeper, had discovered that she was wrong.

To despair was now added guilt. Her dreams were full of Roderigo's cries, swearing his innocence, begging her to stay and fight for him. He had been a bad husband, selfish and deceitful, spending her money, turning on her, destroying her life. But her conscience accused her of being a bad wife, deserting him in his hour of need. If she had stayed, perhaps he would be alive…

She had fought back in the only way she could, by denying the past. She resumed her maiden name, blotting out Roderigo from every corner of her life. Her passport, her driving licence, the rent book to the shabby little apartment which was now all she could afford, all proclaimed her Margaret Cortez. Roderigo Alva might never have existed.

It was only sometimes, in the darkness, that she heard him still, shrieking his desperation and fear. Then she would bury her head beneath the pillows and pray hopelessly for an absolution that would never come.

*   *   *

At Malaga Airport a car was waiting to take them the hour's journey through the Andalucian countryside to Granada. Catalina was filled with excitement. 'I'm so glad to be back,' she said. 'You will love it here, Maggie.'

'Whereabouts in Spain did you live before?' Sebastian asked from Catalina's other side.

'In the city of Granada,' Maggie replied briefly.

'So you know this place?' Catalina sounded disappointed. 'You didn't say. But then, you never talk of that time.' She patted her hand sympathetically. 'Forgive me.'

'We're not actually going to the city, are we?' Maggie said, anxious to forestall one of the girl's sentimental outbursts. 'I believe Don Sebastian's house is a few miles outside.'

'In the foothills of the Sierra Nevada,' he said. 'It is the most beautiful place on earth.' And for the first time Maggie thought she detected real emotion in his voice.

He was silent for a few miles, then he said, 'There,' in the same tone. And she began to understand.

Don Sebastian's 'house' could be seen on one of the lower slopes. It was actually more like a small Moorish palace, sitting serenely overlooking the valley. It seemed to be built on several levels, and even from a distance Maggie could perceive its beauty, how it extended into gardens, towers, rambling this way and that in leisurely style.

The car had begun to climb a road that twisted and turned among elm and cypress, giving her glimpses of the lovely building, that were snatched away almost at once, to be replaced a moment later with a closer look, even more beautiful.

They came at last to some wrought iron gates that

opened, apparently of their own accord, to let them
sweep through. A little more climbing and they were
there, the front doors standing open and a middle-aged
man and woman waiting ready to greet them. Maggie
guessed these were the chief steward and housekeeper.
Behind them there was a crowd of servants, who had
evidently come to see their new mistress arrive.

Hands reached out to open the car doors. Sebastian
slipped a reassuring arm about Catalina's shoulders and
led her forward to meet her household. But he glanced
back to make sure Maggie was close behind, and introduced her with an easy courtesy that prevented any awkwardness.

The housekeeper showed Catalina to her room. It had
a grandeur suitable for the future mistress of this mini
palace, and she danced around it gleefully before seizing
Maggie's hand and taking her along the corridor to another room, almost as lavish as the first.

'This is yours,' she said.

'This?' Maggie echoed, overwhelmed by the gorgeous
red tiles on the floor, the mosaic-inlaid walls and the
huge draped bed. There was history in this room as well
as beauty, and a subtle, ancient magic that elicited her
fascinated response. Along the outer wall were two tall,
horseshoe arches, hung with heavy net curtains. Set between the arches were floor length windows that opened
onto a balcony.

Dazed, Maggie allowed Catalina to lead her out onto
the balcony with its magnificent view down the valley
and across the distance to Granada, and the hill on which
stood the glorious Alhambra Palace. It was early evening
and darkness had fallen, showing the gleams of light
from the collection of buildings that made up the palace.

Directly under the balcony Maggie could see one of

the courtyards of Sebastian's house, and something struck her.

'This is like a smaller version of the Alhambra,' she murmured. She had visited the splendid Moorish palace several times, and recognised the emphasis on highly decorative mosaics, the arches supported on pillars so impossibly delicate that it seemed as though the building was about to fly away.

'That's what it's supposed to be,' Catalina told her. 'They say that the Sultan Yusuf the First built it for his favourite, in the style of his own palace. All the other concubines lived in the harem, but he kept her here, hidden away from the world. He was murdered by another man who also loved her. When she heard, she came out onto this balcony where she could look across the valley, and stayed here until she too had died from grief. They say her ghost still walks in these rooms.'

'If they say that, they talk nonsense,' Sebastian said from the curtained window. He had come in behind them so quietly that neither of them had heard him. 'Why should any man force himself to travel fifteen miles for one woman when he could reach the harem in a moment?'

Maggie felt her annoyance rising at the sight of him standing there, so assured, his face full of wry amusement at what he plainly considered female fancies. Yet even then she had to concede that his tall body and proud head had a magnificence that matched his surroundings.

'He might want to keep her apart if he loved her very much,' she observed. 'You, of course, would find that incredible, Señor.'

'Totally incredible,' he agreed dryly.

'Oh, you're so unromantic!' Catalina scolded. 'I love to think of the Sultan standing at a window of the

Alhambra, gazing up to where the favourite stood on this balcony, calling her name across the valley. Maggie, why do you laugh? It isn't funny.'

'I'm sorry,' she choked. 'But you said he wanted to keep her hidden from the world. She wouldn't be much of a secret if he was bawling her name across fifteen miles.'

'How unromantic you are!' Sebastian chided her in Catalina's words, but he was grinning. 'And, for the record, Sultan Yusuf wasn't murdered by a jealous lover. He was assassinated by a madman. And no ghost walks these rooms, Señora—don't be alarmed.'

'I wasn't alarmed,' Maggie told him crisply. 'I don't believe in ghosts. Not that kind, anyway.'

The last words were spoken half to herself and made him glance at her with a quick frown. But he said nothing.

'You have no souls, either of you,' Catalina said crossly.

Sebastian stood back, indicating for them to return inside. 'Forgive my intrusion, ladies. Señora Cortez, welcome to my home. I hope the hospitality meets with your approval.'

'It's overwhelming,' she said, indicating the splendid apartment. 'Much too fine for me. I'll get lost in all this.'

'Be sure that I'll send out a search party for you,' he said. And he actually smiled right at her, almost inviting her to share a joke.

He shouldn't do that too often, she thought. It was dangerous.

CHAPTER FOUR

AT THE centre of Sebastian's home was the Patio de los Pájaros, the garden of birds, an enclosed garden, with a pool and a softly plashing fountain. Elaborately carved stone birds sat in silence beneath the trees and between the shrubs, and more birds hovered beside the pool.

Beyond the trees and shrubs were elaborately decorated arches whose twisted pillars seemed too frail for their burden. And yet the total impression was of perfection. Everything here was of peaceful symmetry, joyful harmony.

A moon was rising high in the dazzlingly clear sky as Maggie slipped outside and took a breath of the sweet night air. It was hard to recall that England was under snow. This far south the December nights were often pleasant, although here in the foothills it was cooler than in the city below, and she wore only a thin nightdress and robe. But even the chill was pleasant, and perhaps the harmony of the garden could restore the harmony of her mind.

The evening meal had been awesome. A pack of Sebastian's relatives, living nearby, had flocked to see his bride's return, and they had been joined by some distinguished names from the local government.

The only one who stood out in Maggie's mind was Alfonso, a distant cousin in his twenties, who worked as Sebastian's secretary. He was aloofly handsome, and at first glance he had the haughty demeanour of a de Santiago. But his smile was charming, and when he gazed at Catalina there was a kind of dumbfounded shock in his eyes that made Maggie pity him. He would have been a more suitable husband for her than Sebastian, yet even he, Maggie thought, was too grave and serious for such a flighty creature.

Catalina's butterfly moods changed this way and that with dizzying speed. When they arrived she'd been a girl, so thrilled with her expensive new toys that she'd forgotten the price she must pay. But as the evening wore on the price became more obvious, until she was almost drooping. Both she and Maggie were relieved when they could retire to bed.

Poor Catalina, Maggie thought as she trailed her hand in the water. How right I was to oppose this marriage. It will be terrible for her.

She leaned over, watching her own moonlit reflection, scattering as she moved her fingers, but then becoming one again as the water stilled.

'Like me,' she said to the night. 'All broken up one moment, peaceful the next. But the peace is an illusion; it can be shattered so easily. Why ever did I come here?'

'Why, indeed?' murmured a voice behind her.

In the same moment she saw him in the water, a man's shape, turned to silhouette by the moon. 'I didn't know you were there,' she said, turning.

'I'm sorry I startled you,' Sebastian said. 'It was wrong of me.'

She nodded. 'One should always wander in an enclosed garden alone. Thus you will find truth and paradise.'

He gave a small start of pleasure. 'So you understand the symbolism?'

'I know why so much Moorish architecture is built around places like this,' she said. 'But I'm not sure I agree with it. How can you achieve truth or heaven when the enclosure shuts so much out?'

'But you forget, it also symbolises the whole cosmos, the world and infinity. Here, all beauty can be held in the palm of your hand.'

He dipped his hand and raised it, so that the water streamed down, leaving just a little cupped in his palm, until he opened his fingers, allowing it to trickle away. In the moonlight it glittered like magic, holding Maggie's gaze, almost hypnotising her. 'You can turn the symbolism any way you like,' he said.

She could watch the water for ever, feeling the peace invade her bones. This was a magic place, and it would be fatally easy to surrender to that magic. She too slid her hand into the water and lifted it high, fascinated by the droplets. Sebastian took her fingers between his, holding them lightly.

'Thank you for everything,' he said. 'For calming Isabella's fears and befriending Catalina, for being wise and strong.'

Through the cold water she could feel the warmth of his hand, holding hers in a grip whose power was concealed but inescapable. She tried to speak, but couldn't. Something was impeding her breathing.

'I think you belong in an enclosed garden,' he said.

'Shut away from the world?' she asked, struggling to escape the spell. 'Not me.'

'No, not shut away. You would bring the world inside with you, and contain it here in your hand, and the man who came seeking truth and wisdom would find it in you. Then he could truly shut out the rest of the world, having all he needed here.'

The words were ravishing, seductive, seeming to swim in the air. With an effort Maggie gave herself a little mental shake. 'Is it wise to make so much of symbolism?' she asked softly. 'If we blind ourselves with symbols, where is the reality?'

'I wonder which reality you are speaking of?'

'Is there more than one?'

'There are a million, and each man chooses his own.'

'Each man, perhaps,' she said wryly. 'But how often can a woman choose? Mostly she has a man's reality forced upon her.'

'Was it forced on you? Or did you choose it freely— and then find that you had chosen in blindness?'

'Aren't all choices made in blindness? And we discover too late.' She gave a little shiver.

'You should have been more sensibly dressed to come out here,' Sebastian told her. Swiftly he removed his jacket and draped it around her shoulders. Unconsciously she sighed at the warmth. 'If you become ill I shall be in disfavour with my bride. She's already angry with me for "brutally forcing" you—her words— to come here, where your heart will be broken by memories of your great lost love.'

'Oh, dear! I've told her not to see me through a filter of tragic romance.'

'You're wasting your time. She loves seeing you that way. Next she'll be wanting you to wander the streets of Granada, seeking out the places you knew with him.'

Suddenly she was aware of danger. It had been there all the time, but he'd managed to make her ignore it until almost too late. She stepped back from him. 'You are wasting your time, Don Sebastian. I don't discuss my husband with Catalina, and I won't discuss him with you.'

'And yet you came to Andalucia to find him—or to be finally rid of him. I wonder which.'

'You can go on wondering. It is none of your business.'

'That was what you meant by ghosts, wasn't it?'

'Please drop this subject.'

'How angry you become when he is mentioned!'

'Neither is my anger any of your business!'

'Then let me give you a word of advice. If you wish to keep your secrets, hide your anger. It reveals too much about you.'

The last of the spell vanished. How dare he think he could bemuse her with his pretty nonsense about gardens and truth!

'You know nothing about me,' she said firmly, 'except that I can be useful to you. That's all you need to know, and all you will ever know. My "secrets" don't concern you, my private life doesn't concern you, and if you ever mention this again I will walk out.'

She was dismayed to find herself trembling. To hide it from him she began to turn away, but he detained her with a hand on her arm.

'I'm sorry. I hadn't realised it was as painful as that.'

She took a deep breath. 'Goodnight, Don Sebastian.'

'Don't go yet.'

'I said goodnight.'

His fingers tightened on her arm. But he found himself holding nothing. Maggie had slipped away, leaving him holding the empty jacket.

The time before the wedding was short, and Catalina's first priority was a visit to Señora Diego, a dressmaker in Granada, where she would find a selection of bridal gowns to choose from. The car was ready to take them early next day, and on the journey Maggie noted wryly that the girl's mood had changed again. The gloom of the previous evening had vanished, replaced by excitement at the thought of an expensive shopping trip.

Catalina tried on dress after dress, until at last the three of them agreed on a garment of lace that enhanced her delicate attractions. It was a little too large, but the alterations could be made at once. Catalina flopped down, worn out by her exertions, and prepared to gorge herself on sticky cakes until she was needed for a fitting.

'Would you mind if I left you for a moment?' Maggie asked. 'I'll be back in an hour.'

Catalina, her mouth full, waved her off, and Maggie slipped away. She'd been taken aback to find that the gown shop was only a few streets from the place where Roderigo's business had been located. Now it seemed an excellent chance to lay a ghost. Just two more streets, then one...

At the last moment she almost changed her mind, but something drove her on to turn the corner, and there it was, the building she had once viewed with such dread, wondering what lies it was sheltering, what bills it was generating for her to pay.

It was different now, neater, more prosperous looking. Whoever had taken it over had made a success. The name over the door was José Ruiz, which struck a chord.

Suddenly the door opened and an extremely handsome young man stepped out. As his eyes fell on her an expression of pure delight spread over his face.

'Maggie!' he cried, advancing on her with outstretched hands. He stopped before her. 'Don't you remember me?'

Then she recognised him as the young cousin who had been constantly in and out of her home with Roderigo. 'José!' she said, pleased. 'For a moment I didn't recognise you.'

'I was a boy then, now I am a man,' he said proudly.

The years from nineteen to twenty-three had been kind to José. He had filled out. His shoulders were broader, the set of his head more mature, but there was still laughter in his eyes.

'I'm so glad to see you again,' he told her. 'I've always remembered how kind you were to me.'

Somebody jostled them on the pavement and he took her arm. 'There's a little place in the next street where we can have coffee.'

When they were seated he said, 'I thought you would never come back here.'

'I never meant to. It's only chance that brought me.'

She explained about her employment and José's eyes widened. 'I have heard of Don Sebastian, of course. Who in these parts has not? He is a great man.'

'Hm! That's as may be. I could find other words. I don't think you'd like him any more than I do.'

'Like?' José seemed mildly shocked. 'But Maggie, he is a man of authority, of respect, of *power*. His landholdings are vast, he has orange and lemon groves, vineyards. One does not dare to like or dislike such a man. One merely prays not to come under his disapproval.'

'I've no patience with that kind of talk. He's a man like any other. As a matter of fact I *have* come under his disapproval, but that's fine, because he's come under *mine*.'

José eyed her in fascination. 'Have you told him so?'

'Certainly.'

'How brave you must be!'

'Tell me about yourself. What are you doing in that place?'

'I took over the remainder of Roderigo's lease, and started my own little business. I export fruit from this region, and I import small luxury goods from all over the world.'

'So did Roderigo, I recall, when he bothered to do anything.'

José looked uncomfortable. 'We do not speak of him,' he said. 'Luckily my last name is Ruiz, not Alva, so I renamed the business, and I don't run it the way he did.'

'You're wise. I too no longer bear his name.' She looked at her watch. 'I must be getting back. Catalina will be wondering where I am.'

'She is Don Sebastian's betrothed?'

'Yes. I left her trying on wedding dresses.'

The light of commerce came into José's eyes. 'Let me escort you, Maggie.'

She smiled. 'These luxury goods you import—they wouldn't be suitable for weddings, would they?'

'Many, yes. But I was thinking more of getting an introduction to Don Sebastian. He has influence in the government—not the Spanish government, but the Andalucian.'

Maggie nodded. She knew Andalucia was a self-governing region where contacts and influence were important. Roderigo had been constantly seeking to 'meet a man who knows someone'.

'If you could introduce me to the great man,' José pleaded. 'There are contracts I could tender for—he will know people—please, Maggie.' He took her hand between his and implored, 'In the name of our old friendship.'

'All right,' she said, unable not to smile, 'I'll do my best for you. But remember, to these people I am Señora Cortez. That happened by mistake, but it would take too long to put right.'

'I won't mention Roderigo,' José swore. 'I can't thank you enough.'

'One more thing,' Maggie said firmly, getting to her feet. 'If you ever again refer to Sebastian as "a great man", you and I are no longer friends.'

'Ai, ai, ai!' he said, impressed.

He walked back to the bridal shop with her and they arrived just as Catalina was dancing about in a flurry of white lace.

'Isn't it perfect, Maggie?' Catalina cried. 'Aren't I beautiful?'

'Beautiful,' she said indulgently. 'Catalina, this is José, an old friend.'

The girl gave a theatrical curtsey, becoming a flower of white lace. José responded with a correct little bow.

'José will be coming to see me after supper this evening,' Maggie added.

'Oh, no, you must come much earlier,' Catalina pouted. 'It's going to be such a boring supper, full of elderly aunts. You must eat with us, and then it won't be so dull.'

José accepted gratefully, and they parted on the promise that they would all see each other later. Maggie had qualms about whether she'd done the right thing, but the evening went off better than she had dared to hope.

As Catalina had said, the huge table was filled with elderly relatives. José's behaviour was perfect. He was courteous to his elders, charming the old ladies and listening deferentially to advice from the men. Maggie introduced him to Sebastian, who nodded politely before turning away. José betrayed no impatience, and was finally rewarded with fifteen minutes in Sebastian's study. Before leaving he pressed Maggie's hands and said,

'Thank you,' so fervently that she knew the interview must have gone well.

That night she strolled in the garden again, choosing a different path from last time. She wandered slowly amongst the flowers, finding her way by the moonlight that lit up silver paths that twisted and curved and ended in shadows. Birds called softly in the night, and wherever she turned there was beauty too great to be true.

At last she told herself that she must go indoors in case Sebastian should appear. There mustn't be another encounter like last night. But still she found herself lingering.

'Does my home please you now that you know it better?' came a voice from the darkness. He appeared from beneath the trees, a silvered outline in the moonlight. He was wearing the clothes in which he'd dined, but now the frilled evening shirt was torn open to the waist. His chest was thick with hair, rising and falling as though he had been running.

'I think you live in the most beautiful place on earth,' she agreed.

He was carrying two wine glasses, one of which he gave to her, almost as if he had known that she would be there. 'How does Catalina seem to you?' he asked. 'Is she happy?'

'She is now, because she's surrounded by pretty things and she's going to be the centre of attention on the big day. But after that?'

'After that, I shall spoil her, like the child she is, and she will want for nothing. Of course, she may find life a little short of intellectual pursuits—'

'We've already agreed that Catalina isn't an intellectual,' Maggie said wryly.

'She's a scatterbrain who'll always be content as long as she has a large dress allowance and girlfriends to gossip with,' he said indulgently.

It annoyed Maggie not to be able to dispute the point, but she'd come to see that Sebastian's assessment of his bride was largely correct. That didn't make her agree with him about his marriage, but it did make him hard to fight.

'And what about you?' she asked. 'How will you manage with a wife who cannot share your thoughts?'

He shrugged. 'I share my thoughts with men, not women.'

'For heaven's sake!' she cried to the sky.

'You demand too much of marriage. No relationship can fulfil all needs. Catalina and I will make a home together. I will keep her safe, give her children, and satisfy her need for passion.'

'You're very sure you can satisfy that?' she snapped.

He shrugged. 'I've had no complaints so far.'

'Stop right there. I don't want to hear about your easy conquests.'

'Why do you assume that they were easy?'

'Because I know about you now. I know how they speak of you—Don Sebastian, the man of authority, of respect, of *power*. The man whose eye everyone wants to catch—'

'Like your friend tonight,' he murmured.

'Yes. Good heavens, he nearly jumped through hoops when he heard I knew you.'

'Why, Margarita,' he said softly, 'I didn't realise that I filled so large a part of your conversation—or your thoughts.'

'Don't try to lay traps for me—'

'You lay them for yourself. Why do you dislike me so much?'

'Because—' it was suddenly hard to answer '—because I feel sorry for Catalina. You mean to be a good husband by your lights, but your lights are very narrow. I see her being frog-marched into this marriage without having a chance to find something better.'

'Something better than a home in which she will be petted and indulged, and given safety in which to rear her children? Yes, I shall be a good husband *by my lights*. But my lights include something you never speak of, perhaps because you think it doesn't matter.'

'I don't know what you mean.'

'I think you do. She is beautiful. I am a man who knows how to please a woman, and how to teach her to please him. Strange, how you never allow for passion, Margarita. A man might almost think you knew nothing of it.'

'Oh, I know about passion,' she said with a bitterness she couldn't suppress. 'I know how dangerous it is, and how overrated. You think if you blind her like that nothing else will matter.'

'I think that a man who satisfies his wife in bed is a good husband, and has protected the sanctity of his home.'

Suddenly time rolled back and she was confronting Roderigo again, beating her head against his selfish conviction that his technical skill as a lover should silence all argument. Terrified, she hurled the cruellest words she could find.

'And how will he know if she's truly satisfied, Sebastian? How can he be sure that what he sees isn't a pretence, the prisoner placating her gaoler? That's the trouble when a man has too much power. He's never quite certain, is he?'

The sharp intake of his breath told her that she'd struck home. 'Be careful,' he said harshly.

'It's true. Admit it!'

She didn't know what demon was lashing her on to drive him past the point of safety. She only knew that she would do anything to crack his control and wipe the complacency from his face. And that she was succeeding.

'Stop there,' he said harshly.

'Why should I? What did you think I meant when I spoke of your "easy conquests"? They're very easy, aren't they, Sebastian? I'm sure women flock to your bed, but is it you that pleases them, or your money and power? You'll never be sure, will you?'

'Then you can be the judge,' he snapped.

She read the intention in his eyes and backed off, but too late. His hand was behind her head and his mouth on hers before she had time to think. There was no chance to even try to push him away as his other arm clamped itself around her waist, grinding her body against his. She had driven him too far. Now he had a point to make, and she knew within seconds that he was going to make it with devastating force. No quarter asked or given.

But that went for her too, she thought furiously. What a pleasure it would be to lie, frozen, in his arms, and let him know how little impact he made on a woman who wanted nothing from him. It would be satisfying to teach him a lesson.

She let her hands fall to her side and stood, unresisting, while his lips moved over hers, skilled, purposeful. There was coaxing in those movements, but she ignored it. It was harder to ignore the hot, spicy smell of him and the feel of his body moulded against hers. She was conscious of the lines of his thighs, his lean hips, and the fact that he had come swiftly to full arousal.

To her dismay, that knowledge sent little sparks of excitement through her. That wasn't what she'd meant to happen, and she wouldn't give in to it. She must remember how much she disliked him, because then she couldn't possibly want to press herself closer to him.

He raised his head and looked down at her face, closed against him in the moonlight. He smiled.

'It isn't going to be that easy,' he said softly. 'For either of us.'

'Go to the devil!'

'Of course. That's where you're driving me. Let's go together.'

'*No!*'

'Too late to say no. Too late for both of us. You should have thought of this before you taunted me. Now we have to go on to the end.'

He covered her mouth with a swift, ravishing movement, and she clenched her hands. It was hard to keep them at her side when they wanted to touch him, excite him. She resisted the impulse, but she guessed he must sense her struggle. At all costs she must prove herself stronger than him at this moment.

As though he read her thoughts he murmured against her lips, 'Why do you fight me?'

'Because somebody must,' she said fiercely, trying not to let her voice shake.

Astonished, he drew back and searched her face.

'You have more power than any man should have,' she flung at him. 'But while I'm alive, it will never be complete. I'll never give you power over me. Not for an instant.'

'I believe you really would fight me to the last moment,' he murmured huskily.

'Believe it! Because I've seen through you.'

'And what do you think you see?'

'This is all an act. You don't really want me at all, any more than I want you. You just can't bear someone who doesn't jump when you snap your fingers. If I let you overcome me, you'd shrug at another conquest and forget me the next moment.'

'Are you so sure?'

'Completely sure.'

'Shall we find out?'

'It will never happen,' she said slowly and deliberately. She wrenched herself free and backed away from him. She was breathing hard, but in command of herself. She wasn't so sure of Sebastian's control. There was a wild look in his eyes, and she was suddenly aware how isolated they were in this distant part of the garden. He was a man used to taking what he wanted.

'I'm leaving this house,' she said.

'I forbid it!'

'And you think you have only to give your orders? Don't try to order me, Sebastian. I'm going first thing tomorrow. And think yourself lucky if I don't tell Catalina the kind of man she's marrying.'

'Do you know the kind of man she's marrying?'

'I know that whatever else you offer your wife, it isn't fidelity.'

'I find it hard to think of fidelity when you're around. Perhaps you should blame yourself for that. Why do you incite me if you have nothing to give?'

'Don't try to blame me! I don't incite you.'

'You incite me just by living and breathing. You incite me when you walk in the room, when I see you—'

'Then the sooner you see me no more, the better.'

She walked away from him quickly. As she went she listened for his footsteps coming after her, but there was only the silence and she managed to reach the building. She was shaking with the violence of what had happened to her, not what he had done, but what she had felt. Her heart was thundering and her whole body shook with the force of the sensations he had aroused. Everything he said was true. She was no girl but a woman who had learned the secrets of desire and couldn't forget them. She'd forced them back, tried to deny what she knew, but they were there, waiting for the wrong man to bring them back to life.

She hurried to her room, longing to get out of sight, but suddenly Catalina appeared, smiling at the sight of her. Now was her chance, Maggie thought. She'd wanted to stop this wedding, and if she told the girl the truth about her future husband, that was all it would take.

Or would it? Catalina probably didn't expect perfect behaviour from Sebastian, but she would expect it from her friend. Her revelations might cause pain without doing any good.

'I thought you were in bed and asleep,' she said.

'I can't sleep. I think and think about my lovely dress. I shall be the most beautiful bride.'

'And after? Will he be a good husband?'

The girl shrugged. 'He will take care of me, and I shall have lots of lovely new clothes.'

This was so nearly what Sebastian had said that Maggie was startled. There was something about Catalina's prosaic attitude to her marriage that made the dreadful words die before they could be spoken. The next moment, she knew they would never be said. Catalina put her arms around Maggie's neck and kissed her softly on the cheek. 'I'm so happy you're here,' she said. 'Nobody has ever been as good to me as you.'

She drifted away down the corridor. At her door, she stopped, blew Maggie a kiss, and slipped inside.

'Oh, heavens!' Maggie said to the silence.

'Thank you.'

She whirled at the sound of Sebastian's voice as he reached the top of the stair. 'How long have you been there?'

'Long enough to know that you might have betrayed me, and didn't.'

'For her sake, not for yours.'

'I know that.' In the dusky light of the corridor she could see that his face was gaunt and strained. 'I behaved badly tonight. You are living under my roof—I forgot my honour, the honour of my house. If you will consent to remain, I give you my word that such a thing will not occur again.' She hesitated and he said, 'You will be safe, on my sacred word!'

'Very well, I'll stay. But hear this, Sebastian. I couldn't give you away tonight, but I'll still use every chance I have to undermine you in her eyes. Do you understand me? If I can talk her out of this wedding—I'll do it.'

He inclined his head. 'At least I can see the battle lines. I have no complaints.'

'You may have if she jilts you.'

'She won't jilt me, because you're too honourable to use your strongest weapon. I thank you, for that and for declaring war openly.'

'As long as you remember that war is what it is.'

CHAPTER FIVE

'OH, MAGGIE, it's wonderful up here. I'm so glad we came!'

Laughing, Catalina flopped down into a seat on the terrace café and looked out over the snow. An energetic session on the piste had left her with bright eyes and glowing cheeks.

They had been three days in Sol y Nieve, the chief ski resort of the Sierra Nevada mountains. Here, surrounded by snow, they could be carefree for just a little time, and it was almost possible to forget Sebastian and all the turbulent emotions below. By day there was skiing and shopping, and in the evening there was good food, wine, and music.

A waiter brought them coffee and cream cakes. Watching the girl tuck in, Maggie said, 'If you're not careful, you won't be able to get into your wedding dress.'

'I eat anything and I never put on weight,' Catalina said with a giggle. 'It makes other women so mad.' She leaned back with her eyes closed, letting the sun play on her face. She looked prettier than ever.

'How did you ever persuade Sebastian to let me out of the cage?' she asked, keeping her eyes closed.

Maggie regarded her wryly, no longer impressed by talk of cages. She knew now that this was Catalina's 'line', and it would be dropped the next time she was enjoying being the star attraction in a big, glamorous, set piece.

'There was no problem,' she said. 'He agreed to my suggestion at once.'

That was true, but there had been a silent subtext. She had gone to Sebastian the morning after their fierce encounter in the garden and told him flatly that she wanted to take Catalina away for a few days.

'Is this really necessary?' he'd asked mildly. 'There's much to do—and I gave you my word—'

'I want to get out of this house for at least a week,' she'd replied. When he still hesitated, she said quietly, 'It is a question of honour.'

She knew those words had revealed something that would have been better kept secret. He would guess now that she wasn't as immune to him as she'd claimed. But at the word 'honour' he'd nodded and agreed without further argument.

While she was getting ready to leave there was a phone call for her. It was José, to thank her for her help yesterday, and to ask her to meet him for coffee.

'I'd love to, but it'll have to wait until we return,' she said.

'You're going away?'

'Catalina and I are going up to Sol y Nieve for a few days skiing. I'll call you when we get back,' she promised.

An hour later the car departed, laden with five suitcases for Catalina and two for Maggie, to start the short journey up the mountain to the ski resort.

It had taken less than an hour for them to remove themselves into what felt like another world. Gone was the balmy air of the foothills, replaced by freezing temperatures and dazzling snow as far as the eye could see. In this cheerful place, where the tourist season was just under way, Maggie could lose herself in mindless activ-

ity, and forget that she'd come within an inch of doing
something for which her conscience would have reproached her. Or at least, she could try to forget.

Skiing with Catalina could be frustrating. The girl was
at home only on the 'green' and 'blue' runs, the two
lowest rungs of difficulty. But Maggie had honed her
skills on these mountains in the dark days of her marriage, when she scarcely cared what happened to her.
From difficult 'red' runs she had progressed to hair-
raising 'black'. The Sierra Nevada had five black runs,
two of them almost sheer drops, and she was longing to
return to them, but with Catalina that was impossible.

When they had finished eating they began to head
back in the direction of the ski lift. Suddenly she heard
a voice call, 'Hey, Maggie!'

Turning she saw two young men in ski clothes, making their way towards her. Against the blinding snow
she didn't recognise either of them until Catalina
squealed with excitement, and cried, *'José!'*

'Goodness, yes, it is,' she said. 'I wonder who the
other boy is.'

José's companion was an undistinguished looking
youth with a slightly sloping chin and prominent eyes.
He was extremely tall with long, awkward legs and no
social graces whatever.

'Allow me to introduce my friend Horacio,' José said,
when he'd approached them. 'We are taking a brief skiing holiday.'

His eyes, meeting Maggie's, were too innocent to be
true, and an incredible thought came to her. Once, José
had fancied himself in love with her. Surely it wasn't
possible that…?

'Permit us to buy you both coffee,' José offered
smoothly.

'We've just eaten, thank you,' Maggie said. 'We were about to return to the slopes.'

'So were we. What a coincidence!'

'Yes, isn't it?' she said, her lips twitching.

The four of them skied together for the rest of the day, and after that it seemed natural to meet up for a meal that evening. By now Horacio was smitten by Catalina, and goofily unable to hide it. The girl's natural kindness stopped her snubbing him too firmly. Luckily he turned out to be a good dancer, so she was able to keep him content with a few energetic turns about the floor. This left Maggie and José together at the table.

'Where on earth did you find him?' she chuckled.

'He works for me. He's a good lad, but he doesn't have much social life, so when I hauled him up here he jumped at it.' He smiled at her outrageously. 'Well, I could hardly come on my own. And, now that I'm here—' He held out his hands invitingly.

She laughed and let him lead her onto the floor, discovering that she was in the mood for a harmless flirtation. They danced together a couple of times, then everyone changed partners and she found herself with Horacio. The next few minutes were a trial, as he kept trying to look over his shoulder at Catalina. The sight of her happily dancing and giggling with José reduced him to anguish. Maggie was glad when it was time for them all to say goodnight.

In the privacy of their suite, the two young women indulged themselves in a hearty burst of laughter.

'If only he'd stick to dancing, everything would be fine,' Catalina gasped. 'But he will talk about balance sheets and import regulations.' She went off in another convulsion of mirth, and Maggie joined her. It made a good end to an enjoyable day.

The four of them spent the next morning wandering around the town on a shopping expedition. It was an enchanted place, covered in snow and full of coloured lights. Dazzling Christmas trees stood on every corner, the shop windows were packed with gifts, and silver bells hung overhead. Maggie and José had gotten a little ahead of the other two when it was time to return to the hotel, and they walked up the steps and into the reception area together. There Maggie stopped, astonished.

'Good afternoon, Señora Cortez,' Sebastian said affably.

'Señor, I had no idea that you meant to come here.'

'The snow reports are encouraging, and as both Alfonso and myself are keen skiers, we couldn't resist.'

Alfonso, a little way behind, inclined his head courteously. Maggie brought José forward and there were murmured greetings all round.

'I wonder if that was the only reason,' she challenged Sebastian. 'If I was suspicious, I might think you were checking up on me.'

'And if I was suspicious, I might ask you where your charge is. There seems to be no sign of Catalina.'

'She'll be here in a moment. We've all been on a shopping trip.'

'All?'

'José's friend is also with us. He'll be arriving with Catalina in a moment.'

Sebastian frowned. 'And you've permitted them to be alone together?'

'As alone as anyone can be in this place.'

A hint of amusement in her manner made him bite back whatever he might have said, and the next moment Catalina appeared, accompanied by what seemed to be a mountain of parcels on beanpole legs. She waved to

them and took hold of the mountain's arm, guiding it
gently in the right direction and causing it to halt just in
time. The removal of the top two parcels revealed
Horacio, puffed, amiable and red-faced.

'I apologise for misjudging you,' Sebastian murmured
to Maggie when the introductions were over. 'The most
prurient gossip in the world couldn't associate scandal
with that idiot. But what about the other one?'

'José came to see me,' she murmured. 'I knew him
years ago and he had a boy's infatuation for me.'

'And now he plans to make up for lost time?'

'So it would seem.'

'He's far too young for you.'

'Thank you!' she said, half-laughing, half-indignant.
'It's a matter of three years.'

'Years,' he said dismissively. 'Did you think I was
talking about years?'

'I don't know what you're talking about,' she said
tartly, although she actually knew very well.

She told herself she was annoyed with Sebastian for
coming here. They had agreed that it was a question of
honour. Where was his honour now? But then, where
was hers to have felt that lifting of the heart at the sight
of him? Was it honourable to notice how handsome he
was, how much taller than every other man, and how
everyone looked at him, especially the women?

But then she told herself to stop being melodramatic.
There were six of them. What could happen?

Sebastian gallantly informed the ladies that he would
meet them for lunch in an hour. José and Horacio would
also be welcome. Horacio prepared to carry Catalina's
booty up to her suite, but at a nod from Sebastian
Alfonso firmly removed the parcels.

They ate in the open at the hotel's balcony restaurant,

which seemed to hang over a sheer drop. Above them rose the splendid vista of the mountains, the white broken only by little coloured figures dashing down the slopes.

'How can they do that when it's as steep as a wall?' Catalina squealed, covering her eyes with her hand.

'Catalina is happiest on very easy runs,' Maggie explained to Sebastian.

'But if you want to try the red or black,' Catalina offered, 'I shall—I shall *watch you*.'

She finished with an air of triumph. Everyone laughed at this anticlimax, and Sebastian said something polite about her forbearance.

Catalina was as good as her word. When the meal was over, they all went up to the top of a red run that made her gulp, but raised Maggie's spirits. She looked at it so longingly that Sebastian read her face.

'Go on,' he said, grinning. 'You can leave Catalina with me.'

She needed no more urging, but raced away with José in hot pursuit. It was glorious. For the first time since coming to Spain she felt free, speeding down the slope so fast that her furies were left far behind. José could barely keep up. At the bottom they immediately joined the queue for the ski lift, and reached the top in time to see the other four beginning the descent in a careful convoy, Catalina flanked by Sebastian and Alfonso, with Horacio bringing up the rear.

'This I have to see.' José chuckled. 'Coming?'

'You bet!' she cried, taking off ahead of him.

They passed the others on the way down, reaching the bottom first and waiting for them with grins on their faces. Sebastian scowled. He was an expert skier who'd had his sport ruined by a nervous novice and, since he was no saint but a fallible man whose pleasures were few, he wasn't in the best of moods.

'I'm sorry,' Catalina said, at her most charming.

'It wasn't your fault,' he said resignedly. 'But be off with you to the nursery slopes. I'll see you at dinner. Not you,' he detained Maggie.

'I must go with Catalina,' she protested.

'Horacio can go with her,' he growled. 'So can Alfonso, and José, and every man on the mountain for all I care. Did you say something?'

'Nothing,' she said, trying to keep a straight face.

In the end they separated into two parties. Sebastian and Maggie returned to the top of the 'red', while the other four made their way to a nice, safe 'green'.

'Whose idea was it for Catalina to try that run?' Maggie asked as they settled themselves on either side of the lift and felt the chain tighten, beginning to pull them up again.

'Mine, for my sins,' he growled. 'I thought she just needed a little encouragement, but we proceeded at a snail's pace, then she freaked out and we nearly had a collision with the skiers behind us—stop laughing, damn you!' But he was grinning.

'You'll feel better when you've had a good dash down the slope,' she said cheerfully. 'There's nothing like it for getting rid of the tensions. Mind you, "black" is even better.'

'You ski "black"?' he asked, turning his head and looking at her with interest.

'When I can. How about you?'

'I like it above everything.'

She looked him in the eyes. 'Really?' she said brightly. 'Then I hope you're not planning to spend your honeymoon skiing.'

Sebastian ground his teeth. 'Perhaps you should give your attention to the snow. We're nearly there.'

Skiing with Sebastian was even more exhilarating than with José, who either travelled beside or just behind her. Sebastian edged in front in what might or might not have been a silent challenge. She tested him, urging her skis faster, but he kept just ahead.

He was beautiful to watch, smooth and graceful, turning with ease, never losing his rhythm or his control. It took all Maggie's skill to match him at every point, but she managed it. At the bottom they stood for a moment, leaning on their skis, breathing hard, smiling.

'Again?' he asked.

She nodded.

They took the lift again, and as they glided upwards Sebastian suddenly turned his head and gave her a full-hearted grin. He was almost a different man and she guessed, because it was the same with her, that the hell-for-leather run had done this to him. He too had known the joy of cares left far behind as he flew down the mountain, and for the first time she wondered about the weight of those cares. He was an autocrat, and sometimes a heavy-handed one, but she had seen how he'd looked after Isabella, not merely making phone calls and giving orders, but taking the old woman's hand between his, speaking to her gently, and calming her fears with kindness.

The next moment, almost as though their minds were connected, he said, 'When I was a boy I practically lived in these mountains. Nothing mattered to me but skiing. I lived and breathed it, and dreamed of competing in the Olympics. They say I would have won a medal, perhaps a gold.'

The last words were said without arrogance, only a touch of wistfulness.

'What happened?' Maggie asked.

'When I was eighteen my father died, and I had to take charge of everything.'

'Couldn't you have done the Olympics first?' Maggie asked sympathetically.

'That's what I thought at the time. But the lawyers explained all that I needed to do, how many people on my lands depended on me.' He shrugged. 'And that was that.'

That was that. With this bleak little phrase he consigned the boy's dream to perdition, shouldering a burden years before his time. He had been the same age that Catalina was now.

'How sad for you,' she said.

'Nonsense!' he growled. 'I always knew what my life had to be. My father trained me for it.'

'But you didn't expect him to die so soon, surely? There should have been a few years for your own dreams first.'

'Yes,' he said after a moment. 'There should have been. Here we are at the top.'

The moment had passed. He was Sebastian again, scowling to cover his embarrassment at having given her a glimpse into his heart.

They did the run five times. As they walked back to the hotel through the snow Maggie said wistfully, 'There's a run here that's so steep it's known as the "Wall of Death". I've never dared try it yet, but I'm going to come back and do it just once before I go.'

'Don't!' he said at once. 'I've done that run and it's no place for a woman.'

'How nice to know that you'll be on your honeymoon,' she said tartly, 'well away from me, and unable to give me orders.'

'You take precious little notice of any order of mine anyway.'

'True. And this one I shall ignore completely.'

He stopped in the entrance to the hotel. 'It's not an order, Margarita. It's a plea. I've done that run and it isn't known as the "Wall of Death" for nothing. You're a good skier, and perhaps if there was somebody there with you—a friend to care for you—but there won't be. It would worry me to think of you doing it alone. Promise me that you won't.'

There was an unfamiliar note in his voice, almost the warmth and gentleness of a true friend. It made Maggie say impulsively, 'All right, I promise.'

He took her hand. 'Thank you. That means a lot to me.'

But then she recollected herself, remembered that in a few weeks he would be married to another woman and out of her life forever. She swiftly withdrew her hand and said brightly, 'I'll hire a professional for the day and he'll guard me like a mother hen. Now, shall we get inside? I'm hungry.'

They found the others already in the balcony café. The three young men rose at their approach, and Alfonso went off to find a waiter. Sebastian seated himself beside Catalina, and waved José to the seat on his other side. This left Horacio sitting blissfully next to Catalina. Watching the moonstruck youth strain her good nature to the limit Maggie wondered if Sebastian had more sense of humour than she'd credited him with.

Sebastian turned his attention to José. 'I've been meaning to talk to you. I know someone who's interested in exactly the kind of goods you supply, and would like to arrange an early meeting.' He pushed a small paper over to José. 'That's his number. Call him now.'

José vanished and returned with the news that he had an appointment for the next afternoon.

'Then you should leave immediately and spend this evening with your files,' Sebastian said with a smile of ice. 'This man will expect you to be extremely well prepared. Let's say our goodbyes now, to avoid delaying you.'

Put as bluntly as that, there was no mistaking the message. José forced a smile, nodded and departed, hauling the reluctant Horacio with him.

Catalina was indignant. 'How can you just steamroller over people like that?'

'He practises,' Maggie observed dryly.

'No need—it comes naturally,' Sebastian capped. 'That young man was in the way. Now forget about him. I believe they have ballroom dancing in this hotel in the evenings, is that right?'

'I've got nothing to wear,' Catalina sulked.

'Then go and buy something and charge it to me,' he said with the air of a man patting a child on the head.

Catalina flounced off. Maggie rose to follow her, but Sebastian detained her and nodded to Alfonso, who slipped away.

Maggie glared. 'I just hope that one day I see that girl toss your credit card back in your face.'

'Do you think you will?'

'No,' she snapped. 'Now I'm going up for an early night.'

'You can have a nap, but you're on duty this evening. Someone has to keep Alfonso company.'

Maggie returned to her room in a temper. After their exhilarating afternoon she'd felt charitable towards

Sebastian, but that had vanished in the face of his casual demonstration of power. Her mood wasn't improved by the realisation that she had only her black cocktail dress, and if she wore it tonight Sebastian might think she was sending him a message.

Determined not to let him take another trick, she stormed down to the hotel's boutique, found nothing there that she would have been seen dead in, and stormed back up to her room. In the end she presented herself for dinner, wearing the black dress, in a sulphurous mood and mentally daring Sebastian to react by so much as the raising of an eyebrow. But he gave no sign of having seen it before, or even noticing her particularly.

Which should have made her feel better.

But it didn't.

The four of them met up in the late evening, in the hotel's restaurant and dance area. It was on the second floor, with windows overlooking the main street where coloured lamps glowed against the snow. By day there was also a glorious view up the mountains, but now the summits were cloaked in darkness.

The men, too, had dressed for the occasion, in dinner jackets and frilled shirts. Sebastian's swarthy skin was startling against the brilliant white of his shirt, and his dark eyes seemed almost to swallow light.

When he had ordered, he said, 'Isabella will be flying home next week.'

'I'm so glad she's well again,' Catalina said warmly.

'Not quite. She's recovering very slowly, and she'll have to go into a hospital in Granada for a while. But I hope to have her with us for Christmas. You look surprised.' This was to Maggie.

'It's just that I've spoken to her a few times on the

phone, the last time yesterday, and she didn't mention returning to Spain.'

'She didn't know. It took me a while to arrange, and I only told her this morning. She's thrilled.'

This was Sebastian at his best, Maggie realised— shouldering, without complaint, the duties for which he'd been born. She had a sudden fierce wish that she could have known him as a carefree boy.

The band struck up. Sebastian took the floor with his fiancée and Maggie accepted Alfonso's polite invitation. But he didn't dance well and fairly soon they returned to the table and settled down to talk.

She liked the young man a lot. Perhaps he would never set the world on fire, but she sensed that there was a lot more to him than met the eye. He gave her all his attention—probably, she thought, to avoid having to look at Catalina in Sebastian's arms. This was something she understood. She didn't want to look at them, either.

Sebastian and Catalina came off the floor to find the other two deep in a political discussion.

'Andalucia is potentially the wealthiest part of Spain,' Maggie was saying eagerly. 'You've got the tourist areas, and some of the most fertile ground in the country. Yet this is the poorest region, and that's a scandal—'

Alfonso nodded and rattled off a list of opportunities wasted. She countered with some examples of her own, gleaned from her years in Granada. So deeply absorbed were they that they didn't notice they were no longer alone until Sebastian coughed, and they looked up to find him and Catalina sitting at the table.

'Maggie!' Catalina squealed in horror. 'How can you talk about such boring things?'

'I don't find them boring, and neither should you. This

is your country and what happens in it should interest you.'

Catalina shuddered. 'You sound like a schoolmistress.'

'Exactly,' Sebastian said. 'And when there is wine and music, to sound like a schoolmistress is an unforgivable crime. Come.' He seized her hand and rose. 'I shall dance it out of you.'

To her dismay, a waltz was beginning: the worst possible dance for a woman who wanted to keep a man at a distance. His light clasp on her hand called up the evening of their first meeting. She didn't want to remember that night when she'd been caught off guard, reacting with her body and her instincts instead of her head, like a rational woman.

Well, she was on guard tonight. She would ignore the feel of his hand in the small of her back, and the way his hot breath drifted against her bare shoulder.

One dance and she was through.

Full of resolution, she took the battle into the enemy's camp. 'You thought that was shocking, didn't you?' she challenged him. 'A woman, talking politics! Why doesn't she keep quiet and know her place?'

'Is that what I was thinking?' he asked mildly.

'You know it was.'

He shook his head, smiling. 'You make a brave battle, Margarita, but your technique is flawed. Never try to put words into your opponent's mouth. It merely puts you in his power, which is where he wants you.'

'I don't admit that I am in your power.'

'But you do know that that's where I want you, don't you?'

She recovered herself. 'You'll die wanting.'

He laughed at that. 'Bravo!'

'Anyway, I didn't put words in your mouth. I know what you think because you've said so. "I share my thoughts with men, not women,"' she quoted.

'*Touché!* I'd forgotten that. And now of course I'm supposed to add to my crimes by saying that a woman shouldn't discuss serious matters, that her body counts more than her mind, and that her place is in my bed, using a woman's intimate skills to please me and letting me please her.'

She tried to fight down the heat that rose in her at this frankness, but Sebastian was a devil who knew how to excite her with words alone. Worse still was the stunning ease with which he'd turned the trick against her. This was exactly what she'd resolved not to let happen. And the wretched man knew it.

'That was roughly the script you'd written for me, wasn't it?' Sebastian continued. 'Well, I'm sorry, I can't oblige.'

'Wh-what?'

'I was impressed by the way you spoke to Alfonso. Clearly, you know your subject. There's a lot wrong in this region, and it'll take a great deal of work to put it right. That's my job. For me, that's what it's all about. I've met very few people who understood. You must have learned a lot during your marriage. Was your husband in politics?'

'No, but my father-in-law was a natural moaner,' Maggie said with feeling. 'He would hold the floor for hours, complaining about the national government, the regional government—this was wrong, that was wrong—and nobody else could ever get a word in edgeways.'

The waltz was ending. Immediately the band struck up a tango, which Sebastian swept her into without a pause. Like everything else, he did this well, but so did she. It was like the skiing all over again, a subtle battle for mastery, with the honours even. They were both breathless and smiling when the music ended.

'You dance well,' he said. 'But I always knew you would.'

A wise woman wouldn't answer that. His eyes were dangerous. So was the heat that came from his body, so powerfully that she could feel it.

'I think we should sit down,' she murmured.

'Not until we've had another waltz.'

But to waltz in his arms, held close against him, wasn't for her. She wanted it too much. She must walk away from him, ignoring the tempting look in his eyes. She must be strong. She *must*.

'Margarita,' he said softly.

'Stop this. Stop it.'

'You stop it. Be strong for both of us.'

'Yes,' she said. 'Yes.' But she didn't know what she was saying any more.

Suddenly the cry went up, 'There they are!' And suddenly everyone was hurrying off the dance floor and crowding the windows that looked out onto the street below. Maggie and Sebastian were swept along with the crowd. Catalina was also on her feet, waving to attract their attention.

'What is it?' Maggie asked, bewildered.

'Santa Claus,' Catalina told her excitedly. 'Every night until Christmas he has a torchlit procession, and tonight is the first one. Come along.'

In her eagerness she seized Sebastian's hand and pulled him after her, leaving Maggie to follow more sedately. Someone opened the doors to the balcony and they all crowded out into the night air.

Far up the mountain they could see the glint of coloured lights against the darkness, making a long, wavy tail speeding down the slope. As it neared, the lights seemed to separate, revealing that each one was fixed to the head of a skier. There were fifty skiers, in fancy dress, some elves, some angels, some fairies, forming a guard of honour to a sleigh, drawn by more skiers, wearing horns to suggest reindeer.

The sleigh itself was magnificent, decorated with tinsel that reflected back every light, the back filled with sacks and parcels. And there, holding the reins, was a big, red-garbed, white-bearded, ho-ho-hoing Santa Claus. Swiftly they came on, growing bigger as they reached the village and glided through the main street, a long stream of glittering colour.

Everywhere doors and windows were open and people came out to look, to cheer and applaud while the procession swept on in glory.

And then it was gone, and there were only the lights fading in the distance, until they had vanished altogether. A collective sigh went up, and the spectators suddenly seemed to realise how cold it was. They retreated back into their well-lit buildings, with only memories of the beauty that had lived so briefly.

And that was how it would have been, Maggie realised, if she'd yielded to the pounding in her blood. Sebastian had said she must be strong for both of them, and for a brief instant strength had seemed too hard.

She could have had her moment, but it would have been like the torchlit procession—beautiful, brilliant, fleeting, leaving only a memory in the darkness.

Thank heavens all this would soon be over. Isabella was returning, Sebastian and Catalina would be married, and she could return to her humdrum life in England, and forget.

CHAPTER SIX

As HER wedding grew closer Catalina's mood veered wildly. Sometimes she was calm, and almost indifferent, at other times she would indulge in bursts of tears.

She entered a lively dispute with Sebastian about their honeymoon. Catalina's choice was a trip to New York. Sebastian's idea was a slow tour of his estates, introducing her to his people, and also her new duties. Maggie threw up her hands in despair at this notion of a honeymoon, and she came within an ace of kicking Sebastian's shins before he belatedly saw sense, and gave in.

Isabella arrived amid much rejoicing, and after another week in hospital she was well enough to move into Sebastian's house, with two nurses.

Some of Catalina's responsibilities came with the season. Nearby was the tiny parish church of San Nicolas, where it was a tradition for the de Santiago family to provide the crib. Sebastian drove her and Maggie the short distance to the charming little building, and played his part in setting the scene. At last, everything was finished, except for the manger, which was still empty.

Maggie gently unwrapped the tissue paper and handed Catalina the tiny wooden figure of a child. It was exquisitely carved and painted, with a peacefully sleeping face, and she felt a sudden tremor go through her. There had been another child that had lain in her arms and slept like that. But the baby had not woken again.

Catalina laid the baby in the manger, and turned away

in answer to some remark of the priest's. Feeling sure she was unnoticed, Maggie moved quietly forward and looked into the crib.

'Isn't it beautiful, Señora?' Father Basilio appeared beside her.

'Beautiful,' she said softly. 'And the real miracle was that he lived.'

'I beg your pardon?'

'All that stress, and the journey on the donkey—he was probably born early. Children sometimes die when they're premature.'

The old man's eyes were kind and understanding. 'Yes, Señora. Sometimes that happens. Was your baby blessed with any life at all?'

'Just a few days,' she whispered.

Somebody spoke to the priest. While his attention was distracted Maggie laid her hand gently on the infant. Suddenly she couldn't see properly. She closed her eyes and took a long breath, and when she opened them again she found Sebastian looking at her. For a moment she thought he would speak, but Catalina burst in with, 'Maggie, isn't it just beautiful?'

'Beautiful,' she said brightly, forcing herself back to reality.

'Sebastian, don't you think everything is perfect?'

'Perfect, my dear.'

'Have I performed my duties to your liking?'

'You've done admirably,' he said, and it might have been Maggie's imagination, but she thought he smiled with an effort.

Christmas passed fairly quietly, as was common in continental Europe. On Christmas Eve the entire household attended the great cathedral in Granada, and on Christmas Day they went to the little parish church.

The time for colourful festivities was the New Year, and in particular, the Feast of The Three Kings, in January. This would be celebrated with the jollity that in England was associated with Christmas, with much wine, good food and giving of gifts. Ten days later Sebastian and Catalina would be married in Granada Cathedral, and Maggie would be free to return home.

She was looking forward to that, she told herself many times. Once back in England she would be able to put these strange, hectic weeks behind her and get Sebastian in proportion, a man who loomed large because of his power and arrogance, but who wasn't really very important after all.

Between New Year and the Feast the place was a bedlam of preparation. Of all the parties in town, Don Sebastian's celebration for his bride was *the* party. Anyone who was everyone had been invited. Those who hadn't took to their beds or retired to the country to hide their shame. Even José had received an invitation, although Sebastian drew the line at Horacio.

Extra cooks were brought in to cater for the armies of guests. An internationally famous chef was installed the week before and began the preparations for garlic soup, mussels steamed in sherry, giant prawns cooked in olive oil, roast suckling pig, almond sponge cake and marzipan coated with bitter chocolate. He had several lively discussions with the steward in charge of Sebastian's huge cellar, and the two of them nearly came to blows over the rival merits of Gramona Chardonnay and Solar Gran Blanco Crianza.

Cleaners polished the place from top to bottom. Every lamp was washed until it sparkled and glowed against the tiles and mosaics. With two days to go the weather struck a warm spell and outdoor festivities became possible. Lights were hung throughout the courtyards, throwing into vivid relief the delicate arches and casting reflections in the water.

Catalina was having a new gown created for the occasion by the same establishment that had made her wedding dress, and insisted on buying Maggie a gown also. Catalina helped her study fabrics and styles, but when it came to the fitting she would lose interest and wander out for a quick shopping trip.

The gown was splendid, long, sweeping and made of dark crimson velvet. Most fair-haired women would have had trouble with the colour, but Maggie's Mediterranean eyes set it off perfectly.

Sebastian's expression said he thought so, on the night of the party, when she came downstairs in her glorious creation, and he gave her a heavy, solid gold antique locket, set with rubies, to wear with it.

'Catalina told me how you would look, so that I could choose your gift correctly,' he said, draping it around her neck.

'It's beautiful,' she said breathlessly. 'But—it's too much—'

'Too much for all I owe you? No, Margarita. No gift is good enough for you. How wise you were to keep me at a distance. By doing so, you restored my honour. For you, I would have thrown it away—'

'And regretted it.'

'Perhaps,' he said after a moment.

She met his eyes. 'Yes.'

He didn't answer this directly, but said with a rueful smile, 'You were always wiser than I.'

'Sebastian, can I give you a little advice?'

'Of course.'

'Be kind to Catalina.'

'That was always my intention.'

'No, I mean more. I mean, be faithful to her. She's young and very vulnerable. You could make her fall in love with you—'

'Is it so easy to claim a woman's love?' he asked quietly. 'Well, maybe I thought so once. I will do as you ask—in gratitude. And you? What will you do?'

'Go home as soon as you are married.'

'And then?'

'Get another job.'

'And live alone?'

She hesitated. 'You mustn't ask me that. We must never talk like this again.'

He sighed. 'I think tonight, and the next few days, are going to be very difficult.'

Catalina appeared. She seemed nervous and distracted, but Maggie put that down to the nature of the occasion. Afterwards she was to wonder how she could have been so blind.

First the long receiving line, with Catalina standing beside Sebastian, smiling mechanically, looking tinier than ever. Everything seemed to swamp her, from the way her long black hair had been taken up and elaborately dressed, to the huge diamond engagement ring that flashed on her finger.

Then everyone crowded to the long tables, with Sebastian's immediate household on the raised top table. Isabella was there, and so was Maggie, although she wished she wasn't. She would have been glad to blend in with the crowd, and steal a glance at Sebastian unobserved. But perhaps, she reflected, it was better for her to be near Catalina. The poor girl was looking deathly pale, almost ill.

'You're doing wonderfully,' Maggie whispered as the

meal, and the speeches came to an end. 'Are you all right?'

Catalina turned a distraught face to her. 'Oh, Maggie, this is too much for me. I must be alone for a few moments.'

'Do you want me to come with you?'

'No, no! I must be alone.' She almost ran in her desire to escape.

Soon it was time for the guests to move from one great hall into another. Here stood the tree, nearly twenty feet tall, brilliant with decorations, packed with gifts at the base, with more gifts piled on tables nearby.

'Where is Catalina?' Sebastian murmured to Maggie. 'She must help me distribute the presents.'

'She was feeling a little overwhelmed. She slipped out for a breath of fresh air.'

'But that was nearly half an hour ago. Come, we must find her.'

The search began quietly, for it seemed certain that Catalina would appear at any moment, but soon it became clear that she had really vanished, and Sebastian's brow darkened. Worse still, some of the guests had realised what was happening and joined in the search with half-malicious interest.

'Damn them!' Sebastian said with soft violence. 'I don't want this all over town. Where the hell is she?'

'What about those doors over there?'

'They lead to the part of the house I use for business. Catalina never goes there. Besides, they're always kept locked.'

'This one isn't,' Maggie said, trying a handle and finding herself in a corridor.

A plump middle-aged man called Marcos was advancing on them, an insincere smile on his face. He was a political opponent of Sebastian, and—to quote Catalina—a creep.

'The poor young lady has probably gone to lie down. Is this where you keep your study? A hotbed of secrets, I'm sure.' He headed for the next door.

'No!' Maggie cried. For suddenly everything had become clear to her, and she knew what was about to happen. If only Catalina had had the sense to lock the door behind her...

But she hadn't. The next moment Marcos had pulled Sebastian's study door open, revealing Catalina standing there, locked in a passionate embrace with José.

Time seemed to stop. In that awful pause, a gaggle of fascinated spectators crowded after them into the room. Both Catalina and José seemed too frozen to move. Her elaborately arranged hair had been torn down and hung in disarray about her shoulders. One shoulder of her dress was pushed down, almost exposing a white, beautiful breast. Her lipstick was smeared and her eyes had the cloudy look of a woman driven to madness by kisses.

Of the two, it was the girl who pulled herself together first. Stepping forward, she faced the crowd accusingly.

'What are you staring at? Have you never seen a woman in love before? This is José. He loves me and I love him. I'm going to marry him.' She whirled on Sebastian. '*Him*, not *you*!'

'Be silent!' Sebastian said warningly.

'I won't be silent. Who do you think you are to bring me here and say I must marry you, whether I like it or not?'

'I never—'

'You did, you did! What choice did I have? The great Sebastian de Santiago favours me, and I'm supposed to faint with the honour. Well, I say no! I won't marry you. I hate you.'

A guffaw of laughter broke from the ever-increasing crowd. As though the sound was the last straw, Catalina's courage collapsed and she flung herself, sobbing, into José's arms.

Sebastian took a step forward to Catalina, but in the same moment something snapped in Maggie. Moving quickly, she placed herself in front of the two young people.

'Leave them alone,' she told Sebastian quietly. 'Whatever you have to say, this isn't the time or place. And you—' she addressed the grinning spectators '—have you no pity for her? She's a child. She should never have been brought to this. How dare you stand there and enjoy her misery? You should be ashamed, all of you.'

Sebastian was as pale as death, but when he spoke he was in command of himself. 'As you say, this isn't the time or the place. Please take Catalina away and look after her. You—' he indicated José '—have abused the hospitality of my house and will leave immediately.'

Maggie put a gentle arm about Catalina and led her away. José looked confused. 'Get out of here while you're still safe,' Sebastian told him savagely.

The next moment he'd become the host again, smiling, ushering everybody out, apologising for the early end to the party. It wasn't hard to get rid of the guests. Don Sebastian de Santiago was too rich, too powerful, too handsome, not to have enemies, and they were all eager to start spreading the hilarious news.

When the last guest had gone and Maggie had finished calming first an hysterical Catalina, and then an hysterical Isabella, she returned downstairs and faced Sebastian in his study.

She hadn't known what to expect, but she was unprepared for what awaited her. The man whose gentle resignation had touched her heart earlier had vanished. In his place was a stranger with glittering, hate-filled eyes.

'Do you think I don't know who to blame for this?' he said in a hard, icy voice.

'The only person to blame is yourself,' Maggie told him firmly.

'Who told me that she would make this happen? Who warned me weeks ago that she would work to undermine me, and humiliate me before the world? Like a fool I didn't believe her. I trusted her, and I tell you that never again will I trust a woman.'

As his meaning became clear, Maggie turned on him in outrage. 'Do you mean *me*?'

'Who else? You threatened to do all in your power to make Catalina betray me. Don't deny it.'

'I said I'd try to open her eyes. I never meant anything like this to happen.'

'Don't lie to me!' he said savagely. 'You practically threw her into that pretty boy's arms. You invited him to this house, you told him about your skiing trip so that he could follow, and when I found him there you told me it was you he was chasing.'

'Because I believed it,' she cried. Horrified, she was beginning to see how everything looked.

'You told him you were going to Sol y Nieve.'

'Only in passing. It wasn't a hint for him to follow.'

'To be sure, I believe you,' he said bitterly.

'How dare you call me a liar?' Maggie snapped.

'That is nothing to what I would like to call you. I've

been insulted in front of the world, and that lies at your door, you scheming, manipulative witch.'

'It wasn't like that. It was a chapter of accidents, and—'

'To think that I brought you into this house!' he brooded, not seeming to hear her.

'And I didn't want to come,' she reminded him. 'But you were so set on having your own way that you mowed me down, as you do everyone. You brought me here as your fiancée's chaperone, and I hadn't been under your roof two days before you tried to seduce me.'

'Don't talk like an ignorant girl, because you're not one. You're a woman of the world who'd only take a man to her bed as an equal.'

'But I didn't take you to my bed. And how glad I am now that I didn't. To you it's nothing but a kind of power game and, I told you before, you'll never have power over me.'

'No, you prefer the power to be on your side,' he said, his eyes glinting with a strange light. 'You demonstrated that very effectively tonight.'

'How can I make you believe that it wasn't some kind of conspiracy?' she demanded.

'Don't try. It was all just a little bit too convenient to be an accident.'

Maggie sighed. 'Believe what you like, Sebastian. You will anyway. Let's just make an end of this.'

'And how do you suggest we do that?'

'I'd have thought it was obvious. It's time for me to go. You must be longing to see the last of me.'

He stared at her. 'Do you really think you're going to simply walk out of here without putting right the injury you've done me?'

'How can I do that? If you think I'm going to bully Catalina into marrying you—'

He made a gesture of impatience. 'Of course not. Our marriage is impossible now. But there's still the inconvenient matter of the cathedral, the archbishop and several hundred guests, all arranged for ten days' time.'

'You'll have to cancel them. People will understand.'

'Oh, yes, they'll understand—and they'll laugh themselves sick.'

'Well, what else can you do? It's happened now.'

'Don't be stupid, Margarita. The answer must be as obvious to you as it is to me. I have arranged to be married on the sixteenth, and that's what I mean to do. Anything else would simply give the town more cause for derision.'

'But you haven't got a bride,' she said incredulously, wondering if she was dealing with a deaf man. 'What are you going to do? Call in one of your conquests to make up the numbers? Will any woman do?'

The strange light was there in his eyes again. 'Not any woman,' he said. 'You.'

She stared at him. Then something caught in her throat and she forced herself to give a brief, choking laugh.

'I'm not laughing,' he said quietly.

'You're right. It's the unfunniest joke I've ever heard.'

'I was never further from making jokes in my life. You don't understand Spanish honour. Perhaps your race has no honour, but here it's a deadly serious matter. The one who does the injury is the one who makes reparation. You have injured me, and it is you, and nobody else, who must make it right.'

'I think you must have gone mad,' she said coldly.

He nodded. 'Maybe that's it. My brain is whirling

with so many terrible thoughts that perhaps I've gone mad. But beware my madness, Margarita, because it will brook no opposition. A madman isn't civilised. A madman will do whatever he has to in order to gain his end.'

'Then he'd better listen to some common sense,' she flashed. 'It's not me who's forgotten that this is Spain, but you—this is one of the most bureaucratic countries in the world. First we would have to apply to the authorities for permission, and that can take a month—'

'I have friends who will see that it doesn't.'

'Oh, yes, your friends in high places. Will they also get my birth certificate from England, and translate it into Spanish, and my husband's death certificate?'

'That will be Alfonso's job.'

'It's impossible in the time.'

'He'll leave for England first thing tomorrow morning.'

'And so will I.'

He laid a hand on her arm. 'No,' he said, so quietly that she almost didn't hear. 'You will stay here, because in ten days' time, we are going to be married.'

She began to sense the force of his will. He spoke softly because his steely inflexibility left no need for noise. Sebastian had said what he wanted, and that was what he would have. Meeting his eyes, it was almost possible to believe that she would meekly do his will.

Almost. But she too had a core of strength deep within that would tolerate no surrender. It asserted itself now, making her throw him off.

'We are not going to be married,' she said clearly. 'I'm sorry for what's happened to you, but I think you brought it on yourself. We'll never agree on this, and the sooner I'm gone the better. I'll say goodbye now,

because I'm going very early tomorrow, and we won't
see each other again.'

She half expected him to stop her, but he only stood
in silence as she walked out of the room.

'Are you really going to leave me?' Catalina asked
mournfully as she watched Maggie packing.

'Now, you stop that! You've got your own way tonight, so don't ask me to feel sorry for you.'

'How have I got my own way? Sebastian says he
won't let me marry José.'

'What did you expect him to say, after the way you
dumped him?' Maggie demanded. After having urged
Catalina to just this course, she now found herself exasperated at the girl's youthful egotism.

'You wanted me to dump him.'

'Not in front of nearly six hundred people. Why
couldn't you have spoken to him quietly?'

'I lost my nerve. Anyway, I never meant to be found
like that.'

No, Catalina would never mean anything, Maggie
realised. Despite her fire and charm, she wasn't a strong
character. She would let things drift until they reached
a crisis, but she wouldn't voluntarily confront the crisis.

'I suppose I needn't ask where you went while I was
having dress fittings?' Maggie added.

'I went to visit José. We loved each other from the
moment you introduced us—'

'All right, there's no need to rub it in that I played a
part in this. I suppose he really came up to Sol y Nieve
to see you?'

'Oh, yes, only then Sebastian was there, and we had
to snatch a few moments of love under his nose.'

'If you don't stop seeing yourself as the heroine of a

tragic romance, I shall get cross. Sebastian isn't an ogre, even if he acts like one sometimes. You're eighteen, legally of age. He can hardly stop you getting married.'

'He controls my fortune until I'm twenty-one,' Catalina said tragically.

'Well, if José's so worried about your fortune, you're better off without him,' Maggie said, speaking more sharply than Catalina had ever heard her before.

She had never felt so little charity towards the girl, who seemed to have no understanding of the earthquake she'd caused in Sebastian's life. Despite his outrageous accusations and demands Maggie felt he was entitled to more sympathy than he was getting. He was certainly right about one thing. The world would laugh itself silly at his public humiliation.

Her packing was finished now. In a few hours she would be free of this place, its emotions and tensions that threatened to tear her apart. She switched off the light and stepped out onto the balcony. Down below she could see the lights, and their reflections in the water. After the turbulence of the evening, the place was silent and deserted.

No, not quite deserted. The man who sat by the water was so still that at first Maggie didn't see him. He might have been made of stone, like the birds who flanked the pool. Once she'd discerned his outline she could see him clearly under the lights, a man who had lost his bride, honour, dignity and reputation in one night.

That was nonsense, she told herself. Other men had been jilted before without making a major tragedy of it. He didn't even love Catalina, and much of it was his own fault.

But they were rationalisations, and they had no power to quell her twinge of sympathy. His attempt to coerce her into marriage had been disgraceful, but she should allow for the feelings of a man at the end of his tether. Impulsively Maggie left her room and went downstairs.

The ruins of the party were all around. She found two clean glasses, filled them with wine and went quietly out to the courtyard, moving so quietly that he didn't hear her. For a moment she caught a glimpse of his face and what she saw made her catch her breath. All the arrogance had been stripped from it, leaving behind only a kind of desolation. It was as though he'd retreated into his own inner world, and found nobody there but himself.

And that was true, she thought. He had power, but no warmth. Respect, but no love. Now, perhaps, he didn't even have respect.

He glanced up and saw her, giving her a slight frown of surprise. She held out a glass and he took it. 'Thank you,' he said with a touch of wryness. 'How did you know that I needed this?'

'I guessed.' She smiled to let him know that all was forgiven.

'Have you got one? Yes? Then what do we drink to? Your last evening?'

'It's for the best.'

'If you say so.'

'Well, you must admit, it was a mad idea.'

'It seemed to have some merit at the time.'

'It was the voice of desperation,' she informed him. 'But Don Sebastian de Santiago only listens to the voice of reason.'

'Are you making fun of me?' he asked in a strained voice.

She laid a hand on his shoulder. 'No, I wouldn't do that.'

'Of course, I should have listened to you in the first place. I admit it. Do you think it makes it any easier to know that I set myself up for this?'

'No. It makes it far, far harder to bear,' she said gently.

Suddenly they were in darkness. The lamps around the water had gone out. Sebastian gave a grunt.

'They're on a time-switch. I'd forgotten. Let's go inside. You can go on talking reason to me. Maybe I'll even come to believe it.'

CHAPTER SEVEN

MAGGIE had never been inside Sebastian's study before tonight, and her first visit had been too crowded with incident to leave her time to observe anything. Now she saw that it was decorated in the same style as the rest of the building, but with dark, masculine colours. Although functional, it was beautiful. One wall was taken up by a huge, oriental rug, and a counterpane that exactly matched it lay over a large couch in the corner. Maggie remembered Catalina saying that sometimes Sebastian worked in this room all night, pausing to cat-nap briefly before returning to his desk.

On one wall hung two large portraits of men with sharp eyes and beaky noses. They were sufficiently like Sebastian for Maggie to guess that this was his father and grandfather.

He took a bottle of wine and two clean glasses from a cupboard, handing one to her. 'Tonight I wish I could get very drunk,' he said grimly. 'I won't, but the thought is tempting.'

'Why won't you?'

He shrugged. 'I never do.'

'Perhaps you should,' she said sympathetically. 'Stop being so much in control all the time. Drown your sorrows tonight, pass out on that couch and wake up with a hangover that will make you forget your other troubles. It might help you get it in proportion.'

He gave a faint smile. 'You almost make me want to try. But I long ago resolved never to drink more than

103

my capacity. My father's brother was a drunkard. People laughed at him and imposed on him. He was the family fool and I—oh, God!—I swore that would never happen to me. And yet now—*now*!' His voice was suddenly savage. 'It was a really good night's entertainment, wasn't it? There was the groom, throwing open his home, showing off his bride to the neighbourhood, introducing her to friend and foe alike—because there were as many enemies as friends there tonight—so proud, just asking to be cast down and turned into a complete idiot. Oh, yes, let's all have a good laugh at that!'

He rose and went to stand in front of the two portraits.

'If anyone had treated my father so, he would have made them sorry they were born,' he said bitterly. 'If they'd done it to my grandfather, he would have killed them. But me, I have to behave as a modern man. I can only writhe at my shame.'

He turned to look back at her, watching him. 'You don't understand what I'm talking about, do you?'

'A little. My grandfather came from these parts. There's enough of him in me to know that this has to be felt deeply. But murder—'

'It was never considered murder when a man avenged his honour. That's what your cold English blood fails to understand, because you no longer know how to take the tie between men and women seriously. Off with the old, on with the new. People change their minds all the time. Find a new girl next week. That's how you think in your country of mists and fogs.

'But here, we know better. We know that the union of a man and a woman is the centre of life, and all else springs from it.'

'But if the choice was mistaken in the first place,'

Maggie argued, 'isn't it better to pass on and make a new choice, rather than suffer for ever? You're wrong when you say I don't understand. But the choice must be good, so that the foundations are strong.'

He gave a grunt. 'You have a clever way with words. You can always make me doubt my own wisdom.'

'Which makes me a woman to avoid,' she said lightly, and he flung her a suspicious glance. 'Don't brood about it, Sebastian. It'll be a nine-day wonder. Then they'll find something else to talk about.'

He drained his glass, and she took it from him to set down. Somehow her fingers became entwined with his. He looked at their clasped hands for a moment. 'They'll never quite forget to laugh at me,' he murmured. 'I'm too good a target.'

It was true. And he wouldn't be able to cope, because nobody had ever dared to laugh at him before. Maggie felt a wave of pity for him. She had told herself that it was his own fault, but faced with his bleak self-knowledge she suddenly felt as though she had seen a lion brought low by jackals.

He gave her a crooked smile. 'Why don't you help me, Margarita? Rescue me with some of that English humour I've heard so much about.'

'I don't think English humour would be much use in this situation.'

'Can't you teach me to laugh at myself?'

'Could anyone do that?' she asked gently.

'I don't really have a sense of humour at all, do I?'

'I've thought sometimes that there was one fighting to get out, but it isn't a large part of you, no. And to-night—well—you'd have to be a saint.'

'I'm no saint, just a man who wants to lash out at those who hurt him, and use force to make the world do his will. But the world turns out to be one silly little girl, and a boy with a pretty face.'

'And you can't murder them,' she said gently. 'It would be overreacting.'

He managed a half-smile. 'When English humour doesn't work, English common sense. What dull lives you must live in that island.'

'Sebastian—do you really think I made this happen on purpose?'

'No. You'd never stoop so low. I shouldn't have spoken as I did, but I was crazy with anger.' He met her eyes. 'Forgive me.'

'Of course.'

'And shall we part friends?'

'Friends.'

He looked down to where their fingers were still entwined. Lifting her hand, he laid his lips against the back of it, and then his cheek. Something in the defeated droop of his head hurt her.

'Sebastian,' she whispered. 'Please don't mind so much.'

'Of course not. It isn't sensible to mind, is it? Tell me, Margarita, what do *you* mind about?'

She was silent so long that he glanced up, and a fleeting look he saw in her face made him catch his breath. She became aware of him and he realised that a door had closed in her.

'I don't mind about anything very much,' she said softly. 'Not any more.'

'God help you if that's true!' he said at once.

'God help me if it isn't. It's dangerous to mind.'

'There's something in your eyes at this moment that I've briefly glimpsed there before.' He drew a swift breath. 'If you leave now, I'll never know your mystery.'

'There's no mystery, Sebastian. Just a girl who took a wrong turning when she was too young and ignorant to know better, and then found that there was no way back.'

'I refuse to believe that you ever did anything bad.'

'I was worse than bad. I was stupid. That's the real crime, and all the worst punishments are reserved for it.'

'I know,' he said simply. 'I found out tonight, remember?'

He rested his cheek against her hand once more. Her heart aching for him, Maggie rested her own cheek against his black head. This was what she would remember about him—not his imperiousness but his vulnerability. When he looked up she drew a breath at the sight of his eyes, more naked and defenceless than she had ever seen them. Thinking only to comfort him, she laid her mouth against his.

At first he didn't seem certain how to respond. His lips moved slightly, then stilled, waiting for her. A sweet warmth pervaded her. It felt good to kiss him freely, without anger or guilt. It felt right, just as it felt right to stroke his face with her fingertips, and then to relax against him when he reached out to hold her.

His arms had never felt so gentle as he cradled her head against his shoulder, but his lips passed swiftly from tenderness to purpose, as though the feel of her own was a touchlight. His mouth moved over hers again and again, each time a little more intent, while her pulse quickened and she felt her control begin to slip. This was not what she had meant to happen—or was it?

She made one last effort. 'Sebastian—let me go,' she murmured hazily.

'Never. You kissed me, and now you must take the consequences.'

'You must be the devil,' she murmured.

'Only me? There's a devil in you too, Margarita. He taught you how to look at a man with eyes that promise everything, so that he knows what you're thinking, and what you want him to think.'

'Can you read my mind?'

'From the first moment!' he said against her lips. 'Your thoughts are the same as mine—hot, fierce thoughts of the two of us together, naked, enjoying each other and to hell with the world. You know what you want from me—don't you—*don't you*?'

'Yes,' she said mindlessly, scarcely knowing what words she used, or what they meant.

'And you also know what you would do to urge me on to fulfil your desires. I think you're very skilled at the caresses that drive a man to madness. Be damned to the devil in you! He put witchcraft in your lips so that kisses are never enough. There'll be no peace until I have you in my bed.'

There was no doubt of his intentions. She had walked into a trap with her eyes wide open. He was determined to make her marry him—if not one way, then another. When talk failed, he'd taken direct action, giving her a false sense of security while he lured her to come to him. Now he had her where he wanted her, and she knew she wouldn't be allowed to leave until she'd said yes, and meant it.

That would never happen, her mind cried. But her mind drowned in her body's clamour. Part of her—the only part that counted when she was in his arms—was saying yes wildly, determinedly, impatiently. She tried to feel anger but she couldn't convince herself. No man had the right to behave like this, but that thought paled beside the knowledge that he was free. She could give her desire full rein and feel no guilt.

He wasn't an admirable character. He was a harsh, cynical man who seized what he wanted arrogantly and without pity. But his lips possessed ancient skills of persuasion and coercion, and they could drive her to the edge of madness.

His hands were working on the fastenings of the beautiful velvet dress, slipping them open, pulling it down with swift, purposeful movements, until he could toss it onto the floor. Her slip followed, then her panties, and now she was tearing at his clothes, as impatient as he, until the moment when they were both naked.

He pulled her against him, kissing with lips that burned, caressing her with fingers that knew how to touch lightly and be gone, leaving a scorching memory behind. This had been waiting for them both since the night in the garden when she had fended him off and fled. What had she been running away from? The depth of her own response, which even then had alarmed her?

Now she could yield to that response, explore it to its depths, explore him. She felt him drawing her down onto the couch, pressing her naked body against his.

She looked into his face, expecting to see him triumphant. But if there was any triumph in him it was confused by other emotions—shock, bewilderment, alarm at losing control, eagerness to discover the unknown. All these feelings were hers, and for a blazing instant she saw them reflected in his eyes as though she were looking into a mirror.

Then the moment passed as he kissed her again with lips that were hot and fierce as they teased hers, taking her ever closer to the moment of truth. She kissed him back, seeking and demanding as an equal. A strange thing was happening to her. Sebastian had said she would know how to urge him on to fulfil her desires, and now she found that it was mysteriously true. Deep, unfathomable instinct told her about him, what he wanted, what he could give.

New life streamed through her like wine. For four years her body had lain cold and sullen, bitterly resentful of the passion that had betrayed her to a life of misery. Now it was asserting itself again, reclaiming its rights, and its rights included a man who could discover its secrets by instinct, and play on them for his own pleasure and hers: a man to whom seduction was more than a skill, it was a black art. This man, and no other.

He'd spoken of 'the caresses that drive a man to madness', and now she offered him those caresses without shame, with a kind of glory in her own power, lashing his desire on with her own. When he slipped his knee between her legs, she pulled him over her at once.

Then he surprised her yet again. Instead of claiming her in fierce triumph, he entered her slowly, almost tenderly, giving her the time she needed to become familiar once more with the sensation of a man inside her. It was such a good feeling. Once she'd sworn never to know it again. Now she wondered how she had endured so long. She threw her head back in a gesture of total sensual abandon, grasping him and driving herself against him.

Only when he felt that movement and knew that he was welcome, did he allow the last of his control to slip. He knew her now, knew that she was a woman who could match him as a man, returning vigour for vigour, demand for demand in the all-consuming death-in-life of mutual abandon. When the moment came they were at each other's mercy, carrying each other down the long drop to oblivion, while each clasped the other as the only safety in a vanished world.

He parted from her, but only by a little. One arm still lay beneath her shoulders, holding her firmly at the same time that he pillowed her head. Sebastian would always be like that, she thought: enticement, the offering of pleasure and perhaps something even sweeter, and behind it, always the hint of ruthlessness.

It was there in his voice now, saying quietly, 'We will marry on the sixteenth. You know that we must, don't you?'

'I don't know what I know,' she whispered, 'except that you're the last man in the world I ought to marry—if I had any sense.'

'Are you a sensible woman?'

'I try to be.' She gave a little gasp of laughter. 'Sometimes it's hard.'

'And I'm a man of no sense at all,' he growled. 'Because if I had, I'd throw you out of my house as a man would throw a fiend who'd come to torment him.'

She made a slight movement and instantly the arm tightened about her shoulders, drawing her over him again. 'But all my sense seems to have deserted me,' he growled. 'I'm going to keep my fiend here to torment me, in defiance of all sanity.'

'And if she has other ideas?'

He grinned. 'She has nothing to say about it.'

'You're forgetting that I heard you say some pretty damning things about what made a good husband. "Keep her happy in bed and the rest will follow." But that's not good enough for me. I want fidelity, and I think you'd find that hard.'

He eyed her sardonically. 'It might have been hard

with Catalina, but not with you. No other woman, I swear it. Do we have a deal?'

She smiled. 'I guess we have a deal.'

She let her head fall until it rested against his chest. She could hear the soft thunder of his heart and knew that it matched her own. The lines of their bodies fitted well together, and she knew now that together they had a magic that could take them to the brink of ecstasy and beyond. It would be so easy simply to let herself be carried forward by his inevitable momentum.

But it wasn't enough. She knew that, even while she prepared to surrender to it. If only her mind would take command, instead of being in thrall to her treacherous senses. It couldn't, because deep down she didn't really want it too, but as she lay there, pillowed on his chest, she knew that she'd made a terribly dangerous decision, one that she might regret, but couldn't go back on.

Sebastian had predicted no trouble about getting the necessary documents, and sure enough Alfonso visited her next day, saying that he was just about to leave for the airport, and needed her instructions. Maggie explained the confusion over her name, and gave him the dates of her birth and her husband's death.

Slightly to her surprise, he shrugged aside any thought that this might cause problems. But of course, Alfonso was thrilled at the developments. He no longer had to endure the sight of Catalina marrying his employer. True, she'd now set her heart on José, but while Sebastian was forbidding that match, Alfonso could hope. And if Sebastian planned to marry Maggie, Alfonso would make sure that all problems were ironed out.

There were a million matters to be seen to before her

wedding, such a short time away. First Catalina must be told, and Maggie was dreading this job. For surely the girl would now divine the truth about the attraction that had smouldered between herself and Sebastian from the first moment, and feel betrayed?

But Catalina astonished her by exploding with laughter. 'You and Sebastian?' she shrieked. 'Oh, Maggie! Maggie!'

'I know it must seem a bit sudden—' she began awkwardly.

'Oh, but I understand. I know everything,' Catalina gasped.

'You—do?'

'You are doing it for me. OK, perhaps a little bit for yourself, because it's good for you to have "an establishment" of your own, and you must be thinking of these things.'

Maggie remembered how Catalina had dismissed Sebastian as 'old', and realised that she herself now ranked in the same category: a widow who had to be thinking of her future because time was rushing on. She concealed a smile.

'You are such a good friend,' Catalina said eagerly. 'And you will speak to Sebastian about my wedding to José?'

'One thing at a time. Let the dust settle before you say anything about that.'

'But I must marry José,' Catalina pouted. 'I love him desperately, passionately.'

It was a child talking. Catalina still hadn't discovered true passion, and her only desperation was to have her own way. She proved it the next moment when her face fell and she said, 'Oh, but now I don't get to go to New York.'

Maggie nearly tore her hair. 'Since that was to be your honeymoon, I should think not.'

'Perhaps I could go anyway, if—'

'Forget it,' Maggie said wryly. 'I get New York as a consolation prize for taking Sebastian off your hands.'

'You are right,' Catalina agreed. 'You will suffer enough.'

She plunged eagerly into helping with the wedding, especially the making of a new dress. Together they visited Señora Diego and selected a roll of pale cream satin, which Maggie felt was more suitable to her widowed status than white.

Señora Diego pulled in all her seamstresses who had it ready for a fitting in a day. The satin had a special weave that made it extremely heavy, trailing slowly as Maggie walked in a way that spoke of grandeur and magnificence, an effect that was greatly increased by the matching lace with which it was heavily trimmed. When Maggie ventured to demur at the spiralling cost, Catalina was scandalised.

'Do you want people to say I helped choose you a dress that wasn't as nice as my own? And you must also have clothes to wear for your honeymoon, so why don't you try on something else while I—?'

'Slip round the corner to see José,' Maggie finished. 'I've got a better idea. While I try on other clothes, you stay right here and give me your opinion.'

'You have no heart,' Catalina said mournfully.

Then a crisis blew up on one of Sebastian's distant estates. Anxious to get it dealt with before the wedding, he announced that he was leaving for a few days.

'Now's your chance to escape,' Maggie teased him. 'A man who was regretting a rash proposal could use this opportunity to vanish into the mists.'

'If it comes to that, this is *your* chance to escape,' he observed. 'Shall I return to find you fled back to England?'

'I've given my word.'

'And so have I.' He brushed a finger against her cheek. 'I think neither of us is going to seek escape.'

CHAPTER EIGHT

SEBASTIAN was due home two days before the wedding. As the time neared, Maggie found she was anticipating him with an urgency that made her blush. She didn't know whether she loved this man, but she knew that they were bound together by a mysterious power. She'd promised herself that this would never happen again, but she had no regrets. Her feelings could flare into love, perhaps soon. If only...

If only he would let them.

For she knew that something was still unsettled between them, would not be settled for a long time—if ever. She had yet to penetrate the dark secret of the man. She knew his pride, and had glimpsed his gentleness. To the world he showed his strength, but she wanted to know his weaknesses. When he let her see them, she would know that he trusted her.

By the same token, she thought with a little smile, when she showed him her own weakness, she would know that she trusted him.

On the day he was expected a storm blew up. Rain and lightning lashed the house and hadn't abated by the evening. At bedtime there was still no sign of Sebastian. Maggie wished she could sleep, but the wind howled and raged with a violence she'd never heard before. She wondered where he was now: probably stopped somewhere for the night rather than risk the remainder of the journey in this weather.

Suddenly a door banged. It sounded loud, as though

it had come from the corridor outside her room. She sat up for a while, listening intently, but now there was only the wind, a low, insistent moan. She felt uneasy sitting like this, waiting for something, not knowing what. Sliding out of bed, she hurried across the floor and opened her door. Outside the wall lamps glowed, casting soft light, filling the corridor with shadows.

'Is anyone there?' she called.

'Yes,' came a growl from the darkness.

Now she could just make him out, walking from the direction of his bedroom. In the light of the wall lamp above him his eyes were no more than dark sockets with something burning in their depths. He came closer and now she could see that he looked as though he hadn't slept for several nights.

'I'd given you up for today,' she said.

He came to stand beside her in her doorway. He was wearing a long bathrobe that revealed his broad chest that rose and fell as though he was under some tremendous strain.

'I hurried back,' he said. 'I had the strangest fear that you might have gone away, after all.' His eyes were haggard, haunted.

'How could you think that, Sebastian? I promised to stay, and I'm a woman of my word.'

She heard a faint click and realised that Sebastian had closed her bedroom door, shutting out the world.

'Is that the only reason that you're here, Margarita? From duty?'

'No,' she whispered.

'Are you sure? I want only what you can give freely. Tell me to go away, and I'll go.'

He was lying and they both knew it. No power on earth could have made him leave her bedroom now, just as no power on earth could have made her order him out.

'Tell me to go,' he repeated.

For answer she leaned forward and laid her mouth on his. Still keeping her hands at her sides, she turned her head, so that her lips moved against his in soft, inciting movements that made him tremble. Sighing into his mouth, she teased him.

She knew at once that she'd driven him beyond the point of safety. His control had been hanging by a thread, and now she'd done the thing that snapped it. His arms tightened fiercely about her, lifting her just a few inches as he hurriedly crossed the floor to the bed. They fell on it together. Her nightdress had vanished, she didn't know where, and somehow he too was naked. His hands seemed to be touching her everywhere, tracing curves and valleys with skilful fingers that teased and incited her, moving fast because he was driven by an impatience that matched her own.

Tenderness could come later. This was raw, unslaked need, thrilling, imperative, and it had dominated her thoughts since the moment he left. Behind the decorum, the planning, the wedding dress fittings, the demure veil, her being had been secretly concentrated on what was happening here and now, in this bed, in Sebastian's arms. The way he could make her feel, the things he could make her want: nothing else mattered.

Her kiss was as devouring as his, her embrace as fiercely demanding. She twined her legs in his, urging him on with all her power. When she tried to speak his name, no words would come, only a gasp as he entered her and the pleasure mounted fast. She clasped him close, wanting more of him, wanting everything. And when she had everything, she wanted more. Then he gave more, and she gave back, and gave, and gave.

They were both trembling with the vigour of their mating as they fell apart, but not far apart. They still held on to each other while they recovered.

'You were away too long,' she said at last.

'Yes,' he said. 'Yes, I was.'

Suddenly she gave a little gasp of laughter.

'What is it?' Sebastian demanded quickly.

'I was just thinking of me, walking up the aisle in a bridal gown,' she said. 'It hardly seems appropriate somehow—after tonight, and the other night.'

'The things we know are for us alone.'

'Yes, but you have to admit that it has its funny side.'

He only scowled, and she realised he couldn't admit anything of the kind. He was a Spaniard, and Spanish men never understood humour in anything that even remotely touched on sex. She smiled fondly. Sebastian wasn't going to be easy to be married to.

But then he surprised her again, by laying his head between her breasts in a way that spoke of trust and tenderness. She put her arms about him, and held him tenderly.

There would be this too, she thought. Tenderness and the quiet moments when they would grow close in a different way from the wildness of their meetings. And the years would pass, and perhaps they would share love. Or perhaps they would only share something so like love that nobody could tell the difference.

When his head suddenly grew heavier she knew that he had fallen asleep, and then she slept too.

In the dawn light he stirred and sat up in bed. 'I suppose I should go,' he said reluctantly. 'We don't want a scandal.'

'True,' Maggie murmured, still half-asleep. She felt, rather than saw, him stand, shrug his shirt on and wander over to stand looking out of the window.

At last she yawned and stretched, sat up in bed, and realised that he was still there, looking down curiously at a small table by the wall, on which lay some papers.

'It's the paperwork for our marriage,' she said. 'You were right, Alfonso did everything in time—got all the certificates, the translations, the permission.' She became aware of a strange silence. 'What is it?'

'Who is Señora Margarita Alva?' he asked slowly.

'Oh, that's me. Cortez was my maiden name. I took it back after my husband died, but for our wedding formalities I had to give his name. I explained it all to Alfonso. I meant to tell you, but I forgot.'

'You—forgot—'

'Well, it's not important, is it?'

He regarded her strangely. 'All this time, you've let me refer to you as Señora Cortez, when you were really—Señora Alva.'

'I told you, I rejected my husband's name. And it wasn't really anybody's business, after all. I had no way of knowing it would matter. Anyway, all the paperwork is correct, and that's what counts.'

'And your husband was—Roderigo Alva?'

'Yes. It says so there.'

'How did he die?'

'In prison.'

She wished Sebastian would turn and face her, but he stayed as he was, slowly looking through the papers, until at last he laid them back on the desk and left the room.

* * *

Her wedding was a flower-filled dream. By custom a Spanish bride had flowers hung around her home, and Maggie stepped out of her room to find that Catalina and Isabella had been to work. Winter roses were hung about her door, petals were strewn along the corridor as she made her way, more roses hung about the great front doors.

All Granada was in the cathedral. Maggie entered on the arm of one of Sebastian's elderly uncles, and there were gasps of admiration at the sight of her. The heavy cream satin dress suited her tall figure admirably, and, for a veil, Catalina had persuaded her to wear a lace mantilla, which added to her air of magnificence. Everyone agreed that she was a fitting bride for a great man.

She had wondered how he would behave during the service, and wasn't very surprised that his manner was distant. What they knew in the heat of their bed was for them alone, and Sebastian wasn't the man to parade his feelings.

So she imitated his lofty bearing as the great choir sang them to their marriage, and the archbishop pronounced them united for ever. Their time would come, a time of hot lips and fevered bodies gasping, seeking, claiming, uniting. It would concern nobody but themselves.

After the wedding came the reception in the great hall, with five hundred guests standing, cheering as Don Sebastian de Santiago entered with his bride on his arm. As he walked the length of the huge room there was nothing on his face but pride and hauteur.

By tradition there were nine wedding cakes, made of sponge with caramel topping, lavishly adorned with fresh cream, and mounted on a spiral stand. For the wed-

ding festivities of Don Sebastian de Santiago there were
no less than a hundred and eighty cakes, mounted on
twenty stands. Each cake must be officially 'cut' by the
bride, for fear of offending many guests, so Sebastian
led Maggie ceremoniously around the long tables so that
she could briefly touch each cake with a silver knife.

By the time the long reception was over Maggie was
feeling tired, but she knew the feeling wouldn't last. The
mere thought of Sebastian could drive out everything but
eager anticipation.

The wedding dress was gone, its grandeur no longer
needed. In its place was a nightdress of simple white
silk, gossamer thin, an invitation to the man she had
chosen to remove it.

Now, as she prepared for her wedding night, her
thoughts were full of the last time she had lain in his
arms, driven almost to madness by the force of her own
desire. She didn't know what else marriage to Sebastian
might mean, but she knew it meant heart-stopping sensations, her very self burned up in the furnace heat of
the passion they created between them. For the moment,
that would be enough. The rest could come later.

For just a moment she was assailed by qualms. There
was an uneasy echo in her head, an echo of herself in
times past. Once there had been a young girl who tried
to console herself for her failing marriage with the
thought that their passion would bind them until matters
improved. Because passion meant love. Didn't it?

She'd learned better in bitterness and grief, and she
wished that sad little ghost hadn't come to haunt her
tonight. She rubbed her eyes, banishing that other girl
back into the past, where she belonged. Because
Sebastian wasn't Roderigo. He wasn't a weakling, always taking the easy way. He was a difficult man in

many ways, but she could trust his strength and his honesty.

As for herself, she knew that she was mentally the right wife for Sebastian as the scatterbrained Catalina could never have been. And he knew it too. They would have a good marriage.

Then she heard Sebastian's step outside, and something quickened in her. She gave a wry smile of self-mockery. She'd been fooling herself with prosaic talk about mental suitability. She had married Sebastian de Santiago because he could bring her body to life, because the mere sound of his footstep could throw her into a fever. She thought of the night to come, and the joyous pleasure that would soon be hers...

The door opened, and Sebastian stood there with a bottle of champagne and two glasses. Maggie knew a twinge of disappointment. She'd pictured him as he'd been on their last night together, when he'd been as eager for their union as she. But Sebastian was still dressed as he had been all day, except that he'd discarded his tie and torn open the throat of his shirt. Still, she thought, consoling herself, she would have the pleasure of undressing him. She smiled into his eyes and was shocked to find there was no answering light.

She closed the door behind him as he came into the room and set the glasses down. His movements were measured, as though he were under great strain and enduring it with difficulty. He opened the bottle, filled both glasses and handed one to her.

'It has been a long day, filled with toasts,' he said. 'But this is the one I've been looking forward to—with interest.'

How strange his voice sounded, she thought. How flat. How dead. How coldly angry. No, that couldn't be right.

But she'd never known until this moment that 'interest' was such a dismaying word.

'The interest, of course, lies in deciding what she shall drink to,' he continued. 'To deceit, to treachery, to the poor fool taken in for the second time?'

'What are you talking about?'

For answer he held up his glass sardonically. 'I drink to you—Señora Alva.'

The old hated name could still make a cold hand clutch at her heart. And to it was added a nameless fear that he had chosen this moment to say such a thing.

'Surely, I am Señora de Santiago now?'

'To others, yes. But to me, you will always be Señora Roderigo Alva.'

His tone put her on her mettle, and she faced him. 'In that case, it hardly seems worth your while to have married me.'

'I married you because I had no choice. To have cancelled a second wedding within a few days would have given the gossips and the sneerers all they needed. Rather than endure that, I will endure the appearance of marriage to you.'

'Cancel a second wedding?' she echoed, bewildered. 'But—why?'

'Because Felipe Mayorez was my father's closest friend,' he said bleakly.

'Felipe—Mayorez?' she whispered.

'You don't even remember his name,' Sebastian said scornfully.

But she did. Against her will it came shrieking out of the black night of things she didn't dare look at. Felipe Mayorez, a kindly old man, who had surprised an intruder in his house one night, and been left bleeding on the floor.

'He—was the man who—'

'The man your husband half-killed, a man who has never been the same since. Since my childhood he visited our house many times and was a second father to me. And when I visit him and see him staring into space, trapped in his own head—alive and yet not alive—and when I think that I have shared a woman with the criminal who did that to him—*amor de Dios*!'

He slammed a hand down on the table, tormented by some violent emotion. Maggie watched him in horror.

'You knew all this,' she whispered. 'As soon as you saw those papers—'

'I couldn't be sure. There might be two men of that name, but you told me he died in prison—'

'You *knew*,' she flung at him. 'You knew I was the last person you should marry, and you didn't tell me—'

'Because our marriage had to go ahead,' he responded harshly. 'It was too late to change anything.'

'You had no right to make that decision on your own,' she cried. 'It concerned me, too. Did you ever think that I might be as horrified by this discovery as you? Why do you think I changed my name back? Because I didn't want to be the wife of Roderigo Alva. I've spent years trying to hide it even from myself, and now, every time I look at you, I'm going to remember. You should have warned me in time.'

'It was already too late,' he snapped.

'Too late for you, not for me. Oh, God, how could this have happened?'

'It happened because you concealed the truth about yourself,' he grated. 'If I'd known this months ago, I would never have employed you, never have let you near my household. For me, the mere name of Alva is horrible.'

'For me, too, can't you understand? I wanted to escape it.'

'How convenient,' he scoffed. 'Felipe Mayorez can never escape it. He lives in a wheelchair, hardly able to move. Some days he can manage to whisper a few words. Some days not. He has nothing to look forward to but death. That's right, turn away. Block your ears. Shut out the truth. If only he could do the same.'

'I'm sorry for what happened to him, but it wasn't my fault.'

'So you say. And yet you tried to give your husband a false alibi.'

'That's not true,' she said violently. 'Roderigo wanted me to say he was with me that evening, but I denied it. That's why—'

She stopped herself. She'd been going to say that was why she felt so bad about Roderigo's fate. If she had told the lie he wanted, he might have lived. But she couldn't say any of this to the harsh, judgmental man she'd married.

'That's why what?'

'It doesn't matter. You've made up your mind and nothing I could say will change it. Don't judge me, Sebastian. You have no right. You don't know the real truth.'

'I know that my dear friend is a speechless cripple.'

'And my husband is dead. There's your revenge, if you want it.'

'But you're forgetting, I am your husband now.'

'Heaven help us both,' she whispered.

Suddenly she was seized by a burst of racking laughter. It convulsed her until she was almost sobbing.

'What is it?' Sebastian demanded.

'I told Catalina that no woman in her senses would

marry a Spaniard. I thought I'd learned my lesson.
You're not the only one who was duped a second time,
Sebastian. Oh, dear God! I thought you were different.
More fool me! No Spaniard is different. No *man* is dif-
ferent. You had no right to keep this to yourself. I'll
never forgive you for that.'

'And I,' he said bitingly, 'will never forgive you for
your part in this. For you too kept something vital to
yourself, didn't you?'

'I've explained about my name—'

'I don't just mean your name. I mean José Ruiz. He
came here as your friend from the days of your marriage.
Tell me, how did you come to know him? *Tell me.*'

'He's one of the family,' she admitted.

'One of the Alva family?'

'Yes, but his name isn't Alva.'

'His name!' he said contemptuously. 'As though his
name mattered when he carries Alva blood. And you
introduced that creature into my house to corrupt
Catalina.'

'He won't corrupt her; he loves her. He's a nice boy.'

'He is an Alva.'

They looked at each other across a deep abyss.

'We're going to have a very interesting marriage,'
Sebastian said at last.

'Marriage,' she echoed. 'You don't call this a marriage, do you?' She could hardly get out the last words.
A bout of shivering had seized her and her teeth had
begun to chatter. She fought to control it but she was in
shock. Waves of uncontrollable horror swept over her
and she felt as though she were freezing.

Sebastian frowned. With an abrupt movement, he
whisked the counterpane from the bed and tried to put

it about her but she fended him off with one hand flung out and eyes that burned.

'Get away from me,' she said hoarsely. 'Don't touch me. Don't ever try to touch me again.'

'You must put something on against the cold.'

'My robe is behind you. Just lay it on the bed and leave it there.'

He did as she said and stepped back, frowning as she seized up the garment and pulled it on, wrapping it right around her as though seeking protection.

'Now go,' Maggie said.

'I don't want to leave you like this—'

'Can't you understand that I hate the sight of you? Go, and don't try to come near me again tonight.'

'And tomorrow?'

'Tomorrow,' she sighed. 'Yes, tomorrow is going to come, isn't it? I can't think of it now. Go away.' Her eyes fell on the champagne he'd brought in. 'Perhaps you should take that with you. There's nothing to celebrate here.'

She watched as he left the room. She was still shivering, and tried to control it by getting into bed and pulling the covers around her. But it was horror that afflicted her, not cold, and at last she got out of bed and went to sit by the window. She remained there, motionless, for hours.

It was her wedding night, the night she'd looked forward to with joyful anticipation. They should have watched the dawn creep in, wrapped in each other's arms. Instead she watched it alone, dry-eyed, hugging her arms across her chest as though trying to defend herself from some threatened evil.

As the light changed from darkness to grey she could see her bags, ready packed for her honeymoon. A honeymoon that would never take place, she resolved, pulling herself together. At last she forced life into her stiff limbs. She took the smallest bag, emptied it of its beautiful clothes, and began thrusting in a few things that she would need, including nothing that Sebastian had ever bought her. The clothes she had brought to Spain with her would be enough. From now on, she was her own woman, and that was how it would stay.

She showered and dressed quickly. She tried to think of the future, but all she could see was a blank.

At last there was a light knock on her door. Sebastian stood there, fully dressed, his drawn face telling of the night he'd spent, a night that seemed to have been as bad as hers.

'May I come in?'

She stepped back to let him pass.

'You're a little ahead of time,' he observed. 'Our plane for New York doesn't leave until three o'clock this afternoon.'

'I'm not going to New York,' she said bleakly. 'I'm finished with you, Sebastian. I won't stay married to a man who could do something so cruel as going through with this farce and not tell me until afterwards. You can go alone, and don't tell me about your reputation, because I don't care.'

'You may not, but I have to. Wherever you go, we must go together, and people must think we are enjoying a blissful honeymoon. England, then?'

'No, Sol y Nieve. I'm going to ski the "Wall of Death", and find out if it deserves its reputation.'

'You're not going there alone,' he said at once.

'I shall do as I please.'

'Not in this mood. I'm not taking chances on you

being reckless. We'll just alter our honeymoon arrangements and go skiing instead.'

'Whatever you like. But for pity's sake, let's get out of this house.'

CHAPTER NINE

THE ''Wall of Death'' started near the top of Veleta, the second highest peak of the Sierra Nevada, and the highest from which skiing was possible. From here it dropped a distance of four miles, almost sheer in many places, until it ended near Sol y Nieve.

Within an hour of their arrival they had taken the ski lift up the mountain, riding side by side. Now and then Sebastian glanced at Maggie, but he didn't speak. There was something about her brooding silence that he was unwilling to interrupt. But when they stood together at the top of the run he said, 'Wait until tomorrow. You're not ready.'

'I'll never be more ready than I am this minute,' she said, looking down the run, not at him.

'More reckless, you mean. Margarita, listen to me—'

He reached for her arm, but as though his touch had detonated a flash she was off, darting out of his reach so fast that she was almost out of sight before he'd recovered. Cursing violently he sped after her, suddenly full of dread. He'd descended the wall himself often before, but never unless he was stone cold sober. And he knew that to tackle it in her present mood was almost an invitation to injury, or worse.

He managed to catch her but there was little more he could do. To get in front, hoping to slow her down, could bring about exactly the crash he feared.

After her first explosive dash, Maggie knew it was going to take all her skill and concentration to get down in one piece. A jagged rock appeared in her path, threatened her, vanished. She could feel the surface spotted with moguls, bumps left by turns in the snow from other skiers, but her legs seemed to move instinctively, balancing her weight to deal with them. Her excitement rose as she realised that she was good enough to do this. Best of all, she was outrunning her ghosts.

And then the end was in sight. She began to slow as Sol y Nieve appeared and grew larger. She reached the end breathless, and feeling as though a cleansing wind had blown through her mind, leaving it empty of everything. There was no pain, no fear, no despair, no joy, no love. There was nothing.

Sebastian appeared almost at once, watching her face. It seemed to him that the hostility had gone, but he searched in vain for anything softer that might have taken its place.

'Fine, you've done it now,' he said, breathing hard.

'Yes, I have. And I'm going to do it again. You don't have to.'

He took hold of her as she turned away. 'Understand me,' he said grimly. 'If you insist on doing this, then we do it together.'

'There's no need!'

'There's every need, because when you break your neck *I want to be there to say I told you so.*'

'Fine! On that understanding.'

When they reached the top she darted away again, but this time he was ready for her. They took the mountain almost side by side and reached the bottom together.

'That's it!' he said.

'It may be it for you, but I'm going back.'

'What's the matter with you?' he shouted. 'What are you trying to prove?'

'Nothing that you have to prove with me.'

His face was strained. 'You know better than that,' he said harshly.

Stubbornly she returned to the top, but this time she knew that she'd made a mistake. She was tired, and had lost the edge that had carried her successfully through the first two runs. Except that now she had experience of the slope, she assured herself. That would make all the difference.

But she'd miscalculated. This time the drop felt steeper, faster, her reactions slower. She tried to ease up. Would the end never come?

What happened next was too fast to follow. Suddenly, the ground, which had been sloping away steeply, seemed to vanish altogether. She had a sickening view of the long drop down into the valley, of nothingness rushing up to greet her. She fought for some footing but the mountain had become an enemy. She heard Sebastian cry out and the next moment she seemed to be in free fall. She called to her aid everything she knew about falling, not fighting it but trying to control it. Even so, she knew she was lucky to reach the bottom in one piece.

The knowledge did nothing to ease her anger at having failed in front of him. As the world ceased its spinning she sat up and slammed her fist into the snow just as he reached her and dropped to his knees.

'You could have been killed,' he cried hoarsely. He seized her. 'Do you understand me? You could have been killed!'

'Well, that would have solved your problem for you,' she yelled back.

His fingers dug painfully into her shoulders. 'Of all the stupid—idiotic—come on.' He helped her to her feet.

She winced and was forced to cling to him for support, but she freed herself at once.

'As soon as we get back to the hotel you'll see a doctor,' he said.

'I'm all right. Just a few bruises.'

'You're going to see a doctor,' he said with exasperated patience. 'Since you've marked me down as a domineering bully, I may as well act the part.'

She didn't answer. She was trying to hoist her skis over her shoulder, but she was all aches. Silently Sebastian took them from her, and they returned the short distance to the hotel. She found the walk harder than she would have admitted to. The mountains seemed to be still spinning around her and she was looking forward to a long sleep.

They had booked into the most luxurious room of the Hotel Frontera. It had two double beds, both big enough to take three, and a huge fireplace with logs. The actual heating was done by radiators, but the fireplace created the right rustic atmosphere, and the hotel maintained it diligently.

Maggie began to remove her outer clothing, moving slowly, and wincing a good deal. But she couldn't reach her boots.

'Let me,' Sebastian said quietly, and knelt down to work on the straps. Maggie took a long breath as he slipped them off.

'I'm sorry. Did that hurt?'

'No more than I deserve, I dare say,' she replied with a gruff laugh.

'For the sake of domestic harmony, I won't answer that.'

There was a knock on the door. Sebastian answered

it and returned with two glasses of brandy, one of which he gave her. 'It will make you feel better.'

It was a very fine brandy and it did make her feel better. He watched her drink it, then offered her the remaining half of his. She accepted it.

The doctor arrived, a pleasant middle-aged man, who looked her over efficiently and announced that she had no bones broken, or even cracked.

'Lots of bruises, but nothing worse,' he announced. 'Don't try that run again until you are well. I've seen people break their necks on it.'

When they were alone Sebastian asked gravely, 'Will you tell me the truth? Was that what you were trying to do?'

'Break my neck? No, of course not. But—I don't know how to put it—it sometimes feels good to take risks and leave it in the hands of fate. When you don't know what the answer is—just to shrug and say, what will be, will be. It can be the most exciting feeling in the world.'

'I know it can. I've done it myself. Nobody would ever ski a black run if they didn't have a touch of the fatalist about them.'

'When I'm better, I'm going back,' she said firmly.

'Very well, we'll go together. But this time, side by side. No races. Whatever you may think, seeing you get killed would not solve my problem. I don't know what the answer is—perhaps there isn't one. But it's not that. Of course,' he added ironically, 'the broken neck might be mine, and then *your* problem would be solved.'

'No,' she said. 'Roderigo died, but it didn't make me free of him. He just became more and more destructive. I thought I'd escaped from his shadow, but now it looms larger than ever.'

'Because of me?' Sebastian asked tensely.

'In some ways you're just like him.'

His head went up. '*I* am like that shiftless criminal?'

'He did what suited him and told me about it afterwards, just like you with our wedding.'

He frowned. 'I did what I thought was right, but maybe—maybe I was wrong.'

'What about what *I* thought was right? It didn't count, did it? Never mind. It's done now. I'm going to bed.'

She got carefully into her bed and curled up at the edge. Sebastian stayed up, drinking brandy until, about one in the morning, he got into the other bed.

Next day she rested, while Sebastian went out onto the slopes. He took the Wall of Death twice in the morning and twice in the afternoon, wondering what he was trying to prove to himself, and not caring to search too far for the answer. He had lunch out, rather than return to the hotel where he knew he wasn't welcome.

In the evening he found Maggie up and dressed, looking better, although she still moved stiffly. She asked politely after his day, and said she thought she might venture out tomorrow, not to ski, but to wander around the town. This kind of small talk carried them through a full half hour.

'You must be hungry,' he said at last. 'Shall I call Room Service?'

'No need. I'm well enough to come downstairs.'

Of course, he thought. The restaurant, where there were other guests and waiters to be spoken to, and the silence wouldn't yawn so terribly between them.

The carefully polite meal that followed was more dreadful than the most bitter quarrel. When it was over she said she would have an early night, but why didn't he spend half an hour in the bar, if he wished? He

agreed, and when he returned upstairs found the light
out and Maggie apparently asleep.

He was awoken by the sound of water running.
Through the crack in the bathroom door he could see a
light, and her shadow as she stepped into the tub. After
a while he heard what sounded like a gasp of pain, followed by a muttered, 'Damn!' He got up, slipped on a
silk robe and went to the door.

'Are you all right?' he asked.

'No,' she said after a moment.

'May I come in?'

'Yes.' She was sitting in the bath, clasping the sides,
a look of frustration on her face.

'I thought a hot soak would help,' she said. 'But now
I can't pull myself up. It hurts when I try.'

He leaned down. 'Put your arms about my neck.'

She did so and he straightened up slowly, taking her
whole weight. As her naked body came into view he
gave a sharp exclamation. The bruises had come right
out now and she seemed to be black and blue all over.

'There's a towelling robe on the door,' she said.

He draped it carefully around her and helped her out.
Then he picked her up gently and carried her over to the
fireplace, setting her down on the sofa. Then, to her surprise, he fetched a towel from the bathroom and sat
down beside her, taking hold of one of her feet and
beginning to dry it gently.

'I can do that,' she protested.

'You can't. See what happens if you try to reach this
far.' She tried, and gave up, wincing. 'You shouldn't
have to go into that bath alone. Why a bath, and not a
shower?'

'I wanted a hot soak. I though it would make me feel
better.'

'And if I hadn't woken up?'

'I'd have sat there until morning, I suppose. Anyway, thank you.'

'I think we should go home tomorrow.'

'No way. I've had a day's rest and a bath, and I'm feeling better. I'll be out tomorrow.'

'No more Wall of Death,' Sebastian said at once.

'No. I've done that.'

'Did it work?' he asked shrewdly.

'Up to a point.' She fell silent.

'Tell me about him,' Sebastian said at last. He saw her eyebrows rise faintly and said, 'Yes, I should have asked before. But I should like to know what a woman like you saw in such a man.'

'I wasn't a "woman like me", in those days. I was a girl of Catalina's age, and just as ignorant and naive as she is. Now, I'm the woman Roderigo made me: not a very nice one, I often think. I don't really trust anyone—not really, deep down trust with my whole heart—because I trusted him so much.'

She was silent for a long time, before Sebastian said, 'Tell me, please.'

'My parents had died, and I was on my own. I thought Roderigo was wonderful, so handsome and charming. He told me he was on a business trip, buying and selling things.'

'He never made an honest penny in his life,' Sebastian couldn't resist interrupting.

'That's not true,' she said quickly, impelled to defend Roderigo by an impulse that she didn't understand. Or perhaps it wasn't him she was defending but the eighteen-year-old Maggie and everything she had believed in. 'The business was real enough. It just didn't do very well. At the start, he really was trying, I know he was.

And sometimes he pulled off very successful deals. But then he got carried away and spent the profits before he had them.'

'So how did he turn into what he became?'

'He didn't have much head for money, I suppose. He always thought money would turn up, and when it didn't, well—I had a little, only that disappeared too. I kept thinking he'd grow up, become more responsible, but he wasn't a boy. He was twelve years older than me. I guess he just couldn't grow up. And when the money was gone he started to panic.'

'Did he hit you?'

'No,' she said quickly, 'he didn't do that.'

He watched her, wondering if she knew what she'd revealed. The speed with which she'd said, 'No, he didn't do that,' implied that it was virtually the only thing he hadn't done.

'He liked to take the easiest way,' Maggie went on. 'In the end, he couldn't do any work. I think he'd forgotten how. So the only way to get money was stealing.' She gave a mirthless laugh. 'He was quite good at that. So, of course, he went on.'

'Why did you stay with such a man?'

'Maybe it was a kind of stubbornness. I couldn't bear to admit that our love had turned into such a mess.'

'You loved him?' Contempt and disbelief mingled in his voice.

'Oh, yes,' she whispered. 'I loved him once. He'd been everything to me, and it was so hard to let it go. And then—I found I was pregnant.'

She was looking into the fire, and didn't see him start.

'I had such high hopes when I knew about the baby. I thought Roderigo might change, become responsible.' She gave the little mirthless laugh again. To Sebastian it sounded almost like choking. 'As though a man's basic nature could change. He grew worse. He thought it justified him being a thief. He kept saying, "I did it for you and our son," until I wanted to scream.

'He was so sure it would be a son. He kept making grandiose plans for the boy, and then going out to steal. I think that's when I noticed that his face was changing. It became thinner, withered and—mean.'

'I remember seeing him at the trial and thinking how like a rat he looked,' Sebastian said. 'A miserable, cornered rat, twisting this way and that to avoid his guilt. Luckily he didn't succeed. Even his own confederates were disgusted with him. One of them gave evidence against him.'

'Yes, I heard.'

'I never saw you at the trial or I would have remembered you.'

'I wasn't there. The day before it started, I went into premature labour. My baby was born at six months. She lived for a week in an incubator. I stayed with her all that time. I knew the trial was going on, but it was like something on another planet. For me, the whole world was in that little incubator.'

'Now I understand what I saw in your face when you looked at the crib,' Sebastian said heavily.

'That wooden baby was almost the same size as mine. Six-month babies are so tiny—you could hold one in your hand—except that I couldn't touch her, only look.' She sighed. 'Until the end. When she died they took her out and wrapped her in a shawl, and I could hold her. She was still warm, almost as though she were still alive. I kept wanting to tell them there was a mistake. She must be alive because she was so warm. But then I felt her start to go cold, and I knew she was dead.'

When she'd said that there was a long silence. Maggie wrapped her arms about herself and rocked back and forth, her head bent. Sebastian watched her, appalled. Whatever he had expected, it wasn't this. He reached out to lay a gentle hand on her shoulder, but she flinched away from him.

He too dropped his head and covered his face. Helplessness, frustration, the feeling that he'd done harm and couldn't put it right, these were things he found hard to handle. Don Sebastian de Santiago always had the answer. That was why people came to him. But tonight she was hurt beyond bearing and he wanted to punish someone for doing it. But the someone was himself, and he didn't know what to do.

'She was so tiny, and she fought so hard to live,' Maggie whispered. 'I'd have given my own life to save her, but I couldn't. I was her mother, but I couldn't help her. My little girl! My sweet, brave little girl! She never had a chance.' Anguish racked her.

Sebastian reached out to touch her but withdrew his hand at once, knowing that there was nothing he could do or say that wouldn't seem like a crass impertinence. So he stayed as he was, cursing silently, and after a while Maggie raised her head and spoke again.

'Nobody cared but me. She was only a girl. José came to her funeral. Nobody else from the family bothered.

'A strange thing happened then. I stopped feeling. And I was glad, because that way there was no more pain. I knew it was still hurting really, deep down. But I couldn't feel it. I saw Roderigo in prison and he screamed at me. I know he did, but it was as though I didn't hear it. I told him I hated him because our baby was dead but I couldn't feel the hate either, although I knew it was there.

'I went back to England. José took me to the airport. He was only a boy, but he was very kind. None of Roderigo's immediate family would help me. They blamed me for not supporting his alibi.'

'It would have made no difference,' Sebastian said. 'Who would have believed you?'

'That's true. But José wasn't like them. He wrote to me when Roderigo died. And that's when—' She stopped and a shudder went through her. 'That's when I started to feel things again. I began to hear him screaming at me. At night—in my dreams—he was always there—crying out that it was all my fault—'

'But that's nonsense!' Sebastian exclaimed. 'How can it be your fault?'

'You thought it was. When you discovered my real name, as far as you were concerned I was just an Alva, one of a tainted family.'

'I was wrong,' he said at once. 'I behaved badly to you. But can't you forgive?'

'And who will forgive me?'

'For what?'

'He's dead. Perhaps I should have lied and saved him.'

'You can't really believe that.'

'By day I don't believe it. But at night, when he accuses me in my nightmares—' She shuddered and put her hands over her ears.

'Stop it!' Sebastian said urgently. He took hold of her and this time she didn't draw away. He wasn't sure how much she was even aware of him. 'Maggie,' he said, shaking her gently, 'Maggie, listen to me. It's over. He was bad and he was punished. It's over. But you have to get on with your life.'

'What kind of life can an Alva have? Bad stock, tainted, incapable of good—'

'Don't!' he said, in a torment almost as great as hers. 'You're not an Alva. You never were. Your name is de Santiago, and you are my wife.'

'I'm *his* wife!' she cried.

'No. You belong to me, now. Feel my arms about you. Feel how much I want you. Don't let the dead claim you. There's so much life for us.'

He kissed her eyes, her mouth, desperately trying to recall her from the cold place that threatened to suck her in. With all her heart she longed to respond to him. Perhaps Sebastian's passion could recall her to life.

But almost at once they knew the truth. Sebastian looked into her face and saw not coldness but despair. Slowly he released his grip.

'It's too soon,' he said haltingly. 'You're not well. Go back to bed. Try to sleep. We'll talk again tomorrow.'

'No more talking,' she said. 'There's no point.'

She let him help her back to bed and tuck her up, then she turned away at once, closing her eyes.

They stayed a week, skiing until they were exhausted, eating together, talking little but with great courtesy. To their own ears they sounded like strangers shouting across a deep valley. He didn't try to make love to her again.

On the night before their departure, as they were packing, Sebastian said, 'What happens now?'

'We go home. You'd better take me on that tour of your estates, introducing me to people.'

Almost imperceptibly he relaxed. 'Thank you, Margarita, for staying with me,' he said quietly. 'I was afraid you would run away.'

She looked at him in astonishment. 'Where to? There's no escape.'

CHAPTER TEN

THEY returned home to find the house in a state of tension. Isabella had recovered her health well enough to enforce Sebastian's prohibition on Catalina seeing José, and the girl was seething with rebellion. She telephoned José every day, but had been unable to slip out to see him.

'And nor will you,' Sebastian told her furiously. 'He is an Alva, cousin of the man who destroyed my friend. You will not see him, and your marriage is out of the question.'

He didn't think Maggie could hear, but she chanced to be within earshot. To her, he never mentioned Roderigo, and she had come to understand that his restraint grew out of concern for her. His manner to her now was always gentle and kind. But when she heard him speak of the Alva family in such a way she knew that the abyss between them was as wide and deep as ever.

Catalina sought tearful refuge with Maggie, who explained the situation as best she could.

'It's not his fault,' Catalina said passionately.

'No, it isn't José's fault,' Maggie agreed. 'But this goes very deep with Sebastian, so don't hope for him to change his mind.'

'I thought you would be on my side,' Catalina said accusingly.

'I might be if you were a little more mature, and if I thought your love for José was deep and true, instead of being just a reaction to your engagement to Sebastian. Now you're free to make a choice, don't rush to choose the first man you see.'

She told Sebastian frankly that she was going to see José.

'Acting as go-between?' he asked wryly.

'Catalina is no nineteenth-century miss, to be locked in her room until she obeys. If I keep the lines of communication open, you're less likely to have a full-scale rebellion on your hands. I'm not going to help them elope—just trying to keep the situation under control. But I won't do it in secret.'

'Thank you. I appreciate that.'

Her visit to José left her more uncertain than ever. There was no doubt of his true feelings, but he struck her as an infatuated boy rather than a serious man. Maggie explained about Sebastian's friendship with Felipe Mayorez, delivered loving messages from Catalina, advised José to be very patient, and promised to work on Sebastian if possible.

Returning home, she went to see him to put in a good word for José, and found him frowning over a letter, willing to give her only half of his attention.

'What's the matter? Who is that from?'

'From Felipe Mayorez,' he said with a sigh. 'He wants me to take you to visit him.' He saw her horrified look and added, 'Naturally he was invited to the wedding, as a matter of courtesy, but he couldn't attend.'

'What state is he in, these days?' Maggie asked awkwardly.

'Almost like a vegetable. He lives in a wheelchair. He has an attendant, Carlos, who feeds him and cares for his every need. Sometimes he can mumble a few words; some days he can speak clearly for a short time.'

'Oh, God!' she whispered. She began to walk around the room, seeking some release from tension. 'I can't see him. It's too risky. There were photographs in the press at the time—'

'Of you?'

'No—I don't think so—but suppose there was a picture I didn't know about—and he saw it—and recognises me? Think how it would upset him.'

'He was in a coma for months. He never saw anything in the papers. Besides, I read everything the press ever printed, and I never saw your picture. Otherwise I'd have known you from the start.' He looked at her. 'It's all right. I have to go but I'll make some excuse for you.'

'What excuse can you make for such a grave discourtesy?'

'I'll think of something. I won't ask you to do this.'

'You must,' she said calmly. 'It's expected.' She saw him looking at her and added, 'You're a public man. You can't afford not to do what is expected.'

In a land where ceremony still counted, Sebastian had been dreading having to explain his wife's absence on a visit of form. He was grateful to Maggie for making it easy, yet something in her ready compliance troubled him. After her first protest, she had seemed to shrug mentally and decide that it didn't matter, because nothing really mattered to her. The old Maggie, who fought him at every turn, seemed to have vanished, and he would have given anything to have her back.

The thought struck him again when he saw her ready for the visit. She was attired in a conventional dress of sober hue, the very picture of a respectable Spanish matron. But the sight brought him no pleasure. She had said appearances must be preserved, and he knew that sometimes people clung to appearances to cover an emptiness within.

He wasn't usually sensitive to people's moods, but he could sense Maggie's despair and confusion. She was lost in a desert, functioning automatically as she waited for something to happen that would show her the way out. And much as he longed to, he knew he couldn't help her. It was he who had raised her demons to howl at her, but he had no power to calm them again, and he wanted to bang his head against the wall. He would have done so if that would have helped her.

The Casa Mayorez was in the heart of Granada, near the foot of the great hill on which stood the Alhambra Palace. In his own way, Felipe Mayorez was a prince, and he had lived as one until the day four years ago when he had been robbed and attacked. Now he existed unheeding, amidst his magnificent possessions.

Carlos, his carer, came to meet them. He was an amiable young man, devoted to his employer—able to read his every mood, even when the words were blurred. But today the news was good.

'He is much brighter than usual,' he told them. 'And he can speak fairly clearly. It will make him so happy that you have come.'

He led the way to the conservatory where Felipe Mayorez lay in a wheelchair that was half a bed. A heavy rug was laid over his wasted knees, and his head rested on pillows. With a great effort he managed to turn it as his visitors approached.

'Welcome to my house,' he said slowly. 'Welcome, my old friend. And to your wife—a very special welcome.'

Sebastian leaned down and kissed the old man with complete naturalness. Maggie was afraid they would see her trembling, but she forced herself to be calm as her husband introduced her. Felipe Mayorez smiled at her, not knowing that she had been the wife of the man who'd destroyed him.

She made the proper reply, and thanked him for his wedding present, a huge, gold-decorated dinner service of the finest porcelain.

'That was my gift to your house,' Felipe said. 'But I have another gift, only for you. On that table.'

Sebastian handed her a small packet. Inside was a pair of heavy gold earrings.

'They're beautiful,' she gasped. 'But I can't take them. They look like valuable antiques.'

'They are,' Sebastian told her. 'They belonged to his wife.'

'His wife,' she said faintly.

'He gives them to you as a great compliment.'

She drew a sharp breath, longing to run away and hide. Why had she come here, when she could have gotten out of it? Then she saw Sebastian's eyes on her, steadying her, felt the warm pressure of his fingers on her hand, and the dreadful moment passed.

'Help me put them on,' she said, taking them up.

He lifted her hair back and she felt his warm breath on the nape of her neck. Then his fingers brushed lightly against her ears, fastening the gold clasps. Maggie drew a slow breath, startled at the way her heart had started to beat.

It was the first time he'd touched her intimately since the night in Sol y Nieve when he'd tried to make love to her, and given up in the face of her despairing chill. Since then, he'd never touched her except by chance, or to give her his hand formally.

And now, when she was least prepared, her sensations

returned, making the blood rush to her cheeks. She met Sebastian's eyes, and saw there that he'd understood. Something was making her breath come quickly. Then a sigh of pleasure from Felipe forced them back to the present, and it was all over.

'Beautiful,' he said. 'Magnificent.'

'Yes, they are beautiful,' she said. 'Thank you.'

Then the tears came to her eyes. It was so dreadful to see him there, his life ruined, and know that she was deceiving him.

'You must not weep,' Felipe said.

'I can't help it,' she said huskily, touching his wasted cheek. 'I'm sorry—I'm so sorry—'

'No need to be sorry for me—when I have a lovely woman to weep for me,' he said gallantly. He tried to raise his arm and failed. 'Sebastian, comfort her.'

She tried to stop crying but her pity for the old man welled up. She had wept for her baby, for Roderigo, for herself, but now she wept for Felipe and they were the bitterest tears of all. She felt Sebastian's arms go around her, drawing her head against his shoulder, and cried unrestrainedly.

After a moment she forced herself to be calm again, and raised her head, smiling at Felipe.

'You are a lucky man,' he said to Sebastian. 'By now, you might have made a different marriage. But this is the wife for you. She is a good and true woman. No man could ask for better. I, Felipe Mayorez, tell you that.'

'And you are right, old friend,' Sebastian said gravely. 'I have known it, but it pleases me to hear you say it.'

Suddenly the old man gave a sigh. His eyes closed and his head lolled.

'Carlos,' Sebastian called, and the young man appeared so quickly that he must have been nearby.

They said their goodbyes, but Felipe seemed hardly able to hear them, and they left. In the car home Maggie realised that she was still wearing the earrings and started to remove them.

'Keep them on,' Sebastian told her. 'They were given from the heart.'

'I never expected him to be so kind to me.'

'He saw something in you that he loved,' Sebastian said simply. 'This I understand.'

He spoke so quietly that she wasn't sure she'd heard him, and when she looked he was gazing out of the window.

Maggie had moved out of the room she first occupied, into one that befitted the mistress of the house, but Sebastian had kept his own room next door. Sometimes faint noises reached him through the connecting wall. He tried not to listen, but the noises tormented him.

On the night of their visit to Felipe he sat up late, listening and trying not to listen. As midnight passed into the small hours he could hear her walking about the room. But then the movements stopped, and the silence was worse.

He thought of her that afternoon, letting him hold her while she was torn by pity for the old man, but slipping quickly out of his arms again. And tonight, when he might have turned to him, she had pleaded a headache and gone to bed early. That was six hours ago and she was still awake.

When he could endure it no longer he went out into the corridor. There was no sound from behind her door, and at last he pushed it open and closed it quietly behind him. She was standing in the middle of the floor. She turned when she heard the click of the door.

'Can't you sleep?' he asked.

'I don't want to sleep. Not after this afternoon. Every time I close my eyes I see him.'

'Felipe?'

'No—*him*!'

There was no further need to ask who *he* was.

'I can't bear my nightmares,' Maggie said desolately. 'He's always there.'

He came close to her. 'He mustn't be there,' he said. 'Nobody must be there but me.'

'Then drive him away,' she said desperately. 'Can't you make him go?'

'Yes,' he said, taking her into his arms. 'I will make him go away, so that there is only me. Tell me that is what you want.'

'Yes,' she whispered, slipping her arms about his neck. 'It's what I want.'

Still he couldn't be sure, and his uncertainty was reflected in his kiss, gentle and loving, passion held in abeyance. There was something new in her response, a desperation, almost a plea, that hurt him. He kissed her repeatedly, trying to bring her back to him.

'Margarita,' he murmured, 'Margarita—where are you?'

'With you—where I want to be. Hold me.'

'What do you want?' he asked her urgently.

'I want you—*you*.'

He longed to ask her what she really meant by that, but the need was rising in him, making his caresses more urgent, his kisses deeper. As always her beauty entranced him, but tonight it had a special quality. He tossed her night dress away, then his own robe, and held her naked body against his.

'Sebastian—I do want you.'

It was all he needed. He reached the bed first and sat, drawing her against him so that he could lay his head between her breasts, revelling in their sweetness and warmth. They were already proudly peaked, testament to her desire. When he caressed them with his lips, she let out a long sigh of pleasure and satisfaction, clasping her hands behind his head, inviting him.

He leaned back so that she slid down onto the bed beside him and began to bestow subtle, lingering kisses on her face, her neck, silently calling her to return to him.

Maggie could feel the change in him through her skin, her sensations, the beating of her heart. Their other lovings had been wild encounters, each seeking and giving pleasure, almost like rivals. Now Sebastian was using desire to give her something else, something she needed far more than pleasure. With every touch he spoke of tenderness, protection, reassurance, and her terrors began to fade. In her need she reached out to him, and he was there.

His arms had always been strong to excite her, but now they were strong to keep her safe. Nobody had ever offered her safety before, and she reached for it, eagerly, blindly, startling him with the emotional depth of her response.

'Margarita,' he murmured.

'Hold me,' she begged. 'Don't let me go.'

'Never,' he said swiftly. 'I'm here—always—' His face was close to hers, his eyes holding hers. 'Now,' he whispered. *'Now!'*

She drew a long breath and suddenly she was a whirlwind in his arms, calling his name, drawing him closer, seeking something only he could give. For a blinding moment everything was well between them, just as it had been when passion was uncomplicated and all they asked. Then suddenly it was over and his heart was beating as never before. Something had happened, beautiful, alarming and beyond his experience. He wasn't sure of anything, except that passion alone would never be enough again.

He lay on his back, his arm beneath Maggie's neck, while she turned towards him, flinging an arm confidingly across his chest, snuggling against him as though seeking refuge.

He thought she murmured something. It might have been, *'My darling,'* or it might not. He listened, hoping she would speak again, but she had settled against him, sleeping as contentedly as a child. After a while he, too, slept.

He awoke in the small hours to find her asleep on his chest, still in the circle of his arm.

'Margarita,' he said softly, 'are you awake?'

There was no answer, only her soft rhythmic breathing. When he was sure she was still asleep, he kissed the top of her head.

'Where are we now?' he murmured. 'You came to me, but why? Was it only to drive him away? If so, how can I complain? Who should defend you from him but I, who brought him back to torment you?

'I knew in Sol y Nieve that you'd returned to that place you spoke of, the place without feeling that you entered when your baby died. There was no hate there, but no love either, no warmth, no joy. Nothing for Roderigo—and nothing for me.

'But now the feelings have returned, haven't they? Why am I afraid to look into your heart? What would I find there? Love for me? Love for him? Despite everything, is some part of you still his? Is that why he haunts you?

'What would you say if I spoke to you of love? Would that bring you closer to me, or drive you further off? Why haven't I the courage to take the risk?'

He made a sudden convulsive movement, sitting up so sharply that he was afraid she would awaken. But she only rolled over and buried herself more deeply in the bed. He rose, pulled on his robe and went to the window overlooking the garden, opening it quietly and slipping out into the cool night air.

Down below he could see the Patio de los Pájaros, where he'd sat on the first evening and she had come wandering out amidst the stone birds, talking of truth and paradise, and they had mysteriously understood each other. But it had ended in a quarrel, as it always did, because this woman was born to torment him. And now that he'd discovered something of her heart and mind, she tormented him more than ever, posing questions that couldn't be answered in bed, and that undermined everything he'd thought was certain in his life.

'Margarita Alva,' he murmured desperately to the night sky, 'how I wish I had never met you!'

Maggie's tour of the de Santiago estates was a triumphant success. Those she met knew only that she was English and had prepared themselves for the worst. But her fluency in their language disarmed them, and the discovery that she was a Cortez, born in the region and knowledgeable about it, completed her conquest. They even began to use her as a channel to Sebastian.

'Of course, I realise that you find it incredibly boring to discuss these things with a woman,' she teased him one evening.

'No, no, that horse won't run,' he defended himself, grinning. 'Not after things I heard you say to Alfonso in Sol y Nieve. Besides, I only said it in the first place to annoy you.' He glanced at the papers she'd put before him. 'Why didn't Señora Herez bring this problem to me ages ago? She's left it almost too late to do anything.'

'She finds you rather alarming.'

He was perturbed. 'I never knew.'

'Is it really too late?'

'We'll be in Seville next week for the opening of the regional parliament. I'll talk to some people.'

In Seville she found herself at the centre of a new world. Now it was Sebastian's fellow politicians who crowded around, eager to know her. Over a series of tiring but triumphant dinner parties she completed what her husband called, 'the conquest of Seville'. His pride in her was enormous. Their closeness seemed to grow every day. By the time they returned home three weeks later they both felt they could dare to hope that the problems were behind them.

Sebastian reached the Casa Mayorez in the middle of the afternoon. Carlos was waiting for him.

'I don't know if I did the right thing in calling you, Señor,' he said nervously.

'You were very vague and mysterious on the telephone. Why don't you simply tell me what had happened?'

Carlos picked up a newspaper, bearing the picture of a ruffianly, unshaven man, whose face Sebastian found unpleasantly familiar.

'It's him,' Carlos said, indicating the picture. 'His

name is Miguel Vargas, and he's just been arrested for murder. It was on television too, and when my master saw this man's face on the screen he became very agitated.'

Sebastian studied the picture and went cold. Now he knew where he'd seen Miguel Vargas before—at the trial of Roderigo Alva. He was an associate of Alva's and had given evidence against him. According to him, Alva had boasted of having robbed the Casa Mayorez once already—something which Alva had been eager to admit, since his defence had been that the previous burglary accounted for his fingerprints on the scene.

'He said the place was stacked with riches, and he was going back,' Vargas had claimed. But this Alva had frantically denied. The two men had had a screaming match across the court. Vargas was an unpleasant character, but nobody had doubted he was telling the truth about this.

'How—agitated?' Sebastian asked Carlos now.

'He kept saying, "Him", "Him",' Carlos said. 'I asked him what he meant, and he said, "He killed me." And then he began to weep. He kept repeating over and over, "He killed me."'

Sebastian tried not to listen to the thoughts that were shouting at him. It was monstrous, impossible. For if it was true—

If it was true, then Roderigo Alva was innocent of the crime for which he had been convicted. And that meant...

He pulled himself together and read the rest of the newspaper story. Miguel Vargas had been arrested for shooting down a policeman in cold blood in the presence of witnesses. There was no doubt of his guilt, or the fact that he would spend the rest of his life behind bars for this crime alone. Nothing Sebastian did or didn't do would make any difference to that.

'What am I to do, Señor?' Carlos asked. 'I thought of going to the police, but an identification by such a sick man after four years—'

'Would be very little use,' Sebastian agreed.

'And they would question my master and upset him further. Shouldn't I spare him that? Advise me, Señor.'

'Let me think about this,' Sebastian told him. 'In the meantime, say nothing. Try to keep him calm, and if possible, don't let him watch the news. I'll be in touch.'

He spent a troubled evening at home, glad that they were entertaining guests, and his preoccupation might pass unnoticed. When the guests had gone he told his wife that he would work late, and spent the night pacing his study.

On the face of it, there was no doubt where his duty lay. If an innocent man had been wrongly convicted, then, even though he was now dead he was entitled to have his name cleared. It was all very simple. Except that...

Except that the discovery of her husband's innocence would reconcile Maggie to his memory. At just the moment when she had begun to turn to himself, she would learn something that would be like a new barrier between them.

It dawned on Sebastian, with a kind of relief, that he could do nothing without first taking this up with the legitimate authorities. He thought of Hugo Ordonez, a good friend and local politician, influential in police circles. Early next morning he called him, received a warm greeting, and by lunchtime Sebastian was sitting in the man's study.

'It's about Miguel Vargas, who was arrested recently,' he said. 'Or, rather, it's about Felipe Mayorez.'

Ordonez looked surprised. 'However did you get to hear so soon?' he said.

'I don't understand. Hear what?'

'About Vargas having committed the attack on Señor Mayorez. Not that we're sure it's true, but it's hard to see why he should have confessed otherwise.'

Sebastian's head shot up. 'Confessed?'

'Taunted us with it. Why not? A dozen witnesses saw him murder that police officer, so he knows he's got nothing to lose. I suppose he thought he'd treat himself to the sight of authority with some explaining to do. Although, as I say, he may be lying for the hell of it.'

'No,' Sebastian said heavily. 'He isn't lying. Mayorez has identified him.'

He told the story of his talk with Carlos and Ordonez whistled thoughtfully.

'What happens next?' Sebastian asked.

'Hard to be sure. It would still be difficult to charge him on the basis of what we've got. He's just as likely to deny he ever confessed. We'll probably spend so much time arguing about the likely outcome that it will just vanish in the files.'

And then nobody would ever have to know, Sebastian thought as he left. Nobody, including the woman whose burdens would be doubled by the knowledge of Roderigo Alva's innocence.

Hadn't she suffered enough? Wouldn't it be an act of kindness to shield her from this revelation? But his conscience told him that he wanted Maggie kept in ignorance so that she would turn more fully to himself. If she knew what he'd discovered, would she ever truly be his? Fiercely, he longed to keep the truth to himself, and

not risk shattering the closeness that was building between them. But had he the right to stay quiet for his
own sake?

All the way home he struggled with his fears. There
were so many good reasons for doing what suited himself, and as a man of power he was familiar with most
of them. But he was also a man with a rigid moral code,
and he had always found temptation easy to resist.

Until now.

CHAPTER ELEVEN

SEBASTIAN had been wrong in thinking that Maggie hadn't noticed his preoccupation the night before. She'd seen it, and she'd also guessed that he hadn't stayed up to work. So when he returned home that afternoon with a heavy step, she was ready for him.

'What is it?' she asked, rising and coming to stand before him, searching his face.

Until this moment, he'd thought there was still doubt about what he would say. Now he knew the decision had already been taken, because there was no way he could lie to her.

'What has happened, Sebastian? Where have you been?'

'With a man called Hugo Ordonez. He has extensive contacts with the police. I went to ask him about Miguel Vargas, who was arrested the other day for killing a policeman.'

She became very still. 'Do you mean the man who gave evidence at Roderigo's trial?'

'Yes. Now it seems that evidence was false. It was Vargas himself who committed the attack on Felipe.'

She stared. 'What are you saying?'

The words almost choked him. 'I'm saying that Roderigo was innocent. Vargas was the guilty man.'

'Vargas *said* that?'

'Yes.'

'But why would he?'

'Because he has nothing to lose. He's facing a life

sentence, and he knows that this admission will cause trouble for the police but none for him.'

He couldn't be sure how much she had taken in. It was almost as though she were holding the news away from her, the better to examine it, and perhaps defend herself from it.

'And you think he's really the man who attacked Felipe?' she asked at last, slowly.

'I'm sure of it. Felipe saw Vargas' face on television on the day he was arrested, and managed to tell Carlos that he was the man. Maggie—!'

Her face had gone so white that he feared she was about to faint. He reached for her but she backed away, clutching a table to hold herself upright.

'Roderigo was innocent,' she said in a dazed voice. 'He was telling the truth all the time? No—that can't be right. It *can't* be!' The words were a plea.

'I'm afraid it is, though.'

'Oh, dear God!' she whispered. 'What am I going to do?'

'You don't have to do anything. I'll start the proceedings for clearing his name—'

But she hadn't meant that, he realised when he saw her desperate eyes. What was she to do now with her memories and her fears?

She began pacing up and down. 'All this time,' she was saying half to herself, 'all this time I hated him—and he was innocent—'

'You didn't just hate him because of this,' he reminded her. 'Even without it, he's still the man who took you for a very nasty ride.'

'I know, I know. I'm trying to be sensible about it, but it's hard. I deserted him, don't you see? If I'd stayed…'

'Maggie, he brought it on himself.'

She whirled on him. 'Did he bring it on himself that Vargas lied?'

'Yes,' he shouted. 'How did he know Vargas in the first place? Because they were fellow criminals. If he'd been an honest man, they'd never have met. Yes, he brought it on himself, and if you were thinking straight you'd see that.'

'How do you expect me to think straight when I can hear him in my head, begging me not to leave? I could cope with that when I thought him guilty, but— Oh, God! what shall I do now? If I'd stayed—fought for him—he might have had the will to live.'

'And he would have lived in prison. There was nothing to clear him, then. Vargas only confessed now because he's dead. You couldn't have freed him by staying.'

'But he begged me to believe him,' she cried, turning away, 'and I just assumed the worst.'

'Because he'd given you ample cause.'

When she didn't answer, something snapped in Sebastian. He seized her shoulders and pulled her around to face him. 'Listen to me,' he said fiercely, 'I've known you as a strong, sensible woman. That's how you've always wanted me to see you. Well, act like one. See him as he was, a waster and a scoundrel who lived off you and broke your heart. Don't give him a halo because he was innocent of this one crime. That's a piece of sentimentality I didn't expect from you.'

She stared at him, seeming dumbfounded. Sebastian had the dreadful feeling of fighting a mist. Nothing he said or did seemed to have any effect, and as his fear mounted it expressed itself as anger.

'You had the guts to fight me,' he shouted, giving her

a little shake. 'Why haven't you got the guts to fight him? *How much do you want to fight him?*'

'Wh-what?'

'Why don't you admit it?' he demanded bitterly. 'He's still the one. It's true, isn't it?'

'No—what are you saying?—of course it isn't true.'

'Words,' he snapped. 'Everything about your actions tell me you're still holding him in your heart.'

'Suppose I was?' she raged. 'Would you have any right to complain? You married me to ease your pride. Well, you got what you wanted. My feelings are none of your business. *Now, leave me alone!*'

She ran out of the room, leaving Sebastian alone, looking at the wreckage of what he had done.

He never knew where she went, and she never told him of the hours she had spent wandering in the further reaches of the grounds. There was nobody out here to see her violent storms of weeping, followed by trembling calm as she fought to get control of her dreadful thoughts. He'd been innocent, and she'd deserted him.

'He's still the one. It's true, isn't it?'

No, it isn't! Don't look at me like that—as though you saw what I was too appalled to see!

Then another burst of weeping, which went on until she was too tired to cry any more.

In the early evening she went in search of Sebastian and found him in his study.

'We both said a lot of things we didn't mean,' she said.

Tell me you didn't mean it.

His smile was constrained. 'I only wanted to help you through this. I probably did it clumsily, for which I apologise.'

Tell me you no longer love him.

'No, no, you're right,' she said, 'about me building him up now. It's just a matter of common sense.' She smiled. 'Just give me a little time to get my head around this.'

'Margarita, don't pretend just because you feel you have to. I'm your husband. If this is hard for you, I want to share it.'

'You and me? Share this?' She gave a small choking laugh.

'Don't,' he begged. 'Don't shut me out.'

'I'm not,' she said, too quickly. 'There's nothing to shut you out from. I'm all right about it, really I am. It won't make any difference to us.'

His heart sank. He heard the sensible words, and saw her smile, as bright as a shield. And they were like a door slammed in his face.

A week later, Sebastian came into the room as Maggie was setting down the telephone. 'What is it?' he asked, seeing her face.

'I was talking to my landlord, in England. He wants to know what's going to happen. When I left I paid two months rent in advance, but I have to decide what I'm going to do now.'

'What is there to decide?' he asked quietly. 'You're my wife. This is your home now.'

'Yes, of course, I just meant— there are things to be sorted out. When I left, I only meant to be away for a few weeks. You have to spend some time in Seville, so it's a good time for me to return to England to arrange matters.' She gave a shaky laugh. 'I think I may have some overdue library books. The fines must have mounted by now.'

His silence had a bleak quality, as though a dark cloud had settled over him. Looking at his face she saw in it everything that was passing through his mind.

'Call your landlord,' he said at last. 'He can return your books. I'll send someone to collect your things—'

'No—I don't want anyone else going through my belongings. And I have people I must see—old friends—I need to say goodbye—'

'Is it goodbye you'll be saying?'

'Of course,' she said, too quickly.

A tremor shook him. 'Don't go, Margarita. It can all be done by others.'

'I don't—I want to do it myself.'

'Very well,' he said after a moment. 'When will you leave?'

'The sooner the better.'

He drove her to Malaga Airport himself, that very day. Inside the terminal he took her bags and waited while she checked in. Their manner to each other was calmly correct. There was nothing in Sebastian's appearance to suggest that he was consumed by hideous fear.

He came with her as far as he could. 'How long will you be gone?' he asked.

'I don't know,' she said with difficulty. 'How long do these things take?'

'Not very long, if somebody wants to hurry home. I wonder how much you want to hurry.'

'Sebastian—'

'Are you coming back to me?' He was holding her hand tightly.

'If I said I wasn't—what would you do?'

His clasp tightened. 'Margarita—'

A crowd was trying to press through. 'Hurry along there, miss. It's the last call.'

The crowd surged. Her hand was free. She didn't know how or why it had happened. Her last view was of Sebastian, reaching out to her across the barrier, touching only air, his face full of a terrible question. She thought he called her name, but she couldn't be sure, and then she could no longer see him.

As the plane landed in London, Maggie realised how badly she was looking forward to being back in her own little flat. It was small and shabby but it was the place where she was herself. It would welcome her.

But just at first, it didn't. She shivered at the cold as soon as she stepped inside. But of course, the heating had been off throughout the winter. She could soon have it warm again. Quickly she put on all the lights and switched on the central heating. As she felt the air grow warmer she looked around, trying to take pleasure in surroundings as familiar as old friends. Her books, her CDs, everything spoke of her taste, her personality.

But her personality seemed to have undergone a change. She wasn't the same woman she'd been when she left here. That woman lived in the past, the more intensely because she was trying to flee it. She had met Sebastian, disliked him, challenged him, been drawn to him against her will.

Now she was standing on a bridge. A future beckoned but it was still misty, and the past hadn't released her. With Sebastian she'd known the heat of desire, the unexpected thrill of anger. She ought to have left him behind, but he was here with her, filling the silence. He'd never been in this place, but somehow she had brought him with her. Once she had been pursued by Roderigo's ghost. Now, mysteriously, it was Sebastian who haunted her.

Whatever she did, his face was there. Sometimes it was hard and judgmental, as she'd seen it on their wedding night, blaming her. But that expression faded soon—as it had done at the time, she realised—and there was a new Sebastian, shocked by her wretchedness, concerned, puzzled, gentle. This was the man who'd stayed with her on the Wall of Death, refusing to leave her side while she was in danger. No coldness or insult had driven him away, she recalled with a faint smile. Not like Roderigo, who would have flounced off in a sulk with far less provocation.

That same Sebastian was there with her as she curled up on the sofa, listening to music with the lights out. In the darkness she might have been sitting on the sofa in the hotel at Sol y Nieve, where he had carried her in the bathrobe and dried her feet.

This was the other Sebastian, the one she'd longed to know, to set beside the autocrat. And now she saw that when she'd met him, she hadn't even recognised him.

'I had to leave you to know how much I love you,' she murmured. 'And if I return to you—will I love you still? Which man will you be then?'

But then she felt someone else there, a bitter unwelcome presence, reproaching her for her desertion, forbidding her to love again.

'*Go away!*' she screamed. '*I can't help you now.*'

Hurriedly she put the light on and looked around, shivering. But she was alone.

Sebastian stayed in Seville on parliamentary business until the last moment, then returned home just as February slipped into March. There was a pleasurable expectancy in the household, for this month would see Sebastian's birthday, the first since his marriage, and naturally Donna Margarita would wish to make a big celebration. If only she would return soon and start giving instructions.

Working late in his study, Sebastian studied the calendar, noting uneasily how close the day was becoming. If his wife failed to be there, it would announce to the world that something was badly wrong, and his fierce pride rebelled at the thought.

But perhaps she didn't know the date? What could be more natural than that he should call, ask how she was, and slip it into the conversation? It needn't sound like pleading, not if he phrased it carefully.

He got as far as dialling, but at the first ring he slammed the receiver down, driven by sheer masculine stubbornness more than anything. To hell with it! To hell with her, if she could treat him like this!

He put his head in his hands.

He could hear Alfonso moving about outside, and called him. 'Do you know where Catalina is?'

'I, Señor?' The young man responded a fraction too quickly, and when he appeared the flush of embarrassment on his face told its own story.

'Yes, you. You're the one who follows her movements the most accurately.' He added wryly, 'Are you having any success?'

'No, Señor,' Alfonso replied despondently.

'No.' Sebastian added under his breath, 'That seems to be the common ailment around here.'

'Señor?'

'Nothing. See if you can find her.'

Alfonso was gone a long time and when he returned he reported awkwardly that Catalina had vanished.

'You mean she's gone out?'

'She didn't order a car.'

'Then she's still here somewhere.'

After ten minutes searching it was Alfonso who discovered Catalina in the bird garden, concealed behind some trees. She was not alone.

'Why are you spying on us?' she demanded fiercely.

'Señorita—please—' he said in dismay.

'All right, Alfonso. I'll take over from here,' Sebastian said, appearing behind him. 'Good evening, Señor Ruiz.'

'Good evening,' José replied with as much dignity as he could muster. 'If I could explain—'

'No, don't explain,' Catalina said defiantly. 'Our love is nobody's business but our own.'

'You may be right,' Sebastian said surprisingly. 'But you should have let *him* say it, Catalina. I wanted to see you so that you could send for him. Señor Ruiz, no doubt my wife has told you that your cousin has been cleared?'

'She has.'

'Come to my study in ten minutes. That will give you time to wipe the lipstick off your face. I have things to say to you, and then I wish to listen while you do the talking.'

'You mean—about my prospects—to support a wife?'

'That can wait until another time. Tonight I want you to tell me everything you can remember about your cousin. There are questions that I should have asked long ago, but I was too proud. Had I not been—' A shadow, as if of pain, crossed his face. 'Well, some mistakes can be put right and others can only be lived with. Perhaps we never know the difference until it is too late.'

The second day became the third, the fourth, a week had passed. Maggie packed away her belongings, tidied up all loose ends until the only thing left to do was give up her apartment. She put that off for a day, and then another. She wondered if Sebastian would telephone her. Perversely she even wished he was there, bracing her with an argument, laying down the law as of old, even making her angry.

Perhaps he would call to remind her that it was his birthday soon. In that country where proper appearances mattered so much, her absence would cause sniggering gossip of exactly the kind he dreaded. But the phone remained silent, and she understood. He was leaving her to make her own decision with no pressure of any kind.

In the end she found that the decision had already been made, not by her, and not then, but at some moment in the past that she couldn't pinpoint. She waited to be sure, then gave up her apartment, arranged for her belongings to be sent on, and caught the next plane to Malaga.

She told nobody that she was coming, and it was late in the evening when the taxi drove through the gates of the Residenza. She entered the house quietly, looking in on Catalina and Isabella, but only for a moment.

'Thank goodness you're home!' Catalina exclaimed. 'He's been like a bear, working into the small hours and growling at everyone. He's in his study now. Poor Alfonso is half dead.'

Poor Alfonso certainly looked up gratefully as Maggie appeared in the doorway of the anteroom where he had his desk. He beamed but she put her finger over her lips.

'Alfonso,' Sebastian called through the half-open door, 'are you going to be all night with that file?'

Alfonso hurriedly picked up the file but Maggie took it from him and slipped into the study. Sebastian was in his shirt-sleeves and looked not at all like an autocrat, just a weary man with a headache, who needed his bed but was uneasily reluctant to seek it. Maggie noticed that the couch looked rumpled, and she guessed that he'd been mostly living in this room. Beside him on the desk was an empty wine glass and a half-full bottle. Suddenly her heart ached for him.

'Bring it over here quickly,' Sebastian said without looking up.

She came quietly to the edge of the desk and laid the file down without speaking.

'I hope you've read it as I asked,' Sebastian growled. 'What did you think?'

'I think it was about time I came home,' she said.

His head went up, and for a moment he simply stared, as if his eyes couldn't focus. He might have been gazing at an apparition that he longed for, but feared to believe in. Then understanding came, and what Maggie saw in his face made her draw a sharp breath. So that was it! And she hadn't known.

The glass overturned. The file vanished somewhere, his chair crashed to the floor, and Sebastian was round the desk, seizing her in his arms, enveloping her in the fiercest embrace he had ever given her.

'You returned,' he said huskily. *'You came back to me.'*

'Of course I did,' she said when she could speak. 'I had to bring your birthday gift.'

'The gift is you,' he said, kissing her again.

'But I have another. Here.' She took his hand and laid it gently on her stomach.

'What—what are you telling me?' His voice shook.

For answer she just smiled, and drew his head down so that his lips lay on hers. She kissed him tenderly, with reassurance, for that was what he needed most just now.

'When we were in the mountains, you said that you didn't know what the answer was, and that perhaps there wasn't one,' she reminded him. 'I don't know what the answer for us is, either. But I believe there is one. And while I was away from you, I realised that we must find it here—together.'

CHAPTER TWELVE

THE entire household settled to prepare for the birth of Sebastian's son, for it was unthinkable that a man of power and respect would not sire a son first time. The boy would, of course, take his first name from his father, but there were several other names to be chosen, and the cook and the steward argued incessantly about the rival merits of Federico and Eduardo.

Sebastian took no part in this, merely shrugging and saying that fate would send what fate would send. Nobody took this foolishness seriously, but they respected him for his gallantry to his wife. It was clear that they were the perfect couple, which was only to be expected with a great man.

Nobody suspected that behind the ideal façade Don Sebastian and Donna Margarita were holding their breaths. They had their child and their happiness, but something had yet to be resolved. There were thoughts they shared, but never spoke of.

She knew, from José, of the night he'd talked to Sebastian about Roderigo and his behaviour during their marriage, but Sebastian himself made no mention of the matter. And if his knowledge of what she had endured made him gentler than ever towards her, how could she tell? He was always gentle, these days.

Something precious was flowering between them, but it grew slowly and hadn't yet reached the point of mutual confidence. They both realised that on the night a photograph slipped out from the pages of a book Maggie had brought back with her from England.

'I didn't know it was there,' she said, apologetically reaching down to take it before her husband saw. But he reached it first, because she was growing large now, and moving slowly.

It was a wedding picture. The bride was very young, her face open, innocent and adoring. The groom wore a 'suitable' smile. To Sebastian's suspicious eyes, it seemed less adoring than predatory, but he knew better than to voice this thought.

The past was still a threatening shadow, but he knew that Maggie had somehow come to terms with it, and he wouldn't risk disturbing that delicate equilibrium. So he retrieved the picture and handed it to her, smiling to hide his jealousy.

'I thought I'd destroyed them all,' she said.

'There's no need to destroy it because of me,' he said, longing for her to do so.

He thought for a moment that she would, but then she gave a tense smile and slipped the picture away in a drawer.

'You still feel guilty?' he asked.

'Only because I have so much. It seems dreadful to be happy when he's dead.'

'Are you really?' he asked with a touch of wistfulness.

'You know I am.'

'I know only of the joy you give to me,' he said, dropping to one knee and laying his hand over her swelling. 'I wish there was some gift I could give you in return.'

'But you give me everything.'

'I don't mean that kind of gift. I mean peace of mind—the freedom to be happy—'

'The freedom to be happy,' she echoed longingly. 'Does anybody have that?'

'I have it—or rather, I would, if you had it too. I wish—' He stopped and sighed. 'But what can I do?'

'Nothing,' she said, understanding him. 'We must treasure what we have, and not ask for more.'

He couldn't find the words to say that this couldn't be enough for him. Somehow, somewhere, there was a gift of love he could make her, and if he watched for the chance, it would surely come. If only, he thought, it didn't take too long.

Yet when the moment did arrive, he almost missed it.

Catalina was passionately interested in Maggie's pregnancy. She read baby books, she studied diets, she argued about names, and grew closer to Isabella who was similarly absorbed. Sebastian, noting these changes, observed that it was time she married.

'Then you'd better ease up about José,' Maggie observed as Sebastian gave her his arm to cross the short distance to their bed.

'I have. I allow him to haunt the house like a sick donkey. She goes out with him, always returns home later than she promised, and I turn a blind eye. And today I told her that if she wished to become betrothed I could probably put up with it.'

Maggie chuckled as he settled her pillows. 'Done with all your grace and charm, in fact.'

'Well, I told you,' he growled, 'I don't like it, and I'm damned if I'm going to pretend that I do.'

The following evening Catalina had dinner in town with José. When she returned she went straight to Sebastian's study. He looked up, surprised to see her alone. 'Where is José?'

'He didn't want to come in.'

Something constrained in her manner made him frown. 'But isn't this a night for celebration? Didn't you get engaged? Catalina, what has happened?' For the girl shrugged and looked awkward.

'I'm not sure—that is—we don't know each other so well.'

'After all this time? Besides, I thought you were determined to marry him.'

'That was when you were saying no,' Catalina said in a burst of honesty.

Sebastian grinned. 'I see. Now I've said yes, it becomes a boring, conventional courtship, without the spice of drama.'

'The world is full of handsome young men,' Catalina said dreamily. 'I've told José that I will still see him, but we can't be engaged, and I consider myself free to see other men.'

'You've *what*?'

'Alfonso is very nice.'

'Alfonso is a damned sight too good for you.'

Catalina giggled. 'He doesn't think so. He says I'm so far above him that he dare not hope—but I told him no man should give up hope.'

'Spare me the details. So you plan to keep them both on tenterhooks. I begin to pity José. I was thinking of you as his victim, but in fact he is yours. Was he very upset?'

Catalina shrugged. 'I may marry him one day—if I don't marry Alfonso—but I want some fun first.' Then her smile faded and she looked uneasy.

'Is something else the matter?' Sebastian asked.

'José gave me this,' she said, producing an envelope from her bag. 'For Maggie.'

Frowning, he took the envelope. It bore no name, and was sealed. 'Did he tell you what's in it?' he asked.

'Only that it's a letter, *from Roderigo*. He's had it for years, and now he wants her to see it. He says he should have given it to her long ago, but she was so bitter and unhappy that he feared it would make things worse. Oh Sebastian, don't you see what that means? Roderigo must have written this in prison, while he was dying, and entrusted it to José. It's his last letter to her. Let me burn it.'

'*What?*'

'What good can it do her to read it now? You can guess what it says, can't you?'

'Doubtless he repeats his protestations of innocence,' Sebastian said wearily. 'Which we now know are true.'

'But suppose it's worse than that. Suppose he says he loves her? That's just the sort of tricky thing he'd do to spoil everything for her. Maggie is yours, now, but if she reads this—'

Then her husband's last declaration of love, made from his deathbed, would reconcile her to his memory with a completeness and finality that could shut out Sebastian again. He knew the bitter truth.

How much better, then, to do as Catalina said? It could only increase Maggie's grief, while doing no practical good. To destroy it would help him keep her heart for himself, and her heart was the only thing in the world that mattered to him now. He turned away from Catalina's shrewd eyes and went to stand by the window, racked with temptation.

'Why do you hesitate?' Catalina demanded. 'Burn it, now—for both your sakes.'

'For *my* sake? Perhaps she needs to see this.'

'But what good could that do—now that it's too late?'

'I don't know,' he said heavily. 'I only know that not to give it to her would be dishonest. And if two people don't have honesty between them, they have nothing.'

'Is this you talking, Sebastian? I've heard you say that sometimes a man must deceive a woman a little, for her own good.'

'Did I say that? Well, perhaps—a long time ago, in another life.'

'So what am I to do?'

'Leave this with me. And, for the moment, say nothing to Margarita.'

When Catalina had gone Sebastian stared at the blank, unrevealing envelope. Now his own fine words rose up to mock him. Honesty, yes, but at what price? The price of seeing Roderigo Alva's memory vindicated in the heart of the woman who had loved him—perhaps, still did?

His life had been built on fine-sounding principles— honesty, duty, honour. Suddenly they were impossibly hard, demanding an act that could tear the heart out of him. But if it could ease her suffering and bring her peace—what right did he have to deny her that?

Once he had thought it would be so easy to love. A man loved a woman; she loved him. What more was there?

Now he saw that love could devastate a man, and give him nothing in return but the knowledge that he had sacrificed himself for a woman, and that she neither knew nor cared. Should anyone be asked to pay such a price?

He took up the envelope, turning it this way and that between his fingers, wishing he knew what was inside.

At last he rose and went to the fireplace. Summer had come, but in the foothills it was still sometimes chilly at night, and a few logs glowed. He stood for a long time, staring into the flickering light. Then, slowly, he held out the letter to the flames.

Maggie was almost ready for bed when he came to her. He found her sitting by the fire in her own room, looking at the wedding picture of herself and Roderigo that she'd brought from England. It struck him suddenly how often she gazed at that picture when she thought he didn't know.

She looked up quickly as he neared and showed him the picture. 'I was thinking it was time I got rid of it.'

'Don't,' he said. 'Wait until you see this.'

'What is it?' she asked, disturbed by his grave face.

'I've brought you something. José gave it to Catalina tonight, to give to you. It's a letter from Roderigo.'

'A letter—for me?' It seemed to him that she paled.

'He must have written it in prison just before he died and entrusted it to José. He's kept it all this time, waiting for the right moment.'

He held it out to her. Maggie took it with shaking hands, and glanced briefly at the scorch-marks on the envelope before tearing it open. Slowly she slid the letter out, opened it, and lay it flat on her lap. But she didn't read it. Then she said something strange.

'I wasn't a good wife. I was too young, and I knew nothing. If I'd been older I might have coped better with Roderigo, maybe helped him.'

He wanted to shout, 'Don't make excuses for him.' But it was too late. His heart was heavy as he realised that she'd guessed the contents of the letter, even as he had, and was preparing herself. He had given her the thing that would destroy them.

'Shall I leave you to read it alone?' he asked.

She didn't answer and he doubted she'd even heard. A stillness had come over her, like the stillness of death. She stared at the paper in her hands but he couldn't tell if she saw it. At last she lifted it and read what was written. Then she read it again, and as she did so her head sank lower until she covered her eyes with her hand.

A cold fear gripped him. He felt he ought to leave her but he couldn't have gone away if his life had depended on it.

'Margarita,' he whispered. He stepped closer and put his hands on her shoulders, dropping to his knees beside her. 'Tell me, my dearest,' he said.

She raised her head and stared into the distance. 'I always knew,' she said quietly. 'In my heart, I always knew. I wish José had shown me this before. I know he thought he was acting for the best—but if I'd only read this sooner—'

'Would it have made so much difference?' Sebastian asked sadly.

'Oh, yes—all the difference in the world. You can think you know what's in a man's heart, but when you see it set down in black and white, in his own words—' She sighed, and his pain deepened.

'And do you now know what was in his heart?' he asked.

She nodded.

'Margarita, don't be sad,' he begged. 'I know it's hard to read his words of love when it's too late, but what you had can never be taken away. Cling to that. Love him if you must. One day, perhaps, you'll turn to me completely, but until then I can be content with what we have. You are worth waiting for.'

At last she raised her head and looked at him. 'What do you think this letter says?' she asked.

'I think it tells you of his love. That hurts you now, but one day it will bring you peace.'

Maggie pushed the letter towards him. 'Read it,' she said.

'Are you sure—?'

'Quite sure. I want you to read this, Sebastian, because if you don't, you and I will never understand each other.'

Slowly, almost reluctantly, he took the letter and ran his eyes over it. The first shock came at once. 'It's dated eight years ago—before you were married.'

'He didn't write it to me,' Maggie said. 'He wrote it to José, from England, soon after we met. Read it.'

Sebastian began to read.

Hey there, little cousin,

I did it! I found myself a real heiress. Her name's Maggie, she's eighteen, pretty enough in an English sort of way, which means she's a bit insipid for my taste. But she's loaded so I'll just have to put up with her looks. Her parents just died, leaving her a couple of hefty insurance policies, plus a house. You should see that house! It almost makes me want to stay here and live in it, but I guess my creditors would prefer it sold.

You never thought I could manage it, did you? Or maybe you just hoped I couldn't. Get real, boy! When I was your age I put women on pedestals, too, but believe me, that's not where they belong. A man needs money, especially a man like me.

She's young and she adores me. I can mould her,

and I'll be a good husband as long as she behaves herself. Besides, everyone knows women can't manage money. I'll be doing her a favour.

I've written to the most awkward of my creditors telling them money's on its way. That should stall them for a while, and with any luck I'll be back in a few weeks with a new wife and enough to set me up in style.

Life's going to be good. As for 'tying myself down'—who's going to? There are plenty of hot, spicy women who like having fun with a man as rich as I'm going to be. I'll live my own life, and my wife will do as she's told.

There was more, but Sebastian was too disgusted to read on. The whole man was there—selfish, faithless, treacherous, convinced of his own superiority, his divine right over the woman.

And there was something more, something he was ashamed to admit. There were words in that letter that could have been written by himself. *She's young… I can mould her…* Hadn't he said much the same, while preparing to marry a vulnerable young girl that he didn't love?

But that had been a long time ago, in another life, before he'd learned the value of a woman's heart.

Half-afraid, he looked at Maggie. She was staring into space.

'He never loved me at all,' she said quietly. 'I realised very soon that my money was a big attraction for him, but I made myself believe that there was some real love there too. But there was none. Some part of me must have suspected that, but I wouldn't *let* myself know it.

'After he died in that terrible way, I shut out the bad and magnified the good. And, when his name was cleared, I felt so guilty that I made myself forget the truth about him.'

'The truth,' Sebastian said, 'was that he was a very nasty piece of work, who brought his troubles on himself.'

'Yes,' Maggie said. 'That really was the truth. Before we even married he was planning to make me pay for his girlfriends.'

'I wonder,' he said slowly, 'how you ever found the courage to trust yourself to another man.'

'Not all men are the same. I took too long to understand that. But what I still don't understand—' she rose and looked into his face '—is why you gave this letter to me, if you thought it was a love-letter.'

'I thought it might help you find peace. There is nothing I wouldn't give, or do, to bring you that peace.'

She touched his cheek. There was a strange, shining light in her eyes. 'You love me as much as that?'

'Yes,' he said simply. 'I love you as much as that.'

'And thanks to your love, I'm free. It's as though a terrible weight has gone from me. It might have crushed me all my life, but you freed me.'

He was dazed by the memory of how close he'd come to burning the letter, and destroying them both. Or perhaps he merely thought he had. He only knew that when he held it out to the flames some power had drawn him back before it was too late. Looking at her eyes, fixed on him, candid and unshadowed for the first time, he thought perhaps he knew the name of that power.

He couldn't tell her about his temptation. At least, not yet. One day, long in the future, he might say, 'You too set *me* free, and this is how it happened.'

Or perhaps, by then, they would no longer need words.

'Sebastian,' she said softly, 'have I ever told you that I love you?'

He shook his head. 'But then, I have never before told you.'

'Not in words, but in many other ways.'

'You are my whole being and existence,' he said slowly. 'You are my love and my life. You are everything to me. You are more, even, than our child.'

'I lost faith in love. Thank you for giving me back my faith.'

'And—him?'

'You want to know if I love you as I loved Roderigo? No, I don't. And I'm glad of it. You should be too. There was always something wrong with that love, and now I know what. He wasn't worth loving. That's the greatest pain of all, to waste love on someone who isn't worth it. I shall never know that pain with you.'

She tossed the letter into the fire, then lifted the photograph and studied it, while Sebastian never took his eyes from her.

'It's there, isn't it?' she said at last. 'The slyness and meanness—it was there in his face all the time. But I wouldn't let myself see it.'

With a quick movement she cast the picture into the flames where it shrivelled. The last thing they saw was Roderigo's face curling up, blurring, vanishing.

'He's gone at last,' Maggie said. 'Now there is only us.'

'Only us,' he echoed, taking her into his arms. 'Yes, only us. Forever.'

In the church of San Nicolas the Christmas greenery was piled high about the pulpit, the font, up against the walls. Down below, the lights glowed softly over the manger.

The wooden child lay in the crib, his arms stretched slightly upward to the living baby looking down at him from wide dark eyes.

'Look, my darling,' Sebastian murmured. 'He is greeting you. Say hello to him.'

'Sebastian,' Maggie chided him, smiling, 'she's only three months old.'

'No matter,' he said. 'In years to come she'll know that she came here in her father's arms. She may not remember, but she will *know*.'

'A beautiful child,' Father Basilio said, reaching up to lay a finger against the baby's cheek. And then, being—for all his sanctity—a man and a Spaniard, he added consolingly, 'And the next one will probably be a boy.'

'Don't let Sebastian hear you say that,' Catalina laughed. 'He thinks his little Margarita is a queen.'

'Fate sends what fate sends,' Sebastian said, straightening up and settling his baby daughter lovingly against his shoulder. 'Fate sent this little one to be a jewel for her Papa.'

'Who's that in the doorway?' the priest asked, screwing up his eyes against the poor light.

'José and Alfonso,' Sebastian said, 'waiting to see who will be honoured with this baggage's company on the way home. It's time you decided between them, Catalina. You are bringing scandal on my house.'

Catalina went down the aisle to where José and Alfonso waited humbly. The old priest followed her to greet them.

Sebastian looked over the baby's head at his wife. He had more than one jewel, but he never spoke of the other one to outsiders, only to her. Maggie smiled at him, then looked back at the crib, touching the wooden baby with a gentle hand.

'That was how I saw you this time last year,' Sebastian reminded her. 'And I think I understood in that moment that you were far more to me than a woman I had tried and failed to conquer. You touched my heart, and that was when I began to be afraid.'

'Afraid? You?'

'You sought no quarter and you gave none. It was I who yielded. And I have been glad ever since. You took a robot, and brought him to life.' He kissed his child. 'And only life can give life.'

His wife reached up to where his cheek lay against their baby's head, caressing them both at the same time. 'Let's go home now,' she said fondly. 'Life is only just beginning.'

They walked out of the church together. At the door she looked back at the Christmas scene and smiled, but she didn't linger.

It would be there again next year.

SINGLE IN THE CITY...

English heiresses Annis and Bella are as
different as sisters can be. Annis is clever
and quiet, Bella beautiful and bubbly.
Yet with a millionaire father, they both think
they'll never find a man who wants them
for *themselves*....

How wrong can they be!

Don't miss this fabulous duet by rising star

Sophie Weston

THE MILLIONAIRE'S DAUGHTER
January 2002 #3683

THE BRIDESMAID'S SECRET
February 2002 #3687

in

Harlequin Romance®

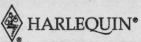

If you enjoyed what you just read,
then we've got an offer you can't resist!

Take 2 bestselling love stories FREE!

Plus get a FREE surprise gift!

CALL THE ONES YOU LOVE OVER THE HOLIDAYS!

Save $25 off future book purchases when you buy any four Harlequin® or Silhouette® books in October, November and December 2001,

PLUS

receive a phone card good for 15 minutes of long-distance calls to anyone you want in North America!

WHAT AN INCREDIBLE DEAL!

Just fill out this form and attach 4 proofs of purchase (cash register receipts) from October, November and December 2001 books, and Harlequin Books will send you a coupon booklet worth a total savings of $25 off future purchases of Harlequin® and Silhouette® books, AND a 15-minute phone card to call the ones you love, anywhere in North America.

Please send this form, along with your cash register receipts as proofs of purchase, to:
In the USA: Harlequin Books, P.O. Box 9057, Buffalo, NY 14269-9057
In Canada: Harlequin Books, P.O. Box 622, Fort Erie, Ontario L2A 5X3
Cash register receipts must be dated no later than December 31, 2001.
Limit of 1 coupon booklet and phone card per household.
Please allow 4-6 weeks for delivery.

**I accept your offer! Enclosed are 4 proofs of purchase.
Please send me my coupon booklet
and a 15-minute phone card:**

Name: _____

Address: _____ City: _____

State/Prov.: _____ Zip/Postal Code: _____

Account Number (if available): _____

---

097 KJB DAGL
PHQ4013

EXPECTING...

She's sexy, successful... and **PREGNANT!**

Relax and enjoy our fabulous series about couples whose passion ends in pregnancies... sometimes unexpected!

Share the surprises, emotions, drama and suspense as our parents-to-be come to terms with the prospect of bringing a new life into the world. All will discover that the business of making babies brings with it the most special love of all....

Look out for our next arrival—coming soon to Harlequin Presents®!

Kim Lawrence

THE ITALIAN'S
SECRET BABY

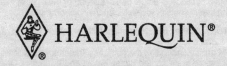

HARLEQUIN®

TORONTO • NEW YORK • LONDON
AMSTERDAM • PARIS • SYDNEY • HAMBURG
STOCKHOLM • ATHENS • TOKYO • MILAN • MADRID
PRAGUE • WARSAW • BUDAPEST • AUCKLAND

ISBN-13: 978-0-373-12741-2
ISBN-10:   0-373-12741-3

THE ITALIAN'S SECRET BABY

First North American Publication 2008.

All about the author...
Kim Lawrence

Though lacking much authentic Welsh blood,
KIM LAWRENCE—from English/Irish stock—was
born and brought up in north Wales. She returned
there when she married, and her sons were both
born on Anglesey, an island off the coast. Though
not isolated, Anglesey is a little off the beaten track,
but lively Dublin, which Kim loves, is only a short
ferry ride away.

Today they live on the farm her husband was
brought up on. Welsh is the first language of many
people in this area, and Kim's husband and sons
are all bilingual. She is having a lot of fun, not
to mention a few headaches, trying to learn the
language!

With small children, the unsocial hours of nursing
weren't too attractive, so, encouraged by a husband
who thinks she can do anything she sets her mind
to, Kim tried her hand at writing. Always a keen
Harlequin reader, she felt it was natural for her
to write a romance novel. Now she can't imagine
doing anything else.

She is a keen gardener and cook, and enjoys
running—often on the beach, because, since she
lives on an island the sea is never very far away.
She is usually accompanied by her Jack Russell,
Sprout—don't ask, it's a long story!

CHAPTER ONE

'I THOUGHT you were going to be late,' his PA said as Roman O'Hagan walked into the empty conference room.

'I don't know if I've ever mentioned this, Alice, but you have a very uptight attitude to timekeeping,' Roman observed, shrugging off his jacket and laying it across the back of a chair. 'And in case it's slipped your mind, I'm the boss so I'm allowed to be late.'

Alice, who had worked for him for four years and had no recollection of him ever being late during that time, planted a cup of coffee in front of him on the long polished table.

'Well, *boss*, I managed to get us on the four-thirty Dublin flight.'

'Excellent.' Swivelling his chair around, Roman stretched his long legs out comfortably in front of him and added with a pained grimace, 'Which is more than I can say for this coffee! And I use the word in the loosest possible sense.' He stared down suspiciously at the pale brown liquid in his cup.

'It's decaff, and in case it's slipped your mind making coffee is not part of my job description. I do it simply because I have a nice nature.'

'I'm a lucky man,' Roman returned, deadpan.

'Yes, you are.' She paused by the door. 'By the way, your brother rang.'

'Did he leave a message?'

'Not for you.'

Roman's darkly defined brows lifted at the cryptic re-

7

sponse. He was as sure as he could be without written proof that his brother, Luca, had a lot to do with the fact his assistant had gone down a dress size during the past couple of months.

It was getting hard to maintain a tactful silence on the subject of his brother not being the marrying kind—*Alice was.*

'He said he'd call back.'

The conference call started off really well, but went rapidly downhill once the second speaker came on the line.

How is it possible for anyone to talk for so long and say absolutely nothing?

Roman interrupted the interminable flow. The response was if anything even more rambling. It also cleared up the question of whether this well-paid individual had grasped the problem or done the necessary research—*he hadn't!*

Roman listened with a half-smile as the man's junior managed to bail out his boss without making it obvious that was what he was doing; he also predicted and responded to the two further questions Roman had planned to ask.

Roman wouldn't forget his name.

'So you think the European market is ready for a project of this—' Before he got to complete his question a female voice, a low, husky, very attractive female voice interrupted him.

'Excuse me, but am I speaking to Mr O'Hagan?'

'Who is that?'

'A Mr *Roman* O'Hagan?'

'How on earth…? I'm afraid this is a private…'

'I'm trying to contact a Mr O'Hagan. Could you tell me who I'm speaking to?'

That combination of selective deafness and persistence,

even if she did have an extraordinarily sexy voice, was going to get wearing very quickly, Roman decided.

F. O'Hagan and Sons had recently been held up as a shining example of firms that employed a higher number than average of females in top-management-level jobs, but none of them was taking part in this conference call today.

Roman didn't have the faintest idea who this woman was or how she had turned up smack bang in the middle of a highly sensitive discussion. He doubted if it was worth the bother of finding out.

Who did people blame for cock-ups before the advent of computers?

'I don't know how you got on this line...' Roman stopped. The lazy smile that formed on his wide sensual mouth held more than a hint of self-derision. Could it be, he wondered, that his display of uncharacteristic tolerance might not be totally unconnected with the fact the gatecrasher had a very attractive voice? In his head those smoky, sultry tones were inextricably linked with long legs, seductive lips and long blonde hair.

'Well, don't ask me! Perhaps it was your turn to fob me off?' came the bitter speculation. 'I've been put through to every other blessed person in the building!'

Goodbye sultry seductress, hello schoolteacher. Oh, well, the harmless fantasy had been nice while it lasted.

'I've been fobbed off and made to wait—'

'Do you mind hanging up? This is a private and confidential discussion.' Some men might like their women bossy—each to his own, that was his motto—only his own taste didn't run in that direction.

Unlike his top management people from across Europe who were hanging on every word of this conversation, the woman on the other end of the line didn't appear to realise that when the head of O'Hagan Construction used this tone the conversation was at an end.

'I've not the *slightest* interest in your discussion,' the owner of the husky voice promised him with considerable feeling.

Roman expelled his breath in a hiss of frustrated irritation. He flicked his wrist, exposing the metal banded watch. 'That's what all the industrial spies say, however—'

'Is that meant to be a joke?' the voice demanded, dropping several degrees below freezing. 'Because I have to tell you I'm really not in the mood. And I warn you if I have to listen to ''The Blue Danube'' one more time I shall not be responsible for the consequences,' she warned darkly. 'Do you want a gibbering female running naked through town on your conscience—?'

'It would depend on the female—'

'I'm so glad you find this amusing.'

'Do you ever let anyone finish what they're attempting to say?'

'For heaven's sake, I'm not asking for a personal audience with the Pope, I just want to speak to Mr O'Hagan.'

Roman leaned his head into his hands. 'Obviously she doesn't—'

'I think it's extremely bad manners to speak about someone in the third person when they…me…I can hear every word you're saying! As I've already explained to *umpteen* people, this really is important.'

Roman's lips twisted in a cynical grimace. Hands clasped behind his head, he leaned back into his upholstered leather chair.

'I'd be surprised if it wasn't,' he observed drily.

The people who wanted to speak to him inevitably considered what they had to say was important. Ninety per cent of them wanted to make him a fortune; all they needed was just a bit of his own money to get their schemes up and running. Very few of these cranks got to tell him about their projects in person because as a rule his calls were screened.

This was one of the concessions he'd been forced to make to security after he'd badly misjudged a situation. He'd turned up at the office one morning to find his stalker—a mild middle-aged woman whom he, in his wisdom, had considered sad, not dangerous—had already been there complete with kitchen knife delusions and a hostage in the shape of his terrified PA.

Alice still had the scar. Unconsciously his hand went to his face. Fortunately you couldn't see hers, but his own reminded him of his poor judgement every time he looked in the mirror.

'*Alice*,' he yelled, swivelling his chair around and positioning it to face the open door, 'I've got a damned crank on this line, can you do something about it?'

'I'm not a crank!' The disembodied voice filled the room with husky outrage.

'Fair enough,' he drawled. 'However, you are on a private line so hang up! If you have a message there are channels you can go through.'

'Haven't you been listening to *anything* I've said? I don't have time for *channels*. Has anyone ever told you that you're an extremely rude man?'

'This has been said, but rarely to my face.'

'*Very ironic*,' came the blighting response. 'But I'm not talking to your face. If I was I might be able…listen, *are* you Mr O'Hagan?'

'I am Roman O'Hagan. If you're not going to hang up, do you think you might get round some time in the next hour to telling me who the hell you are? If only so that I can make sure you never have an opportunity to harangue me in the future.'

This threat produced an audible sigh at the other end. 'Well, I do think you might have said so straight away instead of wasting my time.'

'Wasting *your* time…?' Roman hoped his silent and invisible executives would stay quiet.

'My name is Scarlet Smith.'

Scarlet… Roman found he was thinking long legs again and, definitely, blonde hair. Not that any amount of hair or legs would make the woman who had this runaway mouth someone he'd ask for a second date…or even a first!

'I manage the crèche at the university.'

So he'd been halfway right with schoolteacher.

'Your mother is officially opening it today.'

'My mother is in Rome.' Roman stopped, having a vague recollection, now that he thought about it, of his mother having mentioned she was interrupting her holiday with her family to fly back and fulfil some commitment…it could well have been this one.

'No, she's in my office, and I'm afraid she isn't very well.'

Roman levered his long-limbed frame into an upright position, his languid air vanishing. 'What's happened?'

'I don't mean to alarm you—'

'Well, you are, so get to the point,' he advised tersely.

'Your mother fainted a little while ago. She seems better now.'

His mother didn't faint. 'What does the doctor say?' Roman asked, settling his loose Italian-designed jacket smoothly across his broad shoulders.

'She hasn't seen a doctor.'

Roman picked up on the defensive note that had entered the attractive voice and his brows drew together in a disapproving straight line.

'Why the hell not?' he demanded. 'I need the car,' he

added seamlessly as he turned to his attentively hovering PA, who, like all good assistants, knew when to say nothing. 'And cancel all my appointments for the rest of the morning, then tell Phil to meet me at the university.'

'Our flight…?'

'Cancel.'

'What if Dr O'Connor is busy—?'

Roman turned his head and looked at her; Alice took the hint.

'Right, I'll tell him to drop everything, though that might be hard if he's in the middle of heart surgery.'

'He's a medical man; he doesn't operate,' Roman retorted. 'Just explain to him what's happened, Alice, and tell him to bring his bag.'

'Your mother wouldn't let me call a doctor or an ambulance.'

Roman turned around as if to face the bleating voice. '*Let you?* She was unconscious,' he derided scornfully.

'For less than a minute.'

Roman knew when he heard someone covering their back; there was nothing he despised more. He came down hard on people who preferred to shift the blame because they lacked the guts to carry the can for their own mistakes.

'Let me tell you, *Miss Smith*, if my mother suffers a broken fingernail that could have been avoided if you had called for medical assistance I'll sue the pants off you and your university!' he promised darkly before cutting her off.

His PA was unable to remain silent. 'Really, you can be so mean!'

'What is this? Sisterly solidarity?'

'I don't think you realise how much you terrify people,' she reproved, shaking her head.

'No, Alice, I know *exactly* how much I terrify people.'

He gave a white wolfish smile. 'It's the secret behind my success.'

'Nonsense,' returned Alice. 'The secret of your success is you live for your work and don't have a life,' she observed disapprovingly. 'You lack balance.'

'A little more terror, Alice, and a little less lip would be appreciated,' Roman drawled.

'That poor girl is probably crying her eyes out.'

'Pardon me but I don't empathise with incompetence, especially when that incompetence puts my family in danger,' he explained grimly.

Contrary to Alice's prediction, the 'poor girl' in question was neither terrified nor crying. She was walking down a university corridor where people who would normally have called out a cheery greeting took one look at her usually sunny face and changed their minds.

Others stared curiously when she walked past practising out loud—the acoustics were excellent—one of the cutting home truths she would like to deliver personally to Mr Roman O'Hagan.

'Get to the point,' he'd said. What did he think she'd been trying to do while he'd been cracking jokes at her expense?

Of course she should have called for an ambulance, she knew that—did he think she didn't know that?

David Anderson, the university's vice-chancellor, looked incredibly relieved as she walked through the door.

'I thought you were only going to be a second, Scarlet?' he said, drawing her a little to one side and out of earshot of the pale-faced woman sitting in the chair.

'How is she?' Scarlet asked, responding to his hand signals to keep her voice low.

'Better than she was, I think. She wants me to ask her driver to bring her car around.'

'I wouldn't bother, David; her son is on his way over,' she revealed casually.

On the whole, and considering how stressed David was already, Scarlet didn't see much point explaining that the millionaire property developer in question was in a very vengeful and litigious mood.

Obviously threats were part and parcel of Roman O'Hagan's *modus operandi*. Scarlet knew the type; she had suffered in silence at the hands of bullies during a lot of her school years. Years of unhappiness that she could have been spared if she had realised earlier that all you had to do with a bully was show them you weren't scared—*even if you were*!

It hadn't been bravery in her last year at school that had made her turn around and tell her gang of tormentors exactly what she thought of them, it had been simply a matter of reaching the end of her tether.

The experience had left Scarlet with a loathing of bullies and a determination to never again put herself in the role of victim. Every time she replayed the phone conversation in her head she felt her anger rising. How dared he threaten her? It wasn't just *what* he had said, it was the *way* he had said it.

And that *voice*; she recalled the inexplicable reaction she had had to the low drawl. Incredibly it had actually produced a physical response. She had reacted to it like a cat whose fur had been stroked the wrong way, her skin literally prickling in an uncomfortable way.

He had the sort of voice that could make an eviction notice sound sexy.

The vice-chancellor shot her a look of annoyed disbelief, which she pretended not to notice.

'You called Roman O'Hagan after she *specifically* asked you not to?' He groaned.

'Did she?'

'I know she did, Scarlet, because I was there at the time and I heard what she said, not once, but twice.'

'So maybe she did,' Scarlet conceded. 'But she also *specifically* asked us not to call a medic or ambulance,' she reminded him. 'And I thought that was wrong too.'

'She's a very important woman; we can't go around ignoring her wishes.'

'You didn't; I did.'

David looked somewhat mollified by this reminder. 'That's true.'

'Just call me Scarlet the scapegoat,' she suggested cheerfully.

David shot her a reproachful look from under his half-moon specs. 'I'll just go and organise someone to meet Mr O'Hagan.'

A three-man job at least, Scarlet mused scornfully: one person to grovel, another to sprinkle rose petals in his path and, last but not least, one to stroke the guy's massive ego. She for one didn't envy anyone the task of being nice to him. Even allowing for his concern over his mother, the mega-rich playboy had come across as a nasty bully of a man. Being rich, in her view, did not give anyone carte blanche to be rude.

'Where's a spare red carpet when you need one?'

David shot her a wary look. 'I hope you weren't rude to him.'

Scarlet adopted a puzzled expression, her eyes wide and innocent.

'Don't look at me like that, Scarlet, it worries me. I've known you since you were six years old,' he reminded her drily.

'Why would I be rude to the man? I rang to tell him his mother wasn't well.'

'Hummph.' David left her with a firm admonition not to take any further unilateral decisions if she wanted to keep her job.

'Are you feeling any better?' Scarlet asked, approaching the slim, elegant figure who was dressed in a soft apricot suit that hinted tastefully at a good cleavage.

'Much better, thank you,' Natalia O'Hagan replied in her soft, attractive Italian accent.

She didn't look nearly old enough to have a son the age of Roman O'Hagan.

Unless he had begun his infamous playboy lifestyle when he was still at school he had to be in his early thirties at least to have fitted in all the beautiful women who had reputedly enjoyed his admiration. As aloof and arrogant as he was widely reported to be, he was rarely photographed without some lush beauty gazing adoringly up into his face.

Scarlet smiled at Natalia. She had taken to the older woman immediately. Unlike her son she came across as a warm, genuine woman with no airs and graces. Just thinking about the vile son with his hateful, sarcastic drawl sent a shudder of antipathy down Scarlet's spine.

Maybe Roman O'Hagan had inherited his arrogance from the paternal side of the equation. It was quite a combination of genes, Italian and Irish, Scarlet reflected, and on the evidence so far she'd say the result of that fusion had produced a person who lacked the charm of the Irish and the charisma of the Italians.

Despite her reassurance as she lifted the glass of water, there was a visible tremor in the older woman's hand.

'Let me,' Scarlet said, taking the glass from her and placing it back on her own desk.

On closer inspection she could see that the scary bluish

tinge had receded from around the older woman's lips. This was good news, but despite these small signs of improvement the woman still looked far from well.

'Can I get you anything else?'

Natalia O'Hagan lifted her head, her lips formed a weak smile, but she didn't appear able to respond to the question.

Scarlet's anxiety increased. She privately called herself every sort of weak idiot for not having stood her ground in the first place and rung for a doctor straight off as she'd wanted.

In that at least her wretched son had been right.

She could have insisted, but when the university bigwigs, who had tagged along with David for the official opening ceremony of the crèche, had overruled her, what had she done? She'd meekly rolled over.

As far as the powers that be were concerned they weren't going to risk upsetting the woman whose generous donation had been responsible for the refurbishment and extension of the crèche facilities, not to mention the new state-of-the art IT building. And Natalia O'Hagan had managed to make it quite clear despite her weak condition, that she did not want a doctor.

That was fine and their call to make, but where were they now, those men and women in suits who knew better? Their absence from the vicinity was pretty conspicuous.

Scarlet had only been half joking when she'd called herself a scapegoat. If anything went wrong it wasn't difficult to figure out who would be left to carry the can, especially if Roman O'Hagan had anything to do with it. She couldn't see the men and women in suits leaping up to take responsibility.

'Won't you let me get someone down from Occupational Health, at least—?' Scarlet began, only to be cut off by an impatient, slightly imperious nod of the smooth dark head.

'You sound just like my sons.'

Scarlet had no control over the expression of horror that spread across her face. *'Me?'*

'You know, I consider myself a lucky woman,' Natalia revealed. 'Two sons who I love dearly, and they are so good to me. But,' she explained with a shake of her head, 'they are both ridiculously overprotective. Roman is possibly the worst.

'He has a terrible habit of thinking he knows what is best,' Natalia continued ruefully. 'If I'd let him he'd run my life, I swear he would.'

'You have to stand up to him!'

Natalia's delicate brow lifted at the heat of Scarlet's stern declaration.

Scarlet coloured self-consciously and forced her expression to relax. 'I suppose it's a son's job to be protective of his mother. I expect mine will one day,' she added lightly.

'*You* have a son?' Liquid dark eyes scanned Scarlet's slim figure. She was wearing her usual work garb, jeans and one of the bright child-friendly tee shirts all the helpers in the crèche wore. It had been suggested that, as the manager of the centre, she ought to wear something more in fitting with her management role, but Scarlet, a hands-on sort of manager, had stuck to her guns and her tee shirt.

'Goodness, you look so young, or maybe that's just me getting old.'

'You're not old.'

'When I look at those little ones I feel...' She suddenly went very still as she looked through the plate-glass partition to the room beyond. It should have been empty; the children were enjoying the party on the lawn. 'That child—what is his name?'

It was a casual enough question, but *casual* in Scarlet's experience didn't equate with the lines of tension bracketing the older woman's soft mouth or the tortured twisting of the hands clasped in her lap.

'Which one? We've got quite a few here. Should you lie down, perhaps…?' she suggested tentatively. 'If you're not feeling well?'

'I'm feeling fine.' The strained smile she produced to prove the point did nothing to soothe Scarlet's fears. 'The little boy I'm talking about is the one who gave me the flowers? The one sitting there.'

Scarlet followed the direction of the ashen-faced woman's strangely haunted gaze as Natalie nodded through the glass partition that separated Scarlet's office from the big, newly equipped play room, towards a small dark-haired figure sitting cross-legged on the floor.

Sam was meant to be outside with the other children watching the magician they'd engaged as entertainment. With the party in full swing he had obviously managed to slip away unnoticed. Sam was a very resourceful child.

He had wanted to finish his jigsaw earlier, and when he wanted something, as she knew to her cost, he could show remarkable focus. His little face was a mask of concentration as he slotted the final piece into a complicated wooden jigsaw and gave a triumphant smile.

'Sam,' Scarlet replied, a puzzled frown forming between her brows as she registered the throb of emotion in the other woman's attractively accented voice.

'I hope I didn't alarm him.'

'Sam takes most things in his stride,' Scarlet returned honestly.

'I thought he might,' came the puzzling dry rejoinder. 'His mother…does she work at the university?'

'Sam's my son, the one I mentioned.' Scarlet was trying very hard not to glow too obviously with pride. 'One of the perks of running the university crèche is I get to bring him to work with me.'

This hadn't happened by accident. Early on Scarlet had realised to leave Sam on a daily basis would be too painful, not necessarily for the child, who possessed an adaptable and sunny personality, but for herself.

'*You?*'

Scarlet endured with equanimity the astonished, searching scrutiny that came her way. The reaction didn't surprise her. Sam was an exceptionally beautiful child, and Scarlet knew the only thing exceptional about herself was her ordinariness, but even so the softly breathed, '*Unbelievable!*' did bring a faint flush to her pale cheeks.

As if she realised her lapse in manners, a flicker of something akin to embarrassment flickered across the beautiful features of the VIP guest.

'And how old is Sam?'

'He was three in April.'

'He seems very advanced for his age.'

'Sam is quick,' Scarlet agreed, unable to stifle a flicker of parental pride at this praise.

'You and your husband must be very proud of him.'

'I'm not married.' Even in this enlightened age Scarlet was used to her single motherhood producing disapproval in varying degrees, but the inexplicable flicker of relief she saw in Natalia's brown eyes was not a reaction she'd encountered before.

It only lasted a moment and Scarlet almost immediately put it down to a trick of the light or her imagination. After all, she asked herself, why would her being unmarried make a total stranger relieved?

'Then Sam's father...?'

'There's just me and Sam and we like it that way,' Scarlet explained cheerfully.

CHAPTER TWO

'BUT it must be hard for a woman alone?'

'One-parent families are not exactly unusual.'

'But you've *never* been married?'

Scarlet, who was beginning to feel puzzled with the older woman's pursuit of the subject, shook her head. 'Never.' This might be a good time to change the subject and admit she had contacted the tyrannical son.

'Listen, Mrs O'Hagan—'

'Natalia, please, my dear.'

'*Natalia,* I know you asked me not to.' Scarlet took a deep breath and made a clean breast of it. 'The thing is I called Mr O'Hagan…that is your son, the control freak one,' she explained unhappily.

'I don't blame you being angry with me,' she continued, 'but I really did think that someone should know—' Scarlet stopped in response to a cool hand laid on her arm.

'I'm not angry with you, child.'

Scarlet gave a sigh of relief. 'I'm glad about that.'

'Did you speak to Roman yourself? I ask,' she added, 'because I have a problem doing so myself sometimes.' She gave a light laugh. 'He is guarded zealously.'

You can say that again!

'I did manage to, *eventually*,' Scarlet admitted with a guarded smile.

There was something in the other woman's manner…she couldn't quite put her finger on it, but Scarlet couldn't shake the feeling that she was missing something.

22

'My, you must be a determined girl, or have special access that I don't?' Her laughter had a forced sound to it.

'I could have done with it, but I had to fall back on my natural talent—I'm stubborn.'

Natalia nodded; her expression suggested her thoughts had already moved on. 'I sometimes think this security business has got out of hand, you know. Since the stalker affair Roman is not a very accessible person, but no doubt you know that.'

'Stalker?' Scarlet queried, pausing to briefly wonder why his mother would assume she knew anything at all about her son.

'Oh, I'm sure you read about it. That woman who became obsessed with him? It was about four years ago.'

Scarlet shook her head. She was not about to explain that four years ago her world had narrowed to the bedside of her dying sister.

'Perhaps you were out of the country?'

'Not likely,' Scarlet returned. 'I get seasick and have a phobia of flying.'

'How inconvenient. Actually it was covered quite widely in the papers—this woman developed a thing about Roman.'

'An ex-girlfriend?' That figured. Any woman who went out with him had to be slightly unbalanced to begin with.

'Well, no, that's the thing, they had never actually met, but she became convinced they had a relationship. She wrote to him, telephoned him, sent him gifts...initially Roman felt sorry for her and thought if he ignored her she'd go away. Things came to a head when he arrived at the office one morning to find her holding his PA at knife-point.'

'Gracious!' Scarlet gasped, her eyes widening in horror. 'Was anyone hurt?'

'Roman managed to talk her into letting Alice go and

apparently she was going to hand over the knife when the police arrived. The woman panicked and became quite frenzied. Roman and Alice both got injured, Alice badly. Fortunately they both recovered.'

'That must have been very traumatic.'

'It was, though Roman was more concerned that he had unwittingly put someone else's life at risk. Oh, I know it wasn't his fault.' Scarlet, who hadn't been going to suggest anything of the sort, remained, silent. 'But Roman has a very overdeveloped sense of responsibility.'

Scarlet smiled politely and wondered privately how much a mother's natural bias had coloured this version of events. Certainly this caring, sensitive paragon didn't sound much like the man the newspapers were so fond of writing about or the one she had spoken to earlier!

'Roman admires a woman with spirit.'

Roman manages to hide his admiration pretty well. 'Really…?' she responded, not sure what else she was supposed to say to this apparently irrelevant comment.

'And what did my son have to say for himself?'

Beyond threaten to sue the socks off me? 'Oh, we didn't really chat,' she responded lightly.

'Well, you'll be able to get reacquainted properly when he arrives. The years have changed him, you know, my dear.'

The turn of phrase struck Scarlet as distinctly odd, but she was so relieved that the older woman appeared resigned that her son was coming to collect her that she didn't comment on it.

'Scarlet.' David appeared at the door. 'Could I have a word for a moment? Mrs O'Hagan, it's good to see you looking so much better.'

Now that he said so, Scarlet too saw that the older woman

had perked up considerably. 'I'll be right back,' she promised.

Actually she wasn't right back because David had been informed that Roman O'Hagan was in the building and, as he put it, thought that, 'a more *senior* member of staff should be here when he arrives. No reflection on your abilities, Scarlet, but as a sign of respect.'

Scarlet gave him no argument. 'I think it's the least he would expect,' she agreed.

It suited her down to the ground not to be there when the bullying millionaire put in an appearance. If she had to be nice to him she'd choke.

'I might take that time owing me and nip off now with Sam, unless you want me to hang around?'

Roman ran his long fingers through the gleaming strands of his dark hair in a gesture of impatience. The same impatience was etched in the strong, symmetrical lines of his darkly handsome face as he looked down at his mother.

'Yes, it *was* necessary for me to bring Philip; he is your doctor.'

'And as I have told him, I fainted, nothing more. You are fussing like an old woman, Roman,' she told her son scornfully. Graciously she extended her arm for the suited figure to apply a blood-pressure cuff. 'Normal?' she asked as the medic removed the stethoscope from his ears.

The doctor nodded. 'If all my patients were this healthy I'd be out of business,' he told her cheerfully.

Natalia shot her son a triumphant look. 'I told you so,' she murmured complacently.

'But you will carry out further tests?' Roman addressed his query to his friend.

'I could, but—'

'Do them.'

Natalia gave a sigh of exasperation. 'This is exactly why I didn't want them to ring you. You come rushing here when I'm sure you have a million more important things to do.'

'Several million things, actually,' Roman corrected, the corners of his wide, sensual mouth lifting in a sarcastic smile. 'Naturally all *much* more important than my mother's health.'

'Well, I'm glad to see that family is still important to you, Roman.'

One dark brow quirked as, with slightly narrowed eyes, he scanned his mother's face. Never slow when it came to reading between the lines, he asked, 'Am I missing something here?'

'You spoke to Scarlet on the phone, I believe.'

'Scarlet—the blonde?'

'She is not blonde. Though I suppose she might have been blonde when you knew her, though women usually go from brunette to blonde, not the other way.'

'I don't and didn't know her.'

'Well, why did you say she was blonde?'

'She sounded blonde.'

His mother looked at him blankly. '*Sounded* blonde? Really, Roman, do not insult my intelligence,' she rebuked coldly.

'Did she say I knew her?' He was accustomed to women trying to get to him, but if this one thought she could use his mother to do so she could think again!

'Relax, Roman. She hardly mentioned you at all, which,' Natalia added heavily, 'is hardly surprising,' his mother reproached. 'This must have been a very painful experience for her.'

'Told you I threatened her, did she? Well, she deserved it. How could anyone not have the wit to get medical help?'

Natalia stared at her son for a moment, then appeared to

come to a decision. She turned to the doctor. 'Philip, dear, do you mind? I've got something I need to say to Roman.'

The doctor clicked closed his case. 'Of course, no problem.'

Roman flashed his friend a brief nod. 'We'll see you back at the clinic in fifteen minutes.'

Other than give an exasperated click of her tongue, Natalia did not respond to his comments.

'Is this going to take long, Mother?' Roman asked as the door closed.

'Should I have made an appointment?' Natalia enquired spikily. 'You may be a *very* important man, but you might want to remember that you're running the company because *I* persuaded your father to retire.'

It had actually been his father's heart attack that had persuaded him and his equally reluctant brother to put their careers on hold and divide their father's responsibilities. The injection of fresh blood and new ideas had produced results that had seen the O'Hagan family's fortunes grow rapidly.

Unfortunately the success had increased, not lessened, the tension between father and sons.

'I'll pass on the fact that two minutes ago you were telling me my time was too important to spend it doing anything as frivolous as rushing to my mother's side.'

'Don't change the subject, Roman.'

'I wouldn't dare if I knew what it was. Are you going to tell me any time soon what exactly I've done?' Roman drawled. 'I know all the signs,' he added grimly. 'I've searched my conscience and nothing immediately springs to mind. I must admit I'm curious.'

Natalia's eyes flashed as her son gave a smile that was both cynical and charming in equal measure. She didn't smile back, but instead snatched from his fingers the pen he was idly doodling with and banged it down on the blotter.

'Don't do that.' Her sons had inherited their father's Irish charm, her own dark Italian looks and, sadly, neither had very many scruples when it came to using either to get what they wanted. Roman had been getting pretty much what he wanted all his life, with one notable exception.

A frown formed between his dark, strongly delineated brows as Roman studied his mother's face. 'Has something happened? Dad…?'

Natalia heard the anxiety enter his deep voice, roughening the velvet-smooth tone, and immediately shook her head reassuringly. Eyes trained on his face, she took a deep, shuddering sigh. *'Scarlet Smith.'* She flung the name like an accusation.

'The woman with the smart tongue and the bad attitude who is not a blonde. If you want to know anything else you're going to have to go elsewhere because that about exhausts my knowledge of the woman.'

Natalia searched her son's face for a moment before her body sagged in relief. 'You didn't know, then.' She sighed. 'I didn't think you could have,' she revealed.

'Didn't know and still don't,' he inserted drily.

'She must have changed her name, or maybe she gave you a false name?'

'Are we back on the not-blonde?'

'I don't approve of everything you do, Roman.'

Roman's expression became stoical as he prepared to endure one of his mother's lectures on his lifestyle with a modicum of patience—patience he would not have extended to anyone else who chose to criticise him.

'But I simply couldn't imagine you abandoning your responsibilities and letting your own son grow up not even knowing who you are.'

CHAPTER THREE

ROMAN, whose hard features had begun to relax into a rueful half-smile at his mother's initial comments, stiffened as she delivered her killer punchline.

'*Son!*' Pallor crept up under his even olive-toned Latin complexion. 'If that's your idea of a joke?' he grated.

'I'm hardly likely to joke about such a thing,' Natalia said. 'Look, I can see this must have come as a shock to you.'

'That's very understanding of you.' Roman's irony was wasted on his mother. 'I don't have a son and I've never met a...' his forehead creased as he tried to recall the non-blonde's name '...Scarlet Smith?'

'Yes, lovely girl.' She glanced across at her son and shook her head.

She watched with some sympathy as her son ground his teeth and stalked stiff-backed across the room, his whole manner screaming anger and frustration. She came up behind him and put her hand on his shoulder. Though she was five eleven in her heels, she had to tilt her head to look him in the face.

'Be honest, is this so impossible to believe?'

'Don't you think I'd know about it if I had a son?' he suggested, his tone deceptively mild.

Natalia gave a very Latin shrug. 'Only if the mother chose to tell you, Roman.'

'And always supposing I did actually make a habit—as you obviously believe—of going around impregnating women. Why the hell wouldn't she have told me? Why

29

struggle to bring up a child as a single parent?' A flicker of suspicion crossed his face. 'Or is she married?'

'You sleep with married women?'

Roman's head went back as he looked heavenwards, sending the dark hair he wore a little longer than was conventional against the collar of his pale shirt. 'No, I do not sleep with married women,' he replied between clenched white teeth.

'Never?'

A hissing sound of seething frustration escaped through Roman's teeth as his mother continued to look at him with an expression of disappointment.

'Not knowingly.'

'Ignorance is no defence in law, or so I've always understood. I accept you didn't know you had a child. Now you do. What are you going to do about it?' she challenged.

'For the last time, I do *not* have a child!'

Natalia gave an inflammatory sigh. 'Denial isn't going to get us anywhere.'

'I'm not in denial,' Roman thundered.

'Yes, you are, and there's no need to raise your voice, Roman, I'm not deaf.'

The bitterness died from his face as he saw the unexpected sparkle of tears in his mother's eyes. 'Sit down,' he insisted, his concern coming across as impatience.

'It must have been some story this woman spun you.' Roman's facial muscles tightened. 'You can normally spot a phoney a mile off. Didn't it strike you as odd that she told you, not me?'

'She didn't tell me anything at all. I gave her every opportunity, but in fact Scarlet pretended not to know you.'

A flicker of incomprehension crossed Roman's face. 'Then what the hell is this about?'

'I've seen the child, Roman, and he *is* you at the same age.'

Roman looked at her for a moment, his dark brows raised, before releasing an incredulous laugh.

'This isn't funny, Roman,' she reproached.

'No, it's not funny to see you so upset,' he agreed sombrely as he hunkered down beside his mother's chair. 'All right, this kid looks like I did,' he acceded lightly. 'But I don't know any Scarlet Smith, the only time I've spoken to her was on the phone, I promise you, and I never forget a name.'

His mother nodded. 'People change in four years. You have,' she added, a tinge of sadness in her eyes.

'Scarlet must have changed her name so that you couldn't find her, that would explain you not recognising her name.'

'That would seem a tad excessive, considering I wasn't looking for her.'

'Don't be flippant,' Natalia snapped.

'I know you'd like to be a grandmother, but I'm not going to pretend I've fathered a kid to oblige you.'

'You wouldn't say that if you'd seen the boy, Roman.'

'Do you think I wouldn't remember the name of a woman I slept with?' he demanded.

'If it was four years ago I'd say you could have some problem. There were a lot of women. I know I shouldn't have brought it up…but…'

'You're going to anyway.' Roman's expression was resigned.

'It's not a subject I enjoy discussing.'

'That makes two of us.'

Being deserted by your childhood sweetheart after the invitations for the wedding had been sent out was not an experience he particularly cared to relive on a regular basis, and that was what his mother was trying to remind him of now.

Making a total fool of himself was something a man was allowed to do *once* in his life. When he made marriage plans the next time his decision would not be based on a blind infatuation and starry-eyed fantasies of a happy-ever-after existence.

A marriage based on a mutual respect where neither partner would feel wounded or outraged if the other sought excitement outside the marriage bed was one that would stand a much better chance of survival in the long run.

Natalia determinedly ignored the dry rejoinder. 'What I'm saying is it's not as if you've never had a one-night stand.'

'Can we leave my sex life out of this? I can hardly be surprised strangers believe what they read about me in the tabloids when my own mother does. You're accusing me of indiscriminately fathering children! Do you *really* think I'm that stupid?' he demanded.

'Just go and see the boy, then you'll understand, Roman. That's all I'm asking you to do. Are you trying to tell me that it wouldn't bother you never to know your own son?'

'I don't have a son.'

'One hundred per cent sure?'

Roman's broad shoulders lifted; playing along was clearly the only way he was going to put an end to this once and for all. He gave a sigh. 'So where will I find the mother of my child?'

'Can't *you* see him?'

'Mr O'Hagan asked *expressly* to see you.'

'I really didn't do much.'

'Just what I said…' Dragging his attention from the text message he was reading David added smoothly, 'I told him that we work as a team here, but it seems your name must have stuck in his mother's mind and of course you spoke to him on the phone.'

'That must be it,' Scarlet agreed drily. Oh, God, it would be just her luck if the man had decided to follow up his complaint officially, but if he had there wasn't any reason he couldn't have mentioned it to David straight off.

'It's a very nice gesture.'

'Men like Roman O'Hagan don't make nice gestures unless there's something in it for them,' she responded cynically.

'And you number how many multimillionaires amongst your circle?'

'I don't, but Abby knew a few.' At least Abby's circle of friends had aspired to the millionaire lifestyle, though, as her sister had explained, not all had had the means to support it.

She saw the flicker of sympathy her bitter remark brought to David's face and added quickly, 'The problem is we're so short-staffed with this flu epidemic. I could do without gestures, kind or otherwise.'

'The longer you spend arguing with me…God, Scarlet, what are you wearing?'

David had been her honorary uncle since she was tiny. Scarlet was always scrupulous about not trading on the family friend thing, but unfortunately David didn't feel similarly inhibited when it came to passing the sort of personal comments he wouldn't get away with with other staff members.

'Borrowed. A baby threw up all over me.'

'Goes with the territory, I would imagine,' came the bracing observation. 'And you were the one who insisted on leaving an indecently well-paid job in the City to work with children,' he reminded her.

'Days like this make me wonder why.'

'No, you don't, you love every minute of it. I don't know why, but you do.'

Scarlet conceded his point with a grin. 'I suppose asking him to come back another day is out of the question?' David looked at her over his metal-rimmed half moon spectacles as though she'd lost her mind.

'Come back another day?'

Scarlet shrugged. 'I thought I'd ask.' She caught sight of her reflection in the full-length window. 'God,' she cried, wincing, 'I can't see him looking like a bag lady.'

'I've seen you looking better, but he's not here to ask you for a date, Scarlet, so I really don't see the problem here.'

'I'm representing the university,' she said weakly.

'If you'd been a member of the academic staff I could see your point,' David responded, treating her suggestion seriously.

'How lucky that I'm only a nursery nurse,' she said dead-pan.

'Exactly, and look on the bright side, he's not going to think you made any special efforts for him which should suit your egalitarian principles down to the ground.'

'Very funny,' Scarlet muttered.

'Now, the sooner you go get your shoulder patted, the sooner you get back to help the troops out.'

With a shrug she admitted defeat.

'Mr O'Hagan is in my office.' David turned in the opposite direction.

'Aren't you coming too?' Scarlet protested with a frown.

'I have an important meeting. Has it occurred to you you might actually like the man?'

'No.'

'Then pretend.' It was not a request.

'Mr O'Hagan, can I have your autograph,' she mocked, assuming an expression of brainless adoration.

'See, you can do it when you try,' David approved, banging her on the shoulder. 'Now off you go and remember he's a very important friend to this university, Scarlet.'

Scarlet nodded meekly. 'I'll be very nice to him.'

It didn't seem a too extravagant promise to make, considering it shouldn't take Roman O'Hagan long to go through the motions of thanking her—at least she hoped not!

CHAPTER FOUR

ROMAN glanced at his watch, his eyes slightly narrowed. If he could get the Scarlet Smith thing sorted before lunch he could fly back out to Dublin and join Alice, who was already there.

That was the best scenario, but if things did run over he didn't begrudge the time, not if the end result made his mother happy. Not as happy as being a grandmother would, but his sense of filial duty had limits.

It did not cross his mind for one second that his mother was correct. There was no possibility he had fathered a child. He had been many things in his life, but careless was not one of them.

Not a man given to moody introspection he turned his mind to the pivotal meeting in Dublin later that evening.

Scarlet tapped on the door half hoping that nobody would reply to her timid knock. Nobody did, but the door, already half ajar, swung open. The man revealed standing there, running a long brown finger down the spine of a leather-bound book, seemed oblivious to her presence.

She cleared her throat and his head turned. Dark lashes lifted to reveal eyes that were one shade short of pitch-black and flecked with tiny golden lights. Scarlet's eyes slid away from the most piercing regard she had ever encountered.

She gulped as her heart made a concerted effort to escape the confines of her chest.

In profile he was perfect; an overused term but more than justified on this occasion. Face on, only a purist would have claimed the fine scar that ran from one razor-sharp cheekbone to just below his eye marred the effect.

Scarlet wasn't that purist!

Roman's immediate thought as he stared at the diminutive brown-haired figure hovering uncertainly in the doorway was, *there must be some mistake.* Realistically, he hadn't actually been expecting some blonde goddess with endless legs, but *this*?

The indentation between his eyebrows deepened, the woman he had spoken to on the phone had come across as gutsy and unafraid to speak her mind, not to mention bloody-minded, but this woman looked scared of her own shadow! She couldn't even meet his eyes!

He experienced an unexpected pang of disappointment.

'Mr O'Hagan...?' Scarlet repeated when he didn't respond.

Great, I've struck him dumb, but not with my ravishing beauty!

'Mr O'Hagan, I understand you wanted to speak to me?'

The voice emerging from the slight frame was right, unexpectedly deep and husky with a sexy little rasp, but everything else was wrong, including the scared way she was not quite looking him in the eye and the tongue-tied routine.

Nice voice, shame about everything else.

'Miss Smith?'

Scarlet nodded, and resisted the aggravating impulse to apologise for her appearance.

'Why don't you come in and sit down?'

'I'm fine here.'

He looked at her impatiently. 'I don't bite.'

She flushed at the satirical note in his voice and realised she must look an idiot standing there as if she was ready to run. Straightening her shoulders, Scarlet overcame the strange reluctance she was experiencing to close the door.

She'd been in the room before and it wasn't exactly cramped—her own office would have fitted in it ten times over—but she was experiencing an almost claustrophobic sensation that involved a tightening in the pit of her stomach and an overwhelming desire to turn and run.

The man was here to say thank you, not interrogate her, or even sue her, unless his mother had suffered a relapse? He didn't give a damn what she looked like, so why the sudden panic attack? She didn't subscribe to the populist celebrity culture and was not overawed or impressed just because someone had fame and money. She was neither shy nor lacking in confidence so her irrational nervousness on this occasion annoyed her.

'So, we meet at last.'

Head down, she nodded.

His mother had thought he had slept with this woman?

He repressed a fastidious wince as he checked out the fashion black spot she represented.

He knew women who could look good in the proverbial sack, but this woman wasn't one of that number. That tunic checked shirt thing almost reached her knees, but at least it covered most of the appalling, baggy track-suit joggers she had teamed it with. There was nothing intrinsically dreadful about the sensible flat leather shoes that completed the ensemble, but they didn't do anything to disguise the fact she was small and shapeless.

Who knew what lurked under the androgynous outfit? He, for one, felt no compelling urge to find out. Though he would have liked to bin the outrageously unattractive glasses she wore, which concealed most of her features, simply on the grounds that they were criminally ugly.

Scarlet stood there miserably while his veiled gaze moved over her. He was suitably enigmatic, but not enigmatic enough to prevent Scarlet getting the impression she hadn't lived up to the billing his mother had given her.

She gave a mental shrug…ah, well, she could live with that!

Standing next to him, even if she had been looking her best, she would have felt plain and unkempt. Six feet four inches, give or take an inch, of spectacular male perfection. He more than lived up to his billing. Unbelievably he was even better looking in the flesh than in print!

She responded on two levels to this discovery. On the one hand she was disappointed at being robbed of the opportunity to confide derisively to her friends, It's all air-brushing, you know, he's not nearly as attractive as he looks in the magazines!

On the other level she responded as any woman would being faced with the most sinfully sexy man she had ever seen—or even imagined seeing!

'Miss *Scarlet* Smith?' Smith was a common name; maybe this was the wrong one? She had the awkward slightly be-mused manner of someone who had walked into the wrong office. 'You do know who I am?'

Didn't everyone? Her lowered gaze lifted. Maybe that was his problem; she hadn't asked for his autograph yet.

'I'm Scarlet. The vice-chancellor said you wanted to see me, Mr O'Hagan.'

A small derisive smile formed on her wide and expressive mouth; after their conversation she wasn't surprised to discover he was the type who thrived on public recognition and got irritated when he didn't receive it.

Well, promise to David or not, Mr. O'Hagan was about to learn she was not one of that creepy boot-licking number!

Her lips parted to ask if he wouldn't mind keeping it brief when his dark eyes locked onto her own.

Scarlet breathed in sharply and promptly forgot what she

was going to say. He really did have the most stunning eyes she'd ever seen, deep chocolate-brown, but not like the sweet milk chocolate she adored, but the dark variety that was too bitter for her palate. For a bemused moment she just stared into those dark, mesmerising topaz-flecked depths before pulling clear and closing her mouth with an audible click.

She gave a smile heavy on serene self-possession to correct any impression he might have got that she was a silly, drooling female. The last thing she wanted was to be heaped together with those adoring hordes.

Dating the rich and photogenic Roman O'Hagan had kick-started the career of many a would-be celebrity, and the women who weren't notorious before they shared the spotlight he lived in definitely were at the end of it!

However, considering her own involuntary fit of the fluttery females, Scarlet was now willing to consider that there might have been a few takers whose motives hadn't been purely mercenary.

Maybe it was the dark, smouldering thing, she mused, because, despite his mixed ancestry, Roman O'Hagan's features, colouring and innate elegance were very much that of the Latin male, as was the devastating raw masculinity he projected.

The clothes helped, of course, she decided scornfully as she put a mental price tag on the pale grey impeccably tailored grey suit he wore teamed with a black silky polo shirt open at the neck. Italian men were notoriously vain and she doubted this one could pass a reflective surface without checking himself out. The catty postscript made her feel better about being unable to find a flaw in his tall, broadshouldered, narrow-hipped athletic frame.

Power, money and a good suit—maybe she wasn't so

different from everyone else easily impressed by the trappings of privilege…?

The suit or the man inside it? It's not his position on the social register that's got you hot!

Turning a deaf ear to the debate going on in her head, Scarlet turned her thoughts to her more immediate problem. After a moment's further deliberation she decided against shaking hands; if he didn't accept her hand she was going to look pretty silly and nothing about him suggested he would welcome the gesture.

She decided it would be best all round if she hurried proceedings along.

'How is Mrs O'Hagan?' Scarlet found it a relief to be able to sound genuinely sincere about something. 'Is she feeling better? She's not had a relapse or anything?'

'She is very much better, thank you, and I'm not contemplating any immediate legal action.'

'That's just as well because I've got no assets for you to strip.' You only had to look at the man to see his business tactics were every bit as unscrupulous as his rivals suggested.

A flicker of renewed interest appeared in Roman's deep-set eyes. Now *that*, he decided, sounded much more like the girl he had spoken to on the phone.

'You take an interest in business? I got my MBA from Harvard; where did you get yours?'

'The London School of Economics,' she responded automatically.

Her reply might not have wiped the supercilious smirk off his face, but at least she had the pleasure of seeing him look mildly taken aback.

'You're trying to tell me that you've got a Masters in Business Administration?'

He had one of those perfectly straight patrician noses that

had been specifically designed to sneer down at lesser mortals. Scarlet would dearly have liked to punch it. Physical violence not being an option, she had to fall back on giving as good as she got in the sarcasm stakes.

'Actually I have, but it's not the sort of thing I'd normally drop into the conversation, because it might sound a bit pretentious.' She widened her eyes and adopted an expression of kittenish innocence. 'Don't you think?' she appealed to him. 'And,' she added thoughtfully, 'that sort of showing off might lead people to think I had a self-esteem issue.'

The stunned look in his eyes gave her a moment's intense, gleeful satisfaction.

'I doubt anyone is going to think you have a self-esteem issue,' Roman mused after a moment of startled, static silence. Whatever the hunched-shoulder stuff had been about, it had not been a confidence issue; her present manner made that obvious.

She inclined her head and smiled. 'Thank you,' she said, even though she was well aware his comment hadn't been meant as a compliment.

'Perhaps I didn't get this right. I thought you worked in the nursery?'

'I'm a nursery nurse,' she agreed with pride.

'Aren't you a little overqualified for the job?'

He stopped short of calling her a liar, but she could hear the amused scepticism in his voice. It was only by exerting superhuman restraint that Scarlet stopped herself supplying the names of referees who could confirm her qualifications and tell him how good she had been at her job.

'Actually I was under-qualified,' she explained calmly. 'I retrained. I was looking for job satisfaction.'

'Good for you!' he applauded with teeth-clenching insincerity. 'I've always said there's no shame in admitting you can't hack it.'

Scarlet's cheek muscles ached from maintaining a fixed smile. 'You have no idea how much I value your opinion.'

'I'm beginning to get a pretty good idea,' he returned drily. 'I believe you were very kind to my mother.'

'She's easy to be nice to; *she's* nice…' Scarlet literally bit her tongue to stop the flow of insults.

One perfectly symmetrical brow dark against his even-toned golden skin lifted to a politely interrogative angle.

'A very nice woman indeed,' Scarlet mumbled indistinctly.

She'd promised David—gosh, that seemed a lifetime ago now, not a few minutes—that she'd be on her best behaviour. Cutting the wretched man down to size was a self-indulgence she simply couldn't afford. It was also something she might not be capable of, she conceded.

Scarlet paused for a moment to consider her reckless behaviour objectively. The exercise gave rise to deep concern as she identified a worrying development, the adrenaline rush, the toe curling excitement she got from trading insults with him had a bizarrely addictive quality.

'She was full of praise for you.'

'She's kind; I hardly did anything,' she replied with suitable modesty, and for the second time that morning she had no argument. 'Not even call for an ambulance.' *You just couldn't leave well alone, could you, Scarlet?*

'Well, the best of us panic in a situation like that.'

'That's extremely understanding of you, but—'

'Yes, it is nice of me, isn't it? My assistant is worried I'll make you cry.'

'But,' she added, sending him a glare of simmering dislike, 'I *didn't* panic!' Scarlet announced, her chin lifting. '*Cry…?*' she added as his last comment sank in. 'I'm not going to cry!' she said, sounding insulted by the suggestion.

'I'm extremely relieved to hear it.' His dark head tilted a

little to one side as he examined her flushed, indignant face. 'So you think you made the right call, then, and you're prepared to defend your action, or rather lack of it?'

'Of course I didn't make the right call,' she surprised him by conceding with a grimace.

'But,' she added quickly, 'that wasn't because I panicked, it was because I took notice of—' She stopped abruptly, not wanting him to run away with the idea she was trying to pass the blame to someone else. 'Is this an official complaint? Because if it is I don't think you should be talking to me.'

'It isn't a complaint, official or otherwise, unless you particularly want it to be.'

Scarlet's jaw tightened at the blatant sarcasm in his voice. 'Then you came to apologise for being so rude to me?' she suggested innocently.

The hooded lids lowered in a lazy fashion but there was nothing remotely lazy about the spark in his eyes. *'Pushing it.'*

Scarlet conceded this lightest of warning with a shrug and rubbed the goose-bumps that had broken out over her forearms. When his voice dropped to a husky murmur that way it had an almost tactile quality.

She had the distinct impression that he wouldn't have minded it if she had ignored him. Roman O'Hagan was coming across as a man who enjoyed a fight and enjoyed winning even more. She could see why he didn't lose often, his dark eyes contained a gleam in them that suggested he had the intelligence to match his stunning looks.

The idea of pulverising him verbally was still an awfully attractive one, if deeply unrealistic.

'You made quite an impression on my mother…you and your little daughter…?' As this was just a matter of going through the motions there didn't seem to be any need to be overly subtle about introducing the child into the conversation, Roman thought.

'Son.'

'Right,' he drawled.

He couldn't have sounded less interested. It wouldn't take much effort to make it a little less obvious he was here under sufferance, Scarlet thought, pursing her lips indignantly. 'Sam,' she supplied.

Roman watched her face soften unconsciously as she said the kid's name and thought, *She isn't actually that bad-looking*. His long lashes lowered, half concealing his eyes as he considered her small heart-shaped face—good skin, nice hair; it was a shame about the glasses, and of course the bizarre sense of style.

But he wasn't here to organise a make-over, he reminded himself. He was here to convince his mother she didn't have any grandchildren running around the country.

'My mother was concerned her collapse might have alarmed…Sam.'

'He didn't take it personally.' Her attempt at levity didn't evoke any response. God, this was heavy going. He had two modes; silent and nastily sarcastic. Clearly scintillating conversational skills were not part of his attraction! But then she already knew that his attraction was much more basic.

Her bland smile became strained as she ran her tongue across her dry lips and swallowed to relieve the nervous occlusion tightening her throat. 'Tell her he's fine.' *Oh, God, please let this be over soon*.

Her hazel eyes flickered to her wrist-watch. Ten minutes to lunch time, one of the busiest times of the day in the nursery. She shifted her weight restively from one leg to the other and repressed a sigh as she lifted her head.

She flushed lightly as Roman O'Hagan angled his sable brows expressively.

'Sorry, I should be somewhere else,' she explained, trying hard to make it sound as if this were something she was sorry about.

'Am I boring you?' Women didn't make a habit of looking at their watches when they were in his company. 'Or should I have made an appointment?'

The sardonic note in his rich velvet voice brought the colour rushing back to her cheeks.

'Well, if I'd had a little warning I could have told you that today isn't very convenient,' Scarlet agreed bluntly. 'I realise,' she added, 'that my time isn't as valuable as yours...' It was the total shock she saw momentarily flicker in his eyes that halted the flow of indiscreet observations.

What's wrong with me? I told David I'd be nice to him. It's not like it requires any great skill, just an ability to keep my mouth shut. Getting herself out of this one was going to require some quick thinking, or talking at least.

'Which, of course, it isn't. I'm sure an hour of your time would cost me loads, whereas I only get paid...but I don't suppose you get paid by the hour. And I don't want an hour of it or even five minutes, though it's obviously been an enormous thrill to meet you.' Was that obsequious enough? She lifted a weary hand to her head. *Oh, God...! Do I sound as much of a blithering idiot as I feel?*

'I'm delighted you're thrilled.'

I might die of humiliation, she decided, listening to the amusement in his deep voice.

'And I'm sorry if this is inconvenient,' he continued, 'but the vice-chancellor said there would be no problem.'

'Well, he would, wouldn't he? You're influential and rich and...' Her scornful observation faded as their glances meshed once again. 'That is, you're...*sorry.*' She managed to force her lips into a stiff smile. 'That was rude.'

'Yes, it was.' It was hard to tell from his languid agreement if he was annoyed or amused.

David will kill me. She exhaled noisily and ran her hands, palm-flat, over her face in a brisk scrubbing motion.

'I get the impression you're having a bad day?'

'What makes you say that?' she asked gloomily.

A laugh was drawn from his beautifully tanned throat. Scarlet lifted her face, startled by the deeply attractive sound. He smiled at her, his teeth flashing very white in his dark face. She blinked—for a moment he had reminded her of Sam; the fleeting similarity made her almost feel disposed to think he might not be quite the monster she had imagined.

'Well, if you carry on like this on a regular basis I can't imagine they'd carry on paying you that *enormous* salary you spoke of.'

She let her hands fall away and shook her head. 'I earn every penny I make. Especially today.'

'What's happened to make this a bad day?'

'*You*…well, not just you,' she added with a self-condemnatory grimace. 'And I don't mean you personally, it's just I didn't like leaving the staff to struggle. I've been putting in lots of extra hours this week to cover for sickness.'

'And what happens if you get sick?'

'Oh, I never get sick.'

Her solemn conviction struck him as funny. She must have picked up on his amusement because she added defensively. 'I can't remember the last time I was ill.'

'Aren't you afraid of tempting fate?'

Scarlet suspected he was making fun of her. 'I'm not superstitious,' she told him her expression contemptuous.

'You've never pinched spilt salt over your shoulder, or counted magpies in a field, or crossed your fingers for luck?'

She shook her head. 'Of course not. Don't you believe me?'

'I think everyone's superstitious deep down; it's human nature.'

This point of view amazed her. '*You're* superstitious?' she asked incredulously.

'My father's Irish, my mother's Italian—the odds were stacked.' His broad shoulders lifted. 'What choice do I have?'

'Well, I'm not superstitious, but I am really glad that your mother is better.'

'But you've somewhere else you need to be,' he completed smoothly.

It would be overstating it to call the glint in his eyes annoyance, *but*…! She probably was making the fact she couldn't stick being in his company a bit obvious.

'That's very understanding of you, Mr O'Hagan.'

'Perhaps we could continue our discussion over lunch?'

Scarlet heard his voice through a faint buzz in her ears as she tried to contemplate what he'd just said.

'Lunch…?' she parroted vaguely.

Best to look on this as a reflex—her hormones had gone into primitive autopilot mode and were acting independently of her brain. Hence the weakness in her legs, the warm heat thrumming through her body and the painful spasms knotting her stomach. He was an attractive man, end of story, no need to complicate it further.

'Bring your son, by all means.'

'*Discussion?*' There seemed to be a time delay in her ability to translate what he was saying. 'We weren't having a discussion.' Her straight brows arranged themselves in an interrogative line. '*Lunch!*'

There's no such thing as a free lunch!

'*Good God, no!*'

His eyes widened fractionally, but other than that nothing in his manner revealed his reaction to her response. It wasn't that he was conceited, but a lifetime of being pursued and flattered by women had left Roman ill prepared to have an invitation of lunch rejected in an attitude of blatant revulsion.

'Well, I know where to come if I need my ego deflated.'

Belatedly Scarlet recalled her promise to David. She tried to soften her blunt reply.

'That is…it's very kind of you to offer,' she added, even though every instinct told her this was not a man predisposed to be kind.

She just stopped herself lifting her hand, which would have drawn attention to her face, which felt as though it were on fire. This was a man who never did anything without a reason. Which left the question, why had he asked her to lunch? Did he have some elaborate punishment in mind because she had answered back to him on the phone?

'Like I said the flu epidemic has left us very short-staffed today.'

'But otherwise you'd have been delighted to come?'

In face of this sardonic observation it took all of Scarlet's will-power to conceal her feelings behind a blank expression.

What were her feelings? In one word—shallow; this was biology at its most basic. She knew what lust felt like, and never had it been less welcome or so extreme, but when you came right down to it she really shouldn't have been letting it get to her this way. There was absolutely no need to stress; it wasn't as if she'd never felt sexual attraction before. She knew about the tightening in her stomach and the rest; it was a biological response—like sneezing.

She took a deep breath and was conscious of the fabric of her borrowed top chafing against her erect nipples; lower, the tell-tale liquid heat was even more of a give-away. *Sneezing?* Maybe not the best analogy.

She saw a smile touch his sensual lips. To her horrified eyes it held a knowing quality that suggested she wasn't hiding anything from him; she felt a flare of anger—her condition was entirely his doing.

'If you'll excuse me, I have to go,' she told him abruptly.

'Rain check?'

She looked at him blankly. If he thought she was strange and peculiar, that was fine, because she was. Being attracted, even in a blind, mindless way, to a man like this could quite safely be categorised as peculiar...also wantonly stupid and brainless!

'Fine, whatever...' she mumbled, before virtually throwing herself through the door in her haste to remove herself from the room.

She literally bumped into David about thirty seconds after she had emerged from his office. She suspected he had been lurking there waiting for her to appear.

'Steady, you're in a hurry,' he said, placing his hands on her shoulders to steady her. 'You came around that corner like you had the hounds of hell on your heels.'

After what she had just endured the hounds of hell would be child's play.

'The girls will be missing me. I promised I'd be back to help with the lunches.'

David's right hand remained on her shoulder. 'How did it go?'

'What...? Oh, with Mr O'Hagan? Fine, absolutely fine.'

David looked at her face and groaned. 'Oh, God, you're such a terrible liar, you always were. What did you do?'

'I didn't *do* anything.'

'But you said something.'

Scarlet's expression grew defensive. 'Of course I said something. I may not warm to womanising playboys—' annoyingly this was something that was hard to say without sounding, not only prejudiced, but distressingly intolerant '—but I'm not a total idiot.' Actually the jury was still out on that one.

'Well, this particular womanising playboy finds time in his schedule to run a highly successful international company.' He looked into her stubborn face and sighed. 'Would it hurt you to be nice to the man, Scarlet?'

'How nice would that be? Will treating everything he says as a pearl of wisdom do, or did you want me to sleep with him?'

'Do you have to be facetious, Scarlet?' David demanded, allowing his aggravation with her to surface.

'It's easier than—'

'Easier than what, Scarlet?'

Good question. 'He's not an easy man.'

'I found him perfectly affable, but, easy or not, Scarlet, he is funding a number of bursaries to help students from less-well-off backgrounds.'

The seconds ticked by while Scarlet stood staring at him with her mouth slightly ajar. Finally she gulped and took a deep breath.

'You're kidding!' Her grin faded as no corresponding smile appeared on David's face. 'Oh, God, I feel such a…'

'Narrow-minded, judgemental?'

'Amongst other things,' she admitted miserably.

David shook his head. 'I don't know why you have a problem accepting the man is capable of acting altruistically?'

Scarlet did. It wasn't the man; it was the type of person he represented.

She had no problem seeing past an unattractive face, and she didn't judge anyone by their accent, their bank balance or the car they drove, but when it came to people who lived their lives being seen in the right places wearing the right clothes and with the right people she came over with terminal intolerance. She knew it and wasn't proud of it, but she couldn't help it.

Scarlet knew about people like that. Her sister had been a member of their very exclusive club, and how many of them had visited when Abby had been ill in hospital, losing her hair after intensive chemo? Abby's friends had had more important things to do, when she had contacted the names in her sister's address book and explained the situation and told them how much it would cheer her sister up to see a friendly face.

A few had made vague promises, but in the end not a single one of those *good friends* had turned up to show support, she recalled bitterly. When the going got tough, the Roman O'Hagans of this world disappeared in their fast cars.

'I'm not kidding. This is not common knowledge,' David added, laying a warning finger to his lips and looking as though he was regretting sharing the confidential information with her. 'Mr O'Hagan was most insistent on his name not being made public.' David gave a wry smile as he thought of all the name plaques he had unveiled in his career. 'Which makes him unique in my experience,'

'Really!' she exclaimed, unable to stop the bitchy retort. 'I'd have thought he'd be used to it! Well, he's not exactly publicity shy, is he?' she added defensively. It seemed pretty perverse to Scarlet that someone who lived his life in the glare of publicity would be bothered about his altruism being made public. 'Maybe it's a tax thing?'

She realised that, far from agreeing with her, David was looking annoyed, and added with as much conviction as she could muster, 'Or maybe he's a very modest, generous man.'

CHAPTER FIVE

SCARLET lowered the blinds over the glass partition and removed her borrowed finery before folding it neatly over the back of her chair. Standing there in just her white cotton pants, she shook out her own clean clothes. Creased, certainly, but a whole lot better than what she had been wearing.

If she had looked half decent would she have emerged from her encounter with Roman O'Hagan looking less of a loon?

Such speculation was pointless. Scarlet turned her thoughts firmly away from that traumatic and humiliating interview she had just endured—she never had been a big fan of post-mortems—and pulled her cream slim-cut pedal pushers over her bottom and slid the zip home over her narrow, some might say boyish, hips.

She took her tee shirt between her hands and attempted to stretch it this way and that without much success. A size six now, but it had survived the hot washing cycle in the industrial-sized machine a local firm had kindly donated to them better than her bra, which had come out looking like a dish rag.

She heard the knock on the door just as she was pulling her tee shirt over her head.

'Come in, Angie,' she called out, her voice muffled. 'I just wanted to ask if you'd mind covering for Barbara in the morning.'

Roman, preceded by his entrance card, a giant teddy bear, pushed the slightly ajar door fully open and walked in.

His experience of buying gifts for small children was limited, but he knew enough to know that the case of excellent claret he had put down for his godson on the occasion of his christening and the additions he had generously donated to the child's investment portfolio at Christmas and birthdays would not be suitable on this occasion. Wine and shares being inappropriate gifts he had sought the advice of his PA.

'What sort of gift is appropriate for a child of three?'

'Boy or girl?'

'Boy.'

'How much money do you want to spend?'

'I don't want to be seen as throwing money at the problem.'

'Right, but you do want to be seen as thoughtful; that's always more difficult.'

'Do you like your job?'

Alice grinned. 'All children like teddy bears, Roman,' she told him confidently. 'Yeah, a teddy bear is a good bet. A big one.'

He had followed her advice with some misgivings. Alice's knowledge of fitness videos, football and chocolate was second to none, but she had never struck him as being particularly child-orientated, unless you counted his kid brother, Luca, but you never could tell with women. Some of the most unlikely ones, women who had publicly declared themselves wedded to their careers, one day started looking on you as potential father material.

He had learnt to read the signals. When he became a father he wanted it to be *his* decision.

Roman was perfectly aware of his responsibility to provide an heir and perpetuate the family name…as if the world didn't have enough O'Hagans in it. But just in case it slipped his mind, his father, who seemed to think his eldest son might well walk under a moving bus at any moment, obligingly reminded him of the fact at regular intervals.

He would get round to doing what his father wanted in his own time, but at the moment he didn't have a son, he'd never met this woman before today, and this was a pointless exercise. There were a hundred other things that he could and should be doing.

Despite these facts he was determined to see the farce through to the end, because he always completed tasks he began. But more importantly, this way, when his mother asked, as she would, he would be able to tell her with a clear conscience that he had seen mother and child and they were nothing to do with him.

Nothing less was going to satisfy her.

Also in the short space of time that had elapsed since Scarlet Smith had knocked back his lunch invitation, Roman had totally forgotten that, not only had he regretted issuing the invite the moment he'd made it—did he even know any restaurants where they served dribbling toddlers?—but he had also lost track of the crucial fact that he hadn't issued the spur-of-the-moment invitation out of any desire for her abrasive company, but because he couldn't think of an easier way of getting to see her son.

'I'd be really grateful,' Scarlet said, still thinking she was talking to Angie. She grunted as she groped to insert her hand through the arm hole. 'Hold on a mo, I think this thing has shrunk.'

She clicked her tongue in regret. The tee shirt had been produced at their last fundraising event and it was decorated with self-portraits produced by the older children, including Sam. Now it was shrunk it would be lovingly stored with the growing collection of childhood memorabilia she was accumulating.

'It could have been worse, the machine totally shredded

my bra,' she confided. 'Not that I'm in any position to complain. This is one of those times being flat-chested pays off,' she huffed with a strangulated laugh as she inhaled deeply to allow the over-stretched fabric to cover and compress her small, pointed breasts.

Roman wasn't complaining either; he had no objections to 'holding on a mo.' Beneath the enticing expanse of slender back he had an excellent opportunity to appreciate the curvy shape and firmness of a small but perfectly formed bottom complete with strategically placed dimple above her peachy left buttock. And he didn't think she was flat chested; his entrance into the room had been perfectly timed to coincide with the brief bare-breasted interval.

He'd been taken unawares; the sight of pink-tipped, delightfully bouncy breasts had frozen him to the spot and primitive urges oblivious to the social restraints of being a modern man had surged into painful life.

It was extraordinary but, far from being shapeless, Scarlet Smith had an enticing body, slim with supple, succulent and very sexy curves. The transformation was nothing short of mind-blowing.

That made it official. He did not have a son—no way would he have forgotten sleeping with Scarlet Smith!

Smoothing the slightly creased cotton fabric over her flat midriff, Scarlet turned around. The smile on her face faded as she saw who was standing there. 'You!' she gasped accusingly.

For a horror-struck moment, she peered up at Roman before her brain got back into gear. She forced herself to release the breath painfully trapped in her chest, unfolded her arms, which she'd wrapped across her bosom in an instinctively protective gesture, and groped behind her on the desk for the glasses she'd set aside a few moments earlier.

'*Dio!* It's absolutely amazing.'

It took her several seconds for her slightly unsteady hands to locate her glasses from the table where she had put them. She slid them back onto her nose and his dark, fatally handsome face slipped into focus.

She was tempted to take them off again.

Roman frowned. Before she had replaced the glasses he had seen a red welt across the bridge of her nose, livid against the pallor of her skin. It was obviously caused by those stupid glasses. It was a crime to hide such beautiful eyes behind thick lenses. Didn't she know glasses were meant to be fashion accessories? That you could get paper-thin lenses and attractive frames these days.

'Those spectacles are too big and heavy for your face,' he censured in a gruff, distracted voice.

Scarlet shook her head ruefully. 'I know, but five years ago they were the height of fashion.' She gave a wry grin. 'It was my funky period,' she explained drily. 'I can't wait to put them back in the dark, dusty drawer they were hiding in,' she confessed.

'Then why don't you?'

'They won't let me wear my lenses until my corneal abrasion heals, and it hardly seemed worth forking out for a new pair.'

'*Corneal abrasion!* You injured your eyes?'

'The right one.' She lifted her hand towards her right eye, which showed no visible signs of the injury she spoke of. 'A freak accident—amusing really. A baby hit me in the face with a rattle, would you believe?'

Most people thought it amusing when she explained the circumstances, but not Roman O'Hagan, it seemed. His lips thinned in disapproval and his nostrils flared.

'This *amusing* accident could have cost you your eyesight.'

Her expression reflected her opinion of his bizarre pursuit of the subject. 'Well, I wouldn't go *that* far…'

'That much I can see.' The grim condemnatory note in his voice seemed a bit over the top to Scarlet. 'I suppose you'd have an equally offhand attitude to walking across the road without looking? You only have one set of eyes; it's generally a good idea to look after them,' he reproached sternly.

To hear him talk you'd think I did it deliberately, Scarlet thought.

'I'm as fond of my eyes as the next person.'

'I'm sure a great many people are fond of your eyes— they are beautiful. As is the rest of you.'

Beautiful eyes—? Beautiful rest of me? Before Scarlet had time to properly assimilate this extraordinary information, she saw where his own hot eyes had come to rest, and her arms reassumed their protective position. She breathed deeply as her entire body was engulfed in a wave of mortified heat that to her mind was worryingly out of proportion with the situation.

If he had shown any inclination to say something more on the subject she doubted she would have heard it past the clamour of her hammering heartbeat. Only he didn't show any inclination to speak…he wasn't showing any inclination to do anything beyond look at her in a way that made her go literally weak at the knees.

'Dear God,' she snapped. 'Anyone would think you'd never seen a woman without her shirt on before!'

And from the way you're acting, the voice in her head added snidely, *you'd think you'd never been looked at by a man before.*

It was true, his smouldering stare was making Scarlet's erect nipples pinch hard and burn. It was deeply mortifying that she had no control whatsoever over what was happening to her.

Roman gave a cough of laughter as dark eyes returned to her face. 'Sorry, I wasn't expecting to find you half dressed.' As he spoke his glance slid once more over her slender figure, and his chest lifted as a deep sigh vibrated through his lean, powerful frame.

'My God,' he observed, shaking his head. 'You look different…different in a good way, in case I didn't make myself clear.' Actually Roman doubted he had ever been less articulate in his life. 'I didn't mean to embarrass you.'

'Strange, I got the impression you were quite enjoying embarrassing me.'

One corner of his mouth lifted in appreciation of her comment. 'Do you play chess?'

'Pardon?' she said, sure she must have misheard him.

'Do you play chess?' he repeated.

Warily she nodded, still unsure of where this was going.

Roman's eyes narrowed. 'You either win with style or lose dramatically—?'

This accurate assessment stunned her. 'How could you know that?'

'You're reckless, and you rely on inspiration. Playing an unpredictable partner is always exciting,' he observed. 'Perhaps we could play some time…?'

Play with Roman O'Hagan?

Before she had time to respond to this proposal he added casually, 'And if you're wondering what I saw when I walked in—I didn't see a thing.'

Scarlet was now ninety per cent sure he was lying, which was no comfort to her. If he managed to unsettle his business rivals with this sort of thoroughness, no wonder they talked about him in financial circles as though he were the second coming.

Her chin lifted to a bolshy angle. 'I'm not the slightest bit embarrassed.' *Now that, Scarlet, is really going to convince him.*

'Why should you be? We're both adults...*consenting* adults.'

The throaty 'consenting' sent a secret shiver down her spine. 'I just wasn't expecting to see you standing there.' Despite her best efforts, she was unable to keep the accusatory note from her voice as she added, 'You surprised me.'

Understatement.

If another man, say Jimmy from the post room had walked in and caught her in the middle of getting changed, if she had inadvertently discussed her bra with him she would not exactly have fallen apart. She would have seen the funny side of the situation.

Right now she didn't feel like laughing.

She watched as he shook his head as if to clear his thoughts and released his breath in a soft sibilant hiss.

'If it's any comfort I got a shock too.' Now was not the perfect occasion, but a man couldn't choose when he was going to be overwhelmed by lust.

'I thought you were someone else...a colleague,' she added.

'Shall I go out and come back in again?' he offered.

'Don't be silly,' she snapped. 'Is there something I can do for you?'

Roman scrutinised her warm face thoughtfully for a moment before crossing the room.

Scarlet watched as he sat the ludicrously large teddy bear he was carrying in her chair behind the desk. She looked at it. It wasn't the sort of item that you could miss, but her attention had been so focused on the man himself she hadn't even noticed he was carrying anything until that moment.

She doubted if she would have noticed if he had arrived accompanied by a full male voice choir!

His burden disposed of, Roman looked at Scarlet once more. He ran a hand through his glossy thatch of sleek dark hair. The action, like everything he did, was rivetingly graceful.

'Is this about our telephone conversation yesterday?' he asked.

'I don't know what you mean.'

'I seem to bother you.'

If he knew how much she would have died of sheer mortification. 'I'm assuming you came here for a reason, Mr O'Hagan.'

'Or can you simply not bear to be in the same room as me?'

'I don't want to be rude, Mr O'Hagan, but I'm really in a hurry. You were horrible,' she admitted, despite her previous decision not to refer to the incident, 'but no more than I expected from someone like you.'

'*Ouch...!* But beyond threatening to sue you, have I done something to upset you?' he wondered, a curious frown deepening the lines above the bridge of his masterful nose.

Other than undress me mentally? Not that she imagined for one moment that she had received any special treatment. Roman obviously had a very Latin attitude when it came to ogling women. Especially if they were wearing tight tee shirts and no bra!

'Of course not.' Even she was unconvinced by her tone. 'Now, if you could tell me what I can do to help you? But I really do need to crack on.'

He ignored her interruption totally. 'I didn't really see how I could have offended you given we've not met before—though,' he added, pausing to allow his eyes to traverse the slim, shapely length of her body, 'maybe we have when you were wearing another disguise. I must say I prefer this one.'

She despised his slick patter and the fact it made her heartbeat accelerate.

'Oh, that.' She laughed uneasily, partly because his un-inhibited scrutiny of her body was not something she was comfortable with. She was even less comfortable with her body's response to that scrutiny. A shivery sensation slipped down her spine and she experienced a moment's blinding panic.

Some people became withdrawn when they were nervous. Scarlet talked.

'One of the children threw up all over me this morning—projectile.' *And he really wants to know this.* 'I usually keep some spare stuff here, but it's always the way—the one time you need them they're not here. The girls rallied around and lent me some clothes until mine could be cleaned. Though we do keep a box of spare clothes, for them, the children, obviously, just not for me.' The hearty laugh she heard emerge from her lips sounded just as unbalanced as the babble that had preceded it.

Scarlet closed her eyes. If Roman O'Hagan hadn't lost the will to live after that, she had. The room was filled with the sound of her own laboured breathing.

'I would say that constitutes a bad day.'

The quiver of laughter she heard in his deep voice brought her head up. Hazel eyes shining with indignation through the lenses of her glasses, she glared at him. 'It's not funny.'

'But not a tragedy either.'

'Are you suggesting I can't laugh at myself?' she demanded indignantly. 'Because, let me tell you, I have a *great* sense of humour...' she met his wry eyes and added with a defensive sniff '...normally.'

She didn't know why she was acting like this. She wasn't a naturally aggressive person; her temper was even; she was one of life's natural conciliators. There was just something about this man that brought out a latent combative streak in her nature.

'Is there something I can do to help you…?' she repeated.

He gestured towards the bear sitting in her chair. 'I had left it in my car. My mother thought your son might like it.'

'That's very kind of her.'

'Perhaps I could give it to him?'

She tried, but couldn't come up with a legitimate reason to refuse this casual request. 'He's in the play room. I'll show you the way,' she offered, only partially managing to mask her extreme reluctance to do so.

Halfway through the door she backtracked and pulled her denim jacket off the hook behind the door. 'It's chilly,' she told him, shrugging it on.

CHAPTER SIX

THE play room, normally a scene of organised chaos, was unusually peaceful when they entered. The younger children were sitting on the floor listening raptly to Angie tell a story.

Angie paused when they entered, her eyes widening a little when she identified the man beside Scarlet.

'Children,' she said, rising to her feet, 'we have a visitor.'

Royalty could not have produced more awe in her voice, Scarlet thought cynically.

'Roman O'Hagan.' Roman, his smile all charm, extended his hand to Angie who accepted it with an eagerness that to Scarlet's critical eye was *too* eager, fawning even, she concluded, viewing the older woman's response to their visitor with a jaundiced eye.

'Oh, I know who you are,' Angie replied with a grin. 'It was only yesterday we were looking at photos of you at that film première in Scarlet's magazine.'

Thank you for that, Angie, now he thinks I'm a secret groupie. 'Were we? I don't remember.'

Roman angled her a speculative look and she glared back at him aggressively.

'Sure you do, you put the magazine in your drawer, Scarlet.'

'For the recipe section—I'm going to make the risotto.' There was a layer of frost on Scarlet's words, which Angie seemed totally oblivious to.

'Isn't that a bit ambitious for you? Scarlet can't cook,' she added in a confidential aside to Roman. 'But she can eat for England and never put on an ounce. Me, I put on a

63

pound if I so much as look at a grain of rice.' She shook her head at the injustice of it.

'There's nothing wrong with womanly curves.'

'That's what my Bob says.'

Scarlet, who couldn't believe that any woman could fall for such a corny line, stared at her friend—her old-enough-to-know-better friend—who was visibly preening.

Roman, head tilted to one side, considered the older woman, a smile playing about his fascinating mouth. 'Is that a Donegal accent I'm hearing?'

Angie laughed. 'Not many people here can tell the difference.'

Without any apparent effort, he slipped into a wildly attractive soft brogue. 'I'm a Kerry man myself, on my da's side anyhow.'

'I have to tell you, Mr O'Hagan,' Angie gushed, 'those photos in Scarlet's magazine didn't do you justice.' She turned to her friend for support. 'Did they, Scarlet?'

'Angie, I think it might be an idea if you got back to the story.' Scarlet gave a significant nod towards the children. They were growing restive.

God bless restive children.

To her immense relief the distraction worked.

'Timothy Jones, don't pull Bethany's hair!' Angie exclaimed, wading in to calmly separate two small figures.

'She pulled mine.'

'Angie, if I could just see Sam for a minute.'

'Sure thing, you go with your mum, Sam. Now, children, say goodbye to Mr O'Hagan and thank him for this lovely present. My, isn't he just gorgeous?' she exclaimed.

Scarlet was pretty certain she wasn't talking about the stuffed toy; she certainly wasn't looking at it.

Roman had a choice; he could tell the eager faces that

the toy wasn't for them or he could hand it over. He handed it over.

Scarlet hid a smile as she tucked Sam's hand in her own.

'Don't worry, Sam knows about sharing, don't you, sweetheart?'

Sam, who was looking with saucer-like eyes up at the tall man standing beside his mother, didn't reply.

'However, he doesn't always like it,' she admitted drily. 'Say hello to Mr O'Hagan, Sam. He's not normally so tongue-tied,' she added, bending down to speak in her son's ear. 'Say hello to Mr O'Hagan, darling.'

'Hello,' Sam grunted, looking at his toes.

Scarlet gave an affectionate sigh and ruffled his dark hair before standing up.

'Hello there, Sam.'

Scarlet happened to be looking at Roman O'Hagan at the moment Sam lifted his head—*so nothing unusual there*—but what she saw was unusual. Unusual and inexplicable. At least as far as she could see there was no immediately obvious reason why the colour would seep out of Roman's face until his vibrant golden skin looked like marble. He stilled, the nerve that throbbed in the hollow of his lean cheek about the only movement in his body. There was no evidence that he was breathing until a deep, soundless sigh shuddered through his body, lifting his ribcage.

As she watched he dropped casually down on his haunches. 'Hello, Sam. I'm Roman.'

He sounded so normal and his whole body language was so relaxed that Scarlet wondered if she had imagined what had gone before.

'Do you like teddy bears, Sam?' Roman ran his hand over the little boy's dark head.

'They're *all right,* but I'm a big boy—I prefer footballs.'

'I'll remember that,' Roman promised.

'I'm going to be a footballer when I grow up.'

Roman made the appropriate impressed noises.

'Are you Mummy's friend?' she was deeply embarrassed to hear Sam ask.

Roman lifted his head; his eyes, which considering his manner with the child had been so relaxed and friendly, were bewilderingly cold. The hostility emanating from his lean body was equally pointed.

He turned back to the boy.

'I'm going to be, Sam, so we'll be seeing each other a lot,' he promised with a smile before he straightened up.

Scarlet held in her indignation until they got out to the corridor.

'Why on earth did you say that to Sam?' she demanded, turning on him angrily. 'He may only be three, but he remembers things.'

'Good. He won't be surprised the next time he sees me.'

'He won't be seeing you and neither will I. To be blunt, Mr O'Hagan, I don't actually like you very much.'

'Actually, Miss Smith, I'm not wild about you either…but I think you'll find you'll be seeing a lot more of me.'

Scarlet stared after him with a baffled expression as he retreated. To say his behaviour was bizarre would have been an understatement.

Still, one thing was certain: if she had anything to do with it neither she nor Sam would be seeing him again, despite his odd claim to the contrary!

CHAPTER SEVEN

SAM was spending Friday night at his best friend Thomas's house. This was the second time he had had a sleep-over. The first time Scarlet had spent the entire night worrying and hanging around the phone just in case an emergency had arisen that necessitated her rushing out of the house.

She had even mentally worked out the quickest routes to the two local hospitals, working on the assumption you couldn't be *too* prepared and it was always better to assume the worst.

The telephone hadn't rung and, far from crying for her, Sam had had a great time. The reciprocal sleep-over had gone equally well.

This time Scarlet was determined not to go weird again; she was not going to let the over-anxious mum thing turn her into a basket case. Instead she was going to look on this as an opportunity to enjoy a few self-indulgent hours alone. She would relax if it killed her! she determined grimly.

Her plans included a long, luxurious soak in a hot bath of decadent bubbles and using the moisturising face mask that guaranteed to bring the youthful bloom back to tired skin. After that there were a box of chocolates and a feel-good video with her name on them.

The opening credits of *It's a Wonderful Life* had just finished when the doorbell rang. She had forgotten that plans were an invitation for things to go wrong, especially when that plan was an evening of unadulterated indulgence.

'Damn!' she swore as she paused the film, hitched up the legs of her slightly too long pyjama bottoms and slid her feet into her slippers. 'Hold your horses,' she muttered crossly under her breath as she trudged to the door.

If Sam had been home she would have been a lot crankier; the chance of him sleeping through the racket their caller was making was just about nil. The doorbell was so insistent that she almost missed the sound of the phone ringing as she passed by.

Scarlet dived for it.

Her heart thudding with trepidation, she lifted it to her ear. *I knew the sleep-over was a daft idea. Three is much too young to be encouraging independence in a child...a child of three should be home with his mother.*

By the time she had politely heard out the person on the line selling double glazing, her heart rate had almost returned to normal and the person ringing the doorbell had begun to hammer on the door with their fist.

It was a very angry sound.

Though not always as security conscious as she might be Scarlet had no problem remembering in this instance to leave the safety chain on as she opened the door a crack. Of all the people she had imagined to discover standing there, Roman O'Hagan had not even featured on the list.

Her exclamation of, 'Gracious!' hardly covered her feelings as she peered up at the tall, commanding figure standing in the hallway.

She swallowed convulsively as her pulse rate shot off the scale. The fluttering sensation low in her belly combined with the difficulty she had breathing made it hard for her to do anything but gape. He was worth gaping at. Gosh, but he looked good, and my, she thought, attempting to nudge her appreciation towards the safer direction of scorn, didn't he know it?

He removed the designer shades he wore and tucked them into the breast pocket of his jacket. The dark, wintry eyes that surveyed her coldly were even less reassuring than the mirrored lenses had been!

It had been ten days since she'd last seen him... *I was counting?* He could not have altered since then, but the hard angles on his face did seem more defined this evening, as though he might have lost weight. But his greyhound-lean frame had not carried any excess flesh the last time. Perhaps it was the black leather jacket and tailored dark trousers that hugged the muscular contours of his long thighs that made him look longer and leaner and just generally harder.

If he'd been auditioning for the part of a dangerous but fatally attractive gangster he'd have got the job on the spot! The sprinkling of designer stubble across his jaw and hollow cheeks only intensified the aura of menace that hung around his sinfully gorgeous person.

The discovery that it was hard to maintain your anger with someone who was blinking innocently up at you did not improve Roman's mood. His jaw clenched because he knew that under baggy pyjamas and the glowing, baby smooth contours of her make-up-free face there lurked a woman who was living a lie.

Even if she didn't know he was the boy's father, she sure as hell knew she wasn't the mother! Besides, what was it his mother had said?

'Ignorance is no defence' Scarlet Smith—if that was her name?—was about to find out it was no defence in his eyes either.

His son was growing up without a father—that wasn't something that had happened by accident. Oh, yes, there were a lot of questions he wanted answered.

Scarlet Smith was going to do the answering.

For all he knew, everything about her was a lie. The curly knot scrunched casually on the top of her head, which made her look simultaneously vulnerable and sexy, was probably contrived to do just that.

'What the hell kept you?' he growled. 'Open the door.'

'I was on the phone.' Scarlet's beleaguered brain having finally accepted the fact that it was actually Roman standing out in the hallway and not some hallucination, she began to move on to other stuff, such as what was he doing here? 'What are you...how...?' She stopped, the blood draining from her face as a possible explanation presented itself to her.

'The Bradleys sent you.' Her worst fears were realised when he didn't deny it.

The Bradleys were exactly the sort of people he *would* know.

Tom was something important in films and Nancy, who wore floaty clothes and cooked like an angel, wrote a foodie newspaper column in a national newspaper; in short the sort of female that left Scarlet feeling sadly inadequate. They lived in a fantastic house, employed an au pair and a gardener, and most likely had dinner guests like Roman.

Her imagination went into overdrive. Oh, my God, it was so bad they hadn't been able to break the news over the phone.

'What's happened to Sam? You can tell me,' she added, an icy calm settling over her as she prepared herself to hear the worst.

Roman's dark eyes scanned her distressed features; the only trace of colour in her face was supplied by her jewel-bright eyes. He appeared about to say something and then changed his mind.

'Just tell me,' she begged. Imagining was so bad, could the reality be worse?

'Let me in.'

'Of course, of course,' she cried, fumbling with the door

chain, her hands trembling. 'Have they taken him to the hospital?' She pushed her fingers into her hair, dislodging one of her hair grips; a section of hair slithered free, falling across her cheek as she flung the door wide and stepped aside for him to enter.

Think, Scarlet, think… 'Now let me think…' she said out loud as she tried to organise her thoughts and keep panic at arm's length. 'Yes, get dressed.' She flashed him a white-faced but encouraging smile. 'It won't take me a minute to get dressed,' she promised, turning to suit her words to action.

Roman closed the front door. 'I don't know who the Bradleys are.'

Halfway to the bedroom door, Scarlet stopped. *'What?'*

'I don't know the Bradleys and, as far as I am aware, Sam is not in hospital.'

Her marble-pale brow creased. 'But you said…'

'No, actually, I didn't, you said.'

She started shaking in reaction as a massive wave of relief hit her. Impetuously she wrapped her arms around him and hugged hard. 'Thank God!' she breathed fervently.

Roman looked at the heart-shaped face complete with misty eyes and trusting sunny smile tilted up to him and felt his focus slipping. He'd come here to uncover some truths, not fantasise about a sexy mouth and what he'd like to do with it.

It wasn't until she encountered his broodingly black and icy cold mesmeric eyes that Scarlet recalled with a rush of scalding embarrassment that she wasn't dealing with someone into spontaneous hugs. Feeling a total idiot, she unpeeled herself from him and stepped away with a self-conscious grimace and a murmur of, 'Sorry.'

She tucked her hands behind her back and resisted the self-indulgent impulse to smooth down the non-existent creases in his jacket, recognizing that the impulse to touch his lithe body no longer had anything to do with spontaneity and a hell of a lot to do with sexual curiosity. It was deeply mortifying to have to acknowledge she had enjoyed the contact with a very well-developed male physique.

She felt she had to offer some sort of explanation for her strange behaviour.

'I know he's perfectly safe with the Bradleys, but when I saw you I thought the worst...' She released a small self-derisive chuckle. 'But I expect you've already gathered that much.'

Her brow wrinkled as an inconsistency she had been too panic stricken to notice earlier struck her.

'Why didn't you say straight off that you didn't know the Bradleys?'

It wasn't as if he could have missed the fact she had been two steps away from hysteria.

'I wanted to talk to you and I wasn't sure you'd let me in.'

Scarlet stared at him. Staggeringly there was no *hint* of apology in his manner. His behaviour was so extraordinary that it took her a while to get her head around what he had done. 'You wanted to come in,' she repeated in a dangerously flat tone as her temper fizzed dramatically into life. 'You wanted to come in.'

Only someone totally callous could act with such calculated cruelty.

'I need to talk to you.'

'Oh, that makes it all right, then!' she said contemptuously.

His classically pure jawline tautened as a dark line appeared across his cheekbones. 'Will you calm yourself, woman?'

'I'm not a woman...well, not your woman, anyhow, and

for that,' she added with incoherent fervour, 'I shall be eternally grateful. *Nothing* makes it all right for you to scare me half to death that way. It was a totally *despicable* thing to do!'

And it also proved her first impressions had been right; he was a man who didn't care about anything but getting what he wanted! If other people got hurt in the process, so what? It didn't matter to Roman.

'You disgust me!' Her voice rose a quivering octave. 'Get out, get out of my home right now!'

'I think you're overreacting just a little here.'

Her eyes flashed pure green fire as she glared up at him. '*Overreacting?* I thought that Sam was—' She broke off, her voice suspended by tears as the nightmare images crowded into her head. 'Maybe I am overreacting,' she conceded huskily. 'But this is only the second time Sam has spent a night away from home and...' She shook her head. 'If you had a child maybe you'd understand.'

His nostrils flared and something she couldn't identify flashed in his eyes. 'I wanted to talk to you.'

From his expression she couldn't imagine he wanted to say anything nice.

'I realise that I should be thanking my lucky stars, but strangely I'm not.' She strode to the door and pulled it open. 'I don't want to talk to you, Mr O'Hagan, and you were right, I wouldn't have let you in.'

Why would she? To allow someone who was broadcasting dangerous and volatile into your home was asking for trouble. Every inch of his powerful frame suggested he was struggling to contain his anger and with limited success.

'If this has something to do with the university you should be speaking to David.'

His dark brows arched. '*University?*' he repeated, his lip

curling. 'You're a nursery nurse. Why would I come here if I wanted to discuss anything involving the university.'

'Frankly, I don't know,' she admitted. 'But it makes about as much sense as anything else I could come up with to explain you being here.'

And it was a lot more feasible than the inspired, but seriously misguided notion that Scarlet was embarrassed to admit she had entertained for a brief mad moment when she had seen him standing there. The one that relied on him having spent the last ten days wrestling with an overpowering attraction for her he could no longer resist.

So it wasn't exactly plausible, but it was a well-known fact that some men liked glasses and flat chests, and if you were going to fantasise you might as well do it properly.

He walked towards her and for a moment Scarlet thought he was going to carry on past her and through the door, but her optimism proved premature. Instead of walking through the door he casually wrenched it from her grasp. It closed with a very decisive click.

'I'm sorry if I alarmed you.' He watched her rub her shoulder and the indentation between his brows deepened. 'Did I hurt you?'

She looked from the closed door to the man—he was alarming her some more and also, much more disturbingly, he was exciting her. 'And that would bother you?' She delivered a brittle laugh. 'Credit me with a little intelligence.' *Even if I've shown precious little of it to date.* 'You obviously get a kick out of bullying women. And you're *not* sorry, so don't say you are,' she hissed furiously.

His eyes narrowed on her belligerent face. 'You make it extremely difficult for a man to be sorry,' he ground out grimly.

'Yes, I know you don't like me, which makes it even more difficult to imagine why you'd want to talk to me or what you'd want to say, and quite frankly I don't want to know!' she lied grandly as she opened the door again. 'Now, if you don't mind, it's late and I'm busy.'

His even teeth flashed white in his dark face as a smile that had nothing whatsoever to do with humour formed on his sensual lips. 'You won't sleep tonight...'

Scarlet froze, her body stiffening as if in anticipation of a blow.

'Curiosity killed the cat and you're going to be wondering what I did it for,' he warned. 'Admit it, you will.'

Scarlet exhaled. She was light-headed with relief and willing to admit almost anything. For a split second she had jumped to the totally irrational conclusion that he possessed some insider knowledge of the dreams that had given her several nights of broken sleep recently.

Dark, erotic dreams.

Angie is always telling me I need to get out more—she's right!

Was it possible that at some subconscious level she was as frustrated as her friend claimed? That could account for the dreams and the fact she hadn't been able to get him out of her head.

'I've told you, I'm busy,' she repeated dismissively.

'Well, you can tell him to clear off.' His fine nostrils quivered in distaste. 'I will not be dismissed.'

He might not know much about bringing up a child, but even he knew that a single mother with a series of boy-friends hardly provided the sort of stable background a child needed—*his* child needed.

She blinked, and tore her eyes from the nerve clenching spasmodically in the hollow of his lean cheek. This con-versation was like walking in halfway through a film after the vital scene when the hero's motivations had been ex-plained.

Roman would be the hero, of course; he had hero written all over him. She, on the other hand, would be one of the character actors, which would suit her—nobody remembered your name and you were always in work.

Fame was not something she craved.

Roman O'Hagan's touch, however, was; you had to face your weaknesses if you were going to overcome them.

'Him who?' she enquired, still without the faintest idea what he was getting at.

He swallowed, the action causing the muscles in his brown throat to visibly ripple, and gave her a look of simmering hostility.

Scarlet heard a door in the hallway outside open and heard the distant murmur of voices.

'Whoever you are so busy with,' he elaborated, totally ignoring the warning hand she raised to her lips.

Scarlet, who didn't want the world to know her business, closed the door. *'Whoever?'*

He shot her an impatient look and strode purposefully towards the bedroom door. Before Scarlet had any clue of his intention or could cry out in protest he yanked it open with such force it thudded loudly against the wall.

'You can't go in there!'

Ignoring her outraged yell, he stepped inside her bedroom. Breathless with anger, she brushed past him. 'What the—?' she began, planting her hands on her hips and glaring at him.

Roman O'Hagan is in my bedroom…talk about a reality-fantasy clash!

When Roman discovered no lover on the bed, but a neat pile of freshly laundered clothes on the bottom of a narrow single bed waiting to be put away, his sneering expression relaxed into bafflement.

'Where is he?'

The fantasy version had not involved him growling at her contemptuously. She pulled back in alarm as her thoughts shifted in the dangerous direction of what he *had* done. It wasn't soon enough to prevent a wave of warm, sexual lethargy working its way through her body.

'Where's who…?' She gave her head a little shake to focus her thoughts.

'The innocent act is quite unnecessary,' he assured her in a cold, clipped voice. 'It's nothing to me who you choose to sleep with.' Even as he said it it struck Roman rather forcibly that his behaviour suggested the exact opposite.

A disinterested observer who didn't know any better might actually have concluded he was the wronged lover. Making a conscious effort, he forced his hands to unclench.

Belatedly Scarlet caught his meaning; her eyes widened. 'You thought…' The low laugh began softly and increased to a full-blooded husky chuckle as the humour of the situation struck her.

She didn't know which was funnier: Roman O'Hagan, the man who had probably slept with more women than she had had hot dinners, having the nerve to get all sniffy because she was entertaining a man, or the idea that she was indulging in an evening of lust!

In these pyjamas too. She looked down at her casual but not sexy attire and released another low gurgle of mirth.

Roman inhaled, his nostrils flaring. 'You think this is funny?'

Scarlet stared at him incredulously. 'Not funny—*hilarious*—!' she corrected, cracking up again.

Bringing up Sam and holding down a full-time job did not exactly leave her with much time or energy for romantic adventures. Dating when you were a single mum was not a simple business and Scarlet had decided it simply wasn't worth the hassle.

As her laughter faded away she weighed the odds; he didn't *seem* drunk, but in view of a dearth of any other possible explanation for his presence, or his bizarre behaviour, she voiced her suspicions out loud.

'Have you been drinking?'

'I have not been drinking.' The denial was issued between clenched teeth.

'Do you mind? Entry to my bedroom is on an invitation-only basis.' She tossed her head and centred her scornful gaze on his devastatingly handsome dark face. 'And you're not invited.'

'I'm devastated.' The derisive look he gave her brought an angry glitter to Scarlet's eyes.

'You would be if you knew what you were missing!' she heard herself jeer.

'If that was an invitation, I'll pass,' he replied, continuing his suspicious visual examination of the room.

'It wasn't.' If he was going to insult her, the least he could do was look at her while he did it.

'You're alone?'

'And this would be your business because?'

He drew an exasperated breath. 'Are you totally incapable of answering a simple question?'

Scarlet shook her head in disbelief. 'I'm not answering any of your questions. Why on earth should I?'

He contemplated her belligerent face for a moment before saying in a placatory manner, 'We can take this into the other room if you prefer.'

Scarlet vented a brittle laugh as she followed him into the living room. '*Wow*, you're all consideration,' she drawled with mock admiration. 'You really have got the most incredible cheek. You barge in here uninvited. You let me think something has happened to Sam and then turn it around and interrogate me!' She gave a weary sigh. 'Will you just go?'

'It's seven-thirty.' His glance rested pointedly on her pyjamas. 'Why are you dressed for bed?'

'Oh, I always wear these when I plan an evening of seduction.'

Her sarcasm brought a dark line of colour to the slashing angle of his incredible cheekbones.

'Then you're alone?'

'I was,' she retorted drily.

He looked around the room, registering the blurred frozen image on the TV screen, the box of chocolates and the untouched glass of wine. His glance reached the box of toys tucked into a corner and he frowned.

'Is...?' He swallowed. 'Where is Sam?'

'Sam is sleeping over at a friend's, the *Bradleys*, which is probably just as well in the circumstances.'

'The circumstances being?'

'Three-year-olds don't react well to being woken up.'

'Ah.' His facial muscles clenched, exaggerating the sharp contours and angles of his face. He really did have bone structure to die for, she thought, despising the weakness that made her incapable of not staring. 'I didn't think.'

'About anything other than what you want? I'd already worked that one out. No doubt it's acting on impulse that makes you such a financial success?'

'I know you're not Sam's mother.'

She waited, her expression attentive but confused, until it occurred to her he was expecting some sort of response. 'Not his birth mother, no,' she agreed. The adoption had made her his legal guardian.

She was cool, he had to give her that. 'You didn't ask me how I knew you weren't his mother?'

She shrugged her shoulders and still betrayed none of the

guilt he had expected her to when confronted. 'I suppose I assumed someone mentioned it in passing. David, maybe?'

'David?'

'The vice-chancellor.'

'You call the vice-chancellor *David*?' His voice was heavy with suspicion.

'He went to school with my uncle, I've known him since I was a little girl so, yes, I do call him David.'

'And he knows Sam isn't your son?'

Scarlet shook her head in total bewilderment. 'It's not like it's a secret. Everyone knows, I suppose.'

He looked at her, his dark brows drawn into a straight line.

'Why? What did you think?'

His eyes were hidden beneath the lustrous sweep of his lashes as he looked across at her, but his attitude suggested he was wary. 'Then who is Sam's birth mother?'

'My sister Abby was Sam's mother.'

CHAPTER EIGHT

COMPREHENSION struck Roman with the force of a tidal wave. Of the scenarios he had imagined—and he had imagined plenty—this one had never occurred to him.

The people he employed on those occasions when he required a background check were both efficient and discreet. He could have had the information she had just provided in literally a matter of hours, maybe less. Instead he had taken a far more tortuous route, and had his DNA compared with the hair sample he had taken from the child.

At the time he had told himself that the fewer people who knew what he was doing, the less chance there was of the story leaking out. He'd wanted to know for certain he didn't have a son without having to involve a whole string of people. Now he was forced to consider the possibility that the *truth* had only been part of what he had wanted—he had wanted someone to blame.

Not just someone.

The stranger who was bringing up his child without his knowledge had to be guilty of *something*—! He had wanted to confront Scarlet, to make this personal—*it was personal*!

His stillness was scary, she thought. It was actually a relief when his shoulders lifted and a soundless sigh shuddered through his powerful frame.

'Was…?'

Scarlet looked away and with a gesture that was intensely weary rubbed the bridge of her nose; the glasses were gone but the habit remained. She blinked hard to clear her blurry vision as tears filled her eyes.

Damn—! She really didn't want to cry in front of him.

It wasn't as if she couldn't talk about Abby without getting upset; she made a point of talking about her with Sam, who had a photo of his mother in his room.

'Here, have this,' he said brusquely.

She released a wry laugh as she automatically took the glass he handed her. 'I was wondering if you ever say please?' she explained in reply to his questioning look.

A puzzled frown developed on her smooth brow as their glances meshed. 'Why are you here, Roman?'

'Your sister is dead?'

Scarlet nodded, and took a swallow of the wine.

'I'm sorry.'

'There's no need to be; you didn't know her.'

She caught a flicker of something in his expression that she couldn't put a name to, but it wasn't there when he walked back from the Welsh dresser with a clean mug in his hand. He proceeded to slosh some wine into it.

'It's cheap supermarket plonk.'

He looked at her, his piercing regard intense. He drew a deep breath and his hands coiled at his sides. 'You'd better sit down,' he said abruptly.

'People say that when they're about to tell you something you won't like hearing.'

He didn't deny it.

Scarlet moved a cushion and sat down on the sofa. Her stomach was churning with apprehension.

'You'd better sit down yourself,' she said with an irritable frown. 'You look terrible,' she added, observing the grey tinge to his olive-toned skin and the definite tautness in the lines around his mouth and eyes.

Her frown deepened.

He still looked pretty damned marvellous.

She watched as he did what she suggested, folding his

long, lean frame into a bucket chair beside the TV. It was laughably inadequate for his length and he ought to have looked silly but he performed the action with his usual inimitable grace. Scarlet loved to watch him move; clearly she was losing her mind.

'It upsets you to talk about your sister?'

Scarlet didn't hear him at first, because she was covetously watching him, imagining the shift of tight, hard muscles in his shoulders as he moved. He had unzipped his jacket and underneath he wore a simple white designer tee shirt. It was fitted enough to suggest the strongly defined musculature of his upper body, a strong body.

Her eyes were drawn to the faint shadow of body hair visible through the fine fabric and she had absolutely no control over the flutter low in her belly. An image of dark, smooth skin came into her head and she swallowed convulsively. It was like walking into a solid wall; the wave of paralysing longing that hit her made her head spin.

The situation called for her to face some facts she'd been ignoring. Since their first meeting she hadn't been able to get Roman out of her thoughts. At first she had tried to resist, but then she had told herself that indulging in the fantasies could do no harm. That had been a mistake, one which she was suffering for now.

She was obsessed!

Given full rein her fantasies had multiplied and got out of control. Now she couldn't look at him without her mind being filled by all kinds of erotic images her feverish imagination had conjured.

Well, it was about time she got her subconscious under control. She took a deep breath. They were talking about Abby, which made her preoccupation with sex all the more shameful.

'*Upset?* Not really, it just hits you sometimes…I miss

her,' she admitted simply. Abby wouldn't have thought her sexual fantasies shameful. If her sister had been here she would no doubt have advised her to go for it, she thought with a smile.

'Was there an illness…or an accident—?' There was nothing in his tone or attitude that she could put her finger on, but the question did not come over as a casual enquiry. 'You don't want to talk about it?' he asked.

'Not especially, but it would seem you do.' She picked up the cushion and hugged it tightly to her body, rocking a little as she pulled her knees up to her chest. 'Why is that? Did you know Abby?' Her eyes widened as she shot him a questioning look.

'I can't recall meeting an Abby Smith.'

'Oh, but Abby didn't use Smith. She said I looked like a Smith but she didn't—she was right,' she reflected, running a hand over the brown hair that Abby had always advised her to bleach. *Blondes darling, definitely have more fun!*

'She was an actress?'

Scarlet shook her head. 'She intended to be one day, but she was a model—Abby Deverell. She was quite successful. Well, actually, she was *very* successful.'

'Your sister was Abby Deverell?'

Scarlet could see him trying to find some similarity in her own features. It would be a fruitless search; Abby had been beautiful.

'People always do that, but we're not alike.'

God, the woman had had his child and he couldn't even recall her face clearly. What sort of man did that make him?

'So you did meet her?' Scarlet wondered why she hadn't considered the possibility earlier. It would certainly explain his brooding expression, she thought, slanting a surreptitious glance at his strong profile.

'Yes, I did meet her,' he returned abruptly.

Now he had a name and face…or he *should* have a face. The woman had fronted a very high-profile publicity campaign just a few years ago. You hadn't been able to walk down the street, open a magazine or switch on a television without seeing her face.

So why, when he tried now to visualise those photogenic features, was he only able to see the face of her younger sister?

Scarlet didn't register the abruptness of his reply. 'She was very lovely, wasn't she?'

He responded to her wistful appeal with an affirmative nod, not because he remembered, to his shame he didn't, but because it was obviously what she wanted to hear. 'Yes, she was.'

He had spent one night at her flat. He knew the date; it should have been his first wedding anniversary. He had woken up fully dressed on her sofa with a raging headache; she had said she had let him sleep it off.

'Did you know her well?'

His silence lasted a long time—a noticeably long time.

Scarlet drew a sharp breath as she suddenly went icy cold all over, convinced that he was about to admit they had been lovers.

'No, I didn't know her well.'

The sigh of relief that whistled through her clenched teeth was silent. If he had been Abby's lover, why would it have made a difference…? What was there for it to make a difference to? It wasn't as if there was, or ever would be, anything between her and Roman.

'So Sam knows you're not his real mother?'

'Of course. You shouldn't lie to children.'

'A very sound principle,' he approved smoothly. 'And when Sam's older and he asks about his parents you'll be able to tell him…?'

Unwittingly, she thought, he had touched upon a subject that had concerned her for some time. Sam would ask about his father, it was inevitable, but what was she supposed to tell him? The truth? Or was she to invent a hero that a boy could be proud of? It was a minefield.

'Sam's very young to understand yet.'

'It's surprising how much children understand.'

'I'll be able to tell him that his mummy loved him very much.'

'Has she been gone long?'

'Abby learnt she had leukaemia when she was first pregnant with Sam,' Scarlet recalled quietly. 'The doctors wanted her to have a termination and start treatment straight away. They warned her that not to do so would seriously reduce her chances of survival.'

Their eyes locked. The shock in his was visible, as was the compassion; the latter made her throat ache, and she swallowed.

'And they were right?'

'Yes,' she admitted softly.

'She ignored them?' he probed gently.

Scarlet nodded.

He released his breath in a long fractured hiss. 'What a decision to be forced to make.' And make alone.

'I don't think it actually was that hard for Abby. I don't think a termination was ever an option for her.'

'How long after?'

'Sam was three months old when she died; most of that three months she spent in hospital,' she imparted quietly.

Roman caught his breath. 'My God.' His brow furrowed. 'She *knew* that having her baby would kill her?'

Anger flared in Scarlet's dark-fringed hazel eyes. 'No, *leukaemia* killed her.'

She was painfully aware that it was possible for a careless

word to plant an idea in a child's head, and she determined that Sam wouldn't grow up burdened with the guilt of his mother's death.

'And I'd be grateful if you didn't say that again—*ever.*'

He inclined his head towards her. 'Of course, I'm sorry.'

Rather taken aback by his apparent sincerity, she accepted it with a grudging but wary nod.

'And you have brought her baby up?' She gave a tiny nod of assent, and his hand came up to his mouth before moving roughly along the angle of his hard, angular jaw.

The bare facts were he had got a woman pregnant and for whatever reason she had not felt able to tell him. That woman had died and if her premature death could not be directly attributed to the birth of his son it had definitely been a contributing factor.

It didn't matter what sort of spin you put on those facts, he did not emerge from the telling of this story looking good. If there was any victim here he wasn't it...not that there was any shortage of victims in this story.

'That must have been hard.' He winced inwardly at the triteness of his words.

'I was terrified of the responsibility at first,' Scarlet admitted. She gave a small laugh. 'I still am sometimes...' Her eyes lifted. 'Does that sound terrible to you?'

As soon as she'd asked the question Scarlet hated the fact she sounded as though she was asking for his approval.

He didn't reply, just continued to look at her with an odd intensity.

'It doesn't sound terrible at all,' he said finally. 'So don't beat yourself up.'

She blinked to clear her blurry vision. It was perverse that after surviving his insults she should be brought to the brink of emotional tears by his kindness.

'Wasn't there someone else you could have shared the responsibility with?'

Scarlet sniffed and dabbed her finger to a spot of moisture in the corner of her eye. 'There was just Abby and me, and our gran who died last year. She was pretty frail.'

He searched her open features, and realised that not only was she *not* canvassing the sympathy vote, she didn't have the faintest idea how poignant her statement sounded.

Dealing with people who normally had an agenda—people who wanted something from him—Roman found himself uniquely ill equipped when it came to a dialogue with someone who said what they meant. Someone who furthermore would have thrown anything he offered back in his face.

'There were no other relatives who could help?'

'No. My uncle and aunty are not really *children* people.'

'But surely they were better situated than you to bring up a baby?'

'Financially maybe, but it's not about money, is it?' she said, taking his agreement on something so fundamental as granted. 'They didn't have a family of their own out of choice,' she went on to explain.

'And I can't imagine them welcoming *anything* which stopped them jumping in the car and driving down to the South of France when they felt like it.' Her nose wrinkled as she looked reflectively at him and her head tilted a little to one side. 'They're a bit like you, really. They do whatever they like without having to consider anyone else…though you're younger, obviously.'

'But equally selfish,' he suggested drily.

'They love one another, so you can't call them *totally* self-obsessed and narcissistic,' she pointed out tolerantly.

'Unlike me.'

Scarlet flushed under his ironic gaze. 'I didn't say that,' she protested.

'You didn't need to. You can't imagine me with children?'

Scarlet frowned at the inflection in his voice. 'You're Italian Irish, aren't you?' She gave an offhand shrug. 'With that background I expect you'll have a big family one day, when you're ready.'

In her head she could see children with Roman's dark eyes and warm colouring running around…children just like Sam.

'Or when I've grown up?'

'I wasn't going to say that. I'm a realist.'

Roman grinned. 'You have a smart mouth.' Lush, lovely and incredibly kissable—!

The fact his dark, devastatingly gorgeous eyes were glued to her lips, and that he was no longer grinning, made Scarlet very nervous.

'I wouldn't worry—a lot of men never grow up. You're obviously enjoying playing the field.' And, my, did he show dedication. She tried to make up for her lack of judgement in speaking her mind with a brittle, blindingly insincere smile.

'But I expect one day you'll get bored with it, and when you meet someone…' Someone beautiful and talented to give him those golden babies.

'You don't sound very convinced.'

'You're right, I've always had my doubts about reformed rakes,' she confided. Her glance skimmed the strong, arrogant lines in his hard-boned features. And if anyone could accurately be described as a rake, it was him.

'Rakes?'

Scarlet, who was warming to one of her favourite themes,

nodded, barely registering the stunned expression on his handsome face.

'I know a lot of women think that with the love of a good woman, the good woman being them,' she qualified drily, 'even the most committed playboy will metamorphose overnight into a faithful husband.' She shook her head and gave an incredulous laugh at the ability of her own sex to fool themselves.

'But you don't share this view?'

'Look at me! Do I look like a hopeless romantic?' she demanded.

He took her reckless offer and there was an extremely uncomfortable interval while he considered the question and her face. The defiant angle of Scarlet's chin increased in direct proportion to the rapid thud of her racing heart.

Finally he delivered his judgement.

'I don't have one hell of a lot of hands-on experience with hopeless romantics but, yes, I'd say you do.'

His dry comment drew Scarlet's eyes involuntarily to the hands he referred to. His long, tapering fingers curled lightly over the arms of the chair; they were square-tipped, suggesting sensitivity and strength. Something low in her belly tightened as she looked at them and imagined them moving over softer, paler flesh.

Colour significantly heightened, she dragged her eyes clear. 'Well, I'm not, and,' she informed him with feeling, '*I'm glad.* I don't see how falling in love can fundamentally change a person's character. Call me a cynic, but, the way I see it, once a faithless love rat always a—' She broke off, her eyes widening. 'Not that I'm calling you a faithless...'

His eyebrows lifted. '*No?* If you say so.' His mobile lips formed a cynical smile as he shrugged.

It was pretty damned hard to refute her observations when

you had fathered a child on a one-night stand and didn't discover it until almost four years later.

In most people's book that qualified as love-rattish behaviour. The fact it had been an accident did not make him any the less an irresponsible bastard.

'Marriage means different things to different people. Some people are more…flexible…' she finished awkwardly.

'I take it "flexible" is a euphemism for sleeping around.'

Scarlet gave an uncomfortable shrug and wondered how on earth she had got onto this subject. 'I guess so.'

His nostrils flared as he looked at her. The expression of chilling hauteur on his dark patrician features sent a ripple down her spine.

'I don't think I'd be at all flexible at the idea of my wife sleeping with anyone else. I happen to consider fidelity an essential component of marriage.'

'Well, it just goes to show you never can judge by appearances,' she responded cheerily. 'Look at me—' she suggested.

When he did her lashes swept down in a protective gesture. 'I used to be the most important thing in my life. I had it all, the job, the flat, the car—'

'And you don't regret giving it up?'

'Not for one second. I earn peanuts by comparison now,' she admitted. 'Not that I ever earned the *serious* money Abby did, but on the plus side nobody treats *me* like I'm a piece of meat, and I don't have to live on lettuce leaves and cigarettes to stay stick-thin! Mostly people appreciate what I'm doing.' *Present company excluded.*

'So your sister left you well provided for?' At least she hadn't spent the last four years leading a hand-to-mouth existence in order to give his son a decent life.

His relief turned out to be premature.

'Abby earned, but she liked to spend too. But, yes, she

had put some money aside for Sam. It will pay for his education and there'll be a little bit left over for a nest egg for him.'

'So you have lived off what?'

'I live within my means, and I don't worry if I'm not wearing this year's designs. I mean, money isn't everything, is it?' A sudden bubble of laughter sprang to her lips. 'Actually, I suppose it is to you.'

'Sure, I sold my soul for a good return on my investments years ago,' he drawled.

'I wasn't being offensive...well, not intentionally, anyhow,' she added with a crooked smile. His rigid expression didn't thaw. 'It was a joke.'

His dark eyes swept across her face. 'Was it?'

'Yes!' she responded, exasperated that he seemed intent on over-dramatising a simple comment. 'You're rich, I'm not, so what I've never had I'm not going to miss, am I?' she pointed out simply.

'Do you plan to go back to your old job?'

'Who knows what the future holds? But it would be good in the immediate future if you revealed a reason for you being here.'

'I'm getting there.'

The ironic twist of his lips troubled her. If she was going to be honest, Roman worried her full stop.

'Where does Sam's father come into all this?' he said casually.

'There isn't one.'

He raised an ironic brow.

'Well, there is, but he isn't in the picture. And not just that one,' she added as he picked up a framed photograph taken of Sam on his first birthday.

This was the point when people who possessed the basics of social skills dropped the subject.

'Have you ever tried to contact him?'

Scarlet shook her head. 'I couldn't if I wanted to.'

'Why's that?'

'I don't know who he is.'

'Surely your sister told you. I'm assuming she knew the seriousness of her condition.'

'Oh, yes, she knew,' Scarlet confirmed bleakly. 'I did ask Abby, I was concerned—' She broke off with a self-conscious grimace. 'She said getting pregnant was her responsibility.'

'Even if it was a one-night stand, that doesn't make it any less the man's responsibility.'

Scarlet shot him a look bristling with suspicion. 'I didn't say it was a one-night stand.'

'Didn't you?' He sounded genuinely surprised. 'Are you sure?'

'Totally.'

'I must have assumed.'

CHAPTER NINE

SCARLET studied Roman with suspicious eyes, bristling at the implied criticism. 'Abby had lots of boyfriends, but she didn't sleep around,' she told him fiercely.

What she didn't tell him, what she had never told anyone, was how Abby, heavily drugged in the final painful stages of her illness, had confessed when pressed for the identity of the father that it hadn't been an accident, that in fact she had planned to get pregnant. That she had wanted a baby and had chosen a father, she just hadn't included him in the plan.

'What if he finds out?' Scarlet asked.

'The only way he'll find out is if someone told him and you don't know who he is.'

'But when he hears you've had a baby, won't it be bound to cross his mind?'

'I doubt if he'll hear, but I thought of that. I told him nothing happened.'

'He was there, Abby.'

'He'd already had several drinks by the time we got back to my place,' Abby recalled, displaying none of her younger sister's awkwardness when it came to discussing the intimate details. 'He actually got quite maudlin and sentimental; I don't think he even noticed I'd added Scotch to his coffee,' she ended on a self-congratulatory note.

Scarlet couldn't believe what she was hearing. 'You got him drunk!'

'But not incapable. Please don't look at me like that, Scarlet, it's not like I raped the man. He enjoyed himself, and I got the impression he had something he wanted to forget. That was why he'd been drinking in the first place...something to do with it being the anniversary of something, I think.'

'But he wasn't a stranger.'

'I didn't want just *anybody* to be my baby's father,' Abby reproached indignantly. 'I did my research beforehand.'

'How long had you been planning to do this, Abby?'

'Let's just say this wasn't an impulse. I finally accepted I was never going to meet Mr Right and settle down. My biological clock was ticking away. I thought about artificial insemination but you don't really get to choose the father that way, and I got pregnant straight off, the first time, which is just as well, because I doubt if...so it must have been meant to be, don't you think, Scarlet?' she asked wistfully.

Scarlet felt unable under the circumstances to tell her sister what she actually thought and so moderated her views. 'You don't think it might be a good idea to tell the father?'

'God, no, a baby would scare the pants off him and I had a hard enough time getting them off the first time. Sorry, Scarlet, I don't mean to embarrass you with the gruesome details.'

'But a baby needs a father.'

'You're thinking about inherited weaknesses...'

'Not specifically,' Scarlet said weakly.

'No worries there, the guy is about as genetically perfect as is possible. When I drew up my list—'

'You had a *list*?'

'Well, it seemed logical, and he was streets ahead of the rest,' Abby revealed, apparently oblivious that she was saying anything out of the ordinary. 'His family on both sides all seem to be disgustingly healthy and live until a ripe old age.'

'You seem to have thought of everything,' Scarlet responded weakly.

'You don't approve, do you, Scarlet? I knew you wouldn't but I was desperate. You have no idea how badly I wanted this baby.'

Scarlet tried to hide how desperately shocked she was when her weak and frail sister went on to describe how she had ruthlessly engineered the seduction to coincide with her fertile period and tampered with the condom! How could you condemn someone who was clinging to life? The guilt of being healthy and strong when someone she loved was dying by inches silenced any protest she might have made.

Abby's spontaneous, warm nature was part of what made her the lovable person she was. But being spontaneous and warm was one thing—what Abby had done was something else! As far as Scarlet was concerned, having a baby was the ultimate expression of love. There had seemed precious little love in the event that Abby described.

'What would you do if the father suddenly appeared?'

The sound of his voice brought Scarlet back to the present.

She blinked her eyes, focusing on Roman's lean, watchful features. Logically danger ought to repel any right-thinking person, but, while there was something distinctly wolf-like in his lean, hungry aspect, it was that same danger that exerted a strange, almost hypnotic attraction.

'I asked what you would do if Sam's father reappeared.'

'Sam's father?'

As always when she thought about the mystery man her sister had callously tricked she was engulfed by a wave of crushing guilt.

There had been a time when she had actually considered trying to discover who he was, but, short of putting an ad in the personal columns, when it came down to it she didn't

The Harlequin Reader Service — Here's how it works:

GET FREE BOOKS and FREE GIFTS
WHEN YOU PLAY THE...

Just scratch off the silver box with a coin. Then check below to see the gifts you get!

SLOT MACHINE GAME!

YES! I have scratched off the silver box. Please send me the 2 free Harlequin Presents® books and 2 free gifts (gifts are worth about $10) for which I qualify. I understand I am under no obligation to purchase any books, as explained on the back of this card.

306 HDL ESJT   **106 HDL ESM5**

FIRST NAME   LAST NAME

ADDRESS

APT.#   CITY

STATE/PROV.   ZIP/POSTAL CODE

7	7	7	**Worth TWO FREE BOOKS plus 2 BONUS Mystery Gifts!**
🍒	🍒	🍒	**Worth TWO FREE BOOKS!**
♣	♣	♣	**Worth ONE FREE BOOK!**
🔔	🔔	🍒	**TRY AGAIN!**

www.eHarlequin.com

(H-P-07/08)

Offer limited to one per household and not valid to current subscribers of Harlequin Presents® books.

Your Privacy - Harlequin Books is committed to protecting your privacy. Our Privacy Policy is available online at www.eHarlequin.com or upon request from the Reader Service. From time to time we make our lists of customers available to reputable third parties who may have a product or service of interest to you. If you would prefer us not to share your name and address, please check here ☐.

have the faintest idea how to go about identifying him. And even if she did, would he thank her? According to Abby he was a man who, given the choice, would not have wanted to know—in fact a man who would have denied paternity.

In the circumstances it was academic. No, her energies were better concentrated on taking care of his son. The son he didn't know he had.

'That's not going to happen,' she told him quietly. There was nothing in his face to explain his motivation in pursuit of the subject.

'But the idea alarms you?'

Her eyes skimmed his face; she was unwilling to allow herself to become entrapped by his dark, mesmeric eyes. 'I didn't say that,' she countered quickly.

'You didn't need to—you have a very expressive face.'

Scarlet was immediately conscious of every facial muscle she possessed as she tried to produce a neutral expression. 'Trust me...I don't want to be rude, but none of this is actually any of your business.'

'It's Sam's father's business,' he replied after a taut silence.

'Sam's father is not going to materialise,' she promised him.

'But if he did...' Roman persisted. 'What would you do if he wanted to be part of Sam's life?'

It seemed much more likely that he would resent the child that he had been tricked into fathering, and who could blame him? Not Scarlet. Non-consensual fatherhood pretty much fitted what had been done to him.

'That's really not at all likely.' His unblinking, glittering scrutiny was making her increasingly nervous.

'Hypothetically,' he inserted smoothly.

'*Hypothetically* I'd work something out for Sam's sake, but this isn't something that's going to happen.'

'You sound very sure.'

'I am.'

'How can you be?'

'Abby didn't tell him,' she revealed abruptly.

'She knew who he was, then?'

Scarlet let out a furious gasp and bounced to her feet. The shocking sound of her hand connecting with his face resounded around the room.

She looked from her extended hand to the mark on his lean cheek. The thin white scar stood out lividly against the reddened skin. Her chest heaved with emotion as her eyes met his.

'You pack quite a punch.'

She had started shaking in reaction. 'I'm sorry.' She was deeply ashamed of the loss of control that had made her resort to violence. 'But you deserved it,' she added with a glare that dared him to disagree with her.

Roman levered himself from the chair in a fluid elegant motion. He looked down at her from his superior vantage point.

'Maybe I do.'

Scarlet looked up at him warily through the protective dark mesh of her lashes. This was not the reaction she had expected.

'What do you mean?'

'You recall when my mother collapsed at the opening ceremony?'

Scarlet nodded. 'Of course I do.' She had not the faintest idea where this was going and, call her a coward, but she didn't actually want to know.

'It was because she saw someone she recognised.'

She still didn't have an inkling. Her smooth brow pleated in a perplexed, wary frown. 'Who did she recognise?'

'She saw Sam.'

An image of Sam, the posy of wilting flowers clutched in his hot, sticky hands, flashed into her head. 'I don't understand.'

He scanned her face for a moment, his own expression broodingly sombre. 'I know you don't. Sam looks exactly the way I did when I was his age. That's what spooked my mother.'

Scarlet was confused but not suspicious, which later on struck her as ironic in the extreme. 'Because Sam looks like you?' Perhaps it was the colouring. Sam did have that Mediterranean glow and the long lashes and, now that she thought about it, at certain angles…

'Because Sam is my son.'

Scarlet was dramatically unprepared for his revelation, which, when at a later date she went over the conversation that had led to it, made her blind, deaf and very stupid!

She was not conscious then or later of his tensing and moving closer in readiness to catch her as the colour seeped rapidly from her skin, leaving it marble-pale.

'For God's sake, sit down.'

Quivering with denial, she kept to her feet. 'You and Abby?' She shook her head, feeling sick. 'You slept with Abby?' she wailed.

Now why did that make her feel as though she were the tragic victim of some betrayal? The victim here was Roman. What he must have felt like discovering he had a son this way she couldn't even imagine! Her well-developed sense of empathy sprang into life, as did her guilt.

'*Apparently.*'

Considering his admission, he was surprised when she didn't deliver the obvious comeback. To father a child accidentally was one thing, to forget about it took the crime to another level.

'She said not, but facts say otherwise,' he related grimly.

'That's ridiculous, you can't be!' she cried shrilly. 'She said he...*you*—' she corrected herself.

'She said what about me?'

Scarlet gave her head a tiny shake; she was having second thoughts about her candour. This was one occasion when the truth was not going to help.

'I don't recall exactly.'

'I'll settle for inexact.'

Scarlet gave an exasperated sigh; he wasn't going to leave well alone. She studied his profile. The light fell from behind, highlighting all the hard angles and intriguing hollows of his face.

'She said the father would have run a million miles if he'd known about the baby.'

Roman flinched.

'You're not running.'

'That's because she was wrong,' he breathed grimly. '*Very* wrong.'

Tears formed in Scarlet's eyes. 'Why are you saying this?' she choked, turning her hands palm upwards towards him in an unconscious gesture of appeal. 'What's the point?'

'*Point?*' he repeated, looking at her as though she were mad. 'I have a son.'

'You don't want Sam. You *can't*. Abby isn't here to punish so leave us alone.' Fighting the rising level of panic that made it hard for her to think, she covered her face with her forearm and swallowed a sob.

'Why would I want to punish the mother of my child? It was my fault.'

Scarlet, who could hear the self-recrimination in his voice, felt so guilty she could hardly look at him. Whatever else Roman was, he was clearly *not* the moral-free zone that Abby had taken him for.

'I'm hardly unable to support a son. Presumably she

thought I'd contest paternity and couldn't stomach the idea of the mud-slinging.' He raked a hand through his dark, sleek hair and fixed Scarlet with an interrogative stare.

She was too stunned by his reading of her late sister's motives that all she could do was stare at him. He appeared to take her silence as confirmation of his explanation.

Why couldn't he be the shallow, selfish playboy Abby had taken him for instead of the owner of a very well-developed set of moral principles? She didn't want to empathise with him, not when he might try and snatch Sam away from her.

She was her nephew's legal guardian but where would she stand legally if he chose to contest her guardianship?

Scarlet was terrified by the thought of a custody battle. Better to let him carry on thinking the pregnancy had been accidental than allow that to happen. Why tell him the truth when there was nothing to be gained except blackening her sister's name?

'Your sister may have been misguided in going it alone.' This admission seemed to be as close as he was going to get to criticising Abby. 'But you've got to admire her. Most women finding themselves in that situation would have wanted to make me pay.'

'Abby didn't want your money.' Her head lifted and there was a flicker of hope in her eyes. 'Couldn't you just pretend you didn't know?' she suggested with a sniff as she wiped the moisture from her face. 'I'm sure it would be a lot more comfortable for you and I wouldn't say anything to anyone.' She dabbed a stray tear from her cheek with the back of her hand.

'You expect me to pretend I don't have a son?' he grated. *'Dio!'* he ejaculated rawly. 'What sort of man do you think I am?' he demanded, every inch of his powerful frame vibrating at the affront.

Scarlet shook her head in a bemused fashion, unable even at this critical moment not to appreciate just how magnificent in a lean, mean way he looked when he was mad. When he lost his temper he was very much the Mediterranean male, all passion and fire.

'This is still just speculation. You can't prove it. Just because you slept with Abby doesn't mean you're Sam's father.' She clung stubbornly to the hope that this might still turn out to be a terrible misunderstanding.

'But DNA sampling does. I wouldn't have come to you unless I was sure. I took a hair sample, Scarlet, the day at the nursery, and had it analysed.'

She sank back into her chair, the fight draining out of her. 'Oh, my God!' she whispered, knowing what was coming.

CHAPTER TEN

'THERE is no doubt about it. Sam is my son, there's no question.'

Scarlet shook her head and, hand pressed to her mouth, ran towards the bathroom. 'Excuse me!' she gulped, polite to the end, and then she bolted.

She was in too much of a hurry to close the door behind her and Roman heard the sound of her painful retching. It was several minutes later when she returned, paler and graver, but her composure was obviously paper-thin.

'If you think you can take him off me... I know you've got money.'

Roman could almost see the sinister plan he hadn't made to snatch the child away from her forming in her mind.

'Don't be melodramatic.'

'I'll run away and you'll never find us,' she threatened wildly. *Now that makes me sound like stable, responsible parent material.*

'I can see you've cast me in the role of evil villain to your wilting heroine.'

'I've never wilted in my life.'

'I'm glad to hear it. I can't abide a clingy female.' He reached out and took her shoulders. When there was no resistance he drew her gently towards him. 'I'm not going to take Sam off you. I just want to be part of his life.'

And he had a right to be part of his life, but what sort of upheaval would that cause for Sam, not to mention herself. Scarlet didn't feel capable of working out the implications of this; she no longer knew which way was up, let alone what was a lie or the truth!

Scarlet, totally focused on convincing him she wasn't going to let him take Sam, didn't even feel the pain as her neatly trimmed nails gouged into the soft flesh of her palms.

'Sam's life is with me,' she asserted loudly.

Roman inhaled sharply and his hands fell from her shoulders. 'He is my son. This will be much easier, Scarlet, if we work together. If we're friends.'

'*Friends?* Even if none of this had happened we could never be friends,' she asserted hotly.

On this at least Scarlet could be totally confident. How could you be friends with someone whose way of life was a total anathema to you, someone with whom you didn't have anything in common and someone who, furthermore, made your hormones act in an indiscriminate and mortifying manner?

Irritation showed in his deep-set shadowed eyes as he heard her out.

'A little bit of give and take here—would it be too much to ask?' he wondered, dragging his hand wearily through his already disordered hair.

Scarlet experienced an irrational urge to smooth down those disordered locks. 'Me give Sam, and you take him! Sam is three—where were you when he had chicken pox? Were you there to hold his hand when they stitched up his head when he fell off his bike?'

'I didn't know I had a son.'

So far he'd only thought about the changes having a son was going to make to his life. For the first time he paused to consider the things he had already missed out on, things he would never see, like the child's first steps. He was unprepared for the feeling of profound loss.

'And now you do, so what? Are you going to change

your entire lifestyle?' *I don't think so.* 'It's obvious you haven't thought this through. What do you plan to do—fit Sam into your schedule between making your next million or wooing your next supermodel? You can't walk in here and demand to be part of Sam's life.'

'I'm not demanding anything.'

'That's not the way it looks from where I'm standing.'

'There are things I can give Sam.'

'Money—?' she suggested scornfully.

'Financial security, certainly,' he agreed levelly.

'Well, that was predictable. I wondered when the pound sign would start flashing.' She raised an eyebrow and produced a disdainful sniff. 'Well, you can put your chequebook away; we don't want your money,' she completed contemptuously.

There was a short simmering silence. Looking down his patrician nose at her, he drew himself up to his full height. 'Does it give you a nice sense of moral superiority to be able to throw my money back in my face?'

'You can't buy me,' she gritted defiantly.

'I'm not trying to, neither am I trying to score points. I'm trying to consider my son's best interests.'

'So am I!' she rebutted uneasily, aware that her responses were becoming increasingly childish.

'*Are you?* I'm a wealthy man—do you expect me to leave my son nothing?'

'Well…I…I hadn't thought…'

'Sam will be the main beneficiary as soon as my solicitor has drafted my new will,' he told her quietly.

She might want to reject his money, but Sam was his son. 'You want to make him a beneficiary. I suppose that's reasonable,' she admitted.

'I want to make him *the* beneficiary.'

'Oh!'

'There is no one else. Obviously I'll reimburse you for any—'

'I don't want reimbursing. Don't you understand? I don't want anything from you! I think you're—'

'Shall we leave your feelings towards me to one side for a moment?'

Scarlet deeply resented him taking upon himself the role of impartial reason. 'Feelings for you!' she parroted. 'I don't have any feelings for you one way or the other.'

'I'm perfectly aware I hardly come out of this looking good.' You couldn't defend the indefensible. 'But it takes two and your sister denied me the right of knowing my son.'

'You leave Abby alone!' Scarlet yelled. 'I'd say she knew what she was doing.'

'So you think she made the right decision?'

'Too right I do,' Scarlet responded with hardly a qualm about lying through her teeth. 'A spoilt, commitment-shy playboy is hardly most people's idea of father material.'

A muscle in his lean cheek clenched more obviously with each successive insult she flung at him. Scarlet knew she was being wildly unfair, but hitting back at him was a knee-jerk reaction she had no control over.

His face went blank, his eyes flat and cold as they scanned her face.

'This isn't a situation of my making, but I'm going to do the right thing whether you like it or not. You're going to have to work with me on this, Scarlet.'

He was obviously very comfortable with issuing ultimatums, but Scarlet was not at all comfortable about meekly acquiescing!

When he got bossy her automatic response was to do the opposite of what he said and, if at all possible, in a manner that would dent his air of ineffable superiority.

'And if I don't?' People must have been doing what he said all his life to make him so damned sure of himself.

His shoulders lifted expressively as his eyes moved briefly across her faintly flushed face. 'We both want what is best for Sam, so you will.'

Scarlet felt a shiver trace its icy path up her spine. The silky words held an unmistakable threat and, even though he never deliberately used his undoubted physical presence to intimidate, it was hard not to be daunted by his tenacity.

'If you wanted what was best for Sam you'd go out that door and forget we exist,' she charged in a furious hiss.

'It's not going to happen.' His tone was not without sympathy, but there was no room for negotiation in his manner. The expression on his lean face was totally implacable. 'I have a son, Sam has a father and a family who will all want to know him. Are you going to deprive him of that?'

She blinked, an expression of confusion spreading across her face. How often had she wished that she could offer Sam a large, loving family? 'Do your family know about Sam?'

'My mother doesn't need the results of a DNA test; she was totally confident from that first moment she saw him that Sam is my son. She's completely over the moon about having a grandchild. I would imagine the champagne is even now on ice.'

'And will she have told your father?' Despite herself, Scarlet found herself interested by his colourful background.

Roman shook his head.

She got the impression he didn't want to discuss his father. It was only a feeling, his cloaked expression was unrevealing, but it was enough to make her speculate.

'But he's not going to be happy about having a grandchild?'

'My father is an inflexible and obstinate man. You understand him better if you accept one thing: he is blind to shades of grey. For Dad things are either right or wrong. You can safely assume that having a child outside marriage will fall into the *wrong* category.'

'He would reject Sam?' The thought that anyone could wish to punish a child for what they, in their narrow-minded way, perceived as the sins of the parents brought a ferocious, protective scowl to her face.

'No, of course not.' Impatiently he brushed aside her anxiety.

His response seemed spontaneous enough, but Scarlet remained unconvinced. Sam's grandfather sounded pretty scary and not at all nice.

She shook her head slowly from side to side. 'You mean not on the surface, that he'll be acting one way and feeling another…?' She shook her head with even more vigour as she thought about it. 'There is no way I'm having Sam exposed to that sort of atmosphere.'

'Dad isn't intolerant.'

'Isn't that slightly contradictory? You're the one who called him "inflexible" and "obstinate".'

'He'd probably say the same thing about me.'

His candour took her aback. 'Well, he doesn't sound like an ideal role model for a little boy to me.'

Roman adopted a mock bewildered expression. 'How can you say that when you can see how well I've turned out?'

Scarlet frowned. She hated it when he made fun of himself that way; it made him almost likeable. She knew it was very important not to like him.

'You don't get on with your father?'

Would it do Sam any favours to be accepted into the bosom of this dysfunctional family? Or am I just grasping at straws? Looking for a reason, any reason, not to co-

operate when deep down I know full well I have no right to deny Sam a father and an extended family.

'That hardly makes me unique, but, yes, we disagree on most things. My father holds some firm views on everything including modern morals—mine mostly.' He rotated his head as if to relieve the tension in his shoulders.

'That's silly; surely he knows most of the stuff in the papers is exaggerated to sell newspapers.' Dear God, if you took every article about him seriously he could be in Paris and New York at the same time!

'Scarlet Smith…are you defending me?' He studied her for several seconds before adding, without the mockery that had laced his previous comment, 'I'm touched.'

Their eyes collided and Scarlet blushed to the roots of her hair. 'Everyone knows that you should take the celebrity stories with a pinch of salt,' she retorted crossly.

Her face got even hotter and her scowl even fiercer as he continued to look at her, one dark brow raised.

'My father believes there's no smoke without fire,' he commented after a painfully long pause—painful for Scarlet anyway.

'People do and I suppose his generation—'

'Sure, there is the generation gap, but it's more than that,' Roman interrupted. 'Before he met my mother, Dad had planned to enter a seminary.'

Scarlet's eyes widened. '*Seminary?* Isn't that where you train to be a priest?'

'It is,' Roman confirmed.

'Gracious!' she exclaimed unthinkingly. 'No wonder he doesn't approve of you!'

'You and he will get on famously,' Roman predicted drily. 'There's also…' Betraying an uncharacteristic inde-cisiveness, he stopped and raked a hand through his dark hair. 'Well, you might as well hear the story from me as you'll undoubtedly hear a version of it from my father when you meet him.'

Scarlet was so curious she let the assumption that she would one day meet O'Hagan senior pass without comment.

'I was engaged to a girl—Sally.'

Her eyes widened. '*You* were engaged?'

'Yes, about five years ago. Why so surprised, Scarlet? Most men of my age have had at least one serious long-term relationship.'

'But I thought you were…'

'A shallow, womanising pig?' he suggested. He observed the surge of guilty colour in her cheeks with a cynical smile. 'Relax, there's no need to totally retrench, the two are not necessarily mutually incompatible.'

'Did your father not approve of her?'

'Far from it, he adored her. He still does. I'd known Sally since we were children—her parents are tenant farmers on the estate. We were always in and out of each other's houses.'

'The girl next door?'

He nodded. 'There was nothing then, but we met up at college and were involved briefly, but it was nothing heavy. Then a few years later we met up at a party. A month later we were engaged. My family, especially my father, was over the moon,' he recalled.

'But you couldn't go through with it.'

Roman's dark, saturnine features clenched. His lip curled into a self-derisive smile as their eyes met.

'No, actually *she* couldn't go through with it. She ran off on the eve of the wedding with my best man.'

'*Gracious!* That's…that's…' She gave a helpless shrug. Very little he could have told her could have shocked her more. Any response seemed hopelessly inadequate. 'I'm sorry. That must have been awful for you.'

'I've had better days, but it happened a very long time ago.'

Despite his apparent indifference Scarlet couldn't help but wonder if behind that casual attitude he was hiding his true feelings. Did he still love this woman who had dumped him so ignominiously? Had he gained his playboy reputation as a result of trying to forget his lost love?

'I don't understand. If she dumped you how come your father blames you?'

'There was a note. She asked me not to tell her parents until she had a chance to talk to them. I'm assuming she never did. Nobody but Mother and I know she ran off with Jake.'

'But—'

'It didn't last…she left for France and came back three weeks later alone. As far as my father is concerned I had the perfect woman and I drove her away. Maybe,' he mused, 'he was right. There's a possibility that you'll meet her in Ireland—she's a teacher at the local primary school these days.'

'When you meet up…' she began, then the implication of his words hit home. 'I won't be going to Ireland.'

'I'm sure Sam will be a lot more comfortable if you do.'

'That's moral blackmail!' she accused angrily.

'It's also common sense,' he pointed out. 'Don't worry, my parents will love Sam,' he promised in a warmer voice. 'There's no sinister reason I haven't spoken to my dad yet, I simply wanted to sort out things with you before I spoke to him.'

'"Sort out?"' she repeated, her mouth forming a twisted smile as she angrily studied his lean face. *As if I can be filed away like a completed contract.* 'Are we *sorted* now?' she asked bitingly.

'I simply meant…' Their eyes made contact, his lashes came down, but not before she had seen the seething frustration in those dark depths. 'You are one prickly female, do you know that?'

'I don't like the idea of being *sorted*.'

'It's a figure of speech.'

'Then maybe you should choose your words with more care.'

'Dear God, I'm already walking on eggshells around you,' he claimed. 'The next logical step would be for us to communicate through a third party. Think about it,' he suggested heavily. 'All I knew for sure when I came here was Sam was my child, and you weren't the mother. I needed some answers.'

'What did you think I'd done, kidnapped him...?' she suggested sarcastically.

'I hadn't ruled out anything. As I've already said, all I knew for sure was you weren't the mother.'

'How convenient I'm not beautiful and blonde,' she jeered. 'Or you might not have realised it was impossible for me to be Sam's mum.'

A dark line of anger appeared along the crest of his cheekbones as their eyes made contact. His were darkly furious as they narrowed to angry glittering slits.

'I'm beginning to think there's an element of jealousy in your hostility.'

'"Jealousy?"' she parroted shrilly. 'You think I'm jealous that you slept with my sister? You must be mad.' Her scornful laugh had a hollow sound to it.

'I was thinking more along the lines of you being jealous because there is someone else with a claim to Sam and you're possessive, you want to keep him all to yourself. But if the other works?' One dark brow quirked suggestively.

A scorching flush travelled over her entire body as she gasped into the static silence that followed his words.

'I wouldn't sleep with a man like you if my life depended on it!'

'Not very original,' he mused, his hooded eyes trained on her heaving bosom. 'But you get full marks for conviction,' he commended.

His tone of amused condescension made her want to throw something large and heavy at his smug face. She hadn't expected the news she didn't want to sleep with him to send him into a deep depression, but there was no need for him to treat it like a joke.

'And,' she continued contemptuously, 'if *I* was choosing a father for my baby, *you* wouldn't even make the list!' She stopped, an expression of horror stealing across her face as she drew back from the very brink of revealing her sister's shameful secret.

As much as Scarlet didn't like the man, she didn't dislike him enough to rub his nose in the humiliating fact that, far from getting accidentally pregnant, her sister had planned the entire thing. If he did go on to become part of Sam's life—and, while she wasn't ready to admit that out loud just yet, deep down she knew it was going to happen—what would she do then? How was she to know that revealing the truth would not colour any relationship father and son might come to have?

Would Roman feel differently about his son if he knew he had been tricked and used…? It wasn't inconceivable a man could resent a child born of such circumstances. No, she decided, nothing could be achieved from coming clean.

For several moments Roman remained silent. When he finally responded he no longer appeared in the mood to be diverted by her comments.

'Having Sam provides you with the perfect excuse for you not getting out there, doesn't it?'

She responded with a grimace of genuine confusion to his observation. '"Getting out there?"'

'Have you always been scared of relationships?'

'You think I use Sam as an excuse? That I'm commitment-phobic?' She released an incredulous laugh. 'What you know about relationships could be printed on a match-box. And if by "getting out there" you mean joining the singles scene and hanging out in bars waiting to be picked up, I'm really not that desperate.'

'I'm happy for you. I wish I could say the same myself, but this conversation is enough to make anyone desperate—' He broke off and heaved a deep sigh. 'Do you think we could concentrate on the main objective of this conversation?'

She watched as he linked his hands behind his head and dropped his head back, the action exposed the long, powerful length of his brown throat. Her tummy muscles quivered.

'What is the main objective of this conversation?' she asked huskily.

Roman unlinked his hands and let them fall to his side. 'I'd like to get to know my son, and before you say anything hear me out.' Their glances locked and slowly, grudgingly, Scarlet nodded. 'I don't expect this thing to happen overnight. Obviously it will be better for Sam if I become part of his life slowly…gradually.'

'If you become part of Sam's life, you're going to become part of mine.'

'Exactly,' he agreed, not reacting to the horror etched on her face. 'Which is why I thought you might have some ideas on the subject.'

Scarlet stared at him incredulously. *'Are you kidding? After what you've just thrown at me I can't even think straight!'*

'Well, we'll just have to put our heads together, won't we?' he gritted.

'I wouldn't be seen dead with any part of my body within thirty feet of the corresponding part of yours!'

His features tautened. 'Listen, my tolerance levels on this are pretty high because I know you think I'm a bastard. That I can accept,' he said heavily. 'But we need... You've got to think of Sam,' he reproached sternly.

As if she had been thinking of anything else for three years! He didn't have the faintest idea.

'You've got to stop turning this into something personal.'

Scarlet planted her hands on her hips and threw her head back. She was literally trembling with reaction.

'Wanna bet?' she drawled.

'Right, you want personal...fine.' He covered the space between them and grabbed the back of her head with one hand; with the other he framed her face. She looked at him with eyes wide and shocked; she smelt of flowery soap, shampoo, and warm woman, and Roman's body reacted violently to the combination.

'Is this the sort of personal you had in mind?'

Even while he was saying it the voice in the back of his head was telling him he'd been looking for an excuse to do this ever since he'd met her. Once he started kissing her the voice wasn't telling him anything, because his brain took a back seat.

In the moment before her soft lips parted to allow his tongue to slide deep inside her warm mouth he heard, or rather felt, the broken whimper in her throat. The erotic little rasp sent a lick of heat through his blood and a corresponding jolt through his already rock-hard body.

She melted into him like warm butter. There was no hint of resistance in the body he had drawn against his, just heat and softness and the promise of more. Greedily he accepted the sweetness so unexpectedly offered him and it was only several hot, frenzied heartbeats later that he lifted his head.

The effort to do so was physically painful.

They didn't immediately step apart, just stood, bodies leaning into each other, breathing hard. Roman's fingers were still meshed into the shiny strands of slightly damp hair on her head and she had hold of his shirt in both hands.

When the drumming in his ears got quieter he could make out the words she kept repeating over and over. 'Oh, my God…oh, my God…!'

'Right, that was stupid,' he said, leaning his chin against the top of her head. 'But inevitable,' he added half to himself. 'Considering the level of attraction.'

His comment succeeded in jolting Scarlet free from the sensual lethargy that had engulfed her. With a cry she tore free of him and backed away, her angry eyes fixed on his taut features.

'The only thing that's inevitable between us is mutual antipathy.' She rubbed her hand across her reddened, swollen lips. The action was purely symbolic; she didn't believe for a moment it would succeed wiping away the memory of his searing kiss.

She had never been kissed that way before, not in a way that had made her crave more than air the pressure of someone's lips on her own. It made her dizzy and breathless all over again to think of his tongue stroking inside her mouth.

His eyes trailed across her face, lingering on the soft, swollen contours of her full lips. He shrugged. 'If you say so,' he said thickly.

'Don't use that patronising tone with me,' she flared, wrenching her hungry gaze from his face. This wasn't the time to indulge in a staring match. 'And don't treat me like a child.'

As she glared straight ahead her eye-line was on a level

with his powerful chest. A chest that moments ago her breasts had been crushed against, softness against iron hardness. Her body had been plastered so close to his that she had been able to feel the heavy thud of his heart mingled with her own. Her eyes lifted as she tried to drag her thoughts clear of the dangerous memories.

Far from saving her, the retreat brought her eyes into direct contact with Roman's dark, deep-set, very angry eyes. Her lashes came down but not before a wave of sheer sexual longing had nailed her to the spot.

'Then don't act like one,' he advised, his manner clipped and impatient. 'I don't force myself on women.'

Scarlet shook her head to clear the sensual fog that made it hard for her to think straight. 'Hell, no, you're irresistible,' she husked sarcastically. 'You don't have to.' *Well, not with me, he doesn't.*

The memory of her total surrender was terrifying. One kiss and she'd been his to do anything he wanted with. She had never relinquished control that way in her life and if the memory of it wasn't enough to terrify her, the fact that she had liked feeling that way, that part of her wanted to recapture the feeling, was!

His jaw tightened another notch in response to her sarcastic jibe. 'You can't pretend that you were some sort of unwilling participant.'

Can and will, Scarlet thought, responding to his claim with a provocative shrug of her slender shoulders.

'That you didn't want to kiss me as much as I wanted to kiss you,' he continued between gritted teeth. 'That neither of us wanted it to stop. You can't pretend those things and expect me to treat you seriously, can you?' By the time he had finished the incredulity in his voice had become scorn.

She looked away from his relentless hard stare and gulped. It had been pretty foolish of her to assume that a man who possessed his vast experience of women would not know how she had felt.

'Like you said, it was stupid.' It was clearly pointless to keep up the illusion that she hadn't kissed him back.

A speculative expression slid across his dark features. 'Possibly...'

She shot him a startled look. 'What do you mean, "possibly"?' she demanded suspiciously. 'There is no way we can go around kissing without it...' Roman raised a quizzical brow as she stopped, flushing to the roots of her hair with mortification.

'Not without it leading to other things,' he finished for her smoothly. 'I realise that.'

Her chin lifted. 'It's not that I couldn't have stopped.' The question was *when*?

'You just didn't want to.' A faint, strangled sound was the only thing that could get past the emotional thickness in Scarlet's throat. 'Neither did I,' he added.

Her eyes widened at his earthy admission.

Their eyes locked. His were filled with a raw hunger that snatched the breath from her lungs. She felt dizzy, and her stomach dipped as though she'd just stepped into a bottomless black hole. The whooshing sound in her ears intensified the sensation of light-headedness.

'You didn't...?' She flushed with mortification to hear the amazed delight in her voice.

It doesn't take much to please you, does it, Scarlet? A man saying he didn't want to stop. As if that is such a life-changing occurrence? Of course he hadn't wanted to stop. Men never did; it was in their nature. They took what was on offer.

Well, I'm not on offer! Once more with a little more conviction, Scarlet.

While she was still thinking he took action and a step that

brought him closer, close enough for her to smell the warm
male scent that rose from his body. The smile, the dangerous
confident smile on his face kick-started her pulse. Now was
the time to tell him she wasn't interested, spell it out once
and for all.

She instinctively knew that with Roman saying no would
be enough.

She opened her mouth to speak but nothing came out to
break the silence. His movements were unhurried, deliberate
even, but for Scarlet he seemed to move in slow motion.
She wasn't aware that she had been holding her breath until
he took her face between his big hands.

Her breath escaped in a series of uneven gasps as his
brown fingers moved along the curve of her jaw.

'You have lovely hair,' he rasped, releasing the clip that
confined her curls on top of her head. Quite deliberately he
fanned it out around her face, running his fingers through
the silky damp strands.

'No.' She shook her head. 'It's brown.'

Roman paused in the act of sliding his hands down her
back. A baffled expression crossed his handsome face. 'This
is something you need to apologise for?'

'And it's too fine. I can't do anything with it.'

She felt his laughter. 'Brown and fine suits your face.'

He tilted her head back to inspect the face he referred to.
Scarlet was very conscious of his other hand, which was
resting very firmly on the curve of her bottom.

'A nice face,' he decided just before he kissed her.

Scarlet gave a sigh as all the strength left her limbs. She
had no choice or, for that matter, desire to do anything but
let her body mould itself to his lithe, lean male frame.

'Please…Roman,' she moaned when his head lifted. She
buried her own in his shoulder with a muffled sob.

He placed a finger under her chin and tilted her face up to him. 'Please what?'

'This is stupid. You know this is stupid. Things are complicated enough without putting...' the colour deepened in her cheeks '...*this*,' she added with an agonised grimace, 'into the equation.'

'*This* is not going to complicate things,' he contradicted, running a finger over the downy soft curve of her cheek. A distracted expression drifted over his hard, strong-boned features. 'God, but your skin is so soft,' he marvelled, his voice a deep, throaty purr. 'So incredibly soft.'

Scarlet dragged his hand from her face. It was so large compared to hers, his brown fingers long and tapering, she could feel the definite suggestion of calluses on his palm. These were not the hands of a man who was desk-bound.

As if reading her mind he offered an explanation. 'The gym bores me. I prefer to climb; it helps me concentrate.'

Once he'd said it she had no problem seeing him clinging to a rock face, using a combination of skill, strength and recklessness, pitting himself against a rock face and the elements, solo because he was not a natural team player.

'There's not much climbing to be had in London.'

'There are some very good climbing walls, though, and I don't live in the city all the time.'

Responding to a sudden crazy impulse, she raised his hand to her mouth and pressed an open-mouthed kiss into his open palm.

She felt his sharp inhalation and with a self-condemnatory groan dropped his fingers as though burnt, which in a way she was. The expression 'playing with fire' could have been created specially to cover this situation.

'Sorry!' she said in an agonised whisper. 'I shouldn't have. This is not sensible.'

A reckless-sounding laugh was wrenched from his throat. 'Who needs sensible?'

Scarlet lifted her head. 'Me.'

His dark, glittering eyes scanned her face. 'Fine, then look at it this way. Let's *use* what we're feeling.'

Scarlet managed to drag her eyes from his mouth. Her brain felt slow and stupid as she parroted, '"Use" it? Use what?'

'The fact there is a strong sexual attraction.'

'I don't understand.'

'What do you normally do when you feel this way?'

A difficult question to answer honestly when she had never felt this way before. She had never longed to plaster herself against a man she barely knew; she had not fantasised about feeling his weight on top of her or wanted to explore every inch of his body with her hands and lips. Honesty was clearly not an option here.

'I don't *do* anything. I'm too busy for relationships and I don't do one-night stands.' She could understand it if he found her last claim difficult to believe after the way she'd behaved.

'I doubt if one night would be sufficient.' Roman slanted her a heavy-eyed look of such sensuous promise that her knees trembled. 'You would date the guy…right?'

'"Date…?"' she echoed as though he were talking a foreign language. 'You're not suggesting me going to dinner or the movies with you is going to help anything?'

'When you are attracted to a man and the feeling is reciprocated that is what most people do…though *dinner* is not essential and personally I'm adaptable and could skip this preliminary stage of the mating ritual.'

'Too much detail!' she interrupted, holding up her hand to halt the flow of information and shaking her head vigorously from side to side.

'Think about it. Sam needs to get to know me, but not in a forced, fake way. If we were dating—'

'Which we're not.'

'If I was the new boyfriend we'd be bound to spend time together.'

He sounded so damned pleased with himself Scarlet was torn between laughter and hysterical tears. 'You're serious, aren't you? You want me to pretend we're going out together so you can get to know Sam.'

Me the girlfriend of Roman O'Hagan—sure, and the world really is going to believe that. Heavens, even a three-year-old would see through that one!

'Not pretend, no.'

The colour seeped out of her face and then flooded back. 'You can't be serious.'

'Sam must be used to seeing your boyfriends around the place?'

She shook her head, still stunned by his suggestion. 'No, he isn't.'

'Don't you have a social life, then?' he asked, clearly not taking her statement at face value.

'Of course I have a social life. I go to a yoga class and I belong to a quilting—'

His dark brows twitched. '*Quilting?* I frequently can't tell if you're on the level or you're trying to wind me up.'

'I don't see why me talking about quilting can possibly be considered trying to wind you up.'

'I'm not talking about *quilting*!' he exploded.

'Quilting is very relaxing,' she informed him with dignity. 'And you have something pretty and practical to show for your efforts at the end of the day. I've not got very far yet, but just because you've no aptitude for something doesn't mean you shouldn't stick with it.'

'I am sticking with it but I can't guarantee for how long.

Will you quit talking about quilting?' he revealed in a low, driven tone. 'I'm talking about sex, unless you've taken some vow of celibacy. Please tell me you've not,' he begged.

An expression of shock spread across his face when, instead of sharing the joke, she looked away. 'You don't date…not at all?'

'Of course I date.'

'I don't see what the problem is, then. Why not date me?'

When he said *'date me'* she was pretty sure it was a euphemism for *sleep with me*. 'You don't see the problem because you're a sandwich short of a picnic and unused to dealing with rejection.'

'Rejection I can deal with, but not from a woman who starts trembling with desire and undressing me with her eyes every time she's in the same room as me.'

The mortified heat rushed to her cheeks. 'My God, you are so colossally arrogant,' she breathed.

A wolfish grin split his dark lean features as he looked down into her outraged face. 'Maybe I am, but also I'm right. Aren't I, Scarlet?'

Scarlet wasn't going down that road.

'You want reasons? Let me see—where shall I start? How do you know I don't already have a boyfriend?'

'You said you don't have time for boyfriends.'

'Well, I don't.'

'That probably explains your short temper.' His fuse was certainly getting extremely short.

He could trace the source with great precision to the moment he had walked into her office and found her struggling into that too-tight top. When you lived in a society where you were constantly bombarded with images of provocatively undressed women it was kind of ironic that he had got so totally hung up over a one-blink-and-you'll-miss-it glimpse of bare flesh.

'Everything is about sex with you, isn't it?' she accused. 'You're obsessed,' she condemned crossly.

It took something as simple as a throw-away comment sometimes. His dark eyes trailed across her face, the soft contours of which he knew were already fixed in his memory. So was the sound of her laugh and her glare and the way…in fact he could access all her facial expressions any time he liked and also sometimes when he didn't like.

'You might not be wrong there,' he agreed.

'I don't know what you mean.'

'I think you do. I think you also know how good sex could be for us,' he rasped in a throaty voice that turned the heavy feeling low in her belly into an actual ache. 'But for some reason you're denying it.'

She closed her eyes and counted to a hundred slowly; all it did was panic her into impetuous speech.

'Actually I don't know a damned thing about sex,' she heard herself announce loudly. 'And before you offer I don't want any lessons from you.'

'Lessons…now that conjures up some very interesting—' He stopped dead, the teasing expression fading dramatically from his face. Eyes narrowed, he subjected her to a hard, searching scrutiny. 'Good God!' he ejaculated hoarsely. 'You're a virgin.'

CHAPTER ELEVEN

'WHETHER I am or not is totally irrelevant and none of your business,' Scarlet was driven by sheer embarrassment to retort.

'It won't be irrelevant to the guy who sleeps with you,' Rowan promised grimly.

Scarlet heard the shaken note in his voice. Well, she'd wanted to turn him off and it would seem she'd succeeded.

'Obviously that changes things,' he added soberly.

Scarlet glared at him indignantly. 'I don't see why. I may not be *vastly* experienced, but I think I'd manage to keep up with you. How hard can it be?'

Something moved at the back of his eyes in response to her challenge. 'There's only one way to find out.' He heard the words come out of his mouth but still he couldn't believe he'd been responsible for them. *A virgin? I'm mad out of my head, insane.*

He watched the rapid rise and fall of her breasts, her lips slightly parted and rosily moist and her eyes—eyes that were frequently a mirror image of her mood—sparkling with reckless challenge.

'What have you been doing—waiting for the right man?' he blasted, suddenly mad as hell with her.

Scarlet blinked, bewildered by his anger. 'Well, that rules you out!'

A nerve jumped along his hard jaw as he leant closer, his voice soft in her ear. 'I may not be the right man, Scarlet, but maybe I'm the wrong man? Sometimes the *wrong* man, like the forbidden fruit, can be more exciting.'

Mesmerised by the erotic rasp of his low voice and spec-tacular pitch-black smouldering eyes, she stared up at him so painfully excited and aroused she had to fight for each individual breath. Her body, every inch of her skin was burning, trickles of moisture formed in the hollow between her breasts and tiny trickles ran down the smooth skin of her back.

'I...I...' she stuttered, staring at him in undisguised long-ing. He was so beautiful she wanted to cry; he was so beau-tiful she wanted to beg him to touch her. Her mind was so consumed by desire that she had no other thought in her head but assuaging the hunger inside her.

He touched the side of her face, and looked into eyes wide and startled. Scarlet returned his stare before sucking in a deep breath and closing her eyes tight to shut out his probing stare.

She felt as if her feelings were written in neon a mile high across her face. She loved him. She who had always scoffed at the idea of love at first sight had fallen madly, deeply and irrevocably in love with Roman O'Hagan.

His fingers barely brushed her skin yet a moan was drawn from deep in her throat. She felt him take her hands within his and she lifted her head. He was standing over her. She trembled as he unfurled her tightly clenched fingers before placing both her hands palm down against his chest. She felt the ripple of taut muscles beneath her fingers and the last vestiges of restraint melted away in the heat of arousal.

Drawing a deep breath, she splayed her fingers and deep-ened the exploration of the hard male contours. She could feel the heat of his skin through the fine fabric of his shirt.

'You're totally incredible,' she breathed.

'I want your hands on me.'

Scarlet, her tongue caught between her teeth as she concentrated all her senses on the tactile sensation, slid her fingers through the inviting gap between the buttons.

'You're warm,' she whispered, trailing one finger slowly along the hard but incredibly smooth muscled ridges of his perfectly developed chest down to his flat belly.

With a mumbled hoarse imprecation Roman took hold of the expensive fabric of his shirt and pulled. There was a harsh ripping sound and buttons flew across the room.

'Your shirt!' she protested.

'I've got other shirts.' With a shrug he dismissed the damaged article that hung loosely open to his waist. 'However I've only one mind and if you don't touch me it could be permanently damaged,' he claimed, taking her wrist.

Scarlet only spent a moment wondering what he was going to do before he placed her hand palm-flat against the broad expanse of softly gleaming golden flesh his violent action had exposed. She felt the sharp contraction of taut muscles beneath her hand and her own stomach muscles spasmed as if in sympathy.

His warm, fragrant breath brushed her sensitive earlobe as he inclined his dark, glossy head. 'No, not *warm*,' he contradicted. '*Hot*. You,' he confided huskily, 'make me hot. From the moment I saw those delicious little breasts of yours I wanted to taste them. I wanted...'

Scarlet, who felt light-headed and strangely removed from what was happening, smiled; it was a smile of anticipation. Perhaps it was that distance, that sense of unreality that enabled her to respond with such devastating honesty? Or maybe something in her instinctively recognised that the situation warranted some plain speaking. Either way she knew this wasn't the time to be sensible or cautious.

Hell! Hadn't she had a lifetime of being both? Didn't she deserve just a little madness?

'No, don't say it,' she begged, directing her passion-glazed slumberous stare to his face. *'Do it!'* she commanded, reaching up to greedily sink her fingers in his hair. The dark waves were ebony and slippery like silk, but she clung hard, yanking his face down to her level.

'It hurts,' she told him, pressing her mouth hard against his. Her eyes were glittering with a feverish brilliance when her head lifted.

'What hurts?' he asked raggedly.

'Wanting to touch you hurts. I've never wanted anything or anyone as much as I want you,' she revealed starkly.

For a long sizzling moment their glances froze, the mutual message of hunger between them a palpable entity. His gasp, the one that moulded his belly into a tight, concave curve, was part of the same fluid movement that scooped her up into his arms.

Scarlet's arms looped about his neck, her legs locked tight around his middle, she kissed him with all the fervour of a mouse totally determined the cat *would* catch her as Roman bore his burden in the general direction of the bedroom.

They collided with several large items of furniture, knocked over a lamp, a framed picture and sundry items, but neither registered the destruction they left in their wake.

Roman didn't bother to detach her from him; instead he fell onto the bed with her on top of him.

He looked up at the woman who sat wantonly astride him… Given what he knew, *could she legitimately be called a woman*? He pushed aside the distracting question and indulged his senses fully in the delicious image—delicious curves, lush mouth and shiny take-me-now eyes.

Scarlet looked around her, her perplexed expression suggesting she didn't have the faintest idea how she'd come to be there.

The sultry, scared smile that she gave him made the ache in his groin almost unbearable. Still holding his eyes, she positioned a hand either side of his shoulders and leaned over him, her hair tumbling over her shoulders.

'What happened to your glasses?'

'Dark drawer time.' She kissed him, a long, deep, languid kiss.

'Pity, I liked them.'

'Liar,' she taunted huskily as she kissed her way up his neck.

'I had this fantasy about taking them off.'

'Really?' She blinked. 'You had fantasies about me?'

He laughed against her mouth. 'Oh, yes, Scarlet.' He gave a grunt of frustration as her luscious lips lifted from his. 'I've had several fantasies about you.'

'You could take something else off instead of the glasses,' she suggested huskily.

'I'd prefer to watch you do it.'

It was as she was unbuttoning the final button on her pyjama top that the wanton reality of what she was doing hit her. Roman, lying beneath her, his dark, intense gaze focused on her every move, saw the feelings of indecision reflected on her face.

'Let me,' he said, taking the white-knuckled fingers that were clutching the edges of the garment tightly together. Her lips parted to protest but their eyes touched and the resistance slid out of her. Still holding her eyes, he gently removed her stiff fingers.

The fabric parted.

Scarlet, overcome by self-consciousness, would have covered herself with her hands but he held them at her sides. The silence pulsated while his eyes feasted on the ivory perfection of her small pink-tipped breasts. He couldn't tear his eyes from the erotic sight; her body was bathed in a rosy flush of arousal that gave her skin a translucent quality.

'*Dio, cara,* you're so incredibly beautiful.' His voice, raw and needy, ached with sincerity.

Head inclined to one side, Scarlet searched his face, not quite confident enough to use the power she sensed she had over him. 'Truly?' she panted wonderingly.

Still holding her wrists, he turned over, pulling her beneath him. 'I never say things I don't mean,' he asserted imperiously.

Though she was only anchored beneath him for a moment before he slid off her and arranged his lean length beside her, it was long enough for her to know that that was where she wanted him. She wanted to feel the hot, heavy weight of his body on top of her. She wanted him to press her body into the softness of the mattress until it could sink no farther; she wanted him to sink into her.

Roman released her wrists but she made no attempt to move them from above her head. She turned her head towards him, and the sultry invitation glowing in her eyes wrenched a primitive groan from his throat before his mouth came crashing down hard and hungry on her lips.

Scarlet gave a soft moan of pleasure as he licked his way into her mouth, skilfully probing the sweet recesses. She welcomed the sensual demand of his lips and kissed him back enthusiastically, drowning in the pleasure as she felt his big hands on her body.

When his fingertips traced a delicate pathway along her straight, supple spine she shivered and stirred restively in his arms. The ripples of hot sensation went all the way to her curling toes. As his exploration shifted to her aching breasts the ripple became an avalanche.

He stroked and teased until her already painfully sensitised flesh felt as if it were on fire, *she* were on fire! She had never in her wildest fantasies come close to imagining the sort of blind, relentless hunger that gripped her at that moment.

When his fingers slid under the waistband of her pyjama bottoms she shivered hard and lifted her hips to help him slide them down her legs.

The air against her bare skin made her shiver. Scarlet opened her eyes and discovered he was propped up on one elbow looking down at her. He shifted his weight while he fought his way out of his damaged-beyond-repair shirt, not taking his dark liquid eyes from her as he casually flung the garment across the room.

Transfixed by the spectacle of perfectly toned muscle and deliciously smooth golden flesh, Scarlet gulped as her greedy eyes ate him up. She was weak with lust just looking at him. He was magnificent, perfect in every way, and the idea of touching that sleek, smooth body made her ache inside.

'You have a beautiful body.' There was a tremor of something close to reverence in his deep voice. 'So pale and perfect in every way.'

Scarlet, who had always compared herself with a beautiful sister, was extremely glad that beauty really did turn out to be in the eye of the beholder after all. But who would have guessed the beholder in question would turn out to be a man like Roman?

She rolled half onto her stomach and Roman's hot eyes zeroed in on the curve of her smooth peachy bottom. He inhaled slowly through flared nostrils when her small hand curved determinedly over him, he released the breath in a slow sibilant hiss as her fingers then tightened over him. Rhythmically she repeated the process again and again.

He was so much harder than she had imagined, feeling him pulse against her hand made the heavy, dragging sensation in the pit of her belly a hundred times more intense.

Her skin had acquired a sheen of moisture by the time he drew her tormenting hand from his body.

His eyes, dark and insolent, touched her face. 'Don't forget your place,' he instructed as he levered himself lightly from the bed.

Scarlet opened her mouth to protest and then saw he was unfastening his belt. The hot rush of desire that zapped through her left her literally panting for breath.

There was an electrified silence as he kicked aside his boxer shorts. Transfixed, she couldn't take her eyes off the hard contours of his taut, toned frame. There were no excess pounds to blur or disguise the perfect muscle definition of his upper body, flat belly and powerful thighs.

He was simply beautiful, a perfect bronzed statue come to life. She felt the prickle of emotional tears behind her eyelids as she feasted her eyes on him.

She was not conscious of moaning his name out loud, but she was conscious of the raw out-of-control light burning in his incredible eyes as he rejoined her. The skin-to-skin contact blasted the last shred of reason, of caution, from her head.

While he kissed her soft lips, deep searing kiss after deep searing kiss, she was all the time conscious of the hardness of his erection grinding into her belly. His skilful hands were moving over her sensitised body. She was equally driven to touch every inch of his smooth golden skin, explore every centimetre of the taut, silky surface.

The air was filled with gasps, hoarse whimpers of pleasure and muted moans.

Ultra receptive to his skilful touch, she writhed and twisted when his hands cupped her breasts; she grabbed his head and cried out when his tongue lashed teasingly across the tight, engorged peaks.

He laughed when she brokenly claimed to be dying—she was only half joking.

'Try and hold on a little longer,' he instructed as he mercilessly began to lick his way down the softness of her quivering belly. She stiffened when his exploration reached the soft fuzz at the apex of her legs.

'Relax, *cara*,' he breathed into her ear.

'But…'

It wasn't his kiss but the unexpected tenderness in his eyes that stilled her protest.

'Don't think, let yourself feel. That's it,' he approved throatily as she pushed against his fingers with a sigh.

'I don't know what I'm doing…in theory I know, but…'

'I know what I'm doing.'

He did.

Because he had had a lot of practice… *He's right, I shouldn't think.*

'And you're not doing so badly, *cara*. Oh, my God, you're so tight,' he breathed hoarsely as he slid a finger inside her.

'That's…*oh, my God*…! Please, Roman, please…'

A considerable amount of pleading and even more indescribable pleasure later, he pulled her knees up and settled between her legs. A shiver of voluptuous anticipation slid through her as she felt the probing pressure of his hard silkiness against the very core of her.

No pain, not really, just pressure and then the mind-expanding miracle of being filled.

He was on top of her and inside her and everything that was happening had a feeling of rightness about it.

That was her last conscious thought as he began to move and the pressure inside her started to build. The first ripples of her orgasm wrenched a deep moan from her parted lips.

I *screamed*! The shocking memory of the feral scream as her orgasm had peaked flashed through her head.

Roman felt the warm body pressed close to him tense. 'Is something wrong?' he asked, stroking the damp hair from her face.

'Nothing,' Scarlet sighed, relaxing back into arms that closed tightly around her.

What could be wrong? She was where she wanted to be. Things like him not loving her could wait until the morning.

It was actually around two in the morning when the shrill ring of the phone roused her. She rubbed her eyes and sleepily reached out only to find there was a large naked male in the way.

She sat bolt upright, suddenly very wide awake. Not daring to look at the shadowy shape in the bed beside her. Carefully she edged her body away from his, difficult in such a narrow bed, and reached over him for the phone.

'Hello…'

'Firstly, don't panic, Sam is fine. Fast asleep, actually.' Tom Bradley went on to explain that it was their son who was unwell. The doctor had been called and he was off to the hospital with suspected appendicitis.

Scarlet expressed her heartfelt sympathy. 'Poor Nancy. How is she?'

'Tearful,' her husband admitted. 'I've told her that kids bounce back but she doesn't cope well with illness.'

Scarlet could hear the stress in his voice. 'So you'd like me to pick Sam up.'

'Well, that's up to you, the au pair is here and he's asleep, but…'

'I'll pick him up now,' Scarlet said, manoeuvring herself out of the bed as she spoke. 'You'll be at the hospital by the time I get there?'

'We're off now.'

'I'm sure he'll be fine, but good luck anyway,' she said before hanging up.

She was halfway across the room when the bedside light was switched on. She froze like an animal caught in the headlights of the car.

'Has something happened to Sam?'

Well, she couldn't complain that he didn't have his priorities right. A naked woman standing less then five feet away and his first thoughts were for his son...as it should be, and very commendable, but she wouldn't have minded being a *slight* distraction.

'Sam's fine.' She walked to the chest of drawers trying to act as if she weren't desperately self-conscious. 'It's his friend from the sleep-over who has suspected appendicitis. That was his dad, Tom Bradley, just now, the *Tom Bradley* you've *never* met,' she inserted drily.

'I'm going to pick Sam up. Could you call me a taxi, please?' She pulled a fresh set of undies from the drawer and stepped into the knickers.

On the whole, she thought she had carried off the entire I'm-perfectly-happy-with-my-body thing really well.

'Don't be stupid, I'll take you.' She heard the creak of bed springs as he got out of bed.

'That's really not necessary,' she started, and froze as she felt his fingers brush her bare back.

'Let me,' he said, snapping the bra catch she had been clumsily trying to fasten first time. She didn't see how he could have failed to feel the shiver that rippled through her body.

'Thank you,' she said huskily. 'Sorry I woke you.' She could no longer avoid looking at him.

'You didn't wake me. I haven't been asleep.'

Unlike her, Roman did not possess any inhibitions about nakedness. Her eyes slid of their own volition down his body and made the discovery that made her blush.

'There will be other mornings,' he promised.

Blushing even more fierily, she looked away and snatched up a shirt that was draped over the back of a chair. 'No,' she contradicted huskily, 'there won't be other mornings.'

Roman's eyes narrowed as she turned her back but he didn't comment on her statement. Any idea she had that he had accepted or not noticed what she'd said was laid to rest when she was safely belted into the passenger seat of his silver Jaguar.

The streets were virtually deserted as he drove through the silent city.

'Why won't there be any other mornings?'

'It was marvellous and so were you, if that's what's worrying you.' Her attempt at light laughter emerged as a croak.

'It wasn't. I'm well aware that what happened between us was special, which is why you're not making sense.'

It was hard to keep her focus when he said 'special' in that sexy, throaty way, but Scarlet knew she had to. He was a passionate, highly sexed man and the chemistry was intense between them, but how soon before she began to see his picture in the newspapers with other women?

Worse still, would she turn into the woman he went back to when there was nothing better on offer? *The sure thing.*

She hadn't wanted to get into this now, but she realised that discussing it while he had to keep his eyes on the road and his hands on the steering wheel was actually not such a bad idea.

'I can't sleep with you again because it wouldn't be good for Sam. He can't see us as a couple and then not—children need continuity. But don't worry, we can work out a schedule for you to visit with him. Though I'd prefer you wait a little while before you have him for the weekend or anything.'

'I'm sure if you dig really deep there is some logic there somewhere.' The amusement in his voice sounded pretty strained as he added heavily, 'Damned if I can find it, though.' The furrows on his brow deepened. 'What has Sam to do with you sleeping with me? Or, for that matter, you *not* sleeping with me?'

'Well, you did imply that it would be convenient if you could sleep over.'

His jaw tightened by several notches. 'I would want to make love to you if there was no Sam. Even in the incredibly ugly glasses I wanted to make love to you. It's called chemistry, *cara*!' he yelled. 'There is a Sam, though, and you can't ignore the fact that us being together will be a good thing for him.'

'When you say "together", that's not what you really mean.' Together to her meant exclusive, it meant commitment, it meant, in an ideal world, love.

'I take it you're going to tell me what I mean.'

The sardonic edge in his voice made her lips compress.

'If you had turned up and found the woman bringing up your child had a string of casual lovers move in with her you'd have been the first to hit the ceiling.'

'That's a totally different thing,' he responded immediately.

'In what way?'

He didn't reply, but a sneaky sideways look told her he was looking explosively angry. Again she was glad he was driving—this way he couldn't throttle her or, much more dangerous, kiss her.

'It would just confuse Sam, Roman. He needs things clearly defined. You can't jeopardise your relationship with him for casual sex.'

'I thought you didn't do casual sex.'

'So did I,' she admitted, her unhappiness showing. She dragged a hand through her hair. 'Obviously you are going to be a part of Sam's life for a long time, and therefore mine.'

'I can see how happy that makes you.'

She glared at his perfect profile. 'This is serious.'

A flash of dark annoyance crossed his taut face. 'I am serious,' he rebutted grimly.

'This is about putting a child's needs first.'

The car slowed at a set of lights and he turned his head. 'A parent's life sounds fun: self-sacrifice and no sex.'

'You're taking what I'm saying out of context and you know it,' she accused. 'Sex within a stable relationship is fine.'

The car behind sounded its horn and Roman cursed softly under his breath as he saw the lights had turned green. 'I'm not surprised you were a damned virgin if you want a marriage proposal before you accept a dinner date,' he observed cuttingly as he pulled away.

He cast a quick sideways glance at her white stricken face and turned his attention back to the road ahead. A few yards farther down the road he released a flood of low impassioned Italian, before heaving a deep sigh.

'Fine, have your schedule, keep me at arm's length. I'll keep my distance for as long as you want me to.'

Scarlet nodded, having decided that on balance it was simpler to pretend she hadn't noticed his get-out clause.

Roman appeared oblivious to the awkward silence that developed and she was relieved when a few minutes later they reached the gate to the Bradley house.

'This is it.'

As they drew up outside the front of the house beside a

BMW and a big four-wheel drive Scarlet unfastened her seat belt.

'Do you want me to wait here?'

She sent him a startled look. 'Not unless you prefer not to come in.'

'I don't want to alarm him. I'm a stranger.'

He was nervous! She felt every kind of insensitive idiot for not realising sooner.

'You're not a stranger, Roman, you're his dad.' She wanted to wrap her arms around him.

Their eyes met and for a moment he stared at her, then he smiled and her heart began to thud. She jumped out of the car before she did something really stupid.

The au pair had obviously been waiting for them.

'Sam's asleep.' Scarlet saw the girl's eyes widen as Roman joined her. It amused her—well, actually, it annoyed her—that as far as the girl was concerned she had become invisible. 'If you'd like to come in, I'll show you the way.'

She went as far as the door of the bedroom and, with a nod, left them. 'I'll be downstairs if you want me.' This was said with a wistful glance at Roman, who, to give him his due, seemed totally oblivious to the effect he had.

Sam was fast asleep, his cherubic face flushed rosily with sleep.

The awed expression on Roman's face as he looked down at the child brought a lump to her throat. Scarlet handed him the fleecy blanket she had brought with her.

'Wrap him up in this, will you? It's his favourite blanket.'

'You want me to carry him?'

To see the ultra-confident Roman look nervous rung her tender heart. 'Yes, please.'

'If he wakes up and sees me...'

She smiled encouragingly. 'Sam doesn't wake easily.'

Sam did wake. He opened his eyes and looked up into the face of the man who was carrying him. He gave a sleepy frown.

'Did you bring me a football?'

'Next time,' Roman promised.

Sam smiled and closed his eyes. 'Good,' he said as he snuggled down into the big man's arms.

Roman shook his head. His eyes were shining; he looked as though someone had just given him the winning Lotto ticket. 'He remembered me.'

There was an emotional lump in her throat that made her voice thick. 'You're not an easy man to forget,' she said, turning away before he saw that she was crying.

CHAPTER TWELVE

SCARLET caught sight of his reflection in the steamy window: a tall man, his lean, long frame filled the doorway. She might only have been feasting her eyes on a reflection, but it didn't stop her receiving the same shocking jolt of sexual longing she always did when he appeared—sleek and sexy and totally out of place, not just in her kitchen, but her life.

Maybe he won't be a presence for much longer?

The prospect of Roman vanishing from their lives should have made her happy. Wasn't it what she'd been praying for right from the start? She felt many things but happiness wasn't one of them.

Since he'd pushed his way into her life she was permanently stressed and edgy. Though she had to admit Roman's behaviour had been impeccable. He had not even raised an eyebrow when she had produced the promised schedule, though when she'd pinned it to the notice-board in the kitchen he hadn't been able to resist a comment about her colour coding.

Three weeks into the arrangement it was hard to remember when he hadn't been a part of Sam's life.

He wasn't the problem; she was!

It had been three days since his last visit. On that visit he'd had a free afternoon and it had been agreed that he would take Sam for a walk in the park. The weather had been perfect, unlike Sam's mood. The toddler had been tired, which always made him cranky, and the fact she hadn't let him watch a programme on the television that looked unsuitable to her had not improved matters.

Roman had not seen his son in this mood before. He had looked uncharacteristically helpless when the toddler had struggled and thrown himself around when he had tried to put his coat on. Acting like a three-year-old who hadn't got his own way, Sam hadn't even looked at the gift Roman had brought for him.

Roman might be intolerant and short-tempered in his dealings with her, but Scarlet had to admit that with Sam he displayed a limitless supply of patience. When, despite his best efforts, the child had remained stubbornly cranky, Scarlet had finally taken pity on the inexperienced father— in truth she had found the usually totally self-possessed and poised playboy looking helpless dangerously appealing.

'I'll come, if you'd like. I could do with some fresh air,' she heard herself offer.

Of course she ought to have let him trail Sam around the park on his own; that would have brought home big time to him that taking care of a young child was not all ice cream and fun games.

Even with her along to retrieve the toy that Sam deliberately threw from the pushchair every few yards the park thing wasn't a raving success. Though it was worth going just to see how horrified Roman looked as he pushed a child who was having a tantrum through town.

'What's wrong with him?' he asked Scarlet in a hushed undertone. 'Is he ill?'

She shook her head. She was amused by his harassed question but, not being a fool, hid the fact. 'Not even possessed by a demon,' she told him cheerfully. 'He's tired, that's all. A nap and he'll be fine. He's fighting sleep—he doesn't want to give in,' she explained knowledgeably.

'He's also fighting me. People are staring.'

Scarlet looked at his heartbreakingly perfect profile. 'You ought to be used to that,' she told him drily.

Despite his discomfort, Roman ironically didn't show any sign of self-consciousness about being the cynosure of curious eyes when a few minutes later he leapt to his son's defence.

She recalled the event with a wry smile. The passer-by who loudly offered the opinion that what that child needed was a firm hand and or good slap got more than he had bargained for when confronted by an icily irate father.

Roman said, in a voice that made Scarlet shiver, that anyone who hit a child in anger was a coward and a bully at the very least. And anyone who hit *his* child would find him or herself regretting the action for the rest of their natural life!

The man's face was a picture.

Since the last visit, Roman had been meant to come around the previous day, but he had cancelled at the last minute. As she had explained to Sam that his daddy wouldn't be coming after all she had wondered whether after the trip in the park he was having second thoughts about the joys of fatherhood.

She didn't turn around immediately even though she could feel his dark eyes drilling into her back. Waiting for her pulse rate to slow to a canter, she continued to dry the dishes stacked on the draining-board as though achieving a shiny finish on the crockery were something she had always wanted to dedicate her life to.

'Had we arranged for you to come over this evening?' she asked, holding a polished glass up to the light to check for smudges.

'I must have lost my schedule,' he returned with an equal amount of irony.

'There's no need to be facetious,' she snapped. 'You can't

just barge in here whenever it suits you. I have a life of my own.'

'The jury is still out on that one.'

Scarlet bit back a retort to this jibe. 'This is only going to work if you accept I have a right to my privacy...'

'To dry dishes? Yes, I can see that it's a uniquely private moment between a plate and a woman. I'm so sorry I intruded.'

Scarlet, the tea towel still clutched in her white-knuckled fingers, spun around, her eyes flashing green. 'You can laugh, but I doubt if you'd like it if I dropped in at your office or home any time I felt like it.'

'And do you feel like dropping in on me often?'

Scarlet refused to drop her eyes in face of the glittering challenge she saw in his. 'All the time,' she drawled sarcastically, 'but so far I'm keeping my impulses under control.'

God knew how long that would last. He looked incredibly gorgeous tonight in a grey designer tee shirt and jeans.

His eyes dropped and lingered on the lush contours of her slightly parted lips. Scarlet felt the predictable debilitating weakness spread through her body. She had no doubt at all that his action was cynically deliberate and indicated nothing more than the fact he got some twisted enjoyment out of seeing her get confused, but she was unable not to react to it.

'Not on my account—*I'm* all for following your natural instincts,' Roman said. Scarlet felt the heat unfurl low in her belly and fought the insidious effects of his warm honeyed voice.

'I'm not interested in your natural instincts except when they result in you letting Sam down.' Anger at her own weakness made her voice harsh. 'Rule number one,' she outlined coldly, 'is you don't make promises to Sam you can't keep. I won't have him disappointed because you had a better offer!' she flared contemptuously.

Roman's chin went up to a haughty angle, his nostrils flared, but the signalled anger didn't arrive. Instead his hard boned features relaxed into a speculative expression as he studied her face with a curiosity that rang alarm bells in her head.

'Is this really about *Sam's* disappointment?'

'Of course.'

'Or are you jealous that I spent the evening with someone else?' he suggested silkily. 'Did you miss me?'

Scarlet swallowed. 'In your dreams!'

'Yes, just lately you are, and the fact is I'd much prefer to have you in my bed,' he acknowledged, his voice roughened with frustration. 'And I'm damned sure you'd like to be there. The question is, why aren't you?'

'I slept with you once.'

'It hadn't slipped my memory.'

His sardonic interruption brought a militant gleam to her eyes. 'And you know perfectly well why it's a bad idea, we've been through all that.'

'Remind me.' His eyes were as hard and unforgiving as slate as they drilled into her.

'I can see you're in a mood…'

His head went back, exposing the strong brown line of his throat, and he gave a derisive snort. 'And you wonder why?'

'I think you're just being awkward for the sake of it!' she accused.

'I can do awkward, but this isn't it.' His dark eyes flashed angrily. 'Where is Sam?'

'Upstairs in number ten playing with Tessa, Isobel's little girl.'

'The woman upstairs?'

Scarlet nodded. 'Her little girl is about Sam's age—they get on really well.'

'That's convenient.'

'Are you suggesting that it's handy for me to have someone to dump Sam on?'

'No.' Without Roman raising his voice the softly spoken denial stilled the angry words spilling from her. 'That's not what I'm suggesting.'

Scarlet's shoulders relaxed but the frown that furrowed her smooth brow remained. 'But you are suggesting something?' she speculated shrewdly.

He shrugged and smiled back at her in that infuriatingly enigmatic way he had.

'I think this weekend might be a good time for a trip to Ireland.'

Very slowly Scarlet finished wiping the mug in her hand and replaced it on the counter. 'Have a nice time,' she said in a voice that was carefully devoid of all expression. *My God, I'm going to miss him!* The recognition of how much was a shock. 'I might invite Isobel over for tea,' she added brightly. 'Sam gets on well with her little girl.'

'So you said.'

'Sorry if I'm boring you,' she returned childishly.

'Scarlet, I'm not going to Ireland alone.'

Stupid me, of course he isn't. With horror she recognised the sickening feeling that stabbed through her as jealousy, which was stupid; she had wanted it this way. Was that why he was spelling it out? Had he picked up before she had on the possessive feelings she was developing…?

'Anyone I know?' she asked casually.

'You and Sam. My father would like to meet you both.'

Scarlet's blinked. 'Me and Sam?' she echoed. 'I don't understand.'

'Neither do I,' he remarked cryptically before taking her

chin in his hand and tilting her face up towards him. The dark spiky lashes lifted off her cheek and big almond-shaped eyes that he knew could vary in shade quite dramatically stared back up at him.

'I'd like you and Sam to come home with me to Ireland,' he repeated patiently. His brows lifted and he gave a lop-sided grin and exasperation slipped into his voice as he asked, 'Who the hell did you think I was going to take home to meet my parents?'

An image of several beauties his name had been linked with flashed through her mind as she shook her head. 'I really don't care.' She moved her head and his light touch fell away.

'Then what do you care about?'

The soft question had a curious driven quality to it that brought her eyes back to his face.

I could look at that face for ever and never get tired of looking. 'The fact that no matter what you promise the moment my back is turned you're there again organising my life, Sam's life, and taking over!' she accused hoarsely.

'You're being ridiculous,' Roman contended, looking genuinely bewildered by her accusation.

'Fine, so you don't expect us to come with you just like that!' She clicked her fingers but the dampness on her skin prevented the action producing a satisfying crack.

Roman clicked his tongue and shook his dark head form side to side. 'Not like that, like this,' he said, taking her empty hand and arranging her thumb and forefinger in the required position. 'It's all in the tension.'

Of that there was plenty!

His touch was light, clinical almost, but the softest touch from him sent every nerve ending in her body awake and screaming for more. A terrible surge of longing welled up in her; it was so intense that she could feel it in her bones.

Their eyes connected and a voluptuous shiver ran all the way to her toes.

Angrily she snatched her hand away and rubbed it up and down against her thigh. Her eyes were wary and fiery as she avoided direct eye contact.

'It didn't occur to you it would have been a nice gesture to *ask* not *inform*?'

The impatience in Roman's face visibly increased as she spoke. 'Or I could have been really subtle and let you think it was your idea all along?' he suggested.

'Only you could call manipulative straightforward.' She shook her head incredulously—he really was a one-off. 'I don't suppose that it occurred to you that I might have made other plans, did it? No,' she added without giving him an opening to respond. 'It wouldn't, because you never consider anyone else but yourself!' she declared angrily.

Roman's eyes lifted. They were smouldering.

'I didn't consider that you'd made plans because as far as I can see you don't have a social life.'

'Not one like yours, certainly.'

'Since Sam was born your life has revolved around him. Can you deny that?'

'Are you saying I smother him?'

'I'd say the possibility of you wearing yourself to a shadow trying to be the perfect mother is a more likely scenario.'

Scarlet threw a hand up. 'You've been a father, what? Five minutes, and you're telling me what I'm doing wrong.'

He opened his mouth to deliver a cutting rejoinder and his gaze settled on her face. Suddenly the anger drained out of him. She looked so tired, he thought, looking at the purplish bruises under her eyes. He experienced a wave of protective tenderness of shocking intensity.

'Consider yourself asked.'

Scarlet looked at him blankly. 'What?'

'I'm *asking* if you and Sam will come to Ireland with me this weekend.'

'It's quite impossible. A trip like that will muck up Sam's routine and I have work on Monday.'

'You're the impossible one!' he flung, literally grinding his teeth in frustration. 'Sam's routine is not engraved in stone. I thought you said it was important with a child to be flexible?'

'This wasn't what I was talking about.'

'Now there's a surprise.' The muscles in his taut jaw tightened another notch. 'As for work, you have four weeks' holiday to take before the end of next month and I happen to know there won't be any objection to you taking some of it next week.'

'And you'd know that because?'

'It always pays to think ahead,' he drawled, seemingly unaffected by the tremble of anger in her voice.

'I can't believe you went behind my back,' she choked. 'How *dare* you interfere in my life this way? This is exactly what I was talking about. I'm not some puppet you can manipulate.'

'How much simpler life would be,' he drawled.

Scarlet shot him a furious glance. 'Well, there's absolutely no way we're coming now. What…what's that?' she said, stopping mid-sentence to stare suspiciously at the newspaper he had drawn from his pocket and thrown on the worktop.

'You'll find the relevant article on page two. It's an evening edition. I think we'll make the front page tomorrow morning. What you read there might make you reconsider your decision. I don't think London is going to be a very comfortable place for you.'

As he spoke his eyes were trained on Scarlet, who was turning the page with considerable trepidation.

'I feel sick!' she declared when the half-page picture headlined DOMESTIC BLISS…? jumped out at her. It was a cosy domestic scene. Roman was manoeuvring Sam's pushchair up a pavement in the park. Sam himself was asleep, his head lolling to one side. Scarlet, her head turned slightly away from the camera, was looking up at Roman and smiling.

'They didn't catch my good side, but you look cute.'

'How can you joke about this?' Scarlet demanded, raising reproachful shell-shocked eyes to his face. She shook her head and protested in a dazed tone, 'We're not going to go public yet.'

'I think we just have.' Roman sounded remarkably philosophical about it. Although you're still the mystery brunette and they've stopped short of saying that Sam is my son, I think it's significant that there are five references to the uncanny resemblance.'

'You didn't arrange this, did you?'

He sucked in his breath audibly. 'No, I did not. I'm pretty sure it was your neighbour upstairs who did that.'

'Isobel wouldn't do that!' she gasped, appalled. 'She's my friend.'

'One who you've known for what? A week?'

'That's only three weeks less than I've known you and you expect me to trust you?'

'And you'd prefer that I was the bad guy. I get your sister pregnant, but it's you who have to be there to hold her hand while she's dying and bring up my son when she's gone. This record is not one to inspire confidence or trust, I can see that, but right now I am here and all I want is to get to know my son.'

'I don't blame you for what happened to Abby.'

'Why the hell not? If the positions were reversed I would.'

Scarlet looked around for something else to dry; this was a subject she didn't want to get into.

With an exasperated grunt Roman snatched the tea towel from her fingers and spun her around to face him.

'Your friend might have nothing to do with this, but when I met her she seemed very interested in my relationship with Sam and you.'

'I didn't know you'd met her.'

'The other day when I was arriving she just happened to be coming out her door and you said yourself that Isobel was hard up for cash. Hasn't her husband lost his job?'

'You're saying she wasn't my friend, she was just using me?' Distress roughened her voice.

'I'm sure she liked you too, but maybe she saw a way to make some money and the temptation was too great to resist. It's incredible how flexible your principles can become when you've no money for the rent.'

'You don't even sound angry!' she gasped, raising tear-filled eyes to his face.

'Do you think nobody who said they were my friend has ever done the dirty on me?' he asked.

'It's awful. No wonder you're so horribly cynical,' she observed. 'Not,' she added with a sniff, 'that I'm going to condemn someone without proof.'

'Quite right, I'm just pointing out a possibility.'

He scanned her ivory-pale face and walked over to the fridge and withdrew a half-open bottle of wine from the door. He filled a glass and wrapped her stiff fingers around it. 'You're in shock and it should be brandy, but I don't suppose you keep any spirits.'

'I have no secrets from you,' she bit back sardonically through chattering teeth.

'Drink the lot,' he insisted, standing over her to make sure she did as he ordered. 'Feel any better?'

'No, just dizzy.' She lifted her eyes to his. 'What are we going to do?'

'We are going to do nothing. We are not going to respond when journalists ask us—'

'But what if—?'

He shook his head. 'We do not respond,' he told her flatly. 'Listen, I know you're not used to handling the media, which is why I thought a few days of time out in Ireland might be a good idea.'

'Don't you mean hiding...running away?'

'No, I don't mean hiding or running away.'

'But that's what it amounts to,' she objected with a frown.

'You'd prefer to be here when the telephone starts ringing or you wake up to find them camping on your doorstep?'

A shudder of revulsion ran through Scarlet at the image his words conjured up. She was an intensely private person; the idea of having her face and name the object of speculation was abhorrent. 'Is that going to happen?' she asked fearfully.

'You'll have a camera lens trained on every window,' he predicted. He looked around the tiny room. 'And this flat could not offer less protection.'

'My entire life can't change because of a silly story in a newspaper,' she protested, her voice rising shrilly. 'Perhaps I should go and stay with a friend?' she suggested.

'You could, if you want to lay them open to the same intrusive media invasion,' he agreed. 'Or you could come with me to Ireland.'

'You think they'll have lost interest in the story by the time we get back?' she suggested hopefully. 'I mean, it's bound to die a natural death really, isn't it, if I go away for a while?'

There was a moment's silence before his dark lashes lifted and he looked directly at her. 'Anything is possible.'

His cagey response didn't sound too comforting to Scarlet. 'But if they want a story or pictures they could follow us to Ireland. Where do you register on the scale of newsworthy?' she demanded. 'Would they follow you to Ireland?'

'Sorry they would, but it wouldn't do them much good. The house is set in the middle of a couple of thousand acres, part of it heavily forested, which means even fly-overs by helicopter are unproductive.

'It's an added plus factor that the neighbours are as unfriendly to the press as the geography. Sometimes,' he mused, 'friends are more effective than a million pounds' worth of security, not that we haven't invested in some of that of late,' he added drily.

'Your stalker?'

'I suppose you read about that.'

'No, your mother mentioned something about it and I've seen the scar, remember?' she added huskily. Her fingertips tingled as she recalled running her fingers along the ridge of scar tissue that stood out pale against his smooth dark skin. Shocking, sensual heat washed over her until she was engulfed from head to toe.

Their eyes touched and locked. *'I remember.'*

A soft, sibilant hiss issued from his lips at the same moment a deep shudder rippled through her body. The sexual tension fed on the electricity that passed between them and became a palpable presence in the room.

Scarlet knew that a gigantic black hole had opened up at her feet and, God, did she want to step into it! Every fibre in her body told her to let go, what the hell? How could this be wrong when it felt so good? From somewhere she dredged up the will-power to cling to the fragments of her self-control.

'It must have been a terrible experience.' Her voice sounded high and brittle to her own critical ears. 'Is she…the woman…?'

'In a psychiatric unit, but making good progress by all accounts. Hopefully she'll be well enough to be released later this year.'

Despite her best intentions this comment brought Scarlet's attention back to his face. If it weren't for the thin line of feverish colour that focused the eye on his high cheekbones she might have thought she had imagined that moment of mutual lust. Now she knew that she hadn't imagined anything—his desire was still there, raw and dangerous…but, worse still, deeply exciting.

Dear God, girl, show a bit of control.

'I don't think I'd be hoping for that in your shoes,' she admitted huskily. The knowledge that give or take a few inches he could have died at the hands of the crazy woman sent a chill through her.

'She was sick, people get sick…'

'But she nearly—'

'But she didn't,' he cut in firmly. 'If we spent our lives worrying about what could have happened we'd never get out of bed in the morning.'

'If we did come with you when we came back the press would still be waiting?'

Roman nodded.

'Wouldn't it be better to get it all over with rather than postpone the inevitable?' The look she directed up at him did not contain the same bold fearlessness of her suggestion.

'You seem pretty adept at avoiding the inevitable,' Roman observed drily. He watched the give-away warm colour bloom on her pale cheeks and smiled.

'Please try and concentrate,' she rebuked.

'It's very hard when you're standing there looking so luscious.'

His voice might have contained a teasing note but there was nothing light-hearted about the raw, needy expression in the eyes that moved in a compulsive fashion over her slender body.

'Don't be silly!' Scarlet found it incredible that someone who had escorted some of the most glamorous women in the country could look at her wearing her oldest jeans and a washed out tee shirt, with no make-up and her hair tied back in a pony-tail, and feel desire.

While her brain told her that it was impossible for him to feel that way about her, her eyes told her differently. Her body—well, actually her body had an agenda of its own. Her body wanted to get as close as possible to this man.

God knew where it came from, but somehow she found the strength not to throw herself at him.

'I need you to be serious for a moment.'

An expression of regret formed on Roman's face as he examined her pale features. She was trying to put a brave face on it in a typically Scarlet way.

He would have given a lot to offer the reassurance she was obviously seeking from him. It frustrated the hell out of him that the matter had been taken out of his hands, but he knew that he would be doing her no favours if he pretended the problem was going to go away.

'I mean, *obviously* I'm not going to go out of my way to provide photo opportunities for these people, but isn't it a cop-out to put your life on hold because of a couple of men with cameras?'

'It's not going to be a couple of men with cameras,' he told her as gently as he could. 'There are going to be a horde of them, a siege. Journos are going to be phoning you offering you money for a chance to tell your side of the story, shoving notes under your front door when you don't answer…'

Scarlet listened to him, growing paler and paler. She held up her hand. 'Don't!' she pleaded. Her lower lip wobbled as a sob rose in her throat. 'Why is this happening?' she wailed. 'It's not fair.' A sigh shuddered through her as Roman's arms drew her against him and then closed around her.

She knew at some level that the safety his arms offered was an illusion, but it didn't actually seem to matter. What mattered was it felt warm and good.

'I know it's not fair,' she heard him murmur into her hair. 'It will pass, I promise, it will pass.' His hand ran down the curve of her back and with a sigh she snuggled a little closer.

She sensed the tension in his lean body as he drew slightly back from her and she lifted a tear-stained face in enquiry.

With a fierce tenderness that stopped her heart in its tracks Roman ran a finger down the curve of her cheek, then smoothed the hair back from her brow.

'So you'll come to Ireland with me.'

Scarlet's heart was beating very hard. 'Right now I'd go anywhere with you,' she confided huskily.

'Does that include to bed?'

'Especially there.'

With a soft cry she walked into his open arms.

CHAPTER THIRTEEN

'WHEN you said you were phobic about flying why didn't you also mention that you get seasick?' Roman asked as Scarlet emerged from the ladies' loo where she had spent ninety per cent of the journey so far.

Scarlet shot him a look of intense dislike, and grabbed the back of the seat to steady herself before she lowered herself on the seat beside the sleeping toddler.

'But this feels like a force-ten gale,' she declared, averting her eyes from the grey heaving waves visible through the window. 'I wish I could sit outside—I always feel better outside. Why isn't there a deck?' she complained querulously.

Roman laughed. 'Do you prefer a conventional ferry with a deck or this fast ferry which halves the crossing time?'

She nodded glumly. 'I see your point.'

'And for the record there isn't a wave to be seen—it's as calm as a millpond. I've crossed when—'

Scarlet lifted a hand to her forehead. 'Spare me the stories of your heroics, please?' she begged sourly. 'I'm surprised you've ever been on a ferry.'

'I did some island hopping when I was a student, but, no, this isn't my preferred mode of transport.' It had taken him ten minutes to convince Alice he was serious when he'd asked her to book three tickets on a ferry across the Irish Sea.

'Sorry you're slumming it on my account.'

'It's been a revelation,' he assured her drily.

'You're such a snob.'

157

'I did crew on a yacht in a cross-Atlantic race once.'

'I suppose you won?'

'No, we came last.'

'How very human of you,' she snapped with bitchy relish.

She closed her eyes. There was no question that she could ever form any sort of meaningful relationship with someone who ate a full English breakfast on board a boat. She opened one eye. 'Thank you for looking after Sam.'

'A pleasure. Perhaps I should have booked us into a hotel overnight before the drive.'

'No, I'll be fine once I'm on land that doesn't move,' she promised him.

Roman considered her pallid complexion but kept his doubts to himself. 'You *really* prefer this to flying?'

'I've never actually flown,' she confided.

'Never?'

The amazement from someone who considered getting on a plane the same way most people thought of getting in a cab brought a wan smile to her lips.

'I tried it once but the stuff the doctor prescribed didn't mix too well with the whisky I drank in the bar before I boarded. I passed out and they had to stretcher me out. Abby was so embarrassed,' she recalled, 'that she pretended she didn't know me.'

'So you got left at home?'

Something in his voice brought her puzzled scrutiny to his face. 'I didn't actually mind. I'm not really a lazing-on-a-beach sort of person.'

'Shopaholic or culture vulture?'

'There are some places I would like to see one day,' she admitted, covering her mouth to conceal a wide yawn. 'Rome, Paris…you know…maybe when Sam is older.'

The hand that brushed the hair from her forehead made her start.

'You're tired.'

She sensed activity to her right just a split second before Roman leapt up from his seat.

She turned in time to see Roman pull a middle aged man who was slumped in his seat down onto the floor. He proceeded to loosen the man's collar and felt at his neck for a pulse before Scarlet's brain had registered what was going on.

The woman who had been sitting beside the unconscious—*please, God, let him be alive*—man began to scream and people began to shout. It said something for Roman's natural air of command that when he lifted his hand to indicate he needed silence, just before he placed his ear to the man's chest, a hush fell.

He straightened up and struck the man with some force on his chest. He then tilted the man's head back and pinched his nose. 'Anybody here know CPR?' he asked in the same non-urgent way he'd done everything else. As he bent to breathe into the man's mouth a scruffy-looking teenager counted him out before applying compressions to the man's chest in an expert way.

They continued this until two members of staff took over from them. Another member of staff politely asked the passengers sitting in the near vicinity to move. Scarlet was struggling to transfer herself and a very sleepy Sam to another part of the boat when Roman appeared at her side.

'Come on up here, champ,' he said, casually lifting Sam up one-handed. 'Give this to me,' he added, indicating the holdall she had looped over her shoulder.

'I can manage.' He treated her to one of his trade-mark ironic looks—the ones that made her feel incredibly childish—and she handed it over with a sigh.

'This weighs a ton. I don't know why women need to cart so much junk around with them.'

Scarlet couldn't let this sexist criticism pass. 'For your information, virtually nothing in there is mine. Sam doesn't travel light. There are the changes of clothes—'

'*Changes*—? You've got more than one set in there?'

'You don't know many three-year-olds, do you, Roman?' she observed, dealing him a superior look. 'Then there's the waterproof in case it rains and drinks...*obviously*. A packed lunch because he's a bit of a fussy eater and some crayons and a—'

A smile tugged at the corners of Roman's mobile lips as he listened to her narrate the contents. 'All right, I get the picture.'

Having secured them alternative seats, he turned to Scarlet, his dark eyes sweeping assessingly over her pale features. 'How are you feeling?'

'Fine.'

He looked less than convinced. 'I admire your stoical attitude—' in Scarlet's opinion his attitude suggested exasperation rather than admiration '—but only this morning I thought turning green was a figure of speech. A boat journey with you has taught me otherwise.'

'That poor man tends to put seasickness into proportion.' She gave a quick glance at Sam and saw he was happily preoccupied. Fortunately he had slept right through the crisis. 'How...how is he? He's not...?' She hardly dared ask.

'He started breathing.'

Scarlet gave a noisy sigh of relief. 'Well thank goodness for that!'

'He's hardly out of the woods yet,' Roman warned.

Scarlet shook her head in agreement. 'But he has a chance, thanks to you,' she added warmly.

'Basic first aid is all.' Roman seemed inclined to make light of his contribution. 'If I hadn't got there first someone else would have done what was needed. The ferry company staff are pretty well equipped to cope until the helicopter arrives.'

'They're going to air-lift him to hospital? Is that possible while we're at sea?'

Roman nodded. 'The bad news is it involves stopping the engine so they can winch him off. I'm afraid this is going to add another half hour at least to the journey.'

Scarlet took a deep breath. 'Right…' Under the circumstances she could hardly complain, even though being on the boat for a minute longer than necessary made her want to weep.

She felt his eyes on her face and lifted her chin. 'Trust you to be a hero,' she condemned with a teasing little grimace.

An amazed laugh was drawn from her throat. 'I'm embarrassing you, aren't I?' It was ironic—she tried her best to discompose him and failed miserably, when all she had to do apparently was say something nice about him.

'Would you like something to eat?'

Scarlet closed her eyes and released a weak groan. 'You really are a horrible man with no heart, you know that, don't you?'

'I'm hurt.'

Even with her eyes closed she could hear the grin in his voice. 'I live in hope.'

'I'm just trying to take your mind off it.' He had thought of other methods but these might have got him arrested in a public place.

'If you're about to suggest that it's all in my mind and all I need is positive thinking, I'll kill you. Also you are totally wrong—it's all in my inner ear; it's a balance thing.' Her eyes flickered open and a deep shudder ran all the way to her toes at a touch of warm air against her sensitive earlobe.

Roman, his hand braced on the head-rest of her chair, straightened up but didn't break eye contact. 'A very nice ear,' he said, his voice doing almost as much damage to her nervous system as his warm breath had. 'I could eat it.'

'You really don't have to do this, you know.' She could barely hear her own voice above the clamour of her thudding heart.

'Do?'

The circles of colour that appeared on the apples of her cheeks looked feverishly bright against her marble pallor.

'Say…stuff. I really don't expect it, you know, just because we slept together once,' she assured him earnestly. '*All right*,' she conceded, 'twice. But you can't really count the last time.'

Her reassurance wiped the smile right off his face. 'You can't… Why?' A nerve clenched hard in his lean cheek as he brought his hand along the side of her jaw. 'Did you have your fingers crossed?'

Scarlet felt the heat rush to her cheeks. She glanced over her shoulder, aware that their conversation was a little personal for so public a place.

Their new seats were directly adjacent to a group of men who all wore rugby kit; the noise they were making made it unlikely they were going to hear anything she said. One of their number she had exchanged a few words with earlier caught her eye and winked.

Scarlet responded to his, 'Hello, lovely girl,' with a grin and a wave before turning back to Roman.

'It's not going to happen again,' she declared in a fierce undertone.

While she spoke he maintained an expression of polite disbelief that made her want to hit him.

'Because you don't want it to?' he suggested in a light conversational tone.

'I've not given it much thought.' Lies didn't get much bigger or more improbable.

'Sure you haven't, as in you've not thought about much else.' He shook his head, the cynical twist to his wide, sensual mouth becoming more pronounced as he looked across at her miserable face. 'Grow up, Scarlet,' he advised tautly. 'There's absolutely no way we could share a bedroom and nothing happen,' he imparted simply.

The thing was his confidence was fully justified. 'That might be true,' she admitted bitterly. 'But I'm not sharing a bedroom with you so we won't find out!'

'I've already explained the sleeping arrangements to my parents.'

'Then you'll have to unexplain them.'

'I can't do that.'

'Why not?'

'Because they expect an engaged couple to sleep in the same bed.'

She stilled and lost what little colour she had. 'What did you say?'

'You heard what I said, Scarlet.'

'Why would your parents think we were engaged?' she enquired in a deceptively mild tone.

'Because that's what I told them.'

She loosed an incredulous peal of laughter. 'Have you lost your mind?' she exploded.

Roman's dark lashes lifted and his eyes glittered with an anger to match her own. 'If I have the blame can be laid directly at your door. Mixed signals don't cover it,' he declared. 'You introduced this ridiculous no-touch policy while at the same time you look at me with those big hungry eyes. It's enough to send the sanest man born round the bed.'

'I do *not* have hungry eyes!'

His brows lifted. 'Sure, and you just hate making love with me. The screams are actually a sign of how much you hate it.'

'I don't scream!' she choked.

'Like a banshee, but I like a woman who can let herself go.'

'You,' she told him in a voice that quivered with outrage, 'are crude and vulgar. A woman would have to be mad to marry you.'

'And are you?'

She stilled, her wide eyes fixed on his face. 'What do you mean?' she asked hoarsely.

'Are you going to marry me, Scarlet?'

'I thought it was a done deal,' she remarked bitterly.

He gave a sardonic lopsided smile but didn't reply.

'You're thinking of Sam?' she suggested.

He opened his mouth as if to say something, then closed it again. When he did speak he appeared to be choosing his words with care. 'I think he would approve. A proper family…maybe a brother or sister.'

She heard the rather worrying sound of slightly hysterical laughter. 'You want a baby?'

He looked mildly surprised. 'Don't you?' he returned.

'Yes,' she heard herself reply. 'Eventually,' she added, trying to retrieve the situation. 'I'm sure you'd get the same answer from most women.'

'I'm not asking most women to marry me, I'm asking you, Scarlet, and I'm still waiting for an answer.'

You had to respect the man for not pretending he loved her, she thought. People in arranged marriages sometimes fell in love and even when they didn't they had happy marriages.

My God, Scarlet, you're talking yourself into this, aren't you?

It would be mad to marry without love.

'Yes, I'll marry you.'

A smile of pure male triumph spread across his face. 'Excellent.' He got to his feet and Scarlet saw that Sam was awake and had his nose pressed to the window. 'Come on, Sam, you'll get a better view of the chopper up there,' he said, taking the little boy's hand.

'I want to fly in a chopper.'

'And you will, Sam,' his father promised.

Just like that, she thought, watching as he led the boy away. She hadn't expected a fanfare or champagne, but *excellent*?

Dear God, what have I done?

CHAPTER FOURTEEN

ROMAN had not exaggerated the remoteness or inaccessibility of the O'Hagan estate. They had driven four miles from the village before they finally reached the gated entrance. They had been travelling along what Roman referred to as the drive, but it wasn't like any drive Scarlet had seen, for at least ten minutes now, and there was still no sign of a house or for that matter a person!

Occasionally there was a break in the trees flanking the driveway affording breath-taking vistas over parkland towards the mountains or sea, and sometimes both. Under normal circumstances Scarlet would have wanted to get out of the car and spend time appreciating the magnificent scenery.

These were not normal circumstances!

She sighed as the next bend revealed no end to the journey. She was still dreading the entire 'meet the in-laws' thing, but she had reached the point where she wanted it over and done with. The reality could not be worse than what she was imagining…*could it*? At least Sam was no longer grouching—he had fallen asleep a couple of miles back, but this almost guaranteed he would be incredibly cranky when he woke up.

'What if they hate me?' They would like Sam. Everyone liked Sam.

Roman slid an amused sideways look at her tense face. 'Well, naturally I will cast you off like a smelly sock.'

'I don't smell!' she protested.

166

His nostrils flared. 'You do,' he contradicted throatily. 'I can smell you on my skin after we've made love.'

She was overpoweringly conscious of the fluid heat in the pit of her belly. 'Like that's happened such a lot,' she retorted, and shifted her position to lessen the pressure on her sensitised breasts.

'It will,' he declared arrogantly.

Now she really was a basket case.

Eyes fixed glassily on the narrow track ahead, Scarlet kept her tongue firmly between her teeth. She had learnt she could say some very reckless things when consumed by lust and right now she was shaking with it! She still was, only hopefully less obviously so, when he spoke a few moments later.

'Why do you crave approval?'

'I don't,' she denied indignantly.

'The only person you need to please is me.' His dark-lashed midnight eyes only touched her face for a split second but it was long enough to send a lick of heat through her body.

'And do I? Because you have no idea how much I would *not* care if—'

'Yes, you do please me...*very much*.'

Scarlet's audible gasp filled the short pause that followed his earthy admission.

She screwed her eyes up tight. 'I *really* wish you wouldn't say things like that.'

'The truth bothers you?'

'*You* bother me!' she exploded resentfully.

'Hold on,' she heard him say.

Scarlet opened her eyes and saw there was a horse just ahead. The rider, a female, twisted around in her saddle as she heard the car engine. Apparently recognising Roman, she started waving madly at them.

Scarlet turned her head, but Roman wasn't looking at her, he was looking at the figure on the horse and he was grinning, an uncomplicated grin of pleasure.

'Someone you know?'

Roman didn't reply; instead he pulled the car up on the grass verge.

'I won't be long.' He was already out of the door when he put his head back inside. 'Has it occurred to you they are probably equally concerned about what you'll think of them?'

'Your family?'

'Our family.'

She lowered her eyes, confused by the possessive glow in his dark eyes. 'Because I'm so very scary.'

Despite her sarcastic retort, actually his comment had made her feel a lot more positive. He was right—what did it matter if Sam was cranky or she looked like an unmade bed? The big picture wasn't about first impressions.

'Scary?' The husky rasp of his voice brought her eyes back to his face. One corner of his mouth lifted in a crooked smile, and there was a warmth in his eyes that made her heart beat faster. 'I think you're delicious.'

Delicious!

The upward surge in her spirits and confidence lasted until she saw that the person on the horse had swept off her riding hat; wavy shoulder-length chestnut hair fell free, and it shone in the weak sun. She lifted the waves off her face with a gloved hand and Scarlet could see she was very pretty.

As Roman approached the horse began to dance around in an alarming fashion—at least it seemed alarming to Scarlet. Casually the rider controlled it. Roman patted the quivering animal's neck as he came level with them.

The rider leaned down in her saddle and, with a hand

behind Roman's dark head, pressed her mouth to his. While Scarlet sat and watched the woman talking in an animated fashion to Roman the tight feeling in her chest got tighter and tighter.

She couldn't remember Roman ever looking that relaxed and happy with her. Several times she threw back his head and laughed out loud.

'That was lucky,' he remarked as he slid back into the car and turned on the ignition. 'I was hoping to bump into Sally.'

The name made Scarlet stiffen. It was several moments before she could trust herself to speak.

'Sally,' she repeated in a conversational tone. 'Would that be the same Sally who left you at the altar?'

'All forgotten.'

Scarlet smiled, her eyes trained on her intertwined white-knuckled fingers. 'How civilised.' The primitive emotions she was experiencing were anything but!

'Well, we're all grown-ups aren't we? And life's far too short to hold grudges. Do you ride?'

Scarlet's head came up. 'Horses?'

'Horses,' he agreed, looking amused by her horrified expression.

'I can't ride.'

'You'll be able to see the house around the next bend. Pity you can't ride—you could have come out with me and Sally tomorrow morning.'

'You're going riding with her?'

'Is that a problem?'

Scarlet released a slow, fractured hiss. 'You bet it's a problem.'

Roman glanced at her rigid profile and stopped the car. He released his seat belt and turned his body to face her. 'Do you mind elaborating on that statement?'

'The fact I need to just goes to prove what a totally insensitive bastard you are. Damn!' she cursed, tears starting in her eyes.

'Let me.' Roman leaned across her, his arms brushing against her aching breasts as he released the seat-belt catch her trembling fingers had been unable to cope with. His warmth, the scent of his body, his nearness—they all conspired to fill Scarlet with an aching longing that went bone-deep.

She held herself rigid until he had straightened up.

'So what's the problem?' he asked, in a *here-we-go-again* tone that sent her temper through the roof.

'We'll put all that guff you gave me about fidelity to one side for a minute, because I didn't believe a word of it anyhow,' she revealed contemptuously.

'Is that fact?' Low and without expression, his voice still managed to leave her in no doubt that he didn't like what he was hearing.

Her chin went up defiantly. If she started screening everything she said for his approval rating she'd probably never open her mouth again.

'There are limits to even *my* gullibility, you know.'

His nostrils flared as he sucked in a breath; his golden chiselled features were a taut mask of anger. She felt despair as she realised that even now his compelling male beauty had the power to touch her deeply.

'But not your stupidity.'

'*My* stupidity? You're the one who expects your family to take us getting married seriously when the moment you arrive you're riding off into the hills with the love of your life!'

'Are we talking about Sally?'

'How many loves of your life are there?'

He gave her a black look. 'Only one.'

The crushing confirmation was like a body-blow. Her pride wouldn't let him see how much she was hurting. 'Am I supposed to turn a blind eye?'

'To what?'

'*To what?* You kissed her!' She stuffed her fist into her mouth to stop the sob that was trying to escape.

'And you didn't like that?'

Scarlet lifted her head and her eyes skated warily across his lean face; he no longer looked angry. It was hard to read from his apparently relaxed expression what he was feeling.

'Would you like it if I went around kissing my old boyfriends? Daft question, I don't suppose you'd even notice,' she ended on a self-pitying sniff. With a deep sigh she closed her eyes. 'God, this was *such* a stupid idea. I don't know how I let you talk me into it?'

'*I would notice.*'

Her eyes widened at the aggressive declaration. 'You would?'

His fingers curved around her jaw, turning her face up to his. 'And I wouldn't like it.' His dark eyes shimmered. 'Actually I *wouldn't like it* quite a lot.'

Her heart started beating very fast. 'What would you do?' she whispered.

A slow wolfish smile spread across his dark, lean face. 'I'd throttle him…just a little, you understand, but enough so that he got the point.'

Suddenly her throat was so dry she could hardly speak. His primitive statement should have appalled her and here she was *excited*…and trying very hard not to let him see *how* excited.

'The point being?'

'That my wife is off limits.'

'I thought we were grown-ups,' she reminded him with

a disgruntled glare. 'Besides, I don't see why I shouldn't kiss whoever I want—you do.'

He laughed. 'That wasn't a kiss…' She read his intent before his head lowered. 'This,' he told her throatily, 'is a kiss.'

With a sigh she leaned back in her seat. Her lips felt tender and her body was gently thrumming with thwarted desire. It had been a kiss, but she had wanted more.

'You know it's very, *very* hard to stop kissing you once I start.' It was some small comfort that his voice reflected some of the strain and frustration she was experiencing.

'Then why did you stop?'

Roman jerked his head towards the back seat where Sam was sleepily rubbing his eyes. 'We have an audience.'

'I want a drink,' Sam announced loudly.

'And you shall have one,' Roman promised. 'Look, there's the house,' he said, starting up the engine.

'It looks like something out of a Jane Austen book,' Scarlet said in an awed voice as the big building loomed ahead of them. She turned reproachful eyes on him. 'You said it wasn't very big.'

'It's only bricks and mortar—don't let the size intimidate you.'

Easy for someone who had been brought up here to say. 'Is it very old?'

'Late Georgian,' Roman explained. 'With some rather ugly Victorian additions. Ask my father about the history…you'll regret it, but you'll score plenty of brownie points.'

'Is that what you want me to do?'

He scanned her pale, tense face with wide, anxious eyes and he exhaled deeply. 'For God's sake, will you stop worrying about what other people want and do what you damned well want?'

His anger made her blink, but it seemed to drain away as fast as it had erupted. He reached across and brushed a strand of hair from her cheek; she shivered as his fingertips lightly grazed her skin. 'Do you like it?'

'Like?' she repeated, fighting the compulsion to rub her cheek against his hand.

'The house.'

'Oh, right…yes…' She pulled back and his hand fell away. 'Like wasn't the right word,' she modified. 'It's big and very beautiful.' *Just like you.* 'I suppose people had lots of children in those days.'

'Mum is trying to persuade Dad to retire to Italy. She's talking of renovating one of the estate cottages for when they come over. She thinks this place is too big for them now.'

Scarlet looked up at the daunting façade and tried but failed to imagine Sam watching Saturday morning cartoons on the telly there…she couldn't. 'I can see her point.' She stiffened as two figures began to walk across the forecourt.

'Oh, God…'

She was in too much of a panic to notice when Roman left the car without comment. He opened the passenger door with Sam secured against his hip with his free arm. He looked at her pale face.

'They'll love you.'

'Says you,' she hissed back, wishing she could share even a fraction of his daunting assurance.

Roman seemed to lack any insight into her feelings. Didn't he understand what it felt like to be here under sufferance, the woman that came with the grandchild they wanted—a package deal?

She slid out of her seat and pinned a smile on her face,

very conscious that his parents were now close enough to hear what they were saying.

Even so they wouldn't have heard what Roman said when he bent close, his lips almost brushing her ear; she barely caught the husky words herself.

'Well, if they don't love you, remember I do, and that's what counts.'

All Scarlet had time to do was shoot him a stunned slack-jawed look before they were knee-deep in hugs and introductions.

It was ironic considering how much she had been dreading this meeting, and how carefully she had planned what she was going to say down to the last detail and inflection, that when it arrived she didn't have the faintest idea what she said or whom she said it to!

The whole thing passed by in a blur, a dream. Her mind was elsewhere.

He said he loved me.

It was possible that saying it out loud might make it seem more real. But Scarlet retained just enough self-control to stop herself trying out the theory.

'I hope you like the room.'

Scarlet smiled a little vaguely. *'Room…?'*

'I hope you like this room,' Natalia repeated patiently.

'Of course, it's a lovely room.' She spared the beautifully furnished bedroom a cursory glance, which lingered longest on the bed she was to share with Roman.

'Sam is in the connecting room—I thought that would be best.'

'Sam!' Scarlet looked around the room, alarm jolting her belatedly to an alert state. 'Where is he?'

Natalia looked at her strangely. 'He has gone to look at

the puppies in the kitchen, remember? You said it would be all right. I can get him if you like.'

Deeply embarrassed, Scarlet blushed. 'Of course…no, that's all right. He's always wanted a dog.'

'All children like puppies and Alice is with him. He'll be fine.'

Alice, Scarlet seemed to recall, dredging through her vague memories of the past few minutes, was the tall blonde who had been introduced as Roman's PA. Roman's father had turned out to have an appearance that matched his intimidating reputation: a big, burly man with a shock of grey hair and an abrupt manner.

'Yes, I'm sure he will.'

'You must be tired after the journey. If you'd like to lie down for a while before dinner you may. Hopefully Luca will be here by then and you'll be able to meet all the family.'

There was only one member of the O'Hagan family she wanted to see at that moment and he was closeted in the study taking a vital call.

She didn't think much of his priorities!

'I am tired,' Scarlet agreed, relieved to have a legitimate reason to explain away behaviour that had to seem pretty bizarre to the other woman. 'Maybe I'll have a shower, or a walk.'

She doubted whether ten cold showers were going to make her any more articulate. It was so typical of Roman to say something like that and then get himself called away.

'Well, I'll be in the drawing room if you want me and I'm sure Roman won't be long,' Natalia said as if reading her mind. 'Would you like some tea brought up to your room?'

'No, thank you, I might wait for Roman.'

CHAPTER FIFTEEN

SCARLET did wait but, contrary to his mother's prediction, Roman *was* long, or at least it seemed that way to Scarlet. She had unpacked her clothes and Sam's in the pretty adjoining room, which looked suspiciously as though it had been recently decorated. Someone, probably their hostess, had gone to a lot of trouble to make them feel welcome and comfortable. She felt a pang of guilt when she realised how ungrateful she must have seemed.

She reached the point where she had half convinced herself he hadn't said anything at all and she had imagined the whole thing when she decided enough was enough. If she sat here any longer, her thoughts going around in circles, she'd go quietly barmy, and she was neglecting her duty as a parent.

She was pretty sure that Sam would be where the puppies were and they were in the kitchen.

Scarlet found the warm cosy room with its original range and modern day appliances, and tried to apologise to Alice for Sam being a nuisance. But Alice, clearly not immune to the charm of his big brown eyes, announced that Sam wasn't bothering her and they were enjoying themselves.

The cook had given them the run of the kitchen so long as they cleaned up after themselves and Alice, with Sam's help, planned to make a batch of scones.

Helping involved a lot of flour and Scarlet left him happily up to his armpits in the stuff.

Making her way back from the domestic offices to the main part of the rambling house was not as easy as it sounded.

When Scarlet found herself back in the boot room for the second time she began to think she might be doomed to wander the below-stairs corridors for ever.

Maybe it was someone's way of telling her that was where she belonged, she thought with an ironic smile. She certainly felt a lot more comfortable in the cosy old-fashioned kitchen than she expected to upstairs in the drawing room.

When she did eventually find herself in the main hallway she wasn't entirely sure how she got there. Her heels were noisy on the gleaming wooden floor as she slowed her pace outside the study door behind which she had seen Roman disappear.

Perhaps Roman wasn't in there. Perhaps he had finished and was even now waiting for her upstairs. The possibility made her heartbeat quicken—and her stride.

It was Sam's name that slowed her down. She could hear voices coming through the slightly open door. She stopped pretending to herself she wasn't eavesdropping when she identified the distinctive sound of Roman's deep voice.

Even this far away it had the ability to raise goose-bumps on her skin. Her weakness brought a smile to her lips; this faded when Roman's voice was closely followed by the deep rumble of Finn O'Hagan's voice raised loudly in anger.

'I suppose it's better late than never...' she heard him observe grudgingly. 'A man should never feel ashamed of his own child.'

Shock held Scarlet frozen to the spot. Had Roman told his father he was ashamed of Sam? Had all the things he'd said been a lie? It was hard for her to believe this, but it was equally hard to read his comment any other way.

'When I look at that poor innocent babe I'm ashamed. Ashamed that I raised a man who can't see beyond his own selfish pleasure.'

Scarlet flinched as there was the sound of something falling...breaking...and Finn's terse instruction to, 'Leave the damned thing alone. Someone will pick it up later.'

'I'm ashamed of you, I'm ashamed I'm your father.'

Scarlet, who now recognised with a sick feeling what was happening, pressed her hand to her mouth.

'I'm sorry to be such a disappointment to you, Father.' In contrast to his father's voice, Roman's was rigidly controlled. 'You shouldn't get excited, Father.'

'I'm not excited, I'm *disgusted*.'

Without thinking about what she was doing, acting purely on an instinct that told her she couldn't let Roman take the blame for something that he was innocent of, Scarlet stepped through the door into the room.

The morning sun was streaming in through the windows of the big book-lined room, and, combined with the glow from the blazing open log fire in the vast carved stone fireplace, it should have made for a warm, cosy atmosphere. But inside the atmosphere was ice.

The two big men, both standing with a large oak desk between them, didn't notice her.

'Sit down, father, and let's discuss this rationally.' From where she was standing she could see the strain in Roman's face. His strongly etched profile was taut and each angle and hollow of his face sharply defined.

'It doesn't matter how *rationally* we discuss it. It's not going to alter the fact that because of you a woman lost her life giving birth to your son.'

A sudden calmness that came from knowing what she had to do settled over Scarlet.

'No!' Her soft voice had a bell-like clarity as she stepped forward into the room. 'This has to stop now.'

The two men turned in unison. 'Scarlet, leave it,' Roman said, moving to block her impetuous entrance.

She shook her head and braced herself against his upper arms with her hands, but he still frustrated her efforts to reach his father, physically blocking her with his own body. Scarlet felt the iron-hard muscles in his well-developed upper arms clench beneath her fingers. Their eyes meshed.

'This isn't right.'

'This isn't your problem, Scarlet.'

'Maybe it isn't, but I'm not going to leave it. I've left it too long already,' she reflected grimly.

'You're defending my son?'

'Well, someone has to,' Scarlet said, stepping back from Roman because there was no way she was going through him.

'After what he did to your own sister.'

The scornful recrimination in the older man's voice brought a flush to her cheeks. 'The point is, he didn't.'

The older man shook his head impatiently. 'Is this what he's told you, girl?'

Roman's deep voice cut angrily across his father. 'Her name is Scarlet, Father. If you want to vent your anger on anyone, I'm here. Leave her out of it.'

The eyes of father and son clashed for a moment. Finn O'Hagan was the first to look away with a slight nod of acknowledgement.

Scarlet's chin lifted. 'I can defend myself,' she told Roman. Then turned to his father. 'Nobody tells me what to think, Mr O'Hagan,' she declared proudly.

'Fine words. You'll be telling me next he isn't the father.'

'Roman is Sam's father,' she admitted.

Roman's father gave an impatient snort. 'Exactly, there's nothing more to be said. The facts speak for themselves.'

'No, actually, they don't, Mr O'Hagan. Roman didn't seduce my sister. None of it was an accident.'

'What are you talking about, Scarlet?' Roman asked.

'Abby *wanted* a baby.'

'I know.'

'No,' she interrupted loudly. 'You don't know. Abby

planned to have a baby and she picked you out as the father.'

'Picked me?' Roman shook his head. 'What are you talking about, Scarlet?'

'Abby picked you out to be the father of her baby. I think having a child became an obsession.' Her trembling lower lip caught between her teeth, she lowered her eyes guiltily.

She couldn't bring herself to look at him. She could only imagine how angry and disgusted he must be feeling and how she was the natural focus for his anger. She couldn't expect him to understand that telling him the truth was a betrayal of her sister's memory.

She took a deep breath before continuing.

'Abby told me shortly before her death that she planned it all. She spiked his drink and…she made sure that any…any *precautions* didn't work. She never had any intention that he would be involved with Sam,' she admitted miserably. 'The morning after,' she added, determined now she had begun to make a clean breast of it, 'to make sure Roman wouldn't suspect anything she told him that nothing had happened, that he had fallen asleep.'

There was a thunderstruck silence. Finn O'Hagan stared at her, then turned to his son. 'My God, can this be true?'

Roman, his dark shadowed eyes still on Scarlet's face, didn't respond to the incredulous question. His impenetrable expression made it impossible to know what to read into his silence.

There was a husky note of appeal in Scarlet's voice as she addressed her words directly to a stony-faced Roman.

'Abby wasn't a bad person,' she faltered huskily. 'She'd had a couple of relationships over the previous year that ended badly. I think she thought that she'd never find a man to love but she wanted a baby.'

'And her solution was to get a man drunk and sleep with him…?'

Scarlet could hear precious little of the understanding she'd been praying for in his voice. She felt her throat close over with unshed tears and drew a deep, slow breath.

'Please don't think badly of her!' she pleaded. Tears stood out in her eyes as she turned towards the door. 'And, Mr O'Hagan, nobody has told you, but it wasn't Roman who called off the wedding to Sally, she did. She ran off with the best man. So you see this isn't the first time you've blamed Roman for something that wasn't his fault. I'd say he's earned the benefit of the doubt...wouldn't you?

'If I were you I'd be grateful I had a son like Roman, not spend my time looking for things to be mean to him about.' She barely managed to get the rebuke out before her self-control snapped and she fled from the room, tears streaming down her cheeks.

For several minutes after she'd gone neither man moved. It was Finn O'Hagan who finally broke the tableau. He looked at his son's profile without comment and went over to the bureau. He poured a generous measure of Irish whiskey from an unopened bottle and drained the glass in one swallow. With a sigh he poured a second, refilled his own and approached his son.

'Is it true about Sally?'

Roman gave a shrug. 'It was a long time ago.'

'I assume that was a yes. It would seem that I owe you an apology.'

Roman's fingers curled around the glass extended to him. 'You thought I'd been a selfish bastard. I thought I'd been a selfish bastard.' His powerful shoulders lifted before he raised the glass to his lips. 'Forget it,' he advised.

'That took some guts...coming in here like she did.'

'You think?'

'Don't you?'

'This isn't about courage,' Roman began forcefully before visibly restraining himself. He ran a hand down his jaw.

'What is it about, Roman?' his father asked quietly. With a groan he lowered himself into a chair. 'I'm as stiff as a damned board,' he complained. 'Your mother might be right, maybe I do need a bit of sun in my old age.' His eyes followed the panther-like, prowling progress of his son as he trod a path down the length of the room and back again.

'The girl must have been torn; it can't be an easy thing it's her sister.'

Roman's dark eyes flared. 'And I'm her bloody husband…or I will be,' he growled, banging the glass down on the desk.

'Oh, that's still on, is it?'

Roman turned on him in a flash. 'What the hell is that supposed to mean? Are you saying I shouldn't marry her?'

Finn appeared to consider the question. 'Well, maybe you could do better.' He silently counted to three before his son exploded.

'*Better?*' he repeated, his eyes narrowed to menacing icy slits. 'I don't want *better*, I want Scarlet.'

Finn smiled up at his glowering son. 'Don't tell me, boy, tell her.'

It was about half an hour later that there was a knock on her bedroom door. Scarlet, who was lying full length on the bed, rolled over and tried to smooth down her hair. It was going to be hard to explain away her bedraggled appearance, she thought, grimacing as she examined the marks twenty minutes of unrestrained weeping had left on her face in the mirror.

'I'll be right there,' she called, sliding her legs off the bed.

The door opened. 'Don't bother.'

Scarlet just sat there awkwardly as Roman came into the room and closed the door behind him.

It was a meeting she had been dreading but one she knew she had to face some time or other. At least now there were no lies or half-told truths between them. A relationship that was built on love could survive the truth. If it couldn't, maybe it wasn't worth saving.

Total rubbish! the voice in her head replied in response to this fatalistic maxim. *Only an idiot stands there and lets their future go down the toilet without at least trying to stop it.*

'I know you must hate me at the moment,' she said, studying the polished floor. Her hair fell forward, the glossy bangs hiding her face and exposing the nape of her neck.

His piercing glance touched the top of her bowed glossy head. His mouth twisted. 'Do I?'

'And I don't blame you,' she hastened to add. 'But I really hope that later on when things are less...*raw* you'll be able to see... It was wrong not to tell you, very wrong— I can see that now.'

'Why tell me now, Scarlet?' Roman demanded, dragging a hand through his dark hair.

'Because I heard your father. I couldn't let him talk to you like that. I couldn't let you take the blame for something when you were innocent.'

'Why not?'

She shook her head. 'I just couldn't.'

'It hadn't bothered you up to that point,' he reminded her. 'You let me...hell, you *listened* and were incredibly supportive to me while I beat myself up, and you didn't say a word. Not one bloody word,' he reiterated in disbelief. 'Did it give you some sort of kick to see me eaten up with guilt?'

Unable to bear the anger in his dark, hostile eyes, she looked away.

'Well, did it?' he demanded harshly.

Scarlet looked up and, numb with misery, shook her head. The sight of the tears rolling down her cheeks seemed to inflame him even farther. 'And there was me unable to believe how you could be so generous in forgiving me.'

Scarlet bit her lips and his lips twisted into a smile that was so bitter and bleak it made her wince. Those same lips had kissed her so beautifully, with such passion, with such tenderness.

'Wondering,' he continued in a voice that throbbed with bitter self-derision, 'what I did to deserve someone so charitable and sweet.'

A strangled sob escaped her lips before she pressed her hand over her mouth.

Roman watched her chin fall to her chest in an attitude of abject misery and his dark features contorted. Scarlet didn't see that or the hand he had stretched out towards her before letting it fall.

'Hell!' he ejaculated rawly as he began to restively pace up and down the room. At the far end of the room he twisted back to face her. *'You must hate me.'*

Scarlet blinked away the hot tears that filled her eyes, her throat felt so emotionally tight she could hardly breathe. She shook her head in denial.

'I love you, Roman.'

He stopped dead.

'I wanted to tell you about Abby.'

'But you managed to stop yourself,' he cut back with dark irony.

'I couldn't tell you what Abby did without—'

'Speaking ill of the dead?' He shook his head. 'That doesn't work.'

'But it's the truth,' she protested feebly. 'At first I didn't think there was any point telling you. Later I wanted to protect you from the truth, and I was worried that, if you knew, you might not feel the same way about Sam.'

'Protect me?'

Head bowed, she didn't look at him. 'I'll explain to your

parents that this is my fault. At least you didn't send out the invitations this time.'

'What the hell are you talking about?' he snarled.

'Well, obviously we can't get married now, not even for Sam.' He was never going to forgive her. Later she would feel regret and pain; right now she felt numb. It was a blessing really.

'I was never marrying you for Sam.'

Her head lifted and what she saw in his face made her heart thud.

'When you said that you loved me, Roman, did you mean it?'

He stilled. *'Love you?'* His eyes closed and he drew a deep shuddering breath.

'Or maybe you did,' she put in quickly—she didn't want to hear him say anything that would spoil that brief perfect moment when she had thought he loved her. 'But now you don't—?'

His eyes opened. 'You don't switch off love like a tap.'

She blinked in bewilderment. 'But you despise me, you'll never forgive me.'

'Do I look that much of a fool?' he demanded, sweeping a strong hand through his dark hair. 'No, don't answer that, I know I do. I…I say things when I'm angry,' he revealed awkwardly. 'I was totally unprepared to hear what you had to say. It's not an ego-enhancing thing to learn that you were used as breeding stock.'

'I know.'

'I'm perfectly aware that you were in an impossible position,' he admitted.

'I should have told you.'

He shrugged. 'It wasn't the fact you didn't tell me that made me so angry,' he revealed. 'It was the fact you thought you *couldn't* tell me, the fact that you thought anything could change the way I feel about Sam.'

'I'm sorry,' she whispered.

A sudden grin spread across his face as he crossed the room to her, his long legs covering the space in two seconds flat. He took her face between his hands.

'Don't do humble, Scarlet; it doesn't suit you.'

'You're not angry with me?'

He shook his head. 'It's not like I haven't been guilty of my share of economy in the truth department. I'm capable of cynical manipulation.'

'Who were you manipulating?'

'You,' he admitted. 'I asked you to marry me because of Sam. I calculated that you were more likely to say yes if I played the happy family card, rather than admit the truth.'

Scarlet ran a finger down the thin white line on his cheek and felt his big body shudder. With a muffled groan he caught her hand and pressed an open-mouthed kiss into the palm.

'What was the truth, Roman?' she whispered huskily.

His lips lifted from her skin, but he retained her hand, rubbing it up and down his jaw. She could feel the prickle of the dark shadowy stubble.

'The truth is I had fallen in love with you, my brave, bolshy and absolutely beautiful Scarlet.' The light of undisguised adoration in his face sent a thrill of wonder through her body. 'I have been half off my head, unable to think about anything else,' he admitted rawly.

'I never guessed!'

'Dear God, I thought I was being obvious enough. Do you actually think I'd travel on a ferry for anyone but you?'

A small gurgle of laughter left her lips before her expression grew grave. 'You miscalculated, Roman.'

His wary eyes scanned her solemn face. *'I did?'*

'The truth would have been much more effective,' she told him simply.

With a smile of fierce relief he drew her to him. He kissed her with a hunger and desperation that made her senses spin.

'I think we should make it a rule to tell each other the truth in future,' he said when his mouth finally lifted.

'But we can tell the odd white lie to other people?'

'Did you have something specific in mind, *cara*?'

'Well, would it be so bad if we made up a little excuse for not going back downstairs straight away?' she wondered with an innocent smile.

'I never need an excuse to make love to my woman,' he declared with breath-taking arrogance. 'And, in addition, in Italy it is common practice to retire into a darkened room in the middle of the day. Siesta is a very civilised custom,' he rasped.

'True, but we're not in Italy.'

'But I'm half Italian,' he reminded her as he scooped her up into his arms and carried her to the bed. 'You'll enjoy being married to an Italian,' he promised.

'I'm beginning to think you could be right,' she agreed with a blissful smile.

'I always am.'

Just this once Scarlet decided she would let Roman get away with this outrageous claim. After all, there would be plenty of other chances for her to point out the error of his ways. Not that she wanted to change her Italian lover; she liked him just the way he was!

Undressed
BY THE BOSS

From sensible suits...into satin sheets!

Even if at times work is rather boring, there is one
person making the office a whole lot more interesting:
the boss! He's in control, he knows what he wants and
he's going to get it! He's tall, handsome, breathtakingly
attractive. And there's one outcome that's never in
doubt—the heroines of these electrifying, supersexy
stories will be undressed by the boss!

*A brand-new miniseries available only from
Harlequin Presents!*

Available in August:

TAKEN BY THE
MAVERICK MILLIONAIRE

by Anna Cleary
Book # 2754

In September, don't miss another breathtaking boss in

THE TYCOON'S VERY
PERSONAL ASSISTANT
by Heidi Rice

HIRED: THE SHEIKH'S SECRETARY MISTRESS

Sheikh Amir has a convenient wife lined up by his
family. His requirements: no love, but plenty of heat in
the bedroom! But he's becoming quite inconveniently
attracted to his sensible secretary...and Amir wants to
promote her—into his bed!

A man driven by desire—who will he make his bride?

*Don't miss the next sizzling installment
of fan favorite*

Lucy Monroe's

Royal Brides series

HIRED: THE SHEIKH'S SECRETARY MISTRESS
Book #2747

On sale August 2008.

REQUEST YOUR FREE BOOKS!

2 FREE NOVELS PLUS 2 FREE GIFTS!

YES! Please send me 2 FREE Harlequin Presents® novels and my 2 FREE gifts (gifts are worth about $10). After receiving them, if I don't wish to receive any more books, I can return the shipping statement marked "cancel". If I don't cancel, I will receive 6 brand-new novels every month and be billed just $4.05 per book in the U.S. or $4.74 per book in Canada, plus 25¢ shipping and handling per book and applicable taxes, if any*. That's a savings of close to 15% off the cover price! I understand that accepting the 2 free books and gifts places me under no obligation to buy anything. I can always return a shipment and cancel at any time. Even if I never buy another book, the two free books and gifts are mine to keep forever. 106 HDN ERRW 306 HDN ERRL

Name	(PLEASE PRINT)	
Address		Apt. #
City	State/Prov.	Zip/Postal Code

Signature (if under 18, a parent or guardian must sign)

Mail to the Harlequin Reader Service:
IN U.S.A.: P.O. Box 1867, Buffalo, NY 14240-1867
IN CANADA: P.O. Box 609, Fort Erie, Ontario L2A 5X3

Not valid to current subscribers of Harlequin Presents books.

Want to try two free books from another line?
Call 1-800-873-8635 or visit www.morefreebooks.com.

* Terms and prices subject to change without notice. N.Y. residents add applicable sales tax. Canadian residents will be charged applicable provincial taxes and GST. Offer not valid in Quebec. This offer is limited to one order per household. All orders subject to approval. Credit or debit balances in a customer's account(s) may be offset by any other outstanding balance owed by or to the customer. Please allow 4 to 6 weeks for delivery. Offer available while quantities last.

Your Privacy: Harlequin Books is committed to protecting your privacy. Our Privacy Policy is available online at www.eHarlequin.com or upon request from the Reader Service. From time to time we make our lists of customers available to reputable third parties who may have a product or service of interest to you. If you would prefer we not share your name and address, please check here. ☐

HP08R

They seek passion—at any price!

A sizzling trilogy by

Carole Mortimer

Two brothers and their cousin are all of
Sicilian birth—and all have revenge in mind
and romance in their destinies!

In July you read Cesare's story in

THE SICILIAN'S RUTHLESS MARRIAGE REVENGE

In August, read Wolf's story in

AT THE SICILIAN COUNT'S COMMAND

Book #2750

Count Wolf Gambrelli annoyed Angelica—and aroused her!
He'd been appointed her live-in protector, and it was clear that
Wolf also desired Angelica, and he'd stop at nothing to bed her.

Don't miss Luc's story in

THE SICILIAN'S INNOCENT MISTRESS

Available September!

BOUGHT FOR HER BABY

Taken for her body...and her baby!

These men always get what they want—
and the women who produce their heirs
will be their brides!

**Look out for all our exciting books
in August:**

#17 THE MARCIANO LOVE-CHILD
by MELANIE MILBURNE

**#18 DESERT KING,
PREGNANT MISTRESS**
by SUSAN STEPHENS

**#19 THE ITALIAN'S
PREGNANCY PROPOSAL**
by MAGGIE COX

#20 BLACKMAILED FOR HER BABY
by ELIZABETH POWER

Harlequin Presents® EXTRA delivers popular themed
collections every month featuring four new titles.